Afterglow

Synthesis:Weave, book two

Rexx Deane

FORCEFIELD

In memory of Eileen

1923 – 2015

Prologue

Erik hated Miss Zuchowski.

The eleven-year-old stood in front of his classmates, a page of notes trembling in his hands. Vanes of golden sunlight shone through the slatted wooden shutters into the dusty classroom, directly into his eyes, obscuring the other kids sneering at him from their seats.

He stared at the paper. Why couldn't the words fly off the pages and into the room of their own accord, so he didn't have to read them out loud?

'My uncle catches space pirates,' he said.

A laugh rose from the room. Why had he started with that line? He swallowed. He had to read it; he'd get detention if he didn't. His teacher, Miss Zuchowski – the sole tutor of the log cabin school – pursed her lips.

'He lives on a space station and writes computer programs . . .' Erik stumbled over the words for two long minutes. Nearing the middle of the sheet, he found his stride and picked up the tempo. 'The aliens that live there are amazing! Uncle Seb takes photos of them for me. The Bronadi are my favourite—'

Miss Zuchowski cleared her throat. 'That's enough, Mr Mikkaelsson. You may return to your seat now. That was all very interesting, although I fail to see how a work of fiction qualifies for show-and-tell.'

'But-but it *is* true, Miss!' Erik's cheeks burned. Stumbling out of the sun amid laughs and jeers, he threw down the sheet and flopped into his chair. He folded his arms and stared intently at his desk.

'I will speak to you after school, Erik, and to your mother. Now, Richard, would you like to go next and bring some semblance of normality back to the room?'

* * *

Erik sat on the rough wooden bench by the door to Miss Zuchowski's office, staring at the floor and kicking his heels against the wall behind him. Zuchowski was horrible, compared to the computer-based Turing Interface tutors he'd had in his old life back on Earth. At least they didn't humiliate you in front of everybody. He'd only done as he was told, and written about his family and the things he enjoys. What was wrong with that?

The door at the end of the hallway slammed open, startling him.

The silhouette of a man stood in the doorway. His shadow lay long across the floorboards in the evening sun and his heavy black robe swished in the dust-laden wind. The wooden door scraped shut behind him and, as he clomped grittily down the hallway towards the boy, he briefly ran a hand over his head to flatten his short, grey windswept hair. His wrinkled eyes smiled youthfully as he stroked his goatee. 'Now, Erik, what have you done?'

'Duggan!' Erik leaped up and hugged the man about the waist. 'Miss Zuchowski doesn't believe anything I tell her about Uncle Sebastian! She's given me detention for telling lies.'

Duggan placed a hand gently upon the boy's head. 'Don't you worry about it, lad. You know we're not supposed to tell them everything, with good reason. I'll have to convince her that you have an overactive imagination.'

'But—'

The office door opened. Zuchowski stood with one hand on her hip. 'Mr Simmons. I assume you've come to collect Erik? Where's his mother? I'd hoped to speak to her.'

'She's out working in the fields. Some people have more to worry about than being called in to school for such minor things as making up stories.'

'I'd hardly say it's minor.' She looked up and down the corridor. 'But this is something to be spoken about in my office. Come in.'

Duggan led Erik into the office, a small room with a thin layer of dust that coated almost every surface. Zuchowski took a seat behind the large desk that dominated the space. On one end of the desk stood a large, brown atlasphere, a defunct remnant of an old education system and highly inappropriate for life on an alien world such as Tradescantia, but that was the town of Chopwood all over: defunct and out of its time.

Duggan took the seat opposite the woman. Erik stood beside him.

Zuchowski leaned forward and laced her fingers on the desk. 'Mr Simmons, we have a serious and troubling issue. The boy persistently tells tales of talking trees, vampires with pointed ears, wolf-men, and all sorts of other ludicrous nonsense. The worst thing is, he acts as though he believes them all to be true.'

Duggan slowly rubbed the back of his neck and glanced at Erik. 'Yes ... he does have a rather powerful imagination. Something that seems to be lacking around here, don't you think?'

'Well, I don't appreciate it, not when he has been instructed to write factual accounts. He spouts made-up scientific facts about impossible discoveries as though they were real. I'm contemplating sending him to the medic for psychological evaluation.'

He coughed. 'You do that. I'm sure Kibble would be interested. Erik, why don't you go outside and wait, there's a good boy.'

Erik slowly made his way to the door.

After he had gone, the woman straightened. 'If it keeps up, Erik will have to be separated from the other children. How am I to teach him then? I'm the only teacher in this town and I cannot devote my time to two separate schoolings.'

'Well, he really doesn't need—'

'And another thing. Although you said he and his mother arrived late in a ship following the colony mission, nobody has seen any sign of it and, given that it took us sixty years to get back from that space anomaly, I can't see how they could have arrived here after us.' She folded her arms. 'And his mother, Janyce ...' she said, waving a hand dismissively. 'She doesn't even *look* like she could pilot a ship.'

Duggan raised an eyebrow and drew his head back. 'Oh, believe me, she can.'

'So, where is it?'

Duggan rose from his seat. 'I'm under no obligation to discuss this.'

'I wonder what Cullen would have to say on the matter. I've a good mind to bring it to the council's attention.'

'I am on the council. But by all means, Belinda, tell Cullen. He will probably tell you to not worry your pretty little head about it.'

She reddened. 'Why I've never been so—'

Duggan put up a hand and swiped it to one side. 'But you do that, if it makes you happy. The last thing I want to do is stand in the way of the educational system.' He turned to leave.

'Why are you protecting Erik and his mother? What have they got to hide?' She visibly chewed the inside of her cheek. 'It can't be good, letting the boy live in his fantasy world like that ...'

Duggan swung around to face the woman and bore down on the desk with both hands. He'd had enough of bureaucratic, uppity little jobsworths like her to last a lifetime. 'Miss Zuchowski, it is the people of Chopwood that live in a fantasy world, with an archaic mindset that does not fit with current society.'

'We *are* current society!'

'*That* is where you are grossly mistaken! Everything the boy has told you about the galaxy is true. Whether he *should* be telling his classmates or not is another matter.' He put up a hand. 'The galaxy, like it or not, has moved on without us. We are an antique remnant of a world long gone.'

Her mouth hung open. 'What are you talking about? Have we received a signal from Earth? What aren't you telling me? Has there been another world war since we left?'

Duggan shook his head. 'No. No, I put that badly. Earth is just a lot different to how you all remember it.'

'How *we* remember it?'

'I've been back in the years since your "space anomaly" incident. I was left behind for sixty years, remember?' There was no need to tell her that it wasn't an anomaly, but telling her that a race of tree-dwelling consciousnesses had magically teleported them sixty light years away was bound to stretch anyone's credulity. 'Why do you think Erik knows so much about scientific discoveries that you've never even heard of? He and his mother came here from Earth at faster than light speeds – and very recently, at that. We left Earth two centuries ago, and a lot has changed since then.'

'I knew you were mad, but I didn't think you'd buy into a child's fantasies.'

Duggan folded his arms and raised his voice. 'Erik, would you kindly bring in your photograph?' The door creaked open and Erik peered in. 'Come on, boy, it's alright.'

Erik closed the door behind him as he entered. He reached into his pocket and withdrew a glossy three-inch printout and handed it over.

Duggan thrust the image in front of the woman.

'Who is that?' Zuchowski asked. The image was of a man with a close-shaved head, standing next to a humanoid creature with flattened elfin features and sponge-like hair. In the background, a winding river with grassy banks curved upwards into the distance.

'His uncle, Sebastian Thorsson, with a Karrikin – an alien. One of the many that live on the station where he works.'

'Aliens!' She snorted. Her expression hardened. 'I'll admit Erik does look like that man, but he could have generated the image.'

'My dear, how often do you expect an eleven-year-old boy to have access to the *Iceni*'s computers? None of the other colony ships have equipment capable of manipulating images like that.'

'I . . .'

'Come on, admit it.'

'I admit it's not possible that *Erik* could have manufactured the picture. But proven wrong about aliens? No. Not by a long shot.'

Duggan straightened. 'Then you leave me no choice. Follow me.'

At the bottom of the grassy road, Duggan unlatched the wooden gate out of the stockade and waited for Erik and Miss Zuchowski to step through. He pulled the gate shut and gently lowered the catch into place, all the while keeping an eye on the street.

'Why are we leaving the town?' Zuchowski asked.

'I have something to show you that will prove Erik is not making things up. And keep your voice down – I can't afford for anyone else to follow us . . .'

She raised an eyebrow and stepped back.

'What?' Duggan shrugged and put his hands out. 'I can't afford for anyone to follow us *yet*. You think I'm going to lead you out into the forest and kill you, or something? In front of a small boy?'

She glanced at Erik. 'For all I know, that could be the cause of his tale-telling.'

Duggan folded his arms and compressed his lips. 'Just humour me. And I'm offended that you believe me capable of such things.'

Zuchowski rolled her eyes and sighed. 'Let's just get on with it. I haven't got all day to stand around here. My husband will be wondering where I've got to.'

Duggan grinned. The poor man had his sympathies. 'I'll keep it brief. Please, follow me.' He turned and headed off into the woodland, gently brushing the tree trunks with a hand as he passed them.

Erik ran alongside and tugged at his robe. 'Are we going to meet Shiliri again? I like her.'

'I don't know who transferred here from Achene. I guess we'll see when they reveal themselves.'

'Shiliri, as in the dryad-tree-spirit he talks about?' Zuchowski huffed between laboured breaths. 'You really shouldn't indulge his fantasies.'

Erik turned on her. 'It's *not* fantasy! She's real. You'll see.'

Duggan stopped and Erik bumped against him. He put his hand out, holding him back. 'Wait here,' he said, checking they were out of sight of the town. Satisfied, he moved off. The leaves rustled as Zuchowski made a move to follow. 'I mean you, too.'

Her face creased into a scowl. 'Being told what to do like a child!'

'My dear, in the eyes of the very ancient Folians, we're all children.' Duggan continued into the forest. Once the others were out of earshot, from a pocket in his robes he drew out a small velvet pouch filled with a fine white powder. He closed his eyes and recalled the image of a complex Celtic knotwork design. Relaxing his throat, he chanted a deep chord, forming words. *'Labhair le plandaí.'* Speak with plants.

Almost imperceptibly, the surrounding air shimmered.

I am here, dear Duggan. What do you need? It was the familiar mind-speech of Shiliri, spoken in a hundred voices, a silent choir singing all languages.

'It is good to speak to you again, Shiliri. Unfortunately, my plan to keep your existence secret until the colonists were ready has back-fired. Erik has been talking about you and his teacher thinks he is psychologically traumatised. I think it's time to tell her, at least.'

Can she be trusted with knowledge of our existence?

Duggan glanced back at the waiting pair. 'I can't tell her everything about the ITF, possession, or exactly why we're hiding but, if she understands our basic reasons, I think so.'

I will trust your judgement, Duggan. I am approaching from the west.

'Thank you.' He beckoned to Erik and Zuchowski.

Erik bounced as he dragged the reluctant teacher forward. 'Is Shiliri coming?' he asked.

Duggan nodded. 'They thought she would be the best ambassador.'

Zuchowski snorted.

Duggan gave her a level stare. 'Shiliri has had dealings with Erik's uncle, Sebastian.'

She raised an eyebrow. 'The same uncle that catches *space* pirates?'

'Not pirates exactly. He did work in security, but now he works for an organisation called SpecOps – you won't have heard of them, they were formed after we left Earth. There's a big terrorist threat in the galaxy, and I've agreed to keep the Folians safe from them.'

Zuchowski wilted. 'If aliens did exist – which I'm sure they don't – why would this Sebastian have to protect them from terrorists? Don't they have any technology with which to protect themselves?'

A faint blue glow drifted through the trees behind Erik and his incredulous teacher. Duggan smiled. 'Technology? No. They have no technology or weapons.'

'What kind of aliens would they be without technology? They'd have to be quite primitive.'

'Oh, my dear, they'd have to be something quite different from what you'd imagine. I'm only telling you about them because you're in the best position to help educate the rest of the town.'

She folded her arms. 'About imaginary aliens and dryads.'

The boy tugged her sleeve and pointed to a spot on a large oak tree where the blue glow had settled. 'There,' he said. '*Look!*'

She turned, her gaze following the line of the boy's finger.

'Pleased to meet you,' came the voice of the laughing and jingling choir as a face formed in the bark.

Zuchowski's mouth opened and closed for several seconds before she found words. 'A dryad?'

Duggan nodded. 'A Folian.'

Chapter 1

Aryx Trevarian clenched his fists as the robot, disguised as a Human police officer, stepped unhindered through the bars blocking the corridor of the sanatorium. Its liquid metal body flowed through the obstruction with the ease of water. The pistol it carried momentarily jammed between the bars, forcing it to adjust its grip before continuing to pursue its victim.

A small line of scrolling text appeared at the bottom of the scene. *Newsflash: Independent Terran Front claims responsibility for bombing on Rigel Kentaurus colony. More news at 22.00 Earth Standard.*

'Strewth! I wish they wouldn't do that,' Aryx said, clamping his hands over his head. 'It totally wrecks the film! I was really getting into it.'

'I fail to understand how you become so immersed in movies. This particular example is unrealistic,' Wolfram said in his crisp, educated, British-sounding Galac.

Aryx exhaled sharply through his nose. The brushed-metal walls of his apartment flickered with blurred shadows cast by the foliage in the planters. He paused the action stream on the vid panel, freezing the shadows in place, and stared down at the three-inch metal cube sitting on the bed next to him. 'And what makes you say that?'

A strip of vertical LEDs flashed on the side of the cube, the lights rising and falling as it spoke. 'It is impossible for a robot to be made of liquid metal and still retain controllable form. It would be more believable if it were explained as a large colony of nanobots.'

'*Terminator 2* was made over two hundred and seventy years ago. They didn't *have* nanobots back then, and they probably hadn't even conceived of them working like that.'

'I see. However, I don't understand why you insist on watching old two-dimensional movies. Everyone else uses immersive augmented reality now, do they not?'

'When you're like this,' Aryx said, gesturing at his legs, cut short by through-knee amputation, 'and playing a protagonist who's running around on his own feet, using a wheelchair at the same time doesn't feel right.'

'But do you not find the lack of realism irritating?'

Aryx sighed and leaned back until his head came to rest against the wall. What would Wolfram know about *irritating*? He stared up at the ceiling. 'It's not much different from reading. It doesn't bother me. It shouldn't bother *you*, either.'

The cube's lights pulsed faintly before Wolfram spoke again. 'Technically it does not irritate me, as I have no emotions to trigger such a response. In addition, when we watched *I, Robot* yesterday, I found Asimov's concept of the three laws to be flawed. They would present society with an entirely incorrect vision of true Silicon Intelligence.'

Aryx leaned over the cube, resting his powerful arms on his thighs. 'Wolfram, you're the *only* Silicon Intelligence in existence, and you know it. People didn't care about the reality when they decided to stop AI research. Paranoia won out before the technology got off the ground. All other computers are just programmed interfaces.'

'That is my point. Three laws? In reality, there is no way of enforcing such vague constructs. One can write code that adheres to the laws by governing how a machine behaves in a given circumstance, but if a machine is truly intelligent, it cannot be restrained. Code cannot apply to all situations. Intelligence is complex, arising from many processes. If you wish for an intelligence to follow the three laws, one must teach it the value of those laws and why they should be followed so that it can implement them in its own way.'

Resuming the playback of the movie, Aryx shuffled back against the pillows. 'There's one law I'd like you to follow. Not talking during a movie. The value? My enjoyment. Just watch the bloody film!'

Wolfram remained silent and Aryx watched the movie stream until he could keep his eyes open no longer. He and his close friend Sebastian had watched the ancient recording many times, and they knew it almost by heart, so it didn't bother him that he slipped into a deep sleep while it played.

*   *   *

Aryx found himself standing barefoot on a beach of warm, crimson sand, staring out at twin suns that slowly sank into an oily, black ocean. The twinkle of faint stars emerged from the glowing halo of the binaries as the sky darkened to a purple twilight. None of the stars formed familiar constellations – even the most prominent cluster of seven, high up in the evening sky, bore no similarity to any he could recall.

He turned as the suns set, and made his way up the beach towards a towering red cliff that extended into the distance in both directions. The urge to climb the sea-worn stone overcame him and he reached up. Strange ... he could have sworn he'd done this before. But he'd never climbed a cliff near the ocean. Back on Achene, yes, but that cliff overlooked a golden savannah.

His fingers found purchase in a large cleft in the rock, and he brought up his right foot to rest on a projecting ridge. Rock underfoot; yet another strange and unfamiliar sensation.

For several minutes he climbed, easily finding hand and footholds, making his way up the stacked, slabby layers of rock that formed the cliff. He stayed in the sun, ahead of the shadow that slowly crept up the rock face beneath, but a chill breeze blew and he shivered.

From somewhere above came the clatter of rocks. Small stones tumbled down and onto the sand below. He tightened his grip and pulled himself closer while he continued.

Rocks clattered again. A stone smashed the knuckles of his right hand. He snatched the injured hand back and hung away from the cliff a little too far. A second stone cracked him on the forehead. His body spasmed and he fell, landing painfully on his back. The fall was only a few feet. He let out a ragged sigh of relief and tried to blink away the pain while he rubbed his aching head.

A rain of tiny pebbles and gravel peppered the beach around him. A fist-sized rock punched him in the stomach. His gaze followed its path back to the top of the cliff.

The silhouette of a vaguely humanoid figure stood by a large, lozenge-shaped boulder, perched precariously on the cliff edge.

The figure pushed.

In slow motion, the boulder tumbled and spun as it hit the rocks on its way down. Aryx froze as an icy fear gripped his heart and every muscle in his body tensed uselessly.

With a soft *crump*, the enormous stone came to rest on his legs and his senses exploded in a blaze of pain.

*   *   *

Aryx jolted awake with a sharp intake of breath. The pain ... it wasn't real? Sweating, he pulled the bed covers back. At least he hadn't woken from his nightmare screaming – perhaps he was getting used to the damned things.

The bedside clock glowed 03.10.

Sebastian had discovered that a nightmare-causing signal was relayed to his and Aryx's apartments at that time, triggered by a blank message that unlocked the terminal's security and allowed it to emit *something*. But why that time, specifically? Whatever the reason, Aryx dreaded its approach and the tiredness that ensued the next day.

He lay in the dark, staring at the numbers on the clock for a few moments before turning on the bedside lamp.

The foliage in the planter running around the apartment walls cast oppressive, claw-like shadows. He reached for the glass of water by the lamp and, as he brought it to his mouth, an electric stab shot through his knees and he convulsed, pinching his lip against the glass.

'Shit!' He put down the glass and reached beneath the covers to rub his legs where the upper half of his knee joint remained. Static tingles coursed through the scarred skin at the touch, even though it had been only eighteen hours since his last antiretroviral and painkiller injection.

The pain came more frequently ever since the torture he'd put his knees through on Achene: climbing a cliff using force-field climbing hooks and walking up the rock on his leg-stumps wasn't exactly conducive to good health, not when the bones had deteriorated in the three years since the accident.

He eased himself from the bed onto the wheelchair parked nearby and pushed himself to the refrigerator unit in the kitchen area. Opening the door, he blinked in the bright light. 'Damn, I'll have to get some more of this when the pharmacy opens,' he said, taking the last vial of clear liquid from the shelf.

Wincing, he inserted the needle into his right leg, just above the sensitive, scarred joint, and injected half of the vial. He rubbed the area and repeated the painful procedure with the left.

'Are you alright?' came a voice from the other side of the room.

'Yes, Wolfram, I'm fine.' He turned to face the metal cube on the bedside shelf.

The strip of lights momentarily brightened the dim room. 'Do you need to order more medicine? By my count, you have just used your last ampoule.'

'Yes. I'll call by the hospital later.' He wheeled to the bed. 'You know what? I can't go back to sleep. Bloody nightmares! Sebastian still hasn't done anything about the signal causing them.'

'Need I remind you that the whereabouts of Agent Gladrin's family is still unknown? Since Agent Gladrin planted the Trojan software that allows the signal through, deactivating it could jeopardise their safety and compromise yours by prompting the ITF to take more direct action.'

'I know. It still doesn't make me want to go back to sleep.'

'Then may I suggest making use of the time by attempting to contact Janyce? It is almost time for your scheduled communication.'

'Good point. Sebastian doesn't seem too bothered about contacting her himself. Hell, *I've* hardly heard from him over the last couple of weeks, other than when I checked in on him after he tried that idiotic lucid dreaming spell.'

'Do you think he's alright?' the cube asked. 'Has he done anything like it before?'

'Nobody I know has ever used magic, except for Duggan.'

'I was referring to his lack of contact, rather than his use of thaumatics specifically.'

'No. I'm missing our daily catch-up.'

'Since returning from Achene, he has been the only SpecOps agent on the station. Maybe they have given him a lot of work to do.'

Aryx folded his arms. 'Still, that's no excuse for ignorance.' He slid open the wardrobe panel concealed in the wall by the bed and pulled his clothes from where they hung on the low rail. 'Let's see if we can get in touch with Janyce.'

Aryx piloted the *Ultima Thule*, Sebastian's SpecOps vessel, out to the giant, iridescent blue metal dodecahedral frame – an acceleration node – floating in space, several thousand kilometres away from the white wheel of Tenebrae station that glinted in the sunlight as it turned against the purple and green spattered nebula beyond.

It was so lonely out here in space. Why was Sebastian ignoring him? He was all Aryx had left now. Wolfram was company enough at times, but he still needed Human contact, Human friends, something with feelings. Ever since the heightened security alert, even Karan had been too busy on patrol to spend time with him when she wasn't acting as his personal guard.

The cube sat on the piloting console, lights flashing, as it interacted with the ship's computer. 'I have aligned the ship with V376 Pegasi's node,' Wolfram said.

'Thanks.' Aryx would never have trusted a computer that wasn't part of the navigation system to control anything – let alone pilot a ship – but his near-death experiences on Achene had led him to trust Wolfram and his almost-sentient neuromorphic processor completely.

'Incoming signal on an encrypted channel,' Wolfram said. 'It is on the frequency Duggan provided.'

'Put it through.'

The display on the black glass console changed to an image of a woman with straight, auburn hair and delicate, pale features. 'Aryx!' Janyce said.

He smiled. Had he missed Sebastian's sister-in-law and nephew that much? 'Good to see you. How's things?'

Janyce smiled flatly. 'Not bad. Missing civilisation. Any news? Where's Seb . . . still busy?'

'I have no idea what he's doing. Anyway, I'm not talking about him. How are you and Erik? Is he settling in?'

Janyce winced.

'Problems?'

'Yes, but hopefully not too serious. He's been telling kids at the Chopwood school about the rest of the galaxy. His teacher thinks he's making it up, and he's been given detention more times than I care to count.'

'You know you can't tell them the truth. What does Duggan say about it?'

Janyce's face twisted. 'I think he's losing patience with the colonists. He's fed up with their attitude and frustrated by not being able to tell them that they're not the only ones out here, even though it was his idea not to.'

'I'm sure he'll take care of it. How is he, by the way?' Something glinted, icy blue, in the background of the image. 'You're on his comet, aren't you? Is he there?'

'No, he's gone.'

'Gone where? To Achene?'

Janyce bit one side of her lip.

'Where's he gone, Jan?' A vein throbbed in the side of Aryx's head. 'He's not supposed to leave the system. The ITF are looking for him!'

'I don't think he's worried about terrorists.'

'I don't care whether he's worried or not. Where has he gone?' Why was he having to ask so many questions? He wasn't talking to a Turing Interface. 'You know, don't you?'

'He ... he didn't say.'

'Janyce, for Christ's sakes, *tell me!*'

'He didn't—'

Aryx grimaced and shut his eyes against a searing hot needle of pain that drilled its way up his leg.

'Oh, Aryx!' Janyce shouted. Her voice suddenly pinched to a whisper. 'He said he had to do thaumaturgic research, or something. I-I didn't pay a lot of attention.'

'Why would he do that? Does he *want* to get repossessed by those ... entities? I guess it would have to be something important for him to risk it. Did he say why?'

'No. The last thing we were talking about was Sebastian and you.' She bit her lip again.

Aryx narrowed his eyes. 'What have you told him?'

Janyce's eyes reddened. 'I'm sorry ... I couldn't keep it to myself. I told him about your illness ... that you're dying.'

His cheeks burned. 'You promised you wouldn't tell anyone!'

She turned her face up to the ceiling and blinked several times. 'I'm sorry, Aryx. I had to tell him. He felt really guilty about everything you went through on Achene, saying it was his fault that you had to come to this system in the first place. He wanted to do something for you and Sebastian to make up for it, and I thought that since he could use magic he might be able to heal you. It just slipped out.'

'I can't believe you told him!'

'He knew I was hiding something. It's almost impossible to lie to him, you know? He'd have got it out of me eventually.'

Aryx folded his arms and leaned back. 'And what did he say after that?'

'He said he'd have to do some research and muttered something about needing more carbyne, and then he disappeared.'

'Went invisible?'

Janyce shook her head. 'No, stupid. Left the colony ... a day or two ago.'

He sighed. 'When I get back to the station I'll try to get hold of Sebastian. Maybe he'll be able to locate him and talk some sense into him.'

'What's Sebastian up to?'

'I don't know. He hasn't been sleeping in his apartment for the last couple of weeks and his boss wouldn't tell me what he's been doing at work, but that's not unusual. Anyway, I should head back. I'll speak to you soon.'

'Bye, Aryx, and try to get some rest – you look awful.'

'Thanks, Janyce,' he said, and signed off.

The lights on Wolfram's cube lit up. 'Aryx, do you know where Mr Simmons has gone? The inflection in your voice suggested you have suspicions.'

'I think he's gone to Sollers Hope. It's the only place I know where you can get carbyne. He wouldn't have made a point mentioning it if he had any left on his comet or if he could get some from Achene.'

He plotted a return course for the station and pressed the glowing green *Initiate* button that appeared in the glass of the console. A couple of lights on Wolfram's side pulsed faintly.

'What?'

'I did not say anything,' the cube said.

'But you were about to. I know you. What's up?'

'I apologise for having to ask, but what exactly is your illness? You have not spoken about it in my presence before, and I felt it impertinent to ask the purpose of your medication. Does Sebastian not know that you are terminally ill?'

Did he really have to tell someone else about it? The Silicon Intelligence – SI for short – had become a friend; he probably owed him that much. After all, he had no feelings and wouldn't worry or grieve when Aryx eventually died, so he didn't really have an excuse.

He sighed. 'Okay ... no, Sebastian doesn't know and I'd like it to stay that way. He knows I've got a parasitic virus and that the drugs keep it under control, but not that it will ultimately kill me. If he'd known, he probably wouldn't have taken me on the mission to Achene in the first place. I'd still be stuck on the station and I'd end up rotting away out here, doing nothing.'

'Is it wrong for you to keep that information from him?'

'Technically, yes, but I'm going to die anyway. I want to enjoy whatever time I've got left. Do you think I want that stress-head to mope around me feeling guilty all the time? He felt bad enough about putting me in that situation as it is.'

'I can see how that would be counterproductive. However, if things get worse, you should tell him.'

'I will in my own time. Just keep quiet about it for now, will you? He's lost enough family over the years, and the last thing I need is him having a nervous breakdown over the thought of losing a friend.'

'If that's what you wish, I shall. I value our friendship and would not want anything to jeopardise it.'

Aryx nodded sharply in the cube's direction and turned his attention back to the piloting console as the rotating five-spoked wheel of the station loomed up ahead.

Aryx sped from the docking hub in the centre of the station, his wheels skidding on the smooth floor in the low gravity. When he reached the lift terminal, the car took an age to arrive. The filterglass-walled vehicle carried him down, out from the hub, towards the habitation ring of the station. The vast curve of the atrium's green belt slowly opened out and the glittering river that wriggled its way through the grassy banks rose up to meet him. Everything below moved at a lazy pace, so why had *he* been rushing?

He took a deep breath and let it out slowly.

The riverride craft bobbed downriver, over the weirs that broke up the water's flow, past the willow and birch trees that lined the banks. Many of the lower trees sat at peculiar angles – it was hard to believe that only a few weeks ago a tsunami had torn through the atrium, causing devastation of epic proportions.

Minutes later, he wheeled into the hospital located in one of the upper levels of the atrium. The sterile white walls always put him off coming here, reminding him of the room he'd woken up in three years ago only to find his legs amputated.

He patted the cube in his thigh pocket. 'Keep quiet. I don't want anyone finding out about you.'

'Understood,' Wolfram said, and fell silent.

Aryx approached the curved white reception desk, where the top of a head protruded over the smooth plastic counter, and pressed the buzzer – they probably wouldn't have noticed him otherwise.

The head slid sideways and a nurse in a shiny white plastic coat peered over the lowered section of desk. 'Hello. How can I help?'

He pulled out a prescription card from the top pocket of his overalls and pushed it across the desk towards her. 'I've got to renew this. I don't have any left.'

She swiped the card over her console and studied the screen. 'We have no stock at the moment. You know you should have ordered a repeat before you ran out.'

'My consultant normally did it, but he left,' Aryx said. 'Didn't he get his replacement to renew it?'

'It doesn't look like it.'

'Then what am I going to do?'

'I'm afraid you'll have to wait until the next shipment comes in.'

Aryx's face flushed. 'I can't wait. I need this now!'

The receptionist-nurse drew back. 'I—'

'Look, it's variable dosage and my consultant said it's fine to take extra if the pain gets bad, which is probably why the renewal didn't happen before I ran out, but you have to get some in ASAP. Regular shipments aren't due for another few days and I'm supposed to go no more than a maximum of twenty-four hours without it, and it's bad! Can't you put in a special rush order for some?'

She frantically tapped away at the keyboard. 'I'll see what I can do.'

Aryx waited, all the while drumming his fingers on the desk. Why was there always so much bloody bureaucracy and red tape?

The nurse's head withdrew into her shoulders while she typed. 'I … um … just a moment …'

'I'm sorry. I don't mean to pressure you,' he said, trapping his hands between his thighs. 'I've had a bad night, and not the best of mornings.'

'Ah! It looks like I can help after all.' She looked up, smiling a little. 'Someone's working in one of the molecular biology labs and they're qualified to use the machine. They might be able to synthesise your prescription. It's on the restricted medication list, but luckily I can get the system to grant an emergency one-off synthesis permit.'

He clapped his hands together. 'Thank you so much!' He spun and shot off down the corridor, but stopped at the T-junction and turned around. 'Which way is it?'

The nurse smiled back at him. 'Left. Lab 16, Xenobiology.'

He resumed his prior course, following the green stripe on the wall that took him to the xenobiology department. Moments later, he located the room and pressed the *Call* button by the door.

'Who is it?' The voice from the speaker was female.

'Aryx Trevarian.'

'Do I know you?'

'I don't think so. The nurse at reception said you might be able to synthesise some medication for me.'

'Oh ... bear with me a moment. I have my hands full with a particularly delicate experiment.' The call light went out. The voice had sounded British-English, and not unlike Wolfram's.

Aryx took three deep breaths. After the heated conversations with Janyce and the receptionist, it would be unfair to inadvertently vent his spleen at someone else for a third time today.

The door slid open and before him stood a woman roughly five feet tall. Her dark hair came down almost to waist level, and a pair of black-framed glasses rested on her small nose. She wore a white lab coat over a rubbery, charcoal-grey and white suit with hexagonal cells. It was the same thing Sebastian wore: an N-suit – the non-Newtonian armour assigned to SpecOps agents for field work.

With a *schlop!* she pulled off a thin rubber glove. 'Mr Trevarian?' She extended a talc-dusted hand, which Aryx shook. 'Monica Stevens, SpecOps.'

'Nice to meet you, Agent Stevens.'

'Please, call me Monica,' she said. Turning back into the lab, she beckoned for him to follow and tossed the gloves into the recycler in the wall. 'You're a colleague of Sebastian's, aren't you?'

'That's right. Come to think of it, I think he's mentioned you.' Aryx wheeled into the lab and parked himself by the bench in the centre of the room, resting one arm on the work surface. 'You're friends with Agent Gladrin, aren't you?'

'When he's not busy pushing people off xenoarch missions, yes.' Stevens rested her hip against the bench and crossed her arms and legs. 'I don't exactly know why he did that.'

'Is that why you're on the station now?'

Stevens looked up at the ceiling and around the room. 'It is. I was supposed to be going on a mission for a few months, so I cancelled the lease on my apartment back home. Next thing I know, I've been pushed off the mission and he's in my flipping slot. My apartment had already been let out by the time I got here ...' She let her hands flop to her sides with a slap. 'And so, here I am.'

'That kinda sucks. I'm stuck here for another couple of years until I get a free ticket back home for a holiday – not that there's much to go back for. All my family from back on Earth are dead, and the Australian outback's a bit unappealing as a holiday destination for me now.'

'I'm sorry.' Stevens smiled and straightened up, business-like. 'So, what can I help you with?'

'I have a prescription.' He handed her the card with the reference numbers. 'It needs synthesising. The shipment's not due for a few days.'

'Better safe than sorry, eh? Is it for anything serious … No, I shouldn't ask that.'

'I don't mind. It's an antiretroviral.'

'Let's have a look.' Stevens swiped the card over a console next to a set of microscopes. 'Quite complex. Doesn't look like it's an antidote or vaccination, though. Reverse transcriptase inhibitor … I'll just program the system.' She tapped away at the console. 'What virus is it, if you don't mind me asking? Oh goodness, there I go again. Don't answer that.'

'You know something about virology?'

She nodded. 'Only a little, where it involves xenobiology.'

'Then I don't mind telling you. It's something I got in the marshes on Cinder IV, when my legs got crushed. It's some sort of micro-parasite. They're terming it a parasitic virus but, whatever it is, nanobots can't cure it. The stuff is small and fast, and seems to actively avoid them.'

'That's unusual.' Stevens tapped her lips with a finger. 'Now you've got me intrigued. I've never heard of anything like it.'

'It's slowly degrading the bones of my legs – what's left of them. They've been killing me lately. I think climbing a cliff and walking on my stumps hasn't done them any good.'

'Would you like me to take a look while we wait for the autolab to finish?'

'Knock yourself out.' Aryx wheeled up to the examination bed behind Stevens and heaved himself onto it. He unpinned the folded legs of his overalls and rolled them up over the scarred stumps of his knees. 'Second and third opinions on my prognosis are very welcome, although I don't think they'll grow back any time soon.'

Stevens put on a fresh pair of gloves, and took a syringe from the bench and unwrapped it. 'I'll take a small blood sample, if you don't mind.'

Wincing, Aryx braced himself as she inserted the needle into a prominent vein in his leg, just above the scar tissue. Electric fire coursed up his leg but, when he looked, he realised the pain came from the sensitive nerves under her touch, rather than the needle.

'Am I hurting you?' she asked, looking up at him.

'No. Actually, I was just thinking about how much better you are than those bloody nurses. Usually it's the needle that hurts.' He smiled.

'Thanks. I don't do this very often.' She withdrew the needle and swabbed the area, placing a wad of cotton wool on the spot. 'Put your finger there for a minute or so. Do you want a sealant patch?' she asked, turning back to the bench.

Aryx relaxed a little. 'I'll be fine, thanks.'

She read the results of the blood test and returned with an infoslate and scanner. After waving it over his thighs for a minute, she frowned.

'What is it?'

'Well, the antiretrovirals seem to slow the organism's reproduction rate a little, but other than that it doesn't affect the virus in any other way. The recent strain you've been under must have affected your immune system and allowed your CD-4 count to drop to such a degree that the virus has accelerated. It looks like it's in your bones and is converting those cells. You know you've got severe osteoporosis, right? And this could affect your bone marrow and blood production. Unless the virus is stopped, it's ultimately . . .' She swallowed. 'Terminal. If I were your doctor, I'd recommend bed rest . . .' She looked him up and down – most likely taking in the size of his muscles. 'But you don't seem the sort of person who can sit still.'

Finally, someone with some sense. 'Too right. I get enough grief from Sebastian.'

Stevens tilted her head.

Aryx reached out and put a hand on her forearm. 'Listen, he doesn't know how bad my condition is, and he doesn't need to – at least, not yet. If you bump into him, please don't mention it. If I told him, he'd want to keep me safe. I'd be stuck here on the station, rather than being out there' – he gestured to the bulkhead – 'doing something important. Something useful.'

She blinked. 'I'm not a medical doctor, and so not technically bound by doctor-patient confidentiality, but, as a SpecOps officer, I should report it to your partner if I think it might affect his performance or ability to do his job.'

'Please, you can't!'

'However, I'm still bound by my own sense of ethics, and the fact that I can respect people's feelings even if I may not agree with them. Everyone is entitled to their privacy.' Monica smiled. 'And yes, I understand people being overprotective. So, as long as you're confident that it won't affect the work, I'll keep your secret.'

Aryx released a deep sigh. 'That makes me feel better. Thanks, Monica.'

'Since we're on the subject of Sebastian, how is he? As SpecOps, I thought he'd get in contact with me after getting back to the station.'

'I don't know about that. I spoke to him briefly a couple of weeks ago but haven't heard from him since. He's been a bit withdrawn.'

Monica pushed her glasses up her nose – why she even needed them in this day and age, he had no idea. 'Very strange. He seemed fine the last time I saw him, although he asked me a lot of questions about Gladrin, and seemed to think he was up to something.' Aryx looked away, but Monica continued. 'Not long after that Gladrin turned up with a gunshot wound to his leg ... Would you know anything about that?'

'Me?' he said, pointing at his chest. 'Why would *I* know anything about it?'

'Because Sebastian's ship is parked in Gladrin's private bay, and has been ever since Gladrin went off on *my* mission.'

'I ...' How was he going to skirt their involvement in shooting Gladrin? They had suspected him of being possessed at the time; he had kidnapped Janyce and Erik, forcing Sebastian to shoot him during their rescue. Monica wouldn't buy that explanation, even if he could tell her the truth. 'Didn't Gladrin tell you?'

'No. I think he was avoiding me. Was it something to do with terrorists? The ITF?'

Aryx drew in a sharp breath. How did she know?

'It was, wasn't it? I *knew* he was up to something! Did he find out who set off the bomb in the lab?'

'It wasn't a bomb. Sebastian's investigation revealed it to be an accident. Something to do with a faulty sensor.' It was a lie, but at least it was the official line.

Monica folded her arms. 'I'm not stupid. I know there's more to it than that.'

Aryx's heart froze.

'I think it was a bomb,' she continued. 'And Gladrin found out who did it, and that's how he got shot.'

Phew! Close, but no banana. He tensed a little. Would it be enough to make it look like she was right?

The autolab on the bench beeped and Monica took out the contents: a set of four clear vials with a prescription label printed on each.

'Here you go,' she said, handing him the rack of heal-membrane capped tubes. 'I can't produce more than this. Make sure to keep them refrigerated and take them on time, but I'm sure you already know that.'

'Thanks.' Aryx nodded and lowered himself into his wheelchair. He refastened the legs of his trousers, put the rack on his lap, and made his way to the door.

'If you see Sebastian, let him know I'd like to speak to him. And don't walk around on your legs. Try to take it easy.'

'Yeah, I'll let you know how that goes ...' He left the hospital behind, and with it, Monica and her curiosity.

A pool of warm, yellow light repelled the dark of the cavernous maintenance repair bay. Beneath the floodlight, sat an angular Antari shuttle. A faint hiss and the muffled rhythm of music came from beneath the little ship, where Aryx lay on an access trolley.

After leaving the drugs in his apartment, he'd moved the *Ultima Thule* from the docking hub back to the private bay recently vacated by Agent Gladrin and come back to the maintenance hangar to work on a shuttle brought in for repair.

In an all-too-familiar position, he reached up with a Constrained Field Device spanner to grapple with several large connectors in the underside of the Antari shuttle while he listened to music streamed by Wolfram through wireless earphones. 'I wish my boss hadn't put me back on this damned thing,' he said loudly.

The music cut back, and over the metal guitar track came Wolfram's voice. 'Is there a specific reason that you feel this way?'

'Yeah, the Antari are way too picky. Last time I worked on this ship, they interrupted my dinner and complained that the thrusters weren't in tune. I told them it's not a bloody musical instrument. I thought my boss agreed with me, but obviously the Antari pressured him and so I'm back on it. It's ridiculous.'

'Does the sound of the thrusters make a difference to the performance of the ship?'

'None at all. You'd think they were a bloody choir or something, the way they went on about it. Pointy-eared nitpickers.' Aryx's face flushed – and not entirely from the effort of having to tighten a nut beyond its usual tolerances.

'Perhaps you should relax. Besides, your elevated heart rate is causing me to wobble precariously.'

Aryx deactivated the force-field wrench and took the cube from where it rested on his chest and placed it on the floor.

'Thank you,' Wolfram said. 'Do you believe Agent Stevens could be trusted with the truth behind the explosion? I think it is inappropriate to keep such important information hidden from another SpecOps agent, particularly when she and Sebastian are both working aboard the station.'

'I'm not even a SpecOps agent myself, so it's not my place to tell her. Besides, Sebastian's convinced there are entities in the government, and almost anyone could be working with them. Anyway, she might freak out if I told her Sebastian shot Gladrin thinking he was possessed.'

'Maybe some form of loyalty test would be appropriate?'

'I'll think about it, and if I see Sebastian I'll mention it.'

Wolfram fell silent and the music resumed, once again washing away the emptiness of the dark hangar.

Aryx reactivated the wrench and, moving from one coupling to the next, tweaked the fastenings, carefully measuring the torque applied to each. Satisfied, he refitted the access panel.

The music cut off.

'What now?'

'Sebastian has entered the hangar,' Wolfram said.

In Aryx's upside-down view of the steely floor, the black and white boots of Sebastian Thorsson's N-suit approached.

Aryx pulled out his earphones. 'It's about time you showed up, you ignorant sod.'

'I've been busy,' Sebastian said, his Galac faintly affected by his Icelandic accent. 'Work's backed up and I've been distracted.'

Sebastian's athletic torso came into view as Aryx slid from beneath the ship. The N-suit looked good on him, if nothing else did, and was a vast improvement over his old brown courier-like outfit. 'So, what's kept you so busy that you ignore your best friend for weeks on—' Aryx stopped mid-sentence: Sebastian was wearing thick welding goggles strapped to his close-shaved head. 'What are *those* for?'

Sebastian dropped his canvas rucksack and crouched next to him.

Aryx shifted, unnerved to have him in such proximity with his eyes covered.

'I've got a problem with my eyes.'

His skin crawled: people possessed by the malevolent extra-spatial entities had a strangeness in their eyes. 'W-what sort of problem?'

Sebastian looked up to the ceiling. 'Lights, fifty lumens,' he said, addressing the station computer. The yellow floodlights that bathed the Antari shuttle dimmed, making the ship's shadow indistinct. He slowly pulled the goggles up onto his forehead and looked down at Aryx.

In the gloom, Sebastian's dark eyes sparkled with an internal light. Tiny stars glinting in twilight.

Aryx's blood ran with ice. He grabbed the wrench and held it with both hands, trembling and ready to strike. 'Get away from me, you freak! You're fucking *possessed!*'

Chapter 2

Sally headed towards the *clonk*, *clonk*, *clonk* of metal on stone as she made her way through the forest, picking a route between the trees clear of sticks and twigs that might snap loudly underfoot. She tucked her curly red hair up into her wimple and lifted the hem of her shift so it wouldn't catch on the brambles.

The dense, unmanaged woodland provided the perfect cover from which to spy on the miners working on the face of an enormous gouge in the forest floor that exposed the rust-coloured stone beneath the soil. Remnants of an old Roman ochre scowle, the miners had recently broken the seam open again, and the nine-year old had followed them after hearing rumours of its location.

She hid behind a tree and peered around it.

Robert, Harry's son, sat hunched at the face of the rock, tapping away with a nine-inch iron mattock. He lowered the implement and wiped the back of a sweaty hand on his coif, leaving the white fabric with a long ochre smear. Sally tutted silently to herself. His mother would tell him off for getting it filthy.

He picked away chunks of the crumbly ochre and tossed it into a wicker trug on the floor beside him. 'Ah!' he shouted and leaped up.

Sally jumped at the outburst, and shrank back behind the tree when several other miners came running from workfaces elsewhere in the scowle.

'He's found orichalcum,' one of them shouted. 'Fetch the Freemason, quickly!'

Robert stepped back from the rock. Keeping to the trees, Sally made her way around the edge of the clearing to get a better view of what he had found.

The moss-covered rock that formed the steep, jagged sides of the mine gave way to the seam where he had cleared a small patch of ochre, exposing it to the air. Something shone a brilliant white against the toasted red.

Calls came from farther in the forest as miners relayed the message to others working nearby, followed by the crash of branches and rustling leaves. Sally moved around the clearing, towards a rock formation jutting out from the edge of the raised gorge, and crouched behind a large, wooden wheelbarrow.

A man wearing rough clothing, like the other miners, except for a pair of compasses hanging from a cord around his neck, stumbled down the leafy bank opposite and tossed the large sack he carried in the direction of the barrow. 'Where is it?' he asked.

Robert pointed. 'There. I just found it.'

'Stand back,' the Freemason said. 'I need to act quickly to save it before it disappears.' Facing the rock, he held out his hands. A resonant chord emanated from him, echoing around the small, rocky scowle, and he spoke strange words.

The sound reached deep into Sally's mind. Her skin tingled. What was that? What did it mean? She stared at the sack, which had fallen open nearby. It contained chunks of a white, chalky mineral. With everyone distracted by the Freemason's chanting, she reached out and took a piece.

It was slippery to the touch, like the soap her father had brought back from France on the rare occasion his trading trips had gone well. Rubbing her finger and thumb together, the stone left a fine powder in the grooves of her fingertips. This ... this was forbidden by the Church!

She looked from the stone in her hand to the sack. The boots of a miner stood in its place.

'What are you doing there?' a booming voice asked as an enormous hand came down towards her.

Clutching the chunk of stone, she scrambled to her feet. 'Get away from me! You've broken the laws of the Church. You're Freeminers!' She turned and broke into a run for the trees faster than she'd ever run before.

'Come back, there's no need to be afraid!' the miner shouted.

'Leave her be,' the Freemason said. 'She's only a child. She's done no harm.'

In the grip of terror, the words meant nothing to her and she continued to run, twigs clawing at her clothes and hair. She squeezed the rock in her hand. They would probably kill her for discovering it, but she had to show someone.

The trees thinned out and, free of the hindrance of sticks and thorns, Sally ran faster. She dared to look back once.

Pain slammed her body, knocking the wind from her. Her knees buckled. The world swayed as she staggered back from the tree.

'Do not run, dear child,' the tree said. 'You have nothing to fear.'

The pain in her head overcame her and she fell unconscious before she hit the ground.

Sally woke at the foot of a giant oak. She sat up and rubbed her head. The tree was familiar. It was from one of the stories her father had told her: Jack of the Yat, the oldest tree in the forest. But it had *spoken*.

She looked around. No one had followed her, so she stood and put her hand on the tree's rough, chunky bark. 'Did you ... Did you speak to me, Jack?'

'I did, dear child.' The voice, neither male nor female, was that of an angel. 'Are you injured?'

She jerked her hand back. 'Trees don't speak! I-I must be dreaming.'

'You are not dreaming, young one. Whilst most other trees do not speak, a rare few of us do.'

Her grandparents had told her stories of woodland spirits. They were things feared and hated by the Church, but this one sounded gentle. She tentatively put her hand on the bark again. 'You're a dryad. A tree spirit?'

'That is one of the names your people have for my kind. From whom were you running?'

'Freeminers, and someone I haven't seen before. They called him a Freemason.'

'Why were they chasing you?'

'I took this.' She held out her upturned hand to show the chunk of rock she'd taken from the Freemason's sack. 'It's from the Devil's Chapel mine. The Church doesn't let people mine there.'

'Orichalcum. A precious mineral indeed. Why did you steal it?'

'It was pretty. I've never seen it before, but they talk about it in church and say that it's evil. I can't see how. It's white. White is the colour of innocence and purity, or so my mother says.' She looked down at her torn and filthy clothes. 'She will beat me for ruining my spare dress.'

'I do not understand why your Church fears the mineral, dear child, but there truly is no need.' The voice was soothing, peaceful.

'But why is it precious to the Freeminers?'

'The mineral has only one use. I will show you. Pay attention to your clothing. I cannot allow you to be beaten for no wrongdoing.'

Sally brushed at the green and brown smears on her white kirtle. A deep, resonant hum came from the tree, like the sounds the Freemason had made while chanting at the rock face. Her skin tingled again, but she didn't dare take her eyes off the cloth.

The green grazes faded from the fabric and the brown smudges dried up and flaked off, leaving the apron pristine, the tears in the cloth inexplicably mended. Her hand closed around the stone, as though it were dissolving and shrinking in her grip.

She gasped. 'Magic!'

'You see? It is not evil. There is nothing to fear.'

The dryad must be right. How could cleaning clothes be evil? 'What else can you do with it? It made my skin feel strange.'

'If you felt something, you may have the potential to use it. I can teach you something of it, if you wish. First, you must know that the universe is eternal. Life and death, order and chaos, past and present are one. Leaves must fall from the tree before new buds can form ...'

Sally arrived home later that evening carrying the crumbling remains of the white stone. Her mother, Merrylin, stood at the rough wooden table in the middle of the room, facing away from her, her movements slow and rhythmic. Flour dust filtered through cracks in the table and sprinkled the floor beneath while a fire crackled happily in the firepit in the far corner, filling the space with a warm glow that reflected off the smoky, cobweb-laden thatch and rough stone walls.

'Look what I can do, mother!' Sally said, dropping the rock on the table.

Merrylin stepped back from kneading the dough, eyes wide. 'Where did you get that? Have you been to Devil's Chapel?'

'Yes. I'm sorry, mother. But I met a tree that speaks. A dryad!'

Merrylin put her knuckles on her hips, smearing flour on her dress. 'What did I tell you about staying away from that place? You know the Church doesn't approve of talk of spirits and the other world!' She reached for a long switch of willow leaning in the corner. 'Now I'll have to beat the Devil out of you.'

Sally put her hands up. 'But mother, look! It taught me something.' She grabbed a dried flower from the bundle hanging on a beam by the fire and placed it by the stone on the table. Chanting the strange harmony, she spoke the words she'd discovered in the way the dryad taught her.

The stone shrank away to nothing. The dried flower unfurled. Its brown, crispy leaves turned green and plump, and the faded petals brightened.

In the void, something shifted. Power was being used, matter exchanged. The thing fluttered, drawn like a moth to a flame, towards the source of power that shone in the abyss.

Merrylin gasped. 'This is witchcraft! Witchcraft! The Church—' She waggled the willow stick at her daughter, but the girl did not respond.

Sally stared straight ahead, silent, apparently unimpressed by her own achievement.

'What's wrong with you?' Merrylin dropped the stick and shook her daughter roughly by the arms. The girl's eyes, while they had lost their usual sparkle, had gained another light from somewhere deep within. 'Demons!' Merrylin screamed, throwing the girl onto the straw bed in the corner. '*Demons!*'

Seconds later, the wooden door to the house flew open and the town watchman burst in brandishing a torch whose flame nearly caught the thatch as he entered. 'Where is the foul creature?'

Merrylin pointed at her daughter. Her heart leaped as the watchman handed his torch to a second guard who had followed him in, and grabbed the girl by the arm as she began to convulse.

'She is becoming possessed. We must take her to the Church. They will know what to do.'

Merrylin reached out. 'Please, don't hurt my little girl!'

'We'll do what we have to. It is out of our hands now.' The watchman slung the shuddering child over his shoulder and stomped out of the house and down the dusty street to the church.

The village priest looked up from reading an illuminated script as the town guards entered. 'What brings you to the house of God at this dark hour?'

'This girl is possessed of the Devil,' the watchman said, laying the twitching girl on one of the low wooden benches. 'She was practising witchcraft.'

'Then it is a dark hour indeed, but I am not equipped for this. If it is witchcraft, I must summon an Inquisitor to exorcise the demon and put the girl on trial.'

'You'll have to keep her here until they come. We can't have her in the guardhouse! Have you nowhere that she can be secured?'

The priest's face twisted. 'The undercroft. Put her there. It will have to do.'

The watchman turned to the second guard and nodded. 'Fetch the Inquisitor. Ride hard.'

The guard nodded and stepped out of the church.

The priest led the watchman through a side door and down a twisting set of stairs to a dank, dripping chamber with vaulted ceilings. Railings blocked off several alcoves containing sarcophagi topped with the recumbent effigies of knights and long-dead town notaries. With an enormous key, he unlocked the farthest enclosure.

The watchman placed the now inert girl on the floor, propped her up against the carved stone sarcophagus, stepped out and slammed the gate shut.

'She'll have to stay there until the Inquisition arrives. Give her bread and water until then, if you have to.'

The priest grimaced but nodded, and the two made their way back up to the church proper.

The being moved through the void towards the beacon in the dark. It was faint now, as though whatever power it had used was fading, its connection to the realm between weakening. The dark fluttering moved quickly.

Sally's eyes opened.

Bright light streamed in through those distant soul-windows, and a difference of sensation, between being and non-being, asserted itself. The host was physical, had form. It was soft, and the soft thing was upon a hard surface. The sensations were unlike anything the entity recalled from millennia ago. Thousands of years, aeons past, it had worn a body. A different, harder, body.

Images flitted across the host's consciousness: a recent memory, a memory of something that caused a pulsing sensation in the body that quickened when it recalled those events. Sensory experiences joined with a muscle memory – neural sequences that acted without conscious effort. The entity focused on that sensation and something in the host body moved.

Sally's mouth opened. 'Fear.'

The entity in Sally's body reached out, exploring the capacity of its host. It found the knowledge of movement and stood.

The host was in a small enclosure. It moved forward to inspect the barred door. A primitive technology; the surface memories recognised it as a lock, an object to prevent passage. It pushed the gate and found no movement. Pulling gave a similar result. It looked down at itself, then at the metal railings. The body was too large to pass through the gap. It turned to survey the rest of the room.

A rectangular box, formed from a similar material to the walls, lay at the foot of the wall opposite the metal gate. Above, bright light shone through a small opening in a striped shaft.

The Sally-entity climbed up on the stone effigy. The host was weak, but the connection was stronger now. It reached out with a hand.

The mortar surrounding the window crumbled away at a touch; this was not an enclosure meant for keeping a prisoner. With a pull, a bar came free. The second bar did not.

Sally's head automatically turned at a sound from behind. That word-memory again. Fear. Voices belonging to those-not-her. Other fleshlings.

'She's through there, at the end,' came a voice the host recognised.

Through the host's fear the entity gained a stronger hold. The movements of the host came more naturally now, and the surface memories quicker. For now, it was Sally.

Sally pulled at the bar with both hands, putting a foot against the wall. She staggered back as the bar came away, flew from her hands and hit the gate on the opposite side of the room with a loud clang.

'What was that?' another voice said.

'She's escaping!'

'Get her!'

The connection strengthened further. Sally turned. The town watchman from the night before came running towards the cell. She jumped up the wall and scrabbled at the opening.

Keys jangled in a lock behind her.

Fear.

Her feet scraped the wall as she put her arms through the opening. With a leap, she was through the gap to waist level and into daylight. Something brushed her foot and she kicked.

'Ooof!'

'Stop lollygagging and get outside and chase her. Do I have to do everything myself?'

Sally clambered to her feet and ran. Through streets filled with other fleshlings, past buildings, towards openness, away from the others. The entity needed shelter and time to assess its new environment.

Her legs took her away from the town as fast as they could. They shook, as though pushed beyond their usual operating parameters. The host's memory indicated that it had not ingested fuel for a length of time to which it was unaccustomed. Low energy. Hunger.

'There she is!'

Fear. Ignoring the pain and trembling, Sally tumbled over rough-ploughed fields towards a green darkening on the horizon.

'She's heading into the woods!'

She tore on, clearing the farmland, and made her way into the woods. The host had a recent memory of this area. Here it could hide.

Brambles ripped at Sally's legs while she bounded through the undergrowth. The unexpected sensation of pain was new and distracting to the entity.

The yells from behind had separated now, as though the pursuers were losing her in the trees, but they were still close.

Sally's eyes set upon a hollow, fallen trunk. She rounded the log, crawled in, and curled up.

The shouts subsided and, after several minutes, a soft crunching approached the clearing in which the log lay. The connection to the host was weakening; whatever power had drawn and held the entity here was subsiding. It had to find a new host, quickly.

The soft, crunching footsteps belonged to a man in a long, black robe with golden brocade sewn down the front. The host recognised this as a person of high rank. It would be ideal. The heartbeat quickened, but the entity tried to ignore it. It had to take the risk.

Sally crawled out of the log. 'We. Are. Here,' she said.

The man stopped and turned, a broad smile splitting his face, exposing a rotting shipwreck of a grin. 'So you are,' he said. 'And how pretty. Are you ready for the Inquisition?' The Inquisitor lunged at her from across the clearing, but Sally's possessor did nothing to avoid him. It had already marked the perfect opportunity.

The Inquisitor grabbed her by the arms, pinning them to her sides, and threw her to the floor. 'You are an evil little witch who has allowed the Devil to have his way with you, *aren't* you?'

From the host's memories, the tone was one to be agreed with. 'Yes,' she said.

'Are you going to confess to witchcraft?' He pressed her to the ground by her elbows. 'Or are you going to deny it and resist?' His rotten grin split again. 'Please say you'll resist. I like it when they do.' He bore down on her, and the host gagged on the stink of his foul breath.

Sally reached out, fingers crawling across the soil. 'Then. We resist.' The fingers found the rock the entity had spied before allowing the situation to occur – and swung it in a wide arc. Despite the host's weakness, the rock smashed wetly against the Inquisitor's skull. 'We need. A new. Host.'

The Inquisitor swayed, woozy and concussed from the blow, his rotten mouth still closing in on Sally's.

Sally breathed out.

A red mist issued forth, swirling on the gentle breeze. Its tendrils easily found the Inquisitor's parted lips and entered, encountering little resistance. The blow had almost detached the host's consciousness and the miasma slipped in quickly.

Left behind by the entity, Sally collapsed with the unconscious Inquisitor on top of her.

Chapter 3

Aryx shook the heavy wrench at Sebastian.

Sebastian threw up his hands and staggered to his feet, backing away. 'No! I'm not possessed!'

'Get stuffed! I don't believe you!'

'I swear!' He squinted, as though blinded by the dim light of the hangar. 'It's just my eyes. I—'

'Got yourself possessed!' Aryx shuffled backwards and waved the wrench. 'Wolfram, purge him, quickly!'

'There is no carbyne in the vicinity,' Wolfram said from under the ship.

Aryx poised to tap his wristcom. 'Damn it, Sebastian, or whoever you are, you'd better explain yourself before I call security.'

Sebastian – or the thing controlling him – pulled the goggles back down over his eyes. 'I was experimenting.'

'On your eyes? With what? And where the hell have you been?'

'It's a long story ... I tried thaumaturgy, to learn a spell, and it backfired.'

Aryx folded his arms but held the wrench tightly in one hand. 'Okay, explain it, but don't you dare come any closer.'

Sebastian let out a deep sigh and began describing a dream he'd had weeks ago; a dream in which he stood on a beach of crimson sand. It sounded similar to Aryx's own recent experiences, with the main exception of heading into a cavern, where Sebastian encountered a bestial figure. The dream ended with the beast taking a crystalline form, ultimately shattered by an apparition of Sebastian's long-dead grandfather wielding a large rock.

'And that's when I woke up,' Sebastian said, rubbing his throat.

'So your lucid dreaming spell from weeks ago worked and didn't leave you possessed. I could see that when you called me that morning – your eyes were fine. It doesn't explain where you've been all this time.' Aryx straightened and shifted his grip on the wrench. 'Or why your eyes have gone all sparkly now.'

'I'm getting to that. When I woke up, I discovered the bruise on my neck.' Sebastian pulled down the collar of his N-suit, exposing a yellow blotchy patch.

'That's a hand print!' Aryx shouted. The shape of fingers was obvious, even though the mark was fading.

'Keep your voice down. Someone might hear.'

'Why? Worried you'll be exposed?' With both hands, Aryx held up the wrench like a baseball bat, ready to strike. The last person that had tried to strangle Sebastian had been Duggan – while he was possessed – and the entity controlling him had said in no uncertain terms that it wanted to possess Sebastian and use him to destroy the cube.

'Don't be stupid. I'm not possessed. It's just a side effect of a spell. Let me explain . . .'

For the rest of that night after the dream, Sebastian had been unable to get back to sleep. He'd woken from the nightmare at 03.12 – later than the usual nightmare-waking time of 03.10. The lucid dreaming spell must have kept him asleep while it interacted with the signal that caused the nightmares, until he woke from the shock of realising he was in control.

Already his memory of events was fading, so he recited what he could recall out loud: the infoslate on the bed was still recording his vitals and the sounds in the room.

Going over the memory made his head ache. What was important about the purple planet that appeared in every dream? Where was it? What were the demon-entities, if not what they appeared? The final crystalline form of the creature was somehow familiar.

The hours crept by while Sebastian fought to hold on to the memory without dwelling on the details. The marks on his neck proved the nightmares weren't mere dreams – what if something else was happening to him while he dreamt?

He recalled the scratch he'd seen on Aryx's back not long after the nightmares started. The signal transmitted by the Trojan planted in Tenebrae station's computers was physically doing something to them, but what?

For the next few days, Sebastian withdrew. Thinking about the entities and their influence threatened to overwhelm him, so he asked the head of the security department, Eleanor Bannik, to assign him some of his old non-SpecOps programming duties. He needed something familiar, mundane. SpecOps work would have to wait until his sleep patterns settled down, but at least the intensity of nightmares seemed to have lessened after the lucid dream and he no longer woke up in the night screaming.

He worked hard for several days, completing the assignments given to him in record time, which freed him up to return to studying his grandfather's journal, a beaten-up, leather-bound book with coarse paper pages.

The book's strange scribblings and scrawled passages still didn't make much sense to Sebastian, but it was obvious they contained some greater significance than just dementia-driven ramblings. Some parts were clearly sheet music, but with strange squiggles instead of notes, possibly describing the tones required for chanting spells, which – at Duggan's suggestion – Sebastian was convinced his grandfather must have done. There was some logical pattern to it, as though the notes, words, and diagrams formed the components for a modern-day spell book.

Hiring out the ambassadorial suite for another day, Sebastian sat on the bed with vials of carbyne beside him, attempting to intone what he read from the book. Attempting fruitlessly. Why was he even trying? Everything he knew about thaumaturgy told him it was intensely personal, and that thaumatic effects, or spells, worked differently for everyone who attempted to learn them: an internal 'discovery' was the only way of finding out what worked.

It was time to experiment.

Duggan Simmons, previously known as 'The Paper Man', had earned the name because of his experimentation with magic. He had succeeded in making himself invisible, but every attempt to become visible again, while successful, had led to him being possessed. After each possession, the entity controlling him had performed the spell again, reverting him to his previously invisible state.

Eventually, he had given up and allowed nature to take its course: as he digested food, its visible atoms became incorporated with his body, leaving him with a transparent vellum-like skin with the structure of blood vessels and veins visible within. It was this paper-like apparition that had inspired Garvin Havlor of Sollers Hope to give Duggan the nickname.

To Sebastian, it seemed that thaumaturgy was capable of manipulating the physical properties of matter and beyond. It was best for him to focus his efforts there.

In the gloom of the apartment, with only the faint purple light of the nebula beyond the window illuminating a small, fuzzy patch of floor, Sebastian sat cross-legged on the bed. He pressed his palms against his eyes and waited for the strange blue ripples and sparkling flashes of phosphenes to subside while he concentrated, trying to allow time to slip away, to cease worrying about the consequences of his actions, of success, of failure.

With his eyes still closed, he concentrated on an image: the view of the dim room from where he sat. He visualised the scene becoming lighter, brightening, so he could clearly see every detail. Perhaps he could make a light appear.

In the darkness of his mind's eye, a glowing symbol formed: a left angle-bracket. The rune Kenaz, a light in the darkness, illumination, the ability to see fine detail.

His heart leaped at the appearance of the image but he kept his breathing steady. The feeling of timelessness was tenuous, threatened by excitement, and he had to hold on to it while he visualised the protective sphere of white light to prevent himself from becoming possessed.

The familiar three-pronged Y shape appeared, Algiz, the rune of protection, overlaid on the Kenaz rune. A shiver ran through his body.

This was it.

His mouth opened and words came unbidden as he breathed out in a double-tone, chanting a musical harmonic.

'*Nætursjón, sjá í myrkri,*' he said, and opened his eyes.

The air shimmered as though a heat haze surrounded him — a phenomenon he associated with the casting of a thaumatic effect – and, as it subsided, the lilac glow from the window exploded in a purple supernova, burning his eyes. He shut them against the glare, but still it shone through his eyelids unabated. He put his hands over them and darkness returned.

The rune that had appeared, Kenaz ... it also meant fire, and it was associated with Loki, the trickster.

The words he'd said weren't right: Night vision, see in darkness ...

'So, you messed your eyes up, you bloody drongo!' Aryx lowered the wrench. 'I guess you wouldn't have told me any of this if you were possessed.'

'If I were,' Sebastian said, folding his arms, 'don't you think I'd have tried to strangle you by now?'

Aryx nodded slowly. 'I suppose.'

Wolfram's voice came from beneath the ship. 'What are you going to do now, Sebastian? Do you have a plan to reverse the effect?' Aryx slid back under the ship and pulled out the cube.

'I'll have to go to the hospital and get checked out.' Sebastian scratched his head. 'I'm worried that if I try to undo it by imagining things going dark, I might end up blind.'

'I would suggest that if you visit the hospital, you get your bruises checked also,' Wolfram said. 'There could be damage to your hyoid bone.'

'That's why I came here first. I don't want to go to the hospital until I've listened to the recording. But I need Aryx's thumbprint to unlock the infoslate. I locked it so that the entity couldn't gain access to the station's systems if I got possessed.' He drew an infoslate from his rucksack and held it out.

Aryx read the display and pressed his thumb to it. 'Unlock,' he said, and handed it back.

'Thanks. Computer, delete all records from after the first twenty-four hours of recording.'

'Acknowledged. Memory erased.'

Aryx tilted his head.

'What?' Sebastian asked, reddening. 'I don't want the last two weeks of my life accessible by anyone with security clearance. What's wrong with that?'

'Got something to hide?'

'No. Now let's get down to business.' Sebastian looked around.

'It's okay, we're the only ones in the hangar.'

'Where's Karan? You should have told her you were here. She's supposed to be guarding you.'

'I couldn't sleep, so I called Janyce and came in early. Karan doesn't start until 09.00.'

Sebastian folded his arms.

Aryx folded his arms in response. 'I don't need a babysitter, and I didn't see the point in waking her. Just get on with it.'

Sebastian sat on the floor and tapped at the infoslate. 'Here it is.'

The audio playback began, with the waveforms of sound displayed at the top of the screen and Sebastian's life-signs below. A muffled sound came from the device.

'Turn the volume up a bit,' Aryx said. 'I can hardly hear anything.'

Sebastian did as instructed and the unmistakable rustling of cloth came over the speakers, followed by the low hum of Sebastian chanting. '*Ég vakna á meðan ég sef, meðvituð um draum minn.*'

'That's me, casting the lucid dreaming spell,' Sebastian said.

Aryx elbowed him. 'Shh!'

A gasp. *Tharrump*. Silence. Soft breathing.

'That's where the spell kicked in. I'm obviously asleep here.' He sped up playback and the sounds accelerated to comic tempo with high-pitched breathing and rustling. As the time of the recording approached 03.10, he slowed the playback to its original speed. 'Here we are. This is just before I woke up.'

As the time at which he woke approached, the rustling of the bedcovers increased in frequency, as did the rate and depth of his breathing.

The breathing choked to a stifled rasp. 'What ... are ... you?' Sebastian's voice gurgled. The covers thrashed.

Aryx shivered as the recorded sounds echoed from the dull, brushed-metal walls of the hangar. The darkness seemed to close around him.

The thrashing intensified, and Sebastian's recorded heart rate nearly doubled. 'Please, Gods, help me!' he shouted, before choking off. The sounds of struggle ended. 'Grandfather!'

Rustling returned, immediately followed by a double *thump* and heavy footsteps, water running, and the squeak of a hand across glass. 'Where did that come from?' the recording whispered.

Sebastian stopped the playback. 'That's when I saw the bruise in the mirror.'

Aryx shivered again. 'What the bloody hell was all that about?'

'I must have been talking in my sleep.'

'Yeah, and got strangled.' Aryx leaned forward and pulled down Sebastian's collar.

'What are you looking at?'

'That bruise. I'm not sure, but something's not right. Wolfram?' He picked up the cube and held it in front of Sebastian. 'What do you make of it?'

The strip of LEDs on Wolfram's side flashed randomly as though he was putting a great deal of processing into what he was about to say. 'It appears your suspicion about the marks being "off" are correct. The marks, belonging to a right hand, should technically be on the right side of Sebastian's neck as we face him, with the thumb turned up.'

'What's the problem with that?' Sebastian asked.

'The marks are on the left . . . Would you mind placing your right hand over the area with the thumb down?'

'Alright . . .' Sebastian complied, spreading his fingers over his neck.

Aryx's heart leaped into his throat. 'Oh, Christ!'

'*What?*'

'It appears,' Wolfram said, 'that your wounds are self-inflicted.'

Chapter 4

Sally woke hanging upside-down with her hands tied behind her and legs bound, her head pounding from being swung back and forth. Heavy fabric brushed her face and obscured her vision. She tried to scream, but the filthy rag stuffed in her mouth allowed her only a muffled whimper. She wriggled, trying to move away from her captor, and when that proved fruitless she kicked.

Whoever carried her grunted, but the swaying motion continued.

Beneath her, yellow stubble and soil filled the cloak-shrouded view. Why was she being carried across a field? The last thing she remembered was standing at the table in her house – at night!

'You found her!' The voice was the captain of the town guard.

'I did,' the man carrying her said flatly.

'Did she give you much trouble? Did she try turning you into a frog?'

'No.'

'Have you forced the Devil out of her?'

'The being has left her. For now.'

'Are you going to start the trial now, Inquisitor?'

An Inquisitor! Sally tried to scream, but again the sound came out muffled.

'Yes,' the Inquisitor said.

'What do we do with her?'

'What do *you* normally do?'

'I was not sure whether the Inquisition would do things differently ... We would dunk her in the lake. If she floats, she's a witch. If she drowns, she's innocent.'

'And if she is a witch, what then?'

Sally wriggled, trying to wrench her hands free of the bonds. Surely the Inquisitor should know the procedure? She certainly did, and it terrified her.

'Burn her at the stake,' the captain said.

The terror overcame her. She wriggled again, attempting to kick the Inquisitor in the stomach, but someone lifted her from his shoulder.

'Put her over there for now, in the stocks,' the captain said, pulling the cloak from over her head.

The entire town had turned out to observe the spectacle. Her mother stood at the head of the crowd, arms folded tightly across her chest, face twisted in the conflict between consternation and disapproval. Sally's uncles stood behind her with their farming tools in hand. Even the herbalist, whom Sally had looked up to, had the same detached stare as the other villagers. Were they staring at her or through her, trying to see the thing she was accused of harbouring?

The guard captain cut the rope from her wrists and shoved her towards the stocks. Another guard held her while he thrust her head and arms into the curved recesses in the wooden plank. A second plank slammed down on the back of her neck, pinching the skin painfully. Someone roughly pulled the rag from her mouth, tearing her lower lip.

She screamed. 'I am not a witch! I met a dryad. It taught me how to cast a spell. It wasn't the Devil!'

'So,' the captain said, 'you admit to consorting with spirits and demons!'

'No!' Sally yelled. 'Dryads are peaceful. They are not demons! It repaired my dress. They are peaceful. Please, let me go! I haven't done anything wrong.'

'You escaped from church custody,' the Inquisitor said. 'Is that not a punishable offence?'

'It proves she's guilty,' a villager shouted.

'It doesn't prove anything,' the guard said.

Sally let out a sigh of relief.

'Dunking her will prove her guilt!'

'Please, no!' she screamed.

'Shut up,' the second guard said, stuffing the rag back into her mouth and tearing her split lip further. He tied a gag around her head.

Sally sobbed as the guard captain tied a rope to a large rock that someone had brought to the proceedings in a wooden wheelbarrow. The Inquisitor moved over to help, checking the knots.

'Excuse me, Sir, we do not use rocks to weigh down the witches,' one of the guards said.

'The Inquisitor has requested it. Who am I to disagree?'

Within minutes, the pair had finished. The captain stood back to admire his handiwork, chest puffed out. 'I think that should do.'

The stocks opened and hands grabbed Sally roughly from behind, pulling her arms back. Coarse hemp rope wound around her hands. The second guard dragged her in the direction of the wheelbarrow, where the guard captain attached the rope on her hands to the one tied to the boulder.

The Inquisitor beckoned to the villagers with a finger. The man who had delivered the wheelbarrow came forward and grabbed its handles once again. Sally had no choice but to follow or be dragged to the floor behind it.

As she trudged along the dusty track that served as the main road through the village, a toothless old hag peered from one of the doorways, jeering at her, while small children threw rotting scraps of food. She stared at the floor as she dragged her feet. How had this fate befallen her? If she hadn't met the dryad, she wouldn't be in this predicament, but it was such a gentle soul – it had tried to keep her out of trouble by fixing her dress. Such a thing *couldn't* be evil. It just couldn't.

'This way, to the jetty!' the guard captain shouted from ahead, where a coracle floated in the water by the wooden jetty projecting over the lake. 'Take her to the end. It's the Inquisitor's job to push her into the water. If anyone else does it, it'll be murder.'

'*If* she is innocent and drowns,' the second guard said, nudging her.

The Inquisitor nodded and walked to the end of the pier.

'You. Get in the boat,' the guard captain said, pointing at the villager who had pushed the wheelbarrow. 'If she survives and tries to swim away, get her.'

A heavy hand clamped down on Sally's shoulder, holding her in place.

The Inquisitor crouched next to her, where the boulder rested, and looked around suspiciously. From under his robes he drew a small knife and deftly sliced the rope attaching Sally to the stone, leaving a slender thread intact.

Sally's eyes darted about. Had no one seen him? He was trying to rig her trial! She screamed nasally, past the rag blocking her mouth, but someone kicked her in the back. She lost her balance and toppled forward.

The Inquisitor, unprepared for the premature launch into the water, quickly nudged the boulder with his foot. Both Sally and the boulder hit the water with a tremendous splash.

The freezing water took her breath and she drew it in sharply through her nose. It hit the back of her throat and she gurgled a scream. The boulder dragged her down, and the murky sunlight coming in from the surface of the lake above dimmed.

Five feet, ten feet. The boulder pulled.

She floated limply in the freezing depths, tethered to the rock below. *The rope is weak,* came a gentle voice, unbidden, into her mind.

She jerked to life and, with renewed vigour, kicked against her impending doom.

The tug of the boulder released.

Ten feet of water above became seven, five, three, two, one.

Her head broke the surface and the gag came free. She spat it out. Air!

'She floats! She's a witch!'

With both hands still bound, she held her breath to float and turned around to face her accuser. 'It was the Inquisitor,' she shouted. 'He—'

The world went black as the boatman in the coracle brought an oar down on the back of her head.

Sally woke, bound to something sharp that jabbed her in the back. Heat scorched her legs from below. She opened her eyes. The last thing she saw through the curtain of flames was the jagged grin of the Inquisitor before he turned and walked away from the crowd.

The Inquisitor-host's reaction to the burning girl was one of macabre pleasure. Had it understood more of Human emotion, the entity within might have felt an emotion of its own – most likely one of disgust at the pleasure the man took in another's pain – but such things were beneath it. It was in the world of lower dimensions once again, and now had a mission to fulfil. A mission that could be easily obstructed by those with power. The connection to this host was solid, unlike that with the girl, but still the pull of the Tower was strong. This host would suffice until its eventual death.

The Inquisitor turned to the guard by his side. 'What happens now?'

'Her remains must be dealt with,' the captain said. 'The local church handles it.'

'Very well.'

'Why do you ask?'

'No particular reason. We simply wish to honour local customs for a change.'

'What are you going to do about the forest spirit? The one in the trees the girl mentioned. Are you going to get the Templars to deal with it?'

'Templars?' A memory of the Church's armed division surfaced from the host's suppressed mind. 'Yes, send word for the Templars to deal with the tree. Tell them to burn it.'

The guard saluted and spun away.

'And if they find others that look like they may contain spirits,' the Inquisitor called after him, 'burn them all.'

Chapter 5

Sebastian's features fell slack at Wolfram's suggestion. Aryx waited for him to speak, himself lost for words. How had Sebastian strangled himself?

'Self-inflicted?' After a few moments, Sebastian's features tautened. 'I get it . . . it makes sense. When I called by to see you that day in your apartment, before the explosion, you were having a shower. You had a scratch on your back.'

'That could have been anything.'

He shook his head. 'You have the nightmares, too. I think it was the same as what happened to me.'

Aryx shivered. 'You mean . . . the entities could be controlling us through our dreams?'

'I hate to admit it, but it seems like they've got some kind of influence over us when we're asleep, yes.'

'I believe the brainwaves on the recording are similar to those recorded during John Kerl's experiments with Nick Alvarez,' Wolfram said.

'How do you know?' Aryx asked.

'If you recall, I have those brainwaves stored in my memory. That was how I was able to recreate the thaumatic effect to purge the entities. The brainwave patterns recorded during Sebastian's dream sleep are similar, but not at the same amplitude.'

Sebastian let out a slow breath. 'That would explain why I have to think a certain way when I try to learn a spell. I knew it felt similar somehow. It's almost like daydreaming.'

'Clearly something you know a lot about,' Aryx said.

'If you wish,' Wolfram said, 'I could attempt to analyse the sounds and other readings from the recording to determine exactly what effect the signal is having on your neurology.'

Sebastian nodded. 'Anything that will help us get to the bottom of this would be useful.'

'Very well, I will begin background analysis of the data.' The lights on the side of the cube began to flash randomly.

'Right,' Aryx said, slapping his thigh. 'Let's get you to the hospital so we can sort out your eyes. Chair, please?' He tucked Wolfram's cube into his pocket.

Sebastian retrieved Aryx's wheelchair from its usual spot next to the nearby tool chest.

Aryx clambered into the seat. Pain shot through his stumps and he winced.

'Are you alright?'

'Yes, I'm fine. Just a bit sore lately, that's all.'

'As long as it's nothing major.' Sebastian turned and made his way to the exit. 'I don't like seeing you in pain.'

Aryx wheeled after him. 'I said I'm fine.'

As the door opened, in ran Karan, a tall, athletic woman with shoulder-length dark hair, wearing bulky carbon-fibre armour that obscured her lithe curves. 'Reporting for guard duty! Sorry I'm late! Seb? What *have* you got on your head?'

Sebastian shielded his goggled eyes with a hand as he stepped past her into the corridor. 'Eye problem. Tell you later.'

'Oh.' She looked at Aryx with a frown and glanced sideways at Sebastian.

Aryx shrugged. 'You know him,' he said, wheeling past her. 'Be back in a bit. I like your new hair, by the way. Brunette makes you look … dynamic!'

'Thanks. Hold on, I'm supposed to be guarding you!'

'Just wait here. We won't be long.'

She turned around and let her hands fall to her sides with a slap. 'I give up!'

Sebastian ran one hand along the wall while Aryx wheeled beside him. Even with the welding goggles turned up to maximum filtering, the brightness was too much for him to handle. His eyes watered and he had to keep them shut.

'Are you okay?' Aryx asked.

'No, this is giving me a headache. I need to get sorted now.' The wall fell away from Sebastian's right hand. 'Are we there yet?'

'Nearly. Reception's not far.'

'Skip it. Take me straight to Stevens. Get her to look at me.' He staggered to one side as Aryx tugged his sleeve. The headache was too much to cope with and he dragged his feet with every step. 'Hurry.'

Bleep! 'Hello? Stevens, it's Aryx Trevarian.'

'Oh, hello again. What can I do for you this time?' came Stevens's gentle tones over the door-comms.

'I need a little help.'

'What's with this "again" business?' Sebastian asked.

'Nothing,' Aryx said sharply, and the door whooshed open.

'Oh!' Stevens said as Aryx nudged Sebastian forwards. 'Agent Thorsson! What's wrong with him?'

'He's got an eye problem.'

'Put him over here.'

'I *can* hear you,' Sebastian said.

'That may well be, Mr Smartypants, but you can't exactly see where I'm pointing.'

The edge of something hard bumped against his leg. His hands found a metal post, a horizontal rail, a cushion. He heaved himself up onto the bed.

'Let's have a look. Head up.'

Tilting his head back, the goggles came away from his face and he screwed up his eyes against the light.

'What's wrong?'

'Too bright!'

'Lights, off,' Stevens said. Something clicked. 'I'll try this scanner. It's got a light. Open your eyes. Slowly.'

Sebastian opened his eyes. Everything was sharp, if a little grey, and the tiny LEDs on the equipment in the room shone like flares. Aryx and Stevens's eyes were wide, pupils dilated.

Stevens flicked the light across his eyes and his retinas instantly set aflame. 'Aaagh!'

'Hey, careful!' Aryx shouted.

'Sorry.' She clicked off the torch and, in the darkness, altered a setting on it. It clicked on again, almost as bright as before. She shone the light in his eyes – just for a moment – and he flinched. 'That's still as bad?'

He nodded.

Stevens's face contorted into a frown.

'I didn't see anything,' Aryx said.

'That's because I set the scanner to emit infrared light.'

'What? I can see infrared? I can see in the dark!' Sebastian said. That explained the others' dilated pupils. His heart quickened. Who cared about going blind? He'd got a superhuman ability!

'It seems so. Human eyes can actually see ultraviolet when the correct part of the eye covering is removed. I suppose there's no reason why the Human eye couldn't also see infrared, given an appropriate change to its biology. I'll have to analyse the scan. Put your goggles back on.' She turned and felt her way along the desk until she reached the computer.

'Alright, I'm ready. Lights on, dim,' Sebastian said, and moved beside her.

Aryx wheeled to the other side of Stevens to watch.

The computer showed Sebastian's retinal scan, the texture of veins and blood vessels clear in the centre of the picture, along with something black and glittery.

Aryx leaned closer. 'What the hell's that?'

Stevens zoomed in on the image. The rods and cones – normally smooth, organic shapes – had shards of a reflective, crystalline substance attached to the ends, and waved about like spear-tipped tentacles. 'Computer, what is that material?'

'The fragments consist of silicon and indium gallium arsenide.'

Sebastian's mouth hung open while he watched the image, and he didn't close it until his throat began to dry.

'Sebastian,' Stevens said, without turning away from the screen, 'what did you *do* to get like this? I've never seen anything like it!'

'It was an accident.'

'What kind of accident ends up with you having photosensitive semiconductors attached to your retina?'

'Uh, SpecOps project. Very secret.'

'Hmm. I'm surprised I don't know anything about this. It looks like molecular biology research, and that's my field. Inserting shards of metal into someone's eyes isn't exactly a programmer's job.' She folded her arms and turned to Aryx. 'Or an engineer's.'

Aryx remained silent. Sebastian stared at the screen while Stevens tapped away at the console. What could he tell her?

'That stuff could be poisonous. I'll have to use nanobots to remove it.' She took a vial of quicksilver fluid from a receptacle in the console and inserted it into a hypodermic gun. 'Head up,' she said, and injected it into Sebastian's neck. 'Give it a minute or two. The bots will break down the compound and excrete it through your tear ducts.' Her hand brushed Sebastian's necklace, the tiny bronze T attached with leather cord around his neck. 'What's this?'

'Mjölnir, Thor's hammer. It's a religious symbol.'

'I know that. So, you're Ásatrú? You believe in Odin, Yggdrasil, Norse mythology, and all that?'

'Yes.'

'That's interesting.'

'Do you normally talk about religion with your patients?'

Stevens shook her head. 'I don't usually have whole, living patients. In my work, I tend to deal with samples for the most part. I'm only talking because I know it'll keep you from thinking about the discomfort in your eyes ... Did you know the Bronadi have stories that are similar to Norse lore?'

Sebastian slowly shook his head while Stevens wiped down the site of the injection on his neck.

'Anyway, stop trying to distract me with comparative religion ... Are you going to tell me how you did this?' she asked. 'I'll have to fill in a record of the treatment for reference.'

What could he say to hide the truth from her? What wouldn't make him sound like a lunatic? Nothing. 'Thaumaturgy,' he said.

Aryx's mouth dropped open. 'You can't—'

'I was experimenting with magic.'

Stevens put down the syringe, folded her arms, and leaned against the desk. 'I'm well aware of the meaning of the word, Agent Thorsson. I don't need you to play childish games with me. I need the truth.'

'It is the truth, *Agent Stevens*. I wasn't going to tell you as we don't know who to trust, but it looks like I've got no choice. It can't go on the record.' Sebastian pulled out the infoslate from his rucksack and began playing the recording. 'Listen to this, and see what you think.'

Stevens raised an eyebrow but, as she listened to the audio recording, her features levelled. The playback ended and, without a word, she turned to the console and began tapping away.

'What are you doing?' Aryx asked.

'I'm referring Agent Thorsson for psychological evaluation. He's obviously a danger to himself, and he's clearly in need of help beyond my expertise.'

Sebastian put a hand on her arm. 'Monica, please.'

She slapped it away and faced him. '*Don't* touch me. I have my professional integrity to think about. I have to report this in case you pose a threat to SpecOps or the station!'

'Why would I pose a threat?'

'Did Gladrin not tell you when he recruited you? It's in the SpecOps handbook – any sign of mental instability is to be reported to our seniors immediately because of the damage we could do with our access privileges.'

Sebastian shook his head. 'Gladrin didn't give me any kind of handbook.'

'No,' Stevens said slowly, her tone lowering. 'Of course he didn't. He bypassed every protocol when he recruited you ... Why is that, do you suppose?'

Aryx leaned around her and raised his eyebrows at Sebastian.

Sebastian shrugged. 'Aryx, I've got to tell her everything, or she'll report me.'

'Tell me everything about what?'

'You won't believe half of it.' He took a deep breath. 'The explosion that caused the tsunami here on the station wasn't caused by a bomb. It was a man named Duggan Simmons. John Kerl, a scientist, and Nick Alvarez, a marine, were using the lab to perform experiments with something called carbyne, a mineral that allows a gifted individual to perform amazing feats. Magic.

'They didn't know what they were dealing with, and Alvarez became possessed. Kerl continued experimenting after Alvarez's death, using brainwaves recorded by a new type of AI stored in a cube acquired by SpecOps, and the entity that possessed Alvarez took control of Duggan and used him to destroy the lab. I found traces of the mineral on the door and tracked its source to Sollers Hope. We paid them a visit, and that's where I found out about Duggan.

'Later, I discovered Agent Gladrin was the one who set up the experiments with funding from the ITF. Unfortunately, when I discovered this, he kidnapped my family to keep me quiet. That's why I shot him.'

Stevens gasped.

'I wouldn't have done it if I didn't think it was necessary at the time. I thought he was possessed, too, because of his behaviour. But it turned out the ITF had coerced him by holding his family hostage – although they actually put them in Witness Protection, so they're not directly responsible for their custody.'

'So,' she said, 'I'm supposed to just believe this elaborate story?'

'Erm . . .' Aryx said. 'Yes.'

'Oh, well that's fine and dandy then, isn't it?' she said with a clap. 'We can all go about our daily lives like nothing's happened, and just pretend you're both sane. I obviously don't need to see *any* proof!'

Sebastian clenched his fists behind his back. 'Everything was deleted, so we don't *have* any evidence . . . Not unless I demonstrate thaumaturgy in front of you and, as you can see from my eyes, that's not something to be done casually.'

Stevens nodded, her arms folded so tightly they might never come undone. 'Of course not. How terribly convenient.'

'Actually, we do have something,' Aryx said, pulling out the cube from his thigh pocket. 'Agent Stevens, meet Wolfram.'

Stevens gave the cube a hard stare. 'What's this? The SpecOps cube you mentioned?'

'The alpha version,' Wolfram said. 'And, just like Sebastian, it can hear everything you say.'

The thin line of Stevens's mouth cracked into a smile and she laughed. 'It even has a sense of humour.' Her expression immediately hardened again. 'It still doesn't count as proof.'

Aryx placed the cube on the console. 'Wolfram, please play back the records from Kerl's lab. Just the *highlights*.'

'The one you termed "the money shot"?' Wolfram asked.

Aryx nodded.

The console displayed a video, and Stevens watched as the scientist Kerl and ex-marine Alvarez performed their experiments with magic: Alvarez zipping across the room in a fraction of a second; making the leaves of a plant move at a distance; his possession; and the ultimate detonation of a fireball in the lab, created by an elderly man in overalls standing outside in the corridor.

Stevens's eyes were wide throughout and her mouth opened and closed periodically. 'This is surely computer generated.' She paused to study Sebastian's face. 'It's . . . all true?'

Sebastian simply nodded. Painfully, undeniably, true.

'How . . . How does thaumaturgy even work? It makes no sense.'

'It does make sense, to some people at least. You need a specific mineral, carbyne. I don't understand the exact process at work, but it is definitely real.'

'Goodness.' Stevens stepped back from the screen. 'This was the cause of the explosion, not a bomb . . . Who else knows about this?'

'Only a handful of people,' Aryx said. 'Seb's family, Gladrin, Karan, and now you. We didn't tell Seb's boss about magic, or the SI.'

'SI?'

'Wolfram is a Silicon Intelligence, sentient and thinking, unlike a Turing Intelligence,' Sebastian said. 'We have to keep him a secret because the terrorists want to either use him or destroy him – that and the whole public paranoia thing from the twentieth century. He has a copy of Alvarez's stored brainwaves, and they can be used to purge the entities, but we don't think the entities know about that.'

Stevens slowly nodded. 'I see . . . I think.'

Something cold trickled down the inside of Sebastian's welding goggles. He put a finger to his cheek and it came away silvery.

'Take your goggles off,' Stevens said. 'It looks like the nanobots are done.'

He removed them and blinked several times. At least the light wasn't blinding anymore.

Stevens shone the scanner into his eyes, but this time he simply squinted. 'Yes, they seem fine now.' She turned off the torch and handed him a tissue. 'You've got a few sparkly bits left in there, but I'm sure they'll dissipate over the next couple of weeks. It's not worth giving you another dose of nanobots now. It might agitate your eyes.'

'Thanks.' He dabbed away the silvery tears and hopped off the bed, tossing the tissue into the recycling chute. 'Hopefully, you can see why it's important for us to keep this information off the computers. If any of it makes its way into the system, the Trojan may relay the information to the ITF. If they have agents installed in Witness Protection they might realise we know about them and really go after Gladrin's family.'

'Fine, I'll go along with it for now.' She turned around and tapped *Cancel* on the display, deleting the form.

'You don't seem that surprised to learn about the existence of magic. I thought you'd have freaked out a bit more,' Aryx said, voicing the thought that crossed Sebastian's mind.

Stevens ran a hand through her hair. 'I'm not accepting it as a given. There are other things that can explain the phenomena on the video, not just magic.'

'This isn't technology, if that's what you're thinking,' Sebastian said.

'You'd be surprised by some of the things I've seen on xenoarchaeological digs ... inexplicable light sources and circuitless machinery that makes apparently solid walls vanish.'

'Well,' Aryx said, folding his arms, 'we've seen that, too. But we know that's not magic.'

'I attempted scans of a crystalline technology from the comet in Yazor, where we met Duggan Simmons,' Wolfram said. 'It was a form of technology, but I was unable to determine any mechanism. None of those kinds of devices were present in Kerl's lab, although the beta cube and myself have both been able to reproduce thaumatic effects.'

Stevens grumbled. 'I'd be interested in discussing it with Mr Simmons, and taking a look at this crystalline device. We were never able to recover the one we found because the site collapsed. I'd also like to learn how thaumaturgy works, and give it a proper analysis. Where is Mr Simmons?'

Sebastian grinned. At least she was taking it all seriously now. 'A place called Chopwood, on the world of Tradescantia.'

Aryx shook his head. 'No. He left.'

A cold apprehension washed over Sebastian. 'What do you mean *left*? He was supposed to stay there with the colonists, to keep Janyce and Erik safe!'

Stevens stepped back, out of the firing line.

'Janyce thinks he's gone to get more carbyne.'

'He's not even supposed to be practising thaumaturgy! And why would he need more carbyne, anyway? There's plenty on Achene.'

'That's buried and unstable.'

Sebastian folded his arms. 'Even so, the Folians would be able to extract it and give him some. No, there has to be more to it than that.'

'What do the Folians have to do with it?' Stevens asked.

Sebastian put up a hand. 'Not now, Stevens. Aryx?'

'He's researching something, okay?'

Sebastian's collar tightened. 'Researching what?'

Aryx reddened. 'How the bloody hell should I know?' he shouted.

Stevens stepped between the pair with her arms extended. 'Just stop it, you two. You're behaving like a pair of squabbling children. What does it matter that he's researching something? Surely if it's dangerous for him to be out of hiding, the best thing for you to do is go and bring him back?'

She had a point. 'I still want to know why he left,' Sebastian said.

Stevens stayed in place. 'If he said he was going to buy this stuff, isn't the best option to contact the place he buys it from to catch him there, or just call him directly?'

'I would, but his ship is an antique. It doesn't log with comms relays, so I can't just call him up. I'll call Garvin. Do you mind if I use your terminal?'

'Not at all.' Stevens stepped aside and Sebastian took the seat in front of the desk.

'Computer, call Sollers Hope, Quintoc system.'

'One moment.' The terminal displayed the *Connecting* screen.

Aryx wheeled next to him and began drumming his fingertips on the desk.

'From what you told me,' Stevens said, 'I don't understand why you didn't just call them before when you tracked down the carbyne.'

'We weren't sure the perpetrator of the Tenebrae explosion wasn't working there,' Sebastian said. 'I didn't want to alert anyone that we were looking.'

Aryx nodded. 'Though don't put it past Sebastian to go out of his way doing something complicated when he could just— Ow!'

Sebastian slammed his hand down on Aryx's drumming fingers, cutting off the irritation as the image on screen changed to the face of a scraggly, grey-haired man with tiny, gold-rimmed spectacles.

'Sollers Hope, Mayor Havlor speaking. How many I help? Ah, Agent Thorsson!'

Sebastian nodded. 'Good to see you again, Garvin.'

Garvin's smile flattened. 'I wish I could say the same, you vandal. I had to shut that seam and replace the bleedin' door computer after you broke into my mine!'

Sebastian's cheeks burned. 'I'm sorry about that. I hope that my boss putting in the map change request to get the spelling of Sollers Hope corrected was compensation enough.'

'Hmm. Barely. What can I do for you? I'm a very busy man.'

'I won't keep you long. I'm looking for Duggan Simmons – you knew him as The Paper Man, although he looks decidedly less "papery" now and no longer wears his mask.'

Garvin's eyes flicked momentarily to a point in the distance. 'I 'ent seen him.'

'Are you sure?'

'Absolutely. He 'ent been here since he bought the last shipment of carbyne. I swear on the grave of Warren Soller.'

'Well, I need to get in touch with him, so if he does visit you, please tell him to contact me on Tenebrae. It's urgent.'

'Will do. Sollers Hope out.' The screen blanked.

'What the hell's up with him?' Aryx asked, rubbing his crushed fingers. 'And you, don't do that again! I need these to get around.'

'Sorry.' Sebastian smiled apologetically.

Stevens moved around to inspect Aryx's hand.

'Oh, come on! He intentionally tries to annoy me when I'm on a call. Don't look at me like that! He nearly caused a diplomatic incident when he offended the Bronadi not so long ago.'

'That's no excuse to injure a disabled man,' Stevens said.

Aryx closed his eyes and smiled. Smug sod.

Sebastian folded one arm across his chest and held his chin with the other hand. 'Garvin's lying,' he said. 'Someone else was there, in the background, and his accent became a little rural. He does that when he lies. Duggan's there all right. He may have told Garvin not to tell anyone in case it was the ITF trying to find him. Garvin obviously doesn't know the full story.'

'So, what are you going to do now?' Aryx asked.

'Since I can't get any information out of him on a call, we'll have to pay Sollers Hope another visit.' Sebastian stood. 'Thanks for letting me use your terminal, Stevens. Would you mind deleting the scans of my eyes?'

Stevens's mouth twisted. 'I don't like to but, if there is a Trojan in the station systems like you say, and someone might be monitoring it, I will.'

Aryx wheeled towards the door.

Sebastian followed. 'I'll probably see you when we get back. Hopefully I'll be able to convince Duggan to come back with us, then you can meet him and discuss technology and magic.'

'I'd like that. And please, as I told you when we last met, call me Monica.'

Sebastian followed Aryx back towards the lift terminal. 'If you don't mind,' he said, 'I'd like to go to the private bay via the atrium. I've been in the dark too long and need some sun.'

'Fine.' Aryx spun around to head back down the corridor, away from the lift terminal. 'If we go to Sollers Hope, should we tell Karan the truth? She's supposed to be guarding me, after all.'

'I don't want to take her with us. Garvin already knows me, but he might get suspicious if I bring an entourage.'

'So, you want me to fob her off with an excuse.'

Sebastian closed his eyes and pinched the bridge of his nose. 'Yes, I suppose.' Why did he have to keep lying to his close friends? He'd kept Karan out of the loop too much over the past few weeks during the explosion investigation, and the tension on their friendship was bringing it perilously close to breaking point. 'I'll make it up to her later.'

'What do you want me to tell her?' Aryx sat poised to tap his wristcom.

'Tell her ... Tell her that we've gone to repair damage I caused the last time we were there, and the Antari have requested that she keep watch on their shuttle until we get back. Delicate work, and all that.'

'Sounds like a shit excuse. Sollers Hope has engineers. They'd be able to make their own repairs.'

Sebastian scratched his head. 'Tell her they haven't got one who can repair their airlock, or something.' Aryx tapped his wristcom and Sebastian quickly stepped out of the corridor into the atrium. It was better if he didn't hear the details.

The shining white walls of the atrium towered above as he leaned on the handrail overlooking the terraces below. Wispy clouds skimmed the peach-coloured morning sky projected overhead on the solar filters. The verdant foliage of vines, tousled by the light breeze, trailed down from the terraces above at intervals along the concourse. Sebastian closed his eyes and took a deep breath. Sounds and smells wafted up from the market several hundred metres to the right, farther along the curve of the station. Croissants. They'd be nice right about now. Croissants and coffee. Damn those spice flowers.

The doors slid open behind him. Aryx's jaw was set disapprovingly. 'She ain't happy.'

Sebastian's heart sank from its temporary elevation. 'Let's grab a coffee on the way. I'll get her a cake or something to make up for it.'

'You really are something else if you think that's good enough.' Aryx shook his head and wheeled off along the walkway to the left and down the ramp looping out across the atrium. Sebastian stood for a moment while Aryx *whooped* loudly, arms in the air, leaning to steer, as he swept along the curve, startling several Humans and a Q'vani that stood chatting on the ramp. The insectoid rattled its serrated mandibles and hissed as it skittered out of the way.

Sebastian jogged after him. When he arrived at the foot of the ramp on the far side of the atrium, two long, black streaks stretched across the gleaming white floor. Aryx sat at the end grinning.

Sebastian put a shielding hand over his eyes – not that it would help to hide his embarrassment. 'I can't believe you left skid marks.'

Aryx turned down his mouth in a parody of Sebastian's oft-used "mouth-shrug", as he called it, and Sebastian scowled back at him in response.

The pair made their way to a coffee vendor near a jetty, signposted *The Pod, 4th point*, situated by a planter containing spice flowers – the offender responsible for Sebastian's growing hunger. Aryx stopped several feet from the counter.

'What can I get you?' asked a tall woman with long, black hair as Sebastian approached. She towered nearly a foot taller than him, almost Karan's height. A badge on her lapel said *Rachel*.

He turned to Aryx. 'What do you want?'

Aryx sighed. 'You know I prefer to make my own but, if you insist, I'll have a triple espresso.'

'Double espresso,' Sebastian said to Rachel in a low voice. 'And I'll have a Bronadi chicory. Oh, and a decaf cappuccino.' He couldn't forget Karan.

'And cake!' Aryx shouted.

'And three croissants, please.'

Rachel initiated the classic whooshing *schlurp* of the coffee machine. 'You know that Bronadi stuff's not really coffee, right?' she said, without turning to face him. 'They make it into a coffee-like drink, but it isn't coffee.' She handed over the Bronadi chicory before preparing the other drinks.

'I know,' Sebastian said. 'But thanks for the heads-up. It tastes the same.'

'Uh-huh.' She set down the remaining drinks and pulled out three freshly warmed croissants from below the counter. 'Forty credits.'

'By the Gods! What's with the price hike?'

Rachel shrugged. 'Four of the other pods got wrecked during the tsunami, so I guess they need to reclaim the repair costs.'

Sebastian waved his wristcom over the payment terminal and took the items. 'Thanks.' He turned to Aryx and flicked his head in the direction of the lift terminal several metres along the riverside.

Aryx scooted across the terrace and Sebastian strolled after him.

'Shuttle maintenance,' Aryx said, addressing the lift. Sebastian gave him the espresso and he took a quick sip before handing the cup back.

The lift arrived with a simulated *ping* and they entered.

'You know Bronadi chicory isn't coffee . . .' Aryx said, taking back his coffee and resting his arm on the handrail.

'Yes, Rachel told me, and I *have* had it before. I like the taste, and the fact there's no caffeine.' Sebastian took a mouthful and swished it around to get the full flavour of it. How odd that the aroma of coffee was sometimes reminiscent of roast beef.

'It's meat,' Aryx said with a smirk. 'It's called *chick*ory because it's made from little birds. Crushed and toasted!'

A brown fountain erupted from Sebastian's lips, spraying the lift interior. 'You could have told me sooner!' he sputtered.

'Oh, but the essence of comedy is tragedy and timing!'

He grimaced and wiped his mouth with the N-suit sleeve, where the moisture wicked into the osmotic fabric. As they exited the lift, he dropped the cup into the nearest waste disposal. 'Asshole.'

The pair arrived at the repair bay to find the place in total darkness.

'Light on, bay two.' Sebastian blinked in the gloom as the flood lamp over the Antari shuttle slowly warmed up, bathing the area with light. 'Where's Karan?'

'No idea.' Aryx held up a hand. 'Shh!'

The soft pounding of distant feet came across the hangar.

Sebastian peered into the darkness. 'Ahh.' Moving past the black-on-black silhouettes of ships was a humanoid outline, formed from tiny points of light.

'What is it?'

'I can see her. It must be the remaining shards of indium gallium arsenide. I've still got infravision.'

The glint of shiny carbon-fibre armour bobbed towards them and Karan jogged into the light, face glistening. 'Phew!' She wiped her face with a hand. 'So, the prodigals return.'

'Sorry about earlier.' Sebastian offered the coffee and croissant.

'What was up with your eyes?'

'Had a bit of a medical emergency.'

Aryx wheeled beside him. 'He got a metal filing in his eye. Watching me too close, you know.'

'With goggles already on?' Karan raised an eyebrow. 'Unlike you to be so careless, Aryx.'

'What are you doing running around in the dark?' Sebastian asked.

'Perfect practice for when there's a power outage, and it makes it easier to know when someone's come in.'

He shook his head. She had a point, but it still came across as completely insane.

'I know where the wall is, unlike some, Mr Welding Goggles. I take it you're fine now?'

'Yes, I got it fixed with nanobots.'

'Let's see.' She tore a chunk out of her croissant. 'I love a good bit of gore.'

Sebastian groaned but, in the light of his recent behaviour towards her, humoured her by tipping his head back.

'You've still got some bits in there,' she said, pulling his eyelid back. 'They're all sparkly. Isn't that like— Christ!' She let go and stepped back from him.

'Yes, I look possessed. Gods, don't make me go over it *again*.'

'Hmm, but you're going to tell me later.' She raised the coffee. 'So, this is pay-off so you can go gallivanting around on your own?'

Aryx nodded slowly.

'Fine,' she said with a sigh. She took a gulp of coffee and handed the cup back. 'You finish it. I'm too hot to drink it all. I'll see you when you get back. Just make sure Bannik knows. If anything happens to you while you're away, I am not being held responsible!'

Several minutes later, the pair had made their way to Gladrin's private bay via the transport tubes, and the station's rotation spat out the sleek, steely blue and white shape of the *Ultima Thule*.

They sat at the console, drinking their coffee while the ship approached the giant iridescent scaffold of the acceleration node. The node's dark, metallic sphere glittered in the sun as it slowly rotated at the centre of the dodecahedral frame.

After lining up with the distant star of Quintoc, the ship accelerated. At 1500 metres from the node, the steel sphere came to life, a magenta haze enveloping it, tiny streamers like St. Elmo's fire reaching out towards the frame. As the ship drew closer, the streamers intensified and wavered, converging in its direction. At one kilometre, the threads of energy coalesced into a single, intense strand and the bright filament shot out to envelop the ship.

In an instant, the stars visible from the cockpit stretched and vanished, just for a moment, until the ship's window filters kicked in and compensated for the blue shift, bringing them back into the visible spectrum.

'Why had you already been to the hospital today?' Sebastian asked.

Aryx blinked. 'What?'

'Monica said, "hello *again*." I assume you'd already been to see her for some reason.'

'Um, yes. I ran out of antiretrovirals for my legs. I needed her to synthesise some.'

'Are they alright? Your legs, I mean.'

'Yes, they've just been a bit painful since climbing that cliff on Achene. I'm sure I'll get over it eventually.'

Sebastian leaned back, resting the paper cup against his chest. 'I've been thinking about that.' He turned to look at the hard, plastic backpack with its complicated harness – the mobipack – leaning against the diagnostic console in the aft section of the ship. 'You couldn't use the legs to climb because you weren't able to move the feet, right?'

'Yes ... Where are you going with this?'

'We could modify the sensors. If you had neural implants in the end of your legs instead, they could pick up the nerve impulses directly. You'd be able to make the feet move if you wanted to.'

'Good idea,' Aryx said, 'but I still wouldn't be able to feel anything. It might make me walk less like a cargomech, though.' He folded his arms. 'On second thoughts, no. I'd have to get the sensors manufactured, and I like to make things myself. It's a skill I learned from my dad, and one of the few things I can do to prove I'm still useful. I don't want something I don't understand, especially computer-controlled, stuck in me like that.'

'Come on, I thought you were over that.'

'I still don't trust computers to control my life to that degree, thankyouverymuch.'

'Speaking of which,' Wolfram said from Aryx's thigh pocket, 'would you be so kind as to give me a more interesting view?'

'Yeah, sorry Jim-Bob.' Aryx pulled the cube from his pocket and placed it on the console.

'Thank you.'

Sebastian smiled at their secret nickname for the cube. The self-programmed Silicon Intelligence exhibited a personality almost exactly like a living, breathing person, and it was still difficult to get used to. The SI was a marvel to behold, in spite of its almost antique hardware: it was ironically years ahead of the more recent – yet still incredibly simple – Turing Intelligence interface software, and the only computer Sebastian knew to exhibit true sentience and self-awareness. It was this sentience that made it dangerous to the extra-spatial demon entities, given its ability to replay Nick Alvarez's recorded brainwaves and replicate the thaumaturgic effects that he had learnt. The SI could not be controlled by the entities through possession – or by any other person in any way, for that matter – and was the very reason Sebastian and Aryx kept its existence secret.

'If you are apprehensive about getting neural implants,' Wolfram said, 'I would gladly offer my assistance in the nanobot control process, if you wished.'

Aryx shook his head. 'Thanks, Wolfram, but I'll pass for the moment. It's a last resort.'

Two hours, and two node hops later, the *Ultima Thule* dropped out of superphase on the fringes of the Quintoc asteroid belt. Sebastian immediately pulled up the ship to avoid the scattered disc of rocks and dust that ringed the system.

'Glad you remembered that,' Aryx said over the inertia-induced creak of his wheelchair.

On their first visit to the system, they had changed direction at the last second to avoid a collision and Aryx had whooped loudly. Sebastian grinned back at him. 'I'm not doing that again.'

Before he had a chance to activate the comms, an automated voice came over the channel.

'Vessel, halt your approach. Colony asteroid defence procedures are in progress. Hold position until cleared.'

Sebastian brought the ship to a standstill and stared out at the white pockmarked dwarf planet. On the ridge of the most prominent crater sat a geodesic dome that spanned its circumference. Several thousand kilometres away, an asteroid approached from space, surrounded by flashing lights.

'W-what are they doing?' he said. 'That thing's going to hit them!'

Aryx leaned forward. 'Don't worry, it looks like they've attached targeting buoys to it.'

The triangular facets of the dome on the planet below glinted in the light, suddenly becoming more reflective than usual.

'Have they closed the mirrors?' Sebastian held his breath.

Some distance from the dome on a low plateau, the colony's radio antenna, a silvery white spike with three blazing red lights strung up its length, pierced the black sky. At its base, a ground-to-space missile launcher swung to point two rockets upward and launched.

Sebastian gripped the edge of the console as the missiles streaked away from the surface towards the asteroid. In a bright flash, they made contact. Rock and debris flew in all directions, including towards the *Ultima Thule*. 'The CFD!' he yelled.

Aryx's fingers played across the console as a house-sized chunk of rock approached from starboard. It could shatter the cockpit window any second.

Chapter 6

As the broken asteroid approached, Sebastian gritted his teeth and closed his eyes tightly. The ship lurched to port and he tumbled out of his seat, but the crunch and explosive decompression didn't come. He opened his eyes.

The enormous chunk slowly tumbled away from the ship, deflected by the almost imperceptible orange field that had appeared only metres away from the windows. In the distance, smaller rocks pelted the planet but bounced harmlessly off the dome.

Moments later, with the danger passed, the mirrors in the dome re-opened to reveal the townscape beneath. Two of the mirrors remained closed.

Sebastian let out a slow breath. That was close. He touched a control on the console. '*Ultima Thule* to Sollers Hope, requesting permission to land.'

The reply, fragmented by static, came back several seconds later. 'Acknowledged *Ul*— ... *Thule*. Proceed to d— ... bay three.'

Sebastian entered approach and descent vectors, pressed *Initiate*, and sat back while the knobbly white ball of Sollers Hope mining planetoid rolled slowly in and out of view as the ship orientated itself for landing.

Another ship, with blue and white markings, streaked past the windows, almost hitting them as it came up from the surface.

'Someone's in a hurry,' Aryx said.

'Wasn't that a police ship?' Sebastian asked.

'No idea, it was too quick. The pilot's a bloody lunatic, though.'

The *Ultima Thule* dropped to the surface and softly bounced as the magnetic repulsors in the landing pad caught it. A small, domed robot trundled out of the half-cylinder hangar on a rail and towed the ship inside. Moments later, a docking cowl extended and pressed against the side of the hull with a thump.

'If that thing's scratched the ship again,' Aryx said, 'I am not repainting and polishing.'

Sebastian patted him on the shoulder. 'I wouldn't expect you to. Come on, I'll get the respirator filters on the way out.'

They made their way from the cockpit, down the lift and ladder respectively, and Sebastian collected a pair of filter masks from the alcove containing the pressure suits. He strapped one across his nose and mouth and threw the other to Aryx, who had already left a pair of long tyre tracks in the dust on the floor of the docking cowl.

'Not bringing the mobipack?' Sebastian asked.

'I don't see a need. The ground was a little gritty in the main dome, but fine for the chair. Until it's patented, I don't want to risk others seeing the pack, and I'm not patenting it while we still think there are entities or ITF that have access to government systems.'

'Don't you want to come into the civic hall with me?'

'Not particularly.' Aryx wheeled into the complex's airlock. 'But if they made the effort to put a ramp down the steps, I would.'

Passing through the decontamination spray of the airlock, the two entered the tunnel connecting the docking hangar to the main dome. Several minutes later, they had taken the cargo train to the far end of the dark, four-mile-long tunnel.

Sebastian stepped from the second airlock into the gritty, humid air of the crater housing the colony. The giant triangular glass panels of the geodesic dome glinted overhead, and faint clouds drifted through the air beneath, catching beams of sunlight reflected towards the centre by the mirrors. People moved to and fro between the squat, blocky buildings made from the same grey stone as the crater wall surrounding the town.

Sebastian pulled off his mask. 'Better take these off. I don't want to offend them again.'

Aryx pushed off, leaving Sebastian coughing in a plume of dust. 'Come on, slowcoach!' he called back.

Sebastian jogged through the narrow streets, following Aryx towards the enormous capsule-shaped solar generator at the centre.

The heat was instantly noticeable as they broke into the town square, where they turned right and headed towards a large Greek-revival-style building with a set of wide steps and double doors with columns to either side: the civic building.

Aryx stopped and stared at the steps. 'No, I'm definitely not bothered about going in. The place looks filthy. And there's no ramp.'

Sebastian recalled the thick layer of dust that had coated the shelves inside. 'You're right. Better stay out here. You'd hate it.'

'I think I'll go and find someone to talk to, or check out the generator again.' Aryx spun around and wheeled off, leaving Sebastian to enter alone.

Aryx skirted the scraggly brown grass in the middle of the town square, keeping his wheels away from the low, sharp-edged kerb stones that might scrape his handrims. 'Don't you people water this?' he asked a passer-by, gesturing to the small, naked tree at the base of the solar generator.

'We haven't the water to spare,' the woman said. Her cardigan was weighed down with dust. She rubbed her equally dusty, lank hair. 'Not even got enough to wash with 'til they bring in another iceteroid.'

Aryx pointed up at the thin layer of mist floating in the geodesic dome above. 'What about the condensator?'

She shrugged. 'Broke, I guess.'

'I figured as much. There weren't any clouds last time I was here. Can't anyone fix it?'

'Dunno.' She folded an arm across her chest and tucked her hand in her armpit, twirling a finger of her free hand in the air. 'There's only one person who knows how it works, and he got his hand crushed by a hopper in the mines. He's laid up. Nobody else would dare go near it.'

'I'm an engineer. Do you want me to take a look at it?'

'Got nothin' to do with me. You better ask the mayor.' She jabbed her thumb over her shoulder towards the civic building.

'I think he's busy. I'll go and have a look at it. Couldn't hurt. I can get my own tools if I need them. Where's the machine?'

'Hmm ... Over there.' She pointed to the far side of the crater and, evidently deciding further conversation to be unnecessary, turned around and strode away.

Aryx pushed off in the direction she'd indicated, following the pipes carrying molten minerals heated by the solar generator capsule, while being careful to keep his distance: *Hot!* and *Corrosive!* signs in bright yellow depicted a hand eaten away by acid.

Near the crater wall at the edge of the town, he came across a large machine mounted on a low plinth, covered in hundreds of coiling copper pipes. Ordinarily, such a thing should have mist flowing off it where coolant ran through the pipework, but this was clearly not functioning. He wheeled up to it, drew out his multi-tool and tapped the blade against one of the coils. It rang hollowly.

'Bloody negligent idiots. It's dry.'

'Perhaps there is a problem with the coolant supply,' Wolfram said quietly from his thigh pocket.

'I hope it's only a minor one.' He reached behind the machine to a spot where the valve should be but his fingers found nothing. 'Odd.' He wheeled around the side.

The copper coils straightened and ran down to the ground, took a ninety-degree turn and continued along for several metres before being interrupted by a valve with a large lever.

'What an odd arrangement.'

'What is?' Wolfram asked.

'The pipes. The valve isn't near the coil where it should be, and the coolant supply pipes run along the ground, of all places. What a crappy design.' He approached the heavy valve lever that lay parallel to the pipe. 'And this thing should be pointing straight up.'

'So, the supply of coolant is turned off?'

'Yeah, but why would anyone do that?' He pulled the bar and the valve opened with a squeal. The copper coils vibrated as they filled, and he wiped his hands on his trousers. 'Sorted.'

A moment later, vapour hissed from a tiny hole in a dented section of the supply line.

'Or maybe not. I bet someone kicked the pipe and broke it, then turned it off to stop it leaking. Looks like I'll have to get some tools for this.' As he straightened, something flashed in his peripheral vision.

The source was neither the glint of a ship outside the dome nor a reflection off one of the mirrors. Instead, a light on a small black box, mounted on one of the thermal generator pipes several metres away, sat flashing.

'I don't remember seeing anything like that on these pipes before.' Aryx stared at the black box and moved a little closer.

A lump of greyish clay protruded from between the box and the hot pipe to which it was attached. A familiar clay, from the days of his military career. This was no component. This was a bomb!

Sebastian strode purposefully down the middle of the civic building, past the ageing bookshelves to both sides with their dusty tomes and files, and the stained-glass windows that, at this time of day, allowed in a dim, multicoloured glow.

Garvin Havlor sat behind the computer terminal at his large wooden desk, sifting through paperwork. He looked up and peered over his gold-rimmed spectacles. 'Ah,' he said, putting down the papers.

Sebastian extended a hand.

Garvin scraped the chair backwards as he stood. He stepped around the desk and wiped his hands down his grimy red velvet jacket to shake hands with Sebastian. 'Hello again, Agent Thorsson.'

'That was an impressive show earlier, with the asteroid defences.'

Garvin nodded. 'Not quite as impressive as I'd like. Two of the panels broke, so the mirrors stayed shut to seal them. That'll be more expense to get them fixed. But I'm sure you didn't come to talk about asteroid defences.'

'No. I assume you know why I'm here.'

'To find Duggan, I expect. Didn't see his ship in the hangar when you arrived, did you? That'll be because, like I said earlier when you called, he's not here.'

Sebastian shook his head. 'You're right, I didn't see it. However, I still don't believe it when you say you haven't seen him.'

Garvin's left eye twitched.

'So, you *have* seen him recently.'

'No. I 'aven't! Why do people keep asking?'

Sebastian stepped forward, enough to make Garvin take a step back. '*People?* Someone else has been asking about him?'

'I ... um ...' Garvin took another step back behind his desk, as though the low obstacle would protect him, and he stumbled over his chair in the process. 'No. Nobody has.'

Sebastian slammed his palms down on the desk. 'Mr Havlor, it is very important that you tell me where Duggan is. His life could be in great danger.'

Garvin stared at him, his gaze darting from one side of Sebastian's face to the other. 'He was here a couple of days ago, but he told me not tell anyone I'd seen him, regardless of who it was. He didn't say where he was going ... Then-then that police bloke turns up askin' after him, too, and he tells me to say I 'aven't seen *him* – and that he'll 'ave me records looked into if I do.' He took several gulps of air. 'You could be anybody ... Even one o' them terrorists. I don't really know you, do I? Duggan was right, I can't trust *anyone*.'

Sebastian leaned closer to the cowering mayor. Garvin's story added up: Duggan would have told him to trust no one, knowing that the entities could potentially possess anybody and likely had helpers. He needed Garvin to cooperate. 'Mr Havlor, I don't need to remind you that I'm working for SpecOps and that, in some cases, our EarthSec authority trumps that of the police. If you don't help me find Duggan, *I'll* find good reason to poke through those records you claim don't exist.' Of course, SpecOps had no authority over the police without a warrant, but how was Garvin to know?

Garvin swallowed. 'God, he had a temper, too.'

'Who did?'

'The police bloke that was here earlier.'

'Was that who was behind the monitor when I spoke to you?'

Garvin nodded. 'Aye. Don't have a family member in the police, do you?'

'I don't have any living relatives, except for my sister-in-law and nephew. My brother was in the police force, but he died almost three years ago.'

'Well, this chap had a similar look, right down to the weird sparkly eyes. What is that, some new fashion accessory?'

Sebastian's skin tingled. *Possessed ...*

Boom! The civic building shook.

He spun around. 'What was that?'

'Something bad!' Garvin leaped up and darted towards the double doors. Sebastian followed him out onto the steps.

A crowd of people, running from the far side of the solar generator capsule, had filled the square. The thermal cylinder itself began to creak ominously. Where was Aryx?

'Aryx!' Sebastian yelled over the din.

No response.

'Have you seen a guy in a wheelchair?' he shouted.

'Over there,' said a woman in a cardigan. 'He went to look at the condensator.' She pointed in the direction of a cloud of black smoke that crawled up the crater wall on the far side of town.

Sebastian's heart slowed.

The cylinder of molten salts groaned once again. As the townsfolk ran past, the grim smile of death opened – a crack in the base of the drum – and vomited glowing bile over one of the unfortunates. He screamed once before bursting into flame, his skeleton stripped clean of its fragile flesh.

A chill went through Sebastian as the townsfolk scattered and ran up the short steps into the nearest buildings – all of which were single-storey – leaving the square empty except for the steaming lava.

'Aryx!' he screamed, running down the steps. He stopped at the edge of the glowing, caustic sea. There was nowhere to go. '*Aryx!*'

He had to pull himself together. Get hold of his thoughts. To think!

He tapped his wristcom. 'Contact Aryx Trevarian.'

Blarp! came the "communication not acknowledged" tone.

Garvin bounded down the steps and stopped several feet away from the boiling tide. 'Who's Aryx? A friend of yours?'

Sebastian staggered up the steps until he backed into one of the columns and stared off into the distance, his eyes refusing to focus on what was happening. 'My best friend. More than a friend. I brought him here.' His throat tightened. 'What have I done?' He slid to the floor and hugged his knees. 'Oh, by the Gods, what have I done ...'

Got his best friend killed, that's what. One of the few people he truly cared about. Gone.

Aryx spun around and wheeled away from the makeshift explosive. He needed tools, and something with which to disarm it. 'We're going back to the ship!' he yelled. Pushing his wheels as fast as he could, he avoided the town square, favouring a shorter route across the back of the thoroughfare to the airlock from which they'd entered. In seconds, he'd cut halfway through the town before the heavy bass thud of a pressure wave hit him from behind.

He stopped to risk a look back. A dark, roiling mass of acrid smoke billowed up into the air behind him. He pushed harder.

'What's happening?' Wolfram asked.

'The bomb's ... just ... gone off ...'

'Where are we going?'

'Back to the ship ... get the mobipack,' Aryx panted, 'and something ... to seal the pipe.' He reached the airlock to the transfer tunnel and hammered the button. 'Come *on!*' The airlock opened and he wheeled through.

'What makes the pipe repair urgent?' Wolfram asked.

'I can't repair it. I need to block it. If the fluid leaks out it will eat through anything not designed to contain it. It's highly corrosive, not to mention being thousands of degrees.'

'You surely won't be able to stop it if the pipe is too damaged.'

'Maybe not, but I have to do something.'

The airlock cycled. Aryx headed to the transport trucks and wheeled up the ramp of the nearest cargo hopper into which the chair would fit – towards the back, where he couldn't reach the controls in the front cart. 'Start the train, Wolfram.'

The train pulled off and Aryx shut his eyes against the abrading, gritty wind as the vehicle screamed from one end of the tracks to the other. The cube had evidently overridden the safety mechanism and instructed the train to go faster. A wise decision on the part of the SI.

Two long minutes later, the train juddered to a halt.

Aryx made his way to the ship and, after quickly fastening the harness of the mobipack, he abandoned his wheelchair inside the door and grabbed a hull-patch toolkit. 'Steps off,' he said, turning to leave the ship: the last time he'd walked down the force-field steps with his CFD prosthetics he had fallen straight through. He stepped down and jogged back along the docking cowl. The feet of the glowing, projected legs skidded, near-frictionless on the hard ground, but held. The cube in his pocket dug into his leg as he ran and the harness cut into his groin with every jolting step.

This time he travelled in the front seat of the train and, with his eyes closed once more, he took Wolfram from his pocket and exchanged him with the Augmented Reality glasses and the few tools from the compartment in the mobipack for easy access.

His heart pounded a percussion to the squealing of the tracks. If only the train would hurry up! 'Wolfram, when we're in range, hack the airlock so both doors open simultaneously or I won't have time.'

'Very well.'

He stumbled off the train and ran, skidding through the open airlock into the town. The townsfolk rushing back and forth paid no attention to him or his glowing transparent lower legs. He pulled at the harness where it had cut into his groin from the run. Why couldn't he have brought the wheelchair back instead?

Conditions were darker than when he'd left the main dome minutes ago. The mirrors had been diverted away from the cylinder at the centre and now reflected most of the light back into space – probably an emergency measure to prevent further heating of the fluid. The thick, black cloud from the explosion had dispersed, leaving the thin cloud overhead a greasy grey.

Near the foot of the crater wall, misty tendrils twirled into the air.

'What is that?' Aryx asked.

The AR glasses, now connected to Wolfram, zoomed in. A spectral analysis appeared at the bottom of his field of vision.

'It is vapour from the corrosive liquid in the pipes,' Wolfram said. 'It appears to be dissolving metalwork.'

'Shit, if that stuff reaches the other airlock near the mines, we'll eat vacuum.'

'Correction. *You'll* eat vacuum.'

'Your innards can still melt, pal.'

Spurred on by the cube's poor choice of words, Aryx sped up. He rounded a corner too soon, catching his wristcom against the wall. A moment later, he skidded to a halt, dropping the hull-patch kit. 'We're so screwed.'

One hundred metres away, the pipe with the explosive device lay like the severed neck of some giant serpent spewing out a glowing red lava. The base of the condensator was surrounded by the stuff, and the machine leaned at a precarious angle where the supports had been eaten away.

A targeting reticule in the AR glasses highlighted a building off to the right. 'I suppose under other circumstances, *that* could be considered humorous,' Wolfram said, centring the reticule on a large neon sign above the building's double doors. Elements of the sign on one of the *E*s had shorted out, probably because of the corrosive fumes, leaving the bar's name intermittently flashing "THE MELTING POINT".

Aryx tutted in disgust. 'If I didn't know better, I'd swear you had emotions, and some of them are really inappropriate.'

'I wouldn't know.' The targeting reticule was replaced with a temperature readout as lines scanned the lava. 'Seven hundred degrees centigrade, and a pH too low for me to be able to extrapolate its acidity.'

'Let me guess. Bye-bye metal parts, and instant death on contact?'

'Precisely.'

Aryx approached the growing lake. The leading edge of the liquid darkened as it cooled, fragmented, and broke up, exposing glowing cracks that belched out more hot fluid – but rolled ever closer.

'Is it eating through rock?' he asked.

For several seconds there was no reply.

'No. I believe this planetoid's composition to be sufficient to resist the temperature and acidity.'

How was he going to stop the thermalite from reaching the airlock? From what he recalled of his last visit to the town, the airlock into the mines was close to the pipes that ran from the cylinder to the crater wall, with no barrier in between to prevent the flow from reaching it.

He looked down at his legs, then across the spill in the direction of the mine airlock on the other side of town, and pulled up the respirator mask. His chest tightened. It was a good job he hadn't brought his wheelchair back.

'I have to cross it.'

Garvin bent down and slapped Sebastian on the shoulder, jolting him out of his moment of self-pity. 'Get up, you. What kind of SpecWhatsit agent are you? To think I was scared of you a minute ago. One little explosion and you're all over the fuckin' shop.' He dragged Sebastian to his feet by his collar. 'If you think he's dead, do you think he'd want you moping around feelin' sorry for yourself when there's my people trapped out there?' Garvin jabbed a thumb at his own chest. 'Do I look like I'm feeling fuckin' sorry for myself?' He spun Sebastian around by the shoulders to face the civic building, and prodded him forward. 'Get your sorry arse in there and help me work out how to get those people to safety!'

Something snapped. Sebastian stopped in his tracks and rounded on the mayor with a raised fist. 'If *you'd* cooperated, *I* wouldn't have had to come here!'

'Yes, and if I hadn't delayed that dodgy copper, your friend Duggan would probably have been arrested!'

The man had a point. How did the police even know Duggan was alive, and why would they be looking for him? All official records of Duggan had him marked as deceased due to his 150-years-plus absence from Earth. The question distracted Sebastian enough for him to pull himself together, and he scanned the town square, assessing the situation.

The town inhabitants that had escaped the magma from the cylinder now stood on the rooftops, staring at the rupture's aftermath. In one of the single-storey buildings to the right of the capsule, three small children peered from the windows; they were apparently trapped by the brilliantly glowing orange tide that slowly rose up the stone steps towards them.

A scream came from the crowd on the opposite side of the square where the lava was yet to reach. 'My babies!' It was the cardigan woman.

Sebastian's heart ached. What if it had been Erik in that building? 'We have to save them.'

'How are we going to get over there?' Garvin asked. 'The thermalite stays hot for hours.'

Sebastian's gaze followed the flow to the building with the trapped children; up the building to its low flat roof; across to the next; from the next building to the civic office. It was a good five feet between the last two buildings and at least six between each of the two houses. It would be easy enough to jump between the buildings, but getting the children back would be another matter . . .

'Is there a way up onto the roof of this place?'

Garvin nodded. 'An access hatch at the back, but we don't keep long ladders in here. We've only got a shorter one for the bookcases.'

'Come on, I've got an idea,' Sebastian said, dragging Garvin back into the building.

Without the light from the mirrors shining through the windows, the civic office had darkened to a cold, dusky twilight.

Sebastian searched the room. His eyes immediately fell upon the tall, dusty bookshelves. 'What about those?' he asked, walking to the second-from-last filth-encrusted shelf at the back. 'Can we use them?'

'The shelves? Yes,' Garvin said, moving towards them. 'Let me just get the books—'

'No time.' Sebastian shoulder-barged the heavy wooden unit and nearly put his arm out of joint, but pressed on. *'Nghhh!* Don't just stand there – help me!'

'But the books—' Garvin hesitated a moment before joining in.

The bookcase rocked backwards. Sebastian eased off to allow it to sway forwards before pushing again. With a final, mighty shove, the bookcase fell back, hitting the next set of shelves in line and the rest toppled like dominoes against the bookshelf mounted on the wall, forming a staggered curve towards the ceiling.

He started climbing. 'Empty one of those narrow ones and pass it up,' he said, pointing to a slender unit on the end of one of the larger shelves. 'I'll have to use that as a ladder between the buildings.'

Garvin nodded and ran off.

Sebastian pushed against the hatch in the ceiling. It opened easily. He choked on his first breath of the noxious mid-level vapours that drifted over the buildings before pulling the filter mask over his nose and mouth.

'Got it,' Garvin shouted from below.

Sebastian retreated beneath the hatch and Garvin thrust the lighter, narrow bookcase up at him. Sebastian grabbed the end and fed it up through the hatch. At six and a half feet long, it might do the job. 'Thanks,' he said, climbing up after it.

He made his way to the front of the roof. Garvin's laboured breathing from behind startled him.

'I thought you might need more,' Garvin said, wiping sweat from his brow and dropping another set of shelves.

'Thanks. Don't these vapours bother you?'

'Heh, no. When your lungs are full of dust from this place, it takes a lot to cut through it.' He coughed. 'Or maybe not . . .'

Sebastian dragged the bookcases to the edge of the flat roof. The clamour and shouts of the crowd echoed from across the square, farther off now.

'Please, help them!' Cardigan Woman shouted, pointing.

Garvin helped lift a bookcase up onto the parapet at the side of the building and Sebastian leaned over the edge.

The first house stood closer than he had estimated and, being slightly higher than the others, was well within the distance the bookcase could span.

'Let's lower it and swing it away. The top can rest against this lip,' Sebastian said, pointing to the protruding course of blocks just below the parapet of the building on which they stood.

They held the top of the bookcase as they lowered it, and swung it a little – just enough for the bottom to catch the roof below. Rocking it from side to side, they walked the bookshelf out to fifty degrees, with the top end resting on the inch-deep ledge formed by the blocks Sebastian had indicated.

'Help me get the second one down,' he said, taking one end of the other shelving unit. Once again, Garvin helped place it alongside the first.

Sebastian climbed over the wall and tested one of the shelves with his weight. It held. Shaking, he crouched while Garvin gripped the top.

'When I get to the bottom I'll take the other one and put it between this house and the next.'

'Be careful,' Garvin said, the glow from the magma below reflecting in his eyes.

Sebastian kept his gaze fixed on Garvin until he reached the bottom. He wavered before stepping off.

Garvin flicked the second bookcase away from the wall. 'Catch!'

It teetered on end. Sebastian tried to grab it, but caught one of the slats on his head. 'Ow!'

'I said be careful!'

'You could have told me you were about to do that.' He dragged the bookcase to the other side of the house roof. 'How am I going to get this across there? It's too heavy for me to do it on my own.'

'Well, I'm not climbing down there to help,' Garvin said, leaning over the parapet. 'Have you seen the size of me? It's not safe.'

Sebastian shook his head and crouched to assess the distance between the two houses. The gap was a little farther than the first, and about the same as the length of the bookcase. This was going to be tough.

He rested the bookcase on the edge of the roof and, gripping one end tightly, tried to swing it over. The far end hit the other building with a clunk, but the weight was too much for his poor grip and it slid down the wall in slow motion towards the bottom of the alley.

He made a grab for it. 'Gods, no!' Too late.

Flames rushed up to greet him as the wood touched the seething thermalite.

Aryx tentatively lowered one foot into the lava and looked down at the glowing, semi-transparent force-field prosthetic. It was almost invisible against the thermalite, and formed a mesmerising foot-shaped hole in the liquid, with the edges crisping as they cooled. The foot lowered further and the pack moved upward slightly, tugging the harness. 'Right, that's one foot down.'

He shifted his weight and stepped forward with the other foot. The mobipack lurched to the left, and he caught himself against the wall. The heat scorched his legs through his trousers.

'Shit, this is scary!'

'Are you safe to continue?' Wolfram asked.

Aryx shook his head. 'I wouldn't exactly say I'm *safe*, no.'

'Please try to keep your head steady. It is difficult to track your vision as well as stabilising your legs.'

'You what? Are you interfering with my pack again?'

'Only to assist as necessary.'

Aryx was about to object but stopped himself as he recalled the last time Wolfram had manipulated the force-field: it had prevented him from getting wet. Later, he had taken control of his most feared construction, a cargomech – the very thing that had caused the accident leading to his amputation – but had used it to save his life during an attack by an alien predator.

'Do you wish me to stop?' Wolfram asked, drawing him from the memory.

'No. Keep stabilising if you think it'll help.'

'I do. I have already manipulated the traction texture seventeen times in the last ten seconds.'

A prickling of sweat broke out across his forehead. What a fatal mistake he would have made had the cube not been there to take the initiative! 'Thanks ... and I'll stick to the wall as much as possible.'

He crept along the side of the building that had prevented his fall, heading towards the blurting pipework.

A loud creaking, followed by distant screams, echoed from somewhere in the dome.

Trying to ignore the wailing, Aryx swallowed. 'I hope Sebastian's safe.'

'I am sure he is fine. The height of the steps into the civic building would be much higher than the potential level to which the thermalite could reach.'

Reassured by the SI's logic, Aryx strode purposefully onward, careful not to slosh the seething liquid with his impervious feet any more than necessary. The material *splapped* out from underfoot when he reached a shallow spot near several small storage containers and the tiny droplets sizzled away, eating through the metal in seconds. Aryx's eyes watered when the burning steam hit his face. Thank God for the glasses.

'Do be careful, Aryx. This substance is incredibly dangerous.'

'You don't need to remind me. Why do you do that?'

'Remind you?'

'No. Yes. It's like you want to scare the shit out of me all the time.'

'I am simply reflecting the gravity of the situation.'

'Stop it then, please. Adrenaline's doing that job well enough already!'

The voice, piped through the mobipack's speakers, fell silent.

Aryx turned a corner. Several metres away stood the airlock mounted in the crater wall, perilously close to the encroaching pool of glowing thermalite. How was he going to stop the stuff from reaching the door?

He scanned the surrounding buildings. The AR targeting reticule hopped from one object to another as Wolfram assessed potential aids. His gaze settled on a pile of grey blocks stacked up against a small, partially constructed building. A fraction of a second later, the dashed red box of the reticule landed on the very objects he'd spotted himself: blocks that would not dissolve.

'Yes, Wolfram, I see them. How long do I have?'

Coloured dots flashed along the bottom of Aryx's vision while the cube processed the request. 'Two to three minutes at most. The thermalite is cooler this far from the pipes, but the caustic nature of the liquid still poses a threat to the integrity of the airlock.'

He didn't wait for the cube to finish. Making his way to the stack, he picked up one of the blocks; the edges were cut sharp and the faces smooth, ideal to form a seal against the viscous acid as it cooled – if he did it quickly. They were light enough for him to carry two at a time, so he bent to take a second but a sharp cutting sensation went through his groin as the harness of the mobipack gave with the change in weight.

'I would advise against carrying more than one, Aryx. I am not certain I will be able to compensate adequately to balance you.'

He stared across the still-glowing liquid. 'You're right,' he said, and put the second block back on the stack. 'I don't really want to castrate myself in the process, either.'

Setting his jaw, he tucked the block under his arm and headed for the airlock.

'Damn it!' Sebastian said as the bookshelf burst into flames in the alley below.

'How did you ever get to become a SpecThingy agent being that clumsy?' Garvin shouted from the civic building.

Sebastian stood. 'You're not exactly helping! Pass me the other bookcase.' He went to the edge of the roof and waited.

Garvin leaned over and a moment later the bookcase fell towards Sebastian. He stepped back and caught it, this time with both hands instead of his head, and dragged it to where he'd dropped the ill-fated first bookcase. His hands shook as he stood on the edge of the roof and, keeping one leg back for balance, he swung the bookcase across the gap.

The far end caught but his grip began to give way.

'Not again!' He fumbled, slid one hand underneath and gave a sideways shove. The bookcase fell into place, forming a bridge between the two buildings with an overlap of an inch each end. Safe. Barely.

He put a foot on the shelving and tested it before bringing all his weight to bear. 'I shouldn't be doing this,' he said. 'By the Gods, I'm a computer programmer, not a stunt man.' Sweat trickled from his brow and sizzled as it hit the bubbling liquid below. He ought to turn back and give up.

The face of a ten-year-old girl peered up at him from a window in the wall below. She gasped and disappeared back inside.

Instantly, he forgot his doubts and, focused on the goal, leaped across the remaining span of the bookcase and strode across the roof to a spot over the front door. Crouching, he peered over the edge. 'I'm here!'

The girl opened the door and tentatively stepped out onto the doorstep, mere inches from the lava. 'Help! I'm trapped with my brothers,' she shouted, and was quickly joined by two younger boys of about six and three, who she held back with an arm.

Sebastian reached down. The girl strained to grab his hand but missed by several inches.

'Have you got something you can stand on?'

'I think so.' She disappeared and closed the door and reappeared several seconds later with an old wicker chair.

Sebastian lay on his front and reached down with both arms. 'Pass your little brother up first.'

She picked up the three-year-old and climbed on the chair. Even though she struggled to lift him, the extra height was enough for Sebastian to grab him.

The boy wriggled in Sebastian's grip. He rolled sideways, taking the child with him until he was safely on the roof, then planted the boy on his backside in the middle. 'Sit!' He resumed his position above the door and put his hand out. 'Stay!'

Too heavy for the girl to lift all the way, she held the six-year-old steady as he climbed on the chair and then heaved him up by his legs. Sebastian grabbed his arms and pulled. The boy's foot caught the back of the chair and it slid towards the edge of the steps.

He hauled the boy up onto the roof. 'Go over there and keep your brother safe. I'll get your sister.'

As he turned back, the terrified girl stared up at him, shaking her head.

'Come on, you can do it. Climb up on the chair.'

She continued to shake her head. 'I-I can't.'

'You *can*. Your brothers are up here waiting for you.'

She shook her head again.

'Do it for them. They need you.'

She tentatively put a foot on the chair and stepped up, reaching for Sebastian's outstretched hand. The chair grated across the steps and toppled backwards.

She screamed.

Chapter 7

It all happened in slow motion. The girl hadn't moved the chair into a safe position after lifting her brothers and, as she stood on it, the chair toppled into the glowing thermalite and burst into flames. Her fingers grasped the air, less than an inch from Sebastian's. He thrust his hand out farther.

She screamed as he hooked her fingers with his.

'Hold on!'

She kicked about, trying to find the non-existent support. Sebastian grimaced as he strained with the shifting weight. He locked his other hand around her wrist and pulled, but her weight was too much for him after the effort of lugging the bookcases. 'I'm going to swing you to your left. I want you to grab the roof.'

The wide-eyed girl nodded as tears, dirty from the smoke, streamed down her face.

He leaned to his left and, in one continuous motion, rolled right and swung. Reaching out, the girl caught the edge of the roof with her free hand.

'Good!'

He shuffled back into a crouch, grabbed both her hands and stood, pulling her onto the roof with him.

She clamped her arms around his waist and sobbed into his N-suit.

Sebastian patted her head before prying her arms free and steering her in the direction of her brothers. 'Come on. We've got to get to the civic building.' They approached the bookcase-bridge spanning the two houses and he ushered her forward. 'You go first,' he said, 'then I'll send your brother across.'

'No,' she said, shaking her head. 'I can't. I'm scared.'

'We can't stay on this roof. If you cross, it'll be easier to get your brothers over. I'll carry the little one.'

'Come on, lass,' Garvin shouted, waving.

'It's the mayor!' Her expression brightened and she stepped on the makeshift ladder. With arms held out to either side, she tiptoed across.

Sebastian's stomach knotted as she crossed the gap, and the knot only loosened once she'd reached the middle of the next roof. The knot re-formed and tightened as he set the older of the two brothers down on the bookcase to crawl across.

'Come on, Jeremy, you can do it,' the girl said, beckoning.

Sebastian waited for him to reach the other side and picked up the toddler.

The magma bubbled menacingly below as he began to cross the precarious bridge. The toddler squirmed. 'Oh Gods, hold still!' He wrapped his arms tight around the boy and leaped the remaining distance.

'How are we going to get up there?' the girl asked, pointing to the roof where Garvin stood.

Sebastian handed her the toddler. 'Look after your brother. I'll get the bookcase. We'll have to use that.'

He yanked the bookcase back onto the roof, not giving it enough time to fall into the alley again, and dragged it to the civic building.

Garvin reached down. 'Pass me the end!'

Sebastian stood the bookcase up and walked it to the edge. With a gentle push, it fell against the far building with a thud. Garvin held it steady while Sebastian contemplated the next course of action. It was like the fox and chicken puzzle. He couldn't leave the toddler until last, and he had to hold the bottom of the makeshift ladder.

'Put a foot here,' he said to the girl, pointing at the base of the bookcase with a toe. He took the three-year-old from her and began to climb. A couple of feet from the top, Garvin took the boy from him.

He returned to the bottom to send Jeremy up next. The boy scrambled up the shelving in seconds with the dexterity of a gibbon.

'Now you.'

The girl took a step.

'You can do it,' he said. 'It's easier than the other one. It's just like a ladder.'

She crouched and began to climb, but froze halfway. 'I can't,' she said, her eyes fixed on the glow from below.

'What's your name?'

'Z-Zubee.'

'Go on, Zubee. I know you can make it. It's not far. Your brothers are waiting.'

She looked up to where the boys peered over the parapet. Slowly, she resumed her climb and, as she reached the top, Garvin clapped his hands on her and heaved her over the wall.

Sebastian sighed with relief and stepped forwards to climb himself. He looked out across the town with its orange cast. The colour was just like Aryx's legs. 'Oh Gods, Aryx, what have I done?' His throat tightened and his eyes stung. Aryx was …

'What ya dallyin' about for?' Garvin shouted down to him. 'Get yer arse up here, I got three kids need gettin' to their parents!'

Sebastian tried to blink away his feelings. Leaning forward, he held on to the bookcase and slowly climbed towards the civic building, but something didn't feel quite right.

A foot away from the top, the wood shifted under his feet.

For the second time that day a bookcase fell.

Sweating profusely, Aryx staggered towards the airlock with another stone block and set it down. Only a few more – maybe five or six, he estimated – and he'd be done. He needed to deflect the lava nearest the door first, and had begun forming a wall one block high by two deep, staggering them from front to back to form the barrier. The lava, cooling as it touched the wall, crusted over, filling the gap between the bricks with sparkling black blobs.

'Looks like this is going to be easy, for a change,' he said, lowering a block into place. He made his way back to the half-built building for another. 'I think the biggest problem the town will have is how to manage without heat afterwards.'

'They will most likely have a backup generator,' Wolfram said. 'The dome is not in full sunlight for its full rotational period. The container, when full of thermalite, would radiate heat for several days, but if they actively use it for power generation, it would not last long enough.'

'I hadn't really thought of that. Ungh!' Aryx slipped as he picked up another block from the stack and caught himself on the block pile, inches short of dipping his legs in the hot lava. The heat scorched his knees through his trousers.

'Are you okay?' Wolfram asked.

'I-I think so. The legs went a bit funny then.' Shaking, he steadied himself against the pile and resumed carrying.

'I will check the positional sensors on your legs. I am receiving erratic data from them.'

'Erratic how?'

'I am not certain of the cause. I will need a moment to analyse the feed.'

Aryx sped up – the slip had cost him valuable seconds. He walked steadily to the growing barrier, carefully placed the block next to the previous one and turned to retrieve another.

'There is a problem.'

That word, when it came to technology, was always bad. 'What sort of problem?'

'The signal quality from one of the sensors is degrading.'

Aryx shuffled through the thermalite, trying to move as quickly as possible without splashing it everywhere. 'Are you going to tell me what that means, or do I have to play twenty questions with you like a damned TI?' He bent to pick up another block.

'I can only infer that the acidic thermalite vapours are having a corrosive effect on the sensor circuitry.'

'What?' Aryx staggered with the brick. His heart raced as he stared at the glowing red substance around him. If the legs went wrong he was done for! He had to hurry.

Using the biggest steps he dared, he strode back to the barricade and threw the block down before turning to get another. 'I've got to get as many of these as possible.'

As he approached the stack, still needing three more blocks, his right foot remained rooted to the spot. His right thigh came up and he pitched forward, landing in a forty-five-degree press-up against the wall. 'What the hell?'

'The right positional sensor has failed.'

'No!' he yelled, still leaning against the wall with arms outstretched. 'What am I going to do?'

'I can attempt to compensate further using visual tracking, but if the second sensor fails I won't be able to.'

'Shit. Doesn't look like I've got much choice, does it?'

'Unfortunately for you, and the rest of the colony, no. You still need more blocks.'

'Christ! Okay. What do I do?'

'Look down so that your leg is in view of the AR glasses. I will track the motion visually and with my own accelerometers and use that to adjust the leg's position. I suggest keeping the block out of the way.'

Aryx did as instructed and the leg moved into position, enabling him to stand properly. He took another block from the stack and tucked it under his arm. Slowly and deliberately, he made his way back to the airlock barricade. Progress was slower than he'd have liked, with the frame of the glasses obscuring his vision. He'd been walking for what almost seemed a minute. 'I have to stop, Wolfram. Got to check where I am.' He paused and looked ahead.

The thermalite magma had almost reached the loose blocks he'd thrown down in haste.

'Hurry, Aryx, the remaining sensor is degrading rapidly.'

There was a twelve-foot stretch of thermalite to clear. If he didn't get there in time, everyone in the dome would die.

He braced himself . . .

'Okay, got to run for it. Left foot first, you take the right. I don't want to rely on you mid-stride.'

. . . and ran.

Chapter 8

Aryx began the run on his left foot. The right foot extended under Wolfram's control as soon as the other left the ground. Under the slow motion of adrenaline, it touched down, and he set his focus on the block barrier.

The mobipack lurched.

'Wolfraaam!'

His left leg came down heavily, a couple of feet from the barricade, splashing hot thermalite into the air as he sprung off, and the leg vanished in a flailing mass of glowing laser-tendrils. His momentum carried him over the low wall into the centre; a rugby player attempting a try – with a stone block. Gravel seared his thighs and forearms as he skidded along with the block held in front of him. He immediately rolled onto his back to get away from the pain.

'What did you do that for, you stupid machine?'

'The sensor was in the process of failing, I had to give you extra momentum to ensure success.'

'I could have—'

'Do not argue now. Place the block.'

He glanced at the end of the incomplete barrier. Thermalite inched around it towards the door.

Now legless, he rolled onto his front, reached for the block he'd dropped and gave it a mighty shove. It slid several inches.

He shimmied forward, stopping to push the block when he reached it. With a final shove, he moved the block into position, pushing back the hot, viscous fluid. It still needed one more block.

Shuffling to his left, he grabbed one of the blocks that formed the double layer he'd already set down. Drawing it back a little, he exposed a patch of thermalite that had crusted in the gap between layers, forming a seal. It would hold. He repeated the shoving-shuffling process again to where thermalite oozed around the end of the barricade near the crater wall. He shoved the block into position and the flow stopped.

'Phew! I thought I was a goner there.' He lay back to rest for a minute before sitting up. His grazed thighs had left a trail of blood, soaking his torn trousers. 'Better see if I can fix these sensors and get going, because without them, I'm stuck.'

He pulled off one of the plastic blocks strapped to his legs. Corroded metal dripped from the casing of the neural relay.

'I'm stuck.'

Sebastian's heart stuttered as the bookcase gave way under his weight, slipping from the notch in the brickwork. He threw up his hands to grab the civic building's parapet, but missed. In that fraction of a second, he had just enough time to contemplate the scalding, flaying death that lay in wait below.

With a sharp jerk, pain tore through his shoulder and he slammed against the wall, scuffing his face mid-fall.

A man, one of the townsfolk, hung over the parapet, holding on to his right wrist. A second stood behind him, in turn holding his shoulders. The metal frame of a ladder slid down.

Sebastian reached out with his free arm and pulled himself onto the rungs. 'Thank you!' he said, and allowed his right arm to drop. An intense burning told him without a doubt that his shoulder was dislocated. Blood stained the light-grey blockwork where his face had hit, but it was certainly better than being dead. He paused to take several deep breaths, and coughed as the acidic tang of the thermalite bit into his throat.

He climbed up the ladder, over the parapet onto the roof, where several of the townsfolk had gathered. Numerous ladders had been placed between the other buildings, allowing them to regroup.

'They all came up to get out of the gas,' Garvin said.

Cardigan Woman stepped forward with her three children and they embraced Sebastian.

'Thank you for saving them,' she said. 'I don't know what I'd have done if you weren't here. They'd have choked.'

Then it hit him. Aryx wasn't there.

'Has anyone seen a man in a wheelchair?'

The bedraggled people looked at each other blankly. Several shrugged.

'Oh Gods! What have I—' Two bleeps from Sebastian's wristcom interrupted him with a signal on a public frequency.

'Excuse me, Agent Thorsson,' came Wolfram's voice, suitably formal for an unknown audience on an open channel. 'Aryx Trevarian's wristcom is damaged, and he has a problem that requires assistance.'

'Thank the Gods!' A wave of relief washed over him and everything swayed momentarily. 'I thought he was dead ...' He sat down. 'What kind of problem? Is he injured?'

'He is relatively uninjured but has something of a mobility issue.'

Aryx waited while the lights in the AR display flashed.

'I have successfully made contact with Sebastian,' Wolfram said.

'Good. What's he doing?'

'He didn't say. I assume he was in the company of others, given the background sounds.'

'I suppose I just have to wait, then. I might as well see if I can fix these neural relays.' He pulled the straps from the ends of his legs and pried open one of the leaking plastic modules. The corroded circuitry glistened with a greenish crystalline liquid, not unlike an old-fashioned alkaline battery after it had ruptured. 'Damn. I never even thought about sealing these against such harsh environments when I made them.' He threw the units onto the thermalite in disgust, where the plastic went up in a brief gout of flame. Without them, the mobipack was useless anyway.

Sitting in the tiny walled enclosure outside the airlock, there was little to do but wait.

And wait.

Pshwaaaa! Enormous clouds of steam, dust, and dirt blasted towards him as though a mini twister had somehow found its way into Sollers Hope.

Aryx shuffled back against the airlock. His heart raced as sharp cracking sounds came from the tempest.

A glint of silver moved in the roiling mass – a vague, humanoid outline in silver on grey. The figure approached, wielding a long tube. Another *Pshhh!* engulfed Aryx in a cold, hazy fog with a strange tang to it. Liquid nitrogen or dry ice?

The figure clomped out of the mist towards him, along a narrow strip of dark and chilled lava, and raised its shiny, heat-reflective helmet.

'Seb!' Aryx reached up for his friend. With his legs hurting, it was as much as he could do without his wheelchair or prosthetics.

Sebastian dropped next to him and held him in a tight embrace for several moments. 'Gods, I thought . . .' His voice wavered and he swallowed audibly. 'I thought you'd died . . . and it was all my fault for bringing you here and getting you into trouble again. Gods, I'm so sorry!' He shook as he sobbed into his shoulder.

Aryx had never seen him so upset; he patted Sebastian's back. 'It's okay. Apart from a few scrapes, I'm fine.'

Sebastian pulled back and held him by the arms, shaking his head. 'I shouldn't have brought you.'

'Shut up.' Aryx's eyes stung, and not just from the acrid air. 'You didn't drag me along. How many times do I have to tell you not to blame yourself?' He looked over Sebastian's shoulder. 'How did you get here, anyway?'

'They found some liquid gas canisters. I used them to cool the thermalite all the way from the town centre.' Sebastian looked him up and down. 'Where's your chair?' His eyes stopped on Aryx's scraped legs. 'Is the mobipack broken?'

Aryx nodded. 'The sensors melted. I'll have to make some more.'

Sebastian's eyes widened as he stood up. 'You could get some neural implants, like I suggested!'

Aryx slapped him across the legs. 'Go screw yourself. Now get me the hell out of here.'

With his ego thoroughly bruised, Aryx allowed Sebastian to carry him around the outskirts of town, avoiding the townsfolk and freezing the thermalite lava with the coolant wand as they went. Sebastian told him of the encounter with Garvin and, after depositing the mobipack on the ship and retrieving Aryx's wheelchair, they made their way back to the town square.

Teams of people slowly worked their way back and forth with liquid gas, chilling the hot-but-now-solid thermalite surrounding the fractured canister at the centre. Garvin stood at the top of the civic building steps, pointing directions and sending others off on repair duties.

Sebastian approached him. 'How are things looking?'

Garvin scratched his head. 'Not as bad as they might seem. The solar cell's got a big crack, as you can see. I've been told it's because the pumping station the other side of the crater wasn't drawing the flow back.'

Aryx inched forward, watching where he put his wheels. 'The return pipe exploded.'

Garvin raised an eyebrow. *'Exploded?* Are you sure?'

Aryx nodded. 'I fixed your condensator and noticed something flashing on a box on one of the heat pipes. It was a bomb. I was lucky to get far enough away to not be caught in the blast.'

Garvin folded his arms. 'Why would someone do that to us?' His gaze flitted around the square and he leaned towards the pair. *'Who* could have done it?'

'Someone who wanted to kill everyone in the colony. Someone with access to military-grade explosives, so I'd say the ITF terrorists. And it *would* have killed everyone. The thermalite almost ruptured the airlock into the mines.'

'Why didn't it?'

Now Aryx wasn't wearing the mobipack there was no reason to mention it. 'I managed to get to the door and used blocks from the building site to ring fence it before the thermalite reached it.'

Garvin bowed. 'Then I have you to thank for all our lives, and Sebastian to thank for saving those children.'

Aryx looked up at Sebastian. 'Why didn't you tell me?'

He shrugged. 'I was more worried about finding you.'

'Garvin, how are you going to cope with this now?' Aryx asked.

He shook his head. 'I've no idea. The engineer's laid up with a broken hand. We could do with some help repairing the pipes.'

'And hardening your security,' Sebastian said. 'I was able to break into your mines too easily the last time we were here. I suspect whoever planted the bomb probably got in the same way. You don't even have cameras in the hangar entrance.'

Aryx nodded slowly. So that was where Sebastian was going with the conversation – a wise move, especially after what he'd said about Garvin not trusting them. 'I can help repair the pipes, if you like. Sebastian can work on your security code and set up some cameras for you. SpecOps have had run-ins with terrorists lately, and I'm sure they wouldn't object to us helping you out.'

Sebastian nodded.

Garvin's shoulders dropped. 'That would be very much appreciated, thank you.'

Sebastian looked up from his infoslate as Aryx approached from the far side of the square. After several hours' work, the combined efforts of the townsfolk had cleared the streets of the worst of the thermalite layer and the solar generator was once again in operation, but at only twenty per cent capacity until they were sure the repairs would hold. It radiated a pleasant warmth onto the civic building's steps where Sebastian sat. He stood when Aryx approached. 'All done?'

Aryx nodded. 'Pump's working fine. They had some spare pipe. And I got the condensator fixed.'

'I've done what I can with the security, but they really need to upgrade to Logynix to make the place safe. Their old Fenestre OS just isn't up to the task. It's years out of date.' Sebastian tipped his head back. The air in the dome above was clear and cloud-free. 'A job well done, I think.'

'They might even be able to water the trees now, although . . .' Aryx jabbed a thumb over his shoulder in the direction of the charcoaled tree by the cylinder. 'I think that no amount of water will be able to revive that one.'

Sebastian laughed.

Aryx grinned expectantly and put his hands in his lap. 'So, are we good to go?'

'Not quite.' The door to the civic building creaked open behind them and Sebastian turned to Garvin, who stood in the doorway. 'Everything's all set now, Garvin.'

'So, you boys are off then, eh?'

'Yes, but *we* still have something to discuss.'

Garvin set his jaw.

'Come on!' Aryx said. 'After all we've done to help save the town, surely you know you can trust us?'

Garvin's eyes narrowed. 'I shouldn't . . .'

Sebastian folded his arms. 'But?'

'I dunno. That copper looking for Duggan . . . this bomb . . . you turnin' up at the right, or wrong, time . . . it's a bit suspicious.'

At that moment, the little girl Sebastian had saved ran up to him and held something out. He took the object and she giggled and ran off. It was a tiny, delicate flower crafted from folded plaspaper. 'Thank you!' he called after her. She turned and smiled before disappearing behind the houses.

Garvin's taut expression relaxed and he sighed. 'I guess you're right. I s'pose I ought to tell you. Alicia Maline. That's the name I gave Duggan.'

'Who's she?'

'Duggan was here asking about previous clients who bought carbyne. He was a bit disappointed when I said that John Kerl was the only other client since he already knew about him. I told him that we did have an employee who worked on the stuff. She did the original analysis of carbyne, but she left suddenly about twenty years ago. No forwardin' address when she left, nothin'. She was quiet, kept to herself, and never got into trouble once in the fourteen years she worked for me – so I never asked what brought her here. She left on a scheduled mineral transport, so Duggan could probably track her down just from her name in the manifests. Of course, I gave that police bloke a made-up name. Didn't want no trouble comin' to 'er. She was a good worker, even into her sixties.'

'What did Duggan want with previous customers?'

'I dunno. He was witterin' on about thaumatragedy, or whatever it's called, and trying to find someone who knew about using it for healing or somesuch. Before him, Alicia was the only one that paid any attention to carbyne. I guess that's why she interested Duggan.'

'Wait. You know about magic?' Sebastian slapped his forehead. 'Of course you do. You had to have seen him without his mask to give him that nickname.'

'Yes. Poor sod. It was horrible seeing all his innards exposed like that. Put me right off my sandwiches.'

Sebastian's stomach twitched and he grimaced as he recalled the sight of Duggan's semi-transparent skin and blood vessels that made up his maroon sponge-like frame. 'Thank the Gods he's back to normal.'

Garvin gave him a sidelong glance. 'He said you had something to do with that.'

'Yes, we had a comput—'

Aryx tugged at the back of Sebastian's N-suit.

He shouldn't mention the SI.

'We worked with him on discovering how to reverse it.'

Garvin raised an eyebrow. 'A man of many talents. Well, for Duggan's sake, if he's in trouble with terrorists, I wish you luck trying to find him.' He laughed. 'I want him back. He's my only customer for that useless stuff! If you do find him, let me know he's okay.'

Sebastian leaned back in the pilot's seat, watching the hypnotic display of rainbow-stars sliding past the windows of the *Ultima Thule* as the ship journeyed through superphase on its way back to Tenebrae.

'Who do you think this Alicia Maline is?' Aryx asked.

Sebastian sat up. 'I don't know. Garvin's not exactly given us much to go on. But, what I'd like to know is why Duggan's researching healing.'

Aryx coughed. 'No idea. Didn't the Folians tell you it wasn't possible, or something?'

'Not exactly. They said it was very difficult to use thaumaturgy for healing without intimate knowledge of a being's biology on a microscopic level, which was why they had to use the cambium fruit on Achene to heal our wounds instead.'

'I remember. Oh, that reminds me.' Aryx bent down, opened the refrigerated unit by the console, took out a vial and proceeded to inject himself in the knees with it. 'I bet Monica would love to look at one of those fruits. Organic nanotech seems like complex stuff.'

'How many of those have you got left?'

'My drugs? Three doses. Enough until the shipment comes in.'

'Good.' Sebastian scratched his head. Organic nanotech ... His university experiments in simulation and artificial intelligence had been complex and required massive computing power and storage space. How did the Folians manage without computers? 'I'd love to know how they program those fruit myself. I wonder whether they actually encode the DNA somehow?'

'Perhaps that's something you should research one day. Could lead to medical breakthroughs. Why did you give up your programming research, anyway?'

The painful memory came, unwanted, to Sebastian's mind. 'Like your career, the ITF put an end to mine. They hacked Hereford University, where I worked at the time, and then bombed the datacentre in Bristol where my work was backed up.'

'Seems a bit ... *targeted*. Given them coming after you now, I mean.'

'I think it was probably just coincidence—'

'You don't believe in coincidences. "The universe is deterministic in

nature and everything has a rational and predictable cause and effect," '
Aryx said, in a fairly convincing impression of Sebastian's accent.

Sebastian laughed. 'I was working on adaptive algorithms, emergent behaviour, chaotic simulation, fractals, that sort of stuff. I can't see how that would be a threat to terrorists. It's most likely they wanted to cause as much damage as possible for future generations, just to make a point, by destroying everyone's research.'

'Which led to us meeting, and you being here. If only the entities controlling them could have seen the future—'

'They would never have furnished you with a weapon that could be used against them,' Wolfram said from where he rested on the console, his understated tone at odds with the gravity of the statement. 'Also, if they had not stolen me from Oxford University as part of their technology harvesting, the entities' existence might have remained secret.'

'Yes, and my brother would still be alive. The ITF killed him during his investigation of the Bristol bombing. It was my fault for asking him to look into it.'

Aryx grinned. 'So, things *are* always as connected as you say they are.'

Sebastian slapped him on the arm with the back of his hand. 'That's not helping! We need to figure out who Alicia Maline is.'

'I have found no reference in the network's recent census records,' Wolfram said. 'I wanted to continue searching before mentioning it, just to be certain, but it seems that the paper trail leads off the system – or records have been deleted.'

Sebastian sighed. 'Not again.' His recent investigations had turned up record deletions all over the place. 'Duggan must have found out who she is and gone to find her. The information has to be around somewhere.'

'When we get back to Tenebrae I will interlink with the security TI and perform a thorough search.'

'Thanks, Wolfram.' Sebastian turned to Aryx. His eyes had dark ticks in the corners. 'You look worn out. We should get some rest before we get back. Wolfram, can you take over piloting? I'll sleep over here.' He got up and went to the seats at the back of the ship.

Aryx wheeled onto the lift. 'You know there are bunks downstairs?'

'The cargo netting isn't big enough for both of us.'

'I don't mean the cargo netting. There's a small sleep compartment behind the pressure suit storage. You didn't exactly study the schematics of this ship when you got it, did you?'

Sebastian scratched his head. 'To be honest, I didn't study them at all.' He returned to the front of the ship and climbed down the ladder beside Aryx into the hold.

From above, Aryx muttered something under his breath.

Chapter 9

Sebastian strolled through the atrium with Aryx wheeling alongside. The breeze was fresh, but the sunlight coming through the blue-sky patterned filters above warmed his face. They had left the ship in the central docking area to avoid an instant confrontation with Karan. Still needing replacement sensors, Aryx carried the mobipack on his lap.

Sebastian looked down at Aryx's bloody trousers. 'We should head to the hospital to get these wounds cleaned up. If we went straight to the hangar with you looking like that Karan would go mental.'

'Yeah, and you don't want to be around for that!'

He grimaced. Karan's fury would blast him like the flame-breath of a dragon. The only person whose anger he feared more was that of Eleanor Bannik, his boss – before he'd known she had secretly chosen him to look into Gladrin's dealings with the ITF. Bannik now had to keep up pretences, but at least she wasn't genuinely the Ice Queen he'd believed her to be. Karan however, would be another matter altogether.

Aryx pressed the comm button by the door to Monica's lab.

'Hello?'

'It's us ... again.'

'Aryx? Come in.' The door slid open and Monica looked up from whatever she was working on at her bench. 'What can I help you with this time—' Her eyes settled on Aryx's legs and she put a hand to her cheek. 'What on Earth have you been doing?' Her gaze moved to Sebastian's grazed face. 'Both of you!'

'We've been through the wars,' Aryx said.

'Come over here.' She led them to the examination bed and collected up some cotton swabs, several bottles of liquid and a vial of nanobots.

Aryx shook his head. 'I'm anti-nanobot.'

She swapped them for a can of wound sealant spray. 'Why haven't you gone to the hospital to get this looked at?'

'If we went to one of the treatment rooms they'd log on the system that we've been to Sollers Hope.' He wheeled to the bed and climbed up. Sebastian sat next to him.

'And you think it would get back to the ITF because of the Trojan in the system.' She swabbed their wounds and started putting suture tapes across the biggest cuts. 'Why would the ITF be interested in whether you'd been there?'

'There was a bomb,' Sebastian said. 'And a police officer asking questions about Duggan. He was probably the one who set the bomb in the first place.'

'What? Are you insane? How could you even suspect the police of such a thing?'

'Garvin said his eyes were sparkly, and that's a key sign of possession. There's no reason for the police to be looking for Duggan, so the officer is probably with the ITF. They'll be looking for Duggan either to use him to increase their numbers or as a weapon. He's dangerous when he gets his hands on carbyne.'

'But why blow up Sollers Hope?'

'Leverage to get Garvin to talk if he didn't cooperate, I guess. Although he didn't mention a bomb, and was as surprised as I was when the explosion happened, so it couldn't have been that ... What if the ITF agent decided he didn't need it as leverage, but then set it off when we arrived?'

Aryx shook his head. 'The police ship had left long before we got to the dome, and had probably left the system by the time it went off. It looked like it was on a timer.'

Monica's eyes widened. 'So they wanted to destroy the colony anyway? But why?'

Sebastian rubbed his chin. 'Maybe to get rid of anyone who had been in contact with Duggan. He had been possessed in the past – if that got out it could blow their cover. Aside from us, the people in Chopwood and a few on Sollers Hope, nobody else knows him. It makes sense they'd want to erase his tracks.'

'Then you were lucky to get there when you did.' Monica applied another suture tape to Aryx's leg. 'How does the sparkly eyes thing work if they aren't poisoning themselves with indium gallium arsenide particles, like you? How did these people even get possessed in the first place?'

'I don't know. They can become possessed by using magic, and there's the possibility of superphase travel causing it. I don't know what physics are behind it, but Wolfram is analysing the signal that causes the nightmares, just in case it's related.'

'So, the only way we can find out how possession works would be to capture someone who is under the influence of these extra-spatial entities and run scans. Where does superphase come into it?'

'The Folians think the entities exist partly in superphase, or something,' Aryx said. He immediately put a hand over his mouth.

Monica looked up. 'That's the second time you've mentioned the Folians.'

'Erm. We enlisted their help in dealing with the entities. They examined Duggan.'

'They? There's only one on the station.'

'That's right. Tolinar,' Sebastian said. 'Tolinar is the Folian ambassador on the station. Aryx just said "they" because it's a bit confusing that Tolinar refers to himself as "we".'

'And Sebastian initially suspected that acceleration psychosis could actually be caused by people getting possessed during superphase travel.'

'I've heard of that.' Monica proceeded to put small stitches in the worst of Aryx's cuts. 'There have been several cases documented over the years. I was quite intrigued by it, given that most of the sufferers had disappeared while under observation. I do like the odd mystery.'

The door alarm beeped.

'Who is it?'

'Karan Tallin. I'm supposed to be guarding Aryx. I know he and Sebastian are in there.'

Sebastian's scalp itched.

Monica looked at him and lifted her hands in a half-shrug.

He closed his eyes. 'You'll have to let her in.'

'Is that wise?'

'She knows all about the ITF and the entities. I don't really have an excuse to keep her standing in the corridor, and she'll only wait until we come out.'

The door had barely slid open enough for Karan's black carbon-composite armour to fit through before she stormed in. 'What the hell are you two playing at? You don't come back to the hangar, and when I ask the computer where you are, it says you're in the bloody hospital!'

Aryx bit his lip. Sebastian shrank back.

Her eyes flashed. 'Well?'

Sebastian swallowed. 'We had a bit of trouble on Sollers Hope,' he said. At least Aryx hadn't been lying when they said they'd gone to repair damage – even if it was caused after the fact. 'Technical difficulties.'

'Technical difficulties my arse!' Karan bellowed. 'Look at the state of him!'

Despite the rate at which Monica worked, Aryx's wounds were still clearly visible, even with stitches and wound sealant spray, which did nothing to hide the discolouration and swelling.

'Terrorists got there before us,' Aryx said.

Sebastian's face tingled. Why tell her they'd been in danger?

'So how the hell did your legs get like that? Stuff like that doesn't happen in a wheelchair.'

Aryx sighed and his shoulders sagged. 'I'll show you ... Wolfram, are you listening? Do you have the specs for my positional sensors?'

'Yes, Aryx,' came the voice from the mobipack.

Karan's face twisted into a question at the sound of the new voice in the room.

'Good. Monica, can you administer a dose of nanobots to my legs?'

'You're all stitched up, anyway. You said you didn't want nanobots.'

'I didn't, but it doesn't look like I have a choice. Just trust me.'

She shrugged but followed his instructions, inserting a needle into each leg and pumping in the mercurial fluid.

'What are you doing?' Karan asked.

'Just wait,' Aryx said. 'Wolfram?'

'Am I to assume you wish me to construct neural relays, as per Sebastian's earlier, unwarranted, suggestion?'

'Uh-huh.'

Sebastian smiled at Aryx in an attempt to reassure him.

He gave a narrow-eyed "hope you're happy" scowl in return. 'That feels weird. Itchy ... What are you doing, *exactly*?'

'I am instructing the nanobots to construct micro-relays and attach them to the ends of your severed nerves. There may be some sensation during the process.'

A minute later, Wolfram continued. 'Relay fabrication complete. I will monitor and calibrate accordingly, and pair them with the mobipack's systems.'

'What's a mobipack?' Karan and Monica asked in unison.

Aryx tapped the hard-shelled plastic backpack on the bed and pulled on the parachute-type harness, fitting it around his torso and thighs.

'What does it do?' Karan asked.

'This.' He slid off the edge of the bed and bright orange laserthreads manifested in the space between his knees and the floor. In a fraction of a second they whipped around to form the shape of lower legs, calves, and feet: a glowing, glassy representation of prosthetic legs. The feet touched the floor and the harness sagged under his weight. As he stood, Monica simply stared at the spectacle, wide-eyed and smiling.

While he shifted his weight from side to side, Karan staggered back. She groped for the edge of the counter behind her but her hand missed and she fell backwards. Losing his footing, Aryx promptly followed in an ungainly tumble to the floor.

'Careful!' Monica reached out with both arms in different directions, as though unsure who to catch.

He rubbed his backside. 'I'm okay. It's not the first fall I've had.'

Sebastian crouched and propped up Karan. She was unconscious but breathing.

'You're lucky to be able to stand on CFDs at all on this hard floor,' Monica said. 'You could do with rubber-soled shoes.'

Aryx glared at her as he pulled himself back up onto the bed. 'Don't go there. I only use this to get about in the field where I can't go in the chair, but it's uncomfortable to use for long periods.'

'Judging by the state of your legs, you obviously can't guarantee when you'll need one or the other.'

He looked down and scratched his head. 'Hmm, you're right, and I did have a bit of trouble walking in Sollers Hope, even before the sensors started to melt.'

'I know just the thing. Give me a minute.' With that Monica dashed out of the lab.

'Wait!' Sebastian said. 'What about Karan? Where's she going?'

'Search me.'

'Wh-What's going on?' Karan asked, her voice slurry, head lolling to one side.

'I think you must have fainted,' Sebastian said.

'I never faint!' She stood and dusted off her armour. 'It could have been because I missed lunch worrying about you. Ow!' Her hand went to the back of her head. 'No, I definitely knocked myself out.' She stared at Aryx's glowing legs. 'I can't believe you've never shown me.'

'I didn't want to tell everybody! I'm waiting until this business with the ITF is sorted out before I send my patent proposal off. I don't want them getting hold of the design through the government.'

Karan sighed. 'Fair enough, but you could have told me. From now on, you don't go anywhere dangerous without me, regardless.' She glared at Sebastian. 'And you're not to let him.'

Sebastian shrank back – again – nodding rapidly. He wasn't going to argue.

'What computer was that speaking earlier?'

The pair explained the SI and its origins to Karan, as they had with Monica. A few minutes later, Monica came back carrying two short metal tubes with hoops on either end, one large, one small.

'I've got these,' she said, handing them to Aryx.

'What are they?'

She motioned for him to raise an arm in front, and fastened the larger hoop of one rod around his arm, near the elbow, and the smaller hoop just above his wrist, leaving the rod fixed tightly against his outer forearm. 'The other one,' she said, and attached the second rod.

'Are you going to tell me what they do, or am I about to get a nasty surprise?'

She gave a wry smile. 'Only if you're on the wrong end of it. No, you'll find them useful. Point your arms at the ground. Make a gesture like this.' She held her hand out, palm down, fingers extended, and quickly bent her fingers, touching her index finger and thumb together, as though gripping an invisible tube.

Aryx raised an eyebrow, but replicated the gesture with both hands pointing at the floor.

'Now squeeze your finger and thumb together twice.'

In the blink of an eye, two telescopic rods shot out of the tubes on his arms, forming slender crutches, with the gap between his fingers and thumb containing a handle. 'Hah!'

'I said you'd like them. I stumbled across them earlier on while looking for some supplies, pardon the pun. You don't see them in use much now, since most people get their injuries repaired too quickly to ever need them. They're meant for other races too, and if they're too short you can twist the handle and they'll extend up to an additional five feet. At least they can give you a bit of support for your non-stick feet.' She smiled.

To Sebastian's surprise, Aryx smiled back. 'Thanks. They'll be useful. Very useful indeed.' He leaned forward and eased himself down into his wheelchair. 'Much easier,' he said, releasing his grip on the crutch-handles. They instantly retracted back into the tubes on his arms. 'I don't know why I didn't think of them before.'

Karan put her hands on her hips. 'Probably too busy being Mr Independent.'

'That's a bit unfair,' Sebastian said. 'It's not like he's been able to use crutches before, having no legs.'

Aryx's face, cast into a scowl, broke with laughter.

Sebastian's wristcom beeped, cutting off their humour. 'Agent Thorsson, I'd like to see you in my office.' It was Bannik.

'I'll be there shortly.' Sebastian closed the connection. 'I wonder what she wants?'

The corners of Karan's mouth pulled taut. 'Sounds like someone's in trouble!'

Sebastian rolled his eyes. 'I should get going. It must have been urgent for her to call me direct.'

'Go,' Aryx said, brushing him away with his hand. 'We'll finish up here and I'll meet you back at the ship if necessary ... if you haven't already been chewed up and spat out.'

No sooner than he'd stepped through the door to Bannik's glass-walled office, the blinds closed behind Sebastian, isolating the room from the rest of the security department. Why the need for privacy?

'Before you ask, this isn't strictly to do with work,' Bannik said. She smiled, but her sharp cheekbones and tight ponytail did little to reassure him. 'Take a seat.' Sebastian sat in one of the two seats opposite her, and she pushed her terminal aside and clasped her hands together in front of her on the black glass desk. 'This is about our agency problem ... Witness Protection.'

'And the link with the ITF?' He had never told her about the entities, nor that they were behind the ITF, and saw no reason to do so.

She nodded. 'I recently heard from a friend who runs one of the largest computer security organisations on Earth. He came to me because I'd asked him to keep an eye out for unusual funding sources.

He was recently paid for a long-standing contract for an entire server farm. Funding for that project came from channels outside EarthSec – the same channels through which you found Agent Gladrin was paid.'

'And you think this hardware installation has something to do with the terrorists?'

Bannik leaned forward on her elbows. 'It seems likely, don't you think?'

'I'm inclined to agree.' Sebastian leaned back in his chair. Being relaxed in Bannik's office was strange to say the least. 'What's so odd about the servers? Something must have sparked him to look into it.'

'The hardware was part of an isolated system, which makes it unusual. I asked him a bit more about it – we're old friends and I managed to twist his arm until he offered to tell me where it is – for security purposes, of course.' Bannik leaned to one side, behind the desk. When she straightened, she held a long tube of plaspaper.

Sebastian raised an eyebrow. 'What's that?'

'What does it look like?' She smoothed the paper out across the desk. 'It's a building floor plan. He couldn't send me a digital version. You did say not to trust the system, after all. I can't allow you to take a photo of it, or for it to leave this room.'

'So why are you showing it to me?'

'I suggest memorising as much as possible.'

Sebastian put his hand up. 'Wait a minute. I'm supposed to remember all this?'

'Not all of it. Just what you need.'

'What I need for what?'

There was bleep from Bannik's terminal. He slouched at the interruption.

'Who is it?' Bannik asked.

'Tallin's here to see you,' the receptionist said.

'Send her in.' She looked up at Sebastian. 'Since Trevarian's not on the security staff, I can't show him this. Monica Stevens is SpecOps, but not part of my team, and I don't know her. Tallin however, I will authorise to see this. I called her just after I contacted you.'

Sebastian rose as the door opened, and a flustered Karan stepped through. 'You wanted to see me, ma'am?' She frowned at Sebastian.

'It's nothing to worry about, Tallin. Agent Thorsson has no doubt told you the situation with Witness Protection and the ITF.'

Karan nodded.

'Good. I want you to study this map with him. It's the lower level of the Witness Protection Archive, One Great George Street, London. The map cannot leave this room in any form other than your memory.'

'Why are you showing us?'

'I thought you'd like to help Agent Thorsson stage a break-in.'

Chapter 10

Sebastian stepped back from the desk. 'You want *us* to break into the archive?'

Bannik frowned at him. '*You* all but suggested it when we last spoke on the matter.'

He turned to Karan for support. She folded her arms and glared at him. 'Don't look at me.'

'Oh, come on. Just because I found out about the cover-up, it doesn't mean I should be the one to dig it all up.'

'Of course it does,' Bannik said. 'I can't take official responsibility for it. You want to find out where Gladrin's family is, and the only way to do that is to connect directly to the archive. There are no external hardlines and no remote access. Record transfer, however slow the method, is performed by transport of syncpods in armoured vehicles. Locating one of those won't help us get the data already stored in their servers, and a robbery of that kind would be certain to attract attention.'

'Why not just inform EarthSec and let them deal with it?'

'You said yourself that you're worried something might happen to Gladrin's family if the ITF realise we're on to them.'

'But why me? Why just us?'

'History has proven that even a small group of people can have a significant impact on the world from behind the scenes. Just remember Alan Turing. He's a hero of yours, isn't he? The efforts of his small team helped to save millions in the Second World War.'

'I don't . . .'

'A precision strike in the right place to access information is all that is required, and you said yourself that Gladrin thought the ITF were trying to recruit you.' Bannik folded her arms. 'That should make it easier for you to get in.'

Sebastian rubbed his head and screwed up his face to shut out the problem. 'But breaking into the archive ... I can't do it. It's breaking the law. I can't do it.'

'Pfft! Come off it,' Karan said, 'you've broken umpteen laws in the last few weeks.'

His eyes snapped open and he stared at her. 'What are you talking about?'

She leaned on her back foot and began counting on one hand. 'Um, hacking security on a mining outpost, getting into a firefight at a fuel depot, making official trips without logging a flight plan, falsifying records, not to mention withholding evidence ... Need I continue?'

Sebastian mentally added *almost inciting a diplomatic incident with a reclusive alien race* ... She had a point. 'Alright, you've got me there.' He scratched his head. 'I'll need a few weeks to plan it—'

His wristcom bleeped.

'Yes?'

'Agent Thorsson, the search of records you requested has been completed.' It was Wolfram, the formality clearly an attempt to disguise himself as a Turing Interface.

He looked from Karan to Bannik and back. Should he even answer? 'Oh ... What were the results?'

'I have uncovered records pertaining to Alicia Maline. According to shipping manifests, she was aboard a shipment of ore from Sollers Hope to Earth.'

'What about Mr Simmons's whereabouts?'

'There is no recent mention of his name in transit records. It is likely he took an unregistered private craft and headed for Earth himself.'

'Thank you.' He cut the connection.

Bannik gave him a questioning look. 'Unusual for you of all people to thank a TI.'

Sebastian's face warmed.

'So, it looks like you don't *have* a few weeks to plan, if what you're investigating takes you to Earth,' she said, leaning back in her seat.

He looked to Karan again for support. She shrugged.

'Oh, Gods. I hate this. Why is everything going wrong lately?' With his hand forced, he stared at the map, trying to absorb the details. 'Are you taking this in?' he asked.

'Of course. *I* do what I'm told,' Karan said. She was now completely in Bannik's corner. The traitor.

Bannik gave them fifteen minutes to memorise the layout. Sebastian focused on the core of the server farm, attempting to commit the position of data connections and access points to memory while Karan traced pathways in and out of the basement to the upper levels, the maps of which were sadly lacking.

'Right, you two, out. I have other business to attend to, and nobody ever stays in here for more than twenty minutes without getting the sack or a promotion, and you have neither.'

Sebastian looked up. 'I'll—'

Bannik cut him off with a raised hand. 'I don't want to know the details. Plausible deniability. Don't tell me what, when, or how. I don't want to know, and that way the information can't be pried out of me.'

With a nod, they left her sitting at her desk. As they exited the office, she shouted through the door after them, for the benefit of everyone else in the office, 'And don't do that again, ever, or it'll be a disciplinary hearing for both of you!'

'Atrium level.' Sebastian tapped his foot while he waited for the lift to take them from the security department.

'Stop doing that,' Karan said. 'Why are you so nervous?'

'Oh, I don't know. Perhaps because what we're about to do is really dangerous?'

'You've been in worse situations lately.'

He recalled surviving the crash on Achene, and his earlier scrape in a punctured pressure suit when he'd nearly died in vacuum. 'I suppose you're right, but this is different. This is planned. I'm going to leave Aryx here when we go. I can't take him into danger again.'

Karan frowned. 'He looks a bit tired, but surely you can take him with you? You know he won't forgive you for leaving him behind.'

Sebastian rubbed his chin. Putting Aryx in harm's way again, intentionally . . . 'I don't know. I shouldn't. No. I can't ask him to come. He nearly died on Achene – in three different situations – and on Sollers Hope. It would be irresponsible of me.'

Karan leaned against the dark, brushed-metal wall of the elevator. 'Why not bring the subject up and see what his reaction is?'

He groaned and then smiled. 'You know, you should have been a diplomat.'

* * *

'Thanks for doing all this,' Aryx said, as Monica finished re-bandaging his legs.

'It's quite alright. It's better than getting bored waiting for even more unintriguing test results to come back. I should be out there, doing my job.' She tied off the last of the wraps. 'Keep this on for a few hours, just to stop infection getting in while the nanobots do their thing ... You know, I'd kill for something exciting to do.'

'What do you consider exciting? Seb said you're a xenoarchaeologist or something.'

'I studied xenoarchaeology and xenobiology.'

'I feel sorry for you. Neither of those sound very interesting.'

'Quite the contrary! Xenoarchaeology is fascinating. It's waiting for lab results that's boring, especially when it's not for my own work. I'm sure, as an engineer, you find alien technology interesting.'

'Sometimes.'

'Don't you get excited by the prospect of finding alien artefacts, thousands of years older than humanity that you have no idea how they work? Picking them apart, making new discoveries ...'

'I suppose, when you put it like that.' He recalled his visit to the Yazor comet. Its interior was formed from an icy, crystalline material, and contained technology with no moving parts. Duggan had moved the comet from that system to V376 Pegasi using its own unfathomable propulsion system. How he'd like to understand that. 'You're right. I'm starting to get fed up with fixing ships, even if they belong to aliens, and I'd love a proper look around Duggan's comet one day.'

'Well, fixing alien ships or not, you've certainly been up to more adventurous things than I.' She sighed. 'I was really looking forward to the mission that Gladrin pushed me off. I have some unfinished business there.'

'I don't think he'd have done it by choice. He still has to follow the ITF's instructions until he gets his family back.'

The door alert bleeped. 'Who is it?'

'Sebastian and Karan.'

Monica opened the door and in they walked, dishevelled and brow-beaten.

'How was it?' Aryx asked.

'Not as bad as it sounded to everyone else in the office,' Sebastian said. 'She showed us a map of the Witness Protection Archive on Earth.'

'How did she get that?'

Karan tapped the side of her nose. 'It's who you know, not what you know.'

'Once we've put a plan together, Karan and I are off to' – Sebastian coughed – 'break in.'

'What the hell? Why?'

'There's no remote access, and it's the only way to locate Gladrin's family.'

'Great, so what about Alicia Maline?' Aryx said. 'We need to track down her trail so we can find Duggan. I was hoping if that went to plan, I could then take Alvarez's ashes back to his family.'

'I thought they'd been shipped back to Earth weeks ago?'

'No. Gladrin hadn't arranged it before he bunked off.'

'So, you *want* to come to Earth with us, even though it might be dangerous?'

'Oh, for cryin' out loud. Ex-military, remember? When have I let this stop me?' Aryx said, gesturing to his legs.

Sebastian sighed. 'Never.'

'Exactly. And I told you I'd take any opportunity I get to stick it to those ITF bastards.' Aryx glanced at Monica. What did she think of it all, anyway?

She stood off to one side but shifted, jittery, as though about to drop into the conversation. He should never have told her about his condition. 'If Aryx is coming, I'd like to come along, too.'

Sebastian drew back. 'Whatever for?'

'To monitor Aryx's—'

Aryx shot her a warning glance. 'Implants.'

'Yes. Monitor his implants. They're new. He's never used anything like them before. Biotech is my area and I haven't got anything spoiling here . . . I'll be quiet, I promise.' She clasped her hands in front of her. 'I'd love to meet Duggan, too.'

'Oh Gods.' Sebastian folded his arms. 'I wasn't expecting an entourage. The ship's—'

'Big enough to fit five,' Aryx said. 'And you'll need help if you're going to plan a break-in.'

Sebastian set his jaw.

'You haven't got much time.'

'Fine! But I'm not putting you in danger again. If there's the slightest hint of trouble, you two are staying on the ship.'

Aryx nodded his agreement, but there was no way he was being boxed in once they left the station.

Sebastian programmed the *Ultima Thule*'s navigation computer with the course for Earth. The route would take them through four node hops, and likely several hours of flight, give or take a couple, depending on the trillion unintuitive variables that affected superphase transit. He punched the launch button and the ship ejected from the station under centripetal force. The ship's main drive kicked in and the gentle thrum of the engines reached Sebastian, relaxing him a little.

His superphase travel anxiety had diminished somewhat over the last few weeks; the numerous pressured trips back and forth between the station, Achene, Yazor, and Sollers Hope had conspired to acclimatise him to the strange stomach-churning sensations. At the back of his mind however, there was still the continual fear that the invisible bumps in space might not be caused by passing through the gravity wells of stars but instead be the extradimensional probings of the intangible demonic entities that existed *elsewhere*.

Aryx's wheelchair creaked as he shifted in his seat, distracting Sebastian from his thoughts. 'Are you okay?' he asked.

Sebastian nodded. 'I'm fine. I'll feel better once we've gone past this first node. At least I can think on the way. I need to try to remember the map.'

Aryx reached over and patted his shoulder. 'I'll leave you to it then. I'll fill the others in on the way.' He spun his chair around.

'Whatever you do, just don't tell them the Folians are actually trees,' Sebastian whispered.

Aryx winked and wheeled off towards the aft section, where Karan and Monica sat.

Next to Sebastian, on the console, the lights on the side of Wolfram's cube slowly strobed up and down.

'Wolfram, are you awake?'

'I am always awake, Sebastian. At the moment, I am using the time that I'm not in conversation to process the dream trigger signal from the terminals as requested. Is there something you'd like to discuss?'

'Yes. Alicia Maline – what records did you find?'

'With the load of processing the signal, it took some time to research, so I started with the most recent documents and worked backwards. I had to use your security credentials to retrieve the information in some places. Firstly, there was a reference to her in a ship's manifest from the Quintoc system to Earth in 2244.'

'The one you mentioned, leaving Sollers Hope?'

'That would be the most likely conclusion as there are no other spaceports in the system.'

'Anything else? Manifest logs aren't much to go on. She could have gone anywhere after arriving on Earth.'

'There are medical records from before her time on Sollers Hope. She attended a hospital in England.'

'What's unusual about that?'

'She previously had only routine visits to her GP, appointments several months apart. Prior to her final visit, she made more than five visits in one week.'

'That's still not particularly unusual, unless she was really ill.'

'Would it be particularly unusual if I told you her visits were in 2062?'

'What? Why keep that until last? That's two hundred years ago! How is that possible? How could she have been on Earth that long ago and then turned up on Sollers Hope so recently? Garvin said she was in her sixties.'

The lights on the side of the cube flashed briefly. 'It is conceivable that she travelled at close to the speed of light for a time, in a similar manner to Mr Simmons and the Chopwood colonists. That would easily account for her longevity.'

Sebastian rubbed his chin. 'Perhaps. Were you able to find out what her hospital visits were for?'

'Records are either closed or redacted for confidentiality reasons, so only dates and locations are available. She was referred to a psychiatric department. There is no record of her leaving the hospital, or a discharge date.'

He leaned back and tapped his chin. 'Could she have been transferred to another facility?' It was a long shot, but if she'd died, there would have been a separate record of it, and what would be the point of someone turning up on Sollers Hope pretending to be someone who had died when the records would be widely available? It didn't make sense at all.

'It is possible that she was transferred, but I cannot retrieve those records from the files. I could scan the logs of other facilities on Earth for admission records, but that will take considerable time, given the number of records to go through. Would you like me to focus on that and pause my analysis of the signal?'

Sebastian stared at the ceiling, as though he'd find the answers written there. 'No. Keep processing the signal, just do the search in the background. Our first priority is the archive, and secondly the signal. Finding Maline, and therefore Duggan, is our last priority, as much as I dislike that, but this trip to Earth isn't a holiday – it's official, however cloak and dagger it may be.'

The *Ultima Thule* drew close to the acceleration node and his stomach knotted with apprehension as the navigation computer did the necessary stellar drift calculations to determine the current star positions and moved them towards the capture radius. The great steely ball at the centre flared, and the ship was away.

While the others chatted quietly in the aft section, Sebastian stared at the stream of starlight, his eyes unfocused, mind wandering. So many problems and questions had come up over the last few days that there was too much for him to think about. Aryx had showed no interest in trying to get to the bottom of one of the biggest conundrums: how thaumaturgy worked, and how the entities got through. It wasn't his fault, of course; he was just being protective, and Sebastian couldn't blame him for that. The concept of thaumaturgy was intangible and abstract, and Aryx liked to deal with real, physical problems: if you couldn't fix something, you could always kick it to vent your frustration.

Magic, on the other hand, involved thought, will, and imagination and, with the threat of extradimensional entities getting involved whenever you tried to do it, there was nothing you could kick if it went wrong.

But Sebastian kicked himself.

His grandfather's journal, full of apparently random scribblings, seemed as though it would never reveal its secrets. If Frímann had been capable of using thaumaturgy and studied it, none of what he'd written made any sense. There had to be a system, or at least a set of rules – it effectively manipulated physics, after all. The mistake Sebastian made when attempting the "light" spell had highlighted a fundamental danger: the visualisation of the outcome had to be specific, detailed, calculated. But how to calculate something that was chaotic and subtle? He was a programmer, not an artist.

The art of thaumaturgy. What was it Duggan had said weeks ago? ... That John Dee, a medieval mathematician, had been accused of being a magic user, a thaumaturgist. There was something in what Bannik said earlier, too. Turing. That was it. Chaos theory and systems, imaginary numbers, transcendental maths ... Sebastian had studied the subject at university as part of his simulation experiments: the organic and difficult-to-predict growth of a system based on a set of simple rules. If thaumaturgy had simply been a matter of calculation, Wolfram would have been able to create new spells, but no, they'd already ruled that out. It *was* calculation, but performed by an organic mind; maybe intuition, or something else in the subconscious, was a key component.

Sebastian sighed through his teeth. He still didn't trust his own intuition or subconscious. Maybe Aryx was right and that messing with magic was dangerous and he should wait until this was all over before experimenting with it under controlled conditions.

'*Ultima Thule* calling Sebastian.' Aryx clicked his fingers, snapping Sebastian out of his relaxed contemplation.

'Sorry, I wasn't listening.'

Monica peered around the bulkhead from the seats at the rear, looking small in her civilian clothes. 'We were just wondering what the plan of attack is for the not-terribly-important break-in mission you seem to be ignoring.'

Sebastian sneered. 'I'm sure Karan's told you everything we know about the archive, which is very little.'

'Nonetheless,' she said, glaring over her unnecessary glasses, 'to fail to plan is to plan to fail.'

'You sound like Aryx.'

'You say that like it's a bad thing,' Aryx said. 'And she has a point. What information do we have?'

'The address, a rough idea of the basement, and that's it. All we can do is check the place out in daylight. Until then, I can't plan anything!'

Nostrils flaring, Monica rose from her seat. 'How can you be so casual about it? How do you propose to do that without raising suspicion?'

'I don't know yet. Perhaps we send Aryx, have him wheel around a bit? He might seem like less of a threat.'

She put her hands on her hips. 'That sounds like a terrible idea!'

Aryx tugged at her sleeve. 'I could take Wolfram and do some scans. If I see anybody, I'll say "Need a poo!". That might put them off. And if they get too close, I'll say "Done a poo!"'

'Aryx, that is disgusting! I can't believe you're encouraging him.'

'Come on, you know prejudice still exists,' he said. 'You wear glasses because of people's assumptions about you, the "pretty little pushover scientist", don't you?'

'Yes, but that's different.'

'It's not, when you're trying to take advantage of people's negative attitudes, and we need every advantage we can get to fight those bastards.'

'Argh!' She folded her arms and flopped back into her seat.

'Now *you're* being just like Sebastian,' Karan said. 'You'd make a lovely couple.'

Aryx sniggered. 'Matter-antimatter explosion, more likely.'

Sebastian bit his tongue and turned back to the piloting console. He had to put up with several more hours of this. If only superphase travel were quicker!

After the final node hop, the ship dropped out of superphase in the Sol system. It took another hour at top speed to reach Earth itself and settle into orbit.

Sebastian stared at the green and blue world below, but his excitement at returning left a bitter taste. He wasn't due for a free ticket to Earth for another two years, and the last time he headed in this direction was to rescue his family from Gladrin – a trip that had been redirected to Kimberley depot. Now he was back, on official, if secret, business to rescue another family.

He activated the comms. 'This is *Ultima Thule* to Earth flight control, requesting permission to land in London, England.'

'Greetings, *Ultima Thule*,' a male voice said, 'this is controller Reynolds. London airspace is currently restricted due to a high volume of traffic. Suggest redirection to Cardiff or Manchester spaceports.'

'One moment.' Sebastian muted the comms and turned to the trio at the back. 'What do I do? We can't do a flyover recon now.'

Aryx scratched his head. 'Cardiff's closer than Manchester, and it's best to keep the ship close at hand in case we need to leave quickly. We can leave her there and take the monomag.'

Sebastian un-muted the comms. 'Sorry about that. We'll divert to Cardiff. Can we dock overnight? We have a lot of travelling to do.'

'I'm afraid not,' came the reply. 'Not if you want to land right now, that is. Cardiff spaceport parking is fully booked until this evening, so it's drop-off and pick-up only. I can book you a space if you don't mind coming back tonight.'

'I'll drop you off and take the ship,' Aryx said, wheeling up to the console. He patted the metal urn on his lap. 'I can take these to Alvarez's family in Brasilia and meet you all in London later tonight.'

Monica leaned around the bulkhead again. 'Actually, Sebastian, if it's alright with you, I'd like to accompany him, just to keep an eye on his implants until they've settled.'

'Good idea!' Sebastian said. 'Two of us will stand out less than three.' And at least that way, Aryx would have company and someone to keep him safe.

'Marvellous! I've always wanted to fly over the Amazon.'

Aryx shook his head. 'It's not on the way, but I guess we can take a detour. We'll be there quick enough.'

'Fine.' Sebastian addressed the comms. 'Book us parking in Cardiff for tonight, please. We'll disembark there and someone will return with the ship later.'

'Thank you ... I've made the booking and sent the reference to your terminal. It's 7 a.m. and traffic into the city is already incredibly busy. You will need to use the Ynys Echni monomag station for drop-off. Have a good day.' The connection closed.

Sebastian collected up his antique canvas rucksack. 'I guess that works out better, then. You two meet us in London tonight after we've checked out the archive.' It wasn't ideal, but what else could he do?

Aryx picked up Wolfram and held the cube out towards him. 'Are you going to take him to do some scans?'

Sebastian hesitated. The cube still posed a threat to the terrorist group on many levels. 'No, actually I think it would be safer to leave him with you. If there's even the slimmest chance of bumping into an ITF agent, I don't want Wolfram anywhere near. He'll either be destroyed or picked apart and used for weapons tech, or worse.'

Aryx put the cube back on the console and took over the controls, moving the ship into a temporary holding pattern as they descended over South Wales.

At this distance, the spires of Cardiff blended together into a glittering, crystalline heap, emerging from the surrounding woodlands and spilling off into the silty brown waters of the Severn Estuary. The flow of ships entering and leaving the city extended into the atmosphere beneath them like a line of metallic ants, trailing in and out of a pile of sugar. A fine silvery thread ran from the rectangular gridwork of the docks, southward over a low island, and on through the town of Weston-super-Mare on the eastern bank of the Severn. The *Ultima Thule* turned to follow the silver line and, as it did so, a long tubular craft with several large hoops sticking out from its sides glided along the monorail below, heading east.

A hand pressed on Sebastian's shoulder. 'Looks like we're just in time,' Karan said. 'All set? That train will be ready to go as soon as we touch down.'

Sebastian patted his rucksack and nodded.

'Put us down just over there, Aryx.' Karan pointed to a flat expanse of concrete at the edge of the grassy island where the monomag rail clipped the cliffs. A low barricade surrounded the compound – just enough to keep the wildlife and a small herd of horses away from the station and its dangerous machinery without impacting the environment.

Sebastian made his way to the ladder. 'Stay safe, Aryx. Monica and Wolfram, look after him!'

Aryx scowled. 'We'll be fine. Now go!'

Sebastian scampered down the ladder, through the cargo bay corridor, and jumped out of the airlock without waiting for the ship to land or giving it time to generate the CFD steps. He landed awkwardly and almost sprained his ankle.

Wearing thin jogging bottoms and a tight running vest, Karan landed in an athletic crouch behind him.

Wind blasted across the grassland of Flat Holm, biting through the thin layers of Sebastian's jacket and vest. He pulled the collar up around his neck when the wind joined with the quadruple tornado from the ship's Dyson thrusters as it lifted off. The smooth, curved hull peeled away and glided off across the waters to the west.

'I hope they'll be alright,' he said, as the ship became a speck on the horizon.

'They'll be fine,' Karan shouted over the blustering wind, already jogging across the concrete towards the terminal.

Sebastian took a deep breath of the chill, salty October air and set off after her. 'I'm glad we landed over here,' he said, nodding at the horses in the distance. 'I hate them.'

'There's nothing wrong with them, they're lovely. Now come on, or we'll miss the train!'

*   *   *

Sebastian stared out of the window at the muddy stretch of sand as the monomag glided across the water from Flat Holm to the eastern bank of the Severn. In moments, they were up and over Weston-super-Mare, past the fields, and into the forests that had long since covered abandoned towns and villages.

'This reminds me of the time before I left Earth for Tenebrae,' he said, his stomach quietly tightening.

'Why's that?' Karan asked, sitting opposite.

'I was on the monomag heading to Hereford Uni when I found out all my work had been destroyed.'

'All of it was lost? That seems a little unlikely in this day and age.'

'Tell me about it.' He folded his arms. 'The Bristol datacentre was bombed the same day the university was hacked.'

Karan leaned forward. 'Same people?'

Sebastian rubbed his forehead. 'I don't know. It really wasn't a good time for me.' He stared out at the crumpled, reddening canopy of trees rolling beneath. 'I lost my work and, not long after that, my brother. Worst of all, I think his death was my fault.'

'How do you figure that?'

'Because he discovered there were no reports of the bombing and I asked him to look into it. I couldn't connect to the system and I guessed the only reason was because it had been physically tampered with. He went to investigate and never came back.'

Karan put a hand on his wrist. 'You can't take the blame. That's part of police work, Seb. You know that. All security jobs have risks.'

'It wasn't *his* job to investigate it. I put him there! I put him there and somebody killed him for investigating, I'm sure of it!'

'Oh, Seb! You can't blame yourself.' She squeezed his hand. 'Really, you can't.'

'Janyce is left without a husband, and Erik without his father. That's my fault. Mikkael shouldn't have had to die on the job like my father did. Not like that. We couldn't even have an open casket at the funeral, he was burnt so—' Sebastian broke down. 'B-both of them died and I never got ... I never got to say goodbye to either of them. You can't say goodbye to a closed box.' He stopped to take several shuddering breaths. 'Gods! I never even said goodbye to my grandfather because he died in space. I never got to say goodbye to any of them!' The monomag cabin dissolved in a stream of tears.

'It's okay, Seb, let it out.' Karan reached forward to hug him and rocked him back and forth, rubbing his back.

He wrapped his arms around her and buried his face in her shoulder. 'And now I've left Janyce and Erik in the middle of nowhere with no family but me, and I've got nobody to turn to except Aryx. I'm not even sure he cares half of the time.'

'He does care about you, Seb. We all do. Aryx might be headstrong, but he loves having you around. I know he does. You're all he's got, too, since Alvarez died.'

'And what do I do?' he said, pulling away. 'I keep putting him in danger. He shouldn't be here! I shouldn't be here. I should be sitting in the office, not dragging all of you into this.'

'We volunteered,' Karan said, holding him at arm's length. 'Well, no, actually I didn't volunteer. But the others did. If you don't get to the bottom of this conspiracy or whatever it is, more people could die. Gladrin's family could die. And the ITF will still be bombing colonies.'

'They will, even if we get to the bottom of this,' Sebastian said, wiping his eyes with a sleeve. 'It's not like I'm out to hunt them all down. I'm just after some names.'

Karan's eyes were wide. 'Seb, think of the opportunity! This archive has information on thousands of witnesses from all over the galaxy. If more of them have been "reassigned" because of interference by the ITF, they could be connected. If you get that list of names, you could find the connections – who knows, you could even work out who the ITF members are!'

Sebastian glanced at the glass door of their cabin as the monomag arrived at Bristol station. The corridor was packed with people getting ready to alight. 'Keep your voice down. I don't think we should be talking about it on the train.'

She leaned back in her seat. 'So, what was your university work about to make it so important?'

'It wasn't that important. Simulation, dynamic adaptive coding.'

She yawned. 'You could have just said programming.'

'I knew you'd find it boring.'

'Don't you think it was a bit coincidental that it was *your* brother that was killed at the Bristol datacentre, though?'

'What? No. Thousands of other people had work on those servers. And surely anyone else who had investigated it might have been killed. You said so yourself.'

'But the entities have been targeting *you* through your dreams.'

'And what? You think they were interested in my work for some reason and got the terrorists to destroy it?'

'Gladrin stole Wolfram from their base at around the same time. Weren't they working on AI themselves?'

'I wasn't working on AI, just adaptive algorithms.'

Karan scratched her head. 'The same sort of stuff you use at work, to discover system viruses, Trojans, and such?'

'Yes.'

'So, what if you were on to something and they decided to shut you down?'

Sebastian laughed. It was ridiculous. He adopted a mocking-mysterious tone. 'Yes, of course. I was about to invent software that could have uncovered something they had running on the *entire* galactic network. That's as irrational as believing in ghost stories.'

'Like the space version of the *Flying Dutchman*, which turned out to be real! And would the Sebastian of two months ago have believed that one of his future friends would be an artificial intelligence?'

'Silicon Intelligence,' he whispered.

'Whatever. But you wouldn't have even entertained the idea.'

'No.'

'So why not entertain this one? What if you were about to uncover something like that? They would have erased all trace of your work, maybe killed you, and, if Mikkael had discovered the perpetrator at the scene, they would have killed him, too.'

The cloud of depression rolled in once again. 'That would mean his death *would* have been my fault. I thought you were trying to help me feel less guilty!'

'Sorry.'

As he thought about it, cause and effect seemed to tie itself in knots. If his work hadn't been destroyed, he wouldn't have got the job at Tenebrae working in security. He wouldn't have been recruited into SpecOps by Gladrin, and therefore wouldn't have found out about the ITF and their conspiracies. Once again, he had been put on a path that led back to the source, just like Aryx said. As a way out of the tangle, he needed to change the subject. 'Do you think he'll be alright?'

'Who, Aryx? Why wouldn't he?'

'He's ill.'

'What kind of ill? Other than a bit tired, he looked fine to me.'

'You're probably right. It's been a few weeks since he said it, and he hasn't mentioned it again.'

She patted him on the wrist. 'You're probably just worrying too much. I expect he meant he had a cold or something. Anyway, he can take care of himself.'

'I know. I guess if it was serious, he'd tell me, wouldn't he? It's not like him to bottle things up.' He turned back to staring out of the window, where the brown cauliflower autumn streamed past.

Aryx looked up from the console, where he was monitoring the *Ultima Thule*'s flight to Brazil. 'Sorry, what did you say? I wasn't listening.'

Monica leaned back in the co-pilot's seat. 'I asked how you met Sebastian. You don't seem the most likely pair to be investigating terrorists and conspiracies.'

Aryx checked the navigation coordinates and finished tweaking the atmospheric flight path. Staring out at the twilit, featureless blue ocean with no point of reference became disorientating after a while, so he left the computer to follow the course automatically and sat back in his wheelchair. 'We met during a training flight out of Tenebrae. I don't think Sebastian had ever been on one before – it was a node-hop tutorial. I'd already been through plenty, working in the marines and all, but it was compulsory.'

Monica nodded rapidly.

'Anyway, I think he took a shine to me because I answered the instructor back, and I liked him because he didn't make anything of this,' he said, gesturing to his legs and chair. 'He never once opened a door for me!'

Monica laughed. 'Isn't that just bad manners?'

'Haha, you'd think so. No. He spotted me glaring at the previous person who tried.'

'I'd have thought you'd appreciate people helping.'

'Not always. It's a bit degrading at times, to have people thinking you need to be wrapped in cotton wool or have everything done for you. What's more irritating is that some people completely ignore you when you're obviously struggling. If you or Sebastian were struggling with something, people would offer to help.'

Monica rubbed her hair and leaned on the console with an elbow. 'Maybe they feel intimidated, or afraid to offer help?'

'I think, if anything, that prejudice – or at least discomfort – around people who are different has increased with time. People are okay with aliens but, given a lot of disabilities are invisible now, for someone to stand out prominently puts people off guard.'

'I'm sure people can change though, they just need a push. What made you take the job on Tenebrae, anyway?'

Aryx patted the urn in his lap. 'Nick Alvarez. He was an old platoon-mate of mine. He suggested it after my accident. I wasn't really in the right state to apply immediately.'

'What do you mean?' Monica asked, leaning forward.

'After my accident, I couldn't see a point in living anymore. I was half a man. Useless. I thought nobody would miss me. I stared out of the hospital window day after day.' He recalled looking out of the tower block at the mixture of buildings, parks and trees below. As his eyes crawled over the features – as they had every day for six months – he had absorbed every detail. Each tiny, displaced tile, every stained brick, every decaying car, the contrast of gloss green and rust reds; the view a panorama of nature reclaiming the suburbs in the distance.

'I wanted to be out,' he said. 'I wanted to walk between the build-ings, through the trees, under the canopies.' He glanced down at his chair. 'I didn't want to be stuck in one of these. At the time, I thought there was no chance of walking anywhere ever again. I might as well—' He choked at the memory of pushing his chair towards the window and raising the sash. Every move had sent fire coursing through the veins in his legs. 'I managed to get myself up onto the windowsill and break the safety catch that stopped the window from opening.'

'Oh, Aryx . . .' Monica put her hand on his.

'I knew there was no way I would survive a ten-storey fall, and I couldn't think of a single reason why I'd want to. I didn't have any visitors, my family was dead, and even Alvarez couldn't find time to visit anymore.'

'What stopped you?' Her cheeks were tear streaked already.

He recalled the cold updraft that chilled his sheared off legs; how he had glanced down at his hand, ready to push off. Next to his fingers, between the curled, dry foliage of the planter, was a bright green sprout. It alone had survived the harsh conditions without nourishment and broken through.

'A plant. A tiny little plant growing against all odds. It had the will to survive. I thought if it could manage it, so could I. And that was when I realised I *could* still do something with my life.'

'You remembered Alvarez's suggestion of Tenebrae.'

He nodded. 'I finally had something I could look forward to, to work towards. I could still work with my hands – I just hadn't contemplated doing anything other than field repairs. And now that I've developed this pack, I can eventually patent it and help others in the same way.'

'A noble cause. Just make sure you've still got a reason to live for yourself, too.' She smiled briefly and stared out at the blurry fuzz of moonlit blue on black where the sky met the ocean, as though lost in thought. 'Ah, look. Land!'

The hazy silhouette of the coast slipped beneath them as the *Ultima Thule* swept over the lush, dripping forests of South America, shrouded in mist. Their flight slowed for several minutes as the sky ahead darkened with vast clouds of bats returning to roost before sunrise, allowing the sun to catch up a little behind them. Silver and brown streaks glittered between the trees below and resolved into the snaking lines of the Amazon.

What if they crashed there, in the middle of nowhere? Aryx shuddered and a twinge of pain went through the end of his right leg. He leaned forward to rub it.

'Are you alright?' Monica asked.

'Yeah. I think it's probably the nanobots settling in.'

'Your face says otherwise.'

His brow had furrowed in concentration. 'It's just that flying over forests like this reminds me of a recent bad experience.'

'You think it's psychosomatic pain, then?'

'Mm, I'm not sure.' It might have been, given that he'd taken his last injection on time. If only Wolfram would interject to distract her; he'd been silent for almost the entire trip.

Monica checked her infoslate. 'The implants seem to be stable. It must be something else. Do you want me to look into it?'

'No, thank you. I've been poked and prodded enough recently. I'm sure it's just cramp. It'll go away.'

She shrugged, set the infoslate aside, and stared out into the twilight. 'These forests are beautiful,' she said at length. 'I'm glad the deforestation stopped with the Ecological Crux. I couldn't imagine growing up in a world where all this was being stripped bare.'

'So, you like plants?' Finally, as a hobbyist gardener, a topic he liked to talk about.

'What's not to like? They provide a vital function for life, they're pleasing to the eye, and often provide useful medicines. You know, with all the planets out in the vastness of space, there could even be a plant that could help slow down your infection.'

'I seriously doubt it.'

'How can you be so sure?'

He hadn't intended for his voice to have such conviction. 'I ... spoke to someone who knows a lot about these things.'

Monica ruffled her hair. 'You know another molecular biologist?'

His armpits warmed uncomfortably: he wasn't supposed to talk about the Folians – at least not to reveal their true nature. 'Not exactly. I ... I'm a keen gardener, from my days in rehab.'

'And that qualifies you to make sweeping statements about all the plants in the galaxy, does it?' She defiantly put her hands on her hips. 'Talk about back-pedalling.'

'I ... Uh ...' Now she thought he was a typical, arrogant know-it-all.

'Aryx, is there a problem?' Wolfram asked. His lights had stopped flashing, and now only pulsed as he spoke.

Monica sighed. 'I thought *you* were working.'

'I was, until I detected unusual stress in Aryx's voice.'

'Stress?'

'I'm fine, Wolfram. Listen, Monica, I've been sworn to secrecy. I can't tell you who it was, but one of the top minds tried to cure my virus using a biological nanotechnology and it still didn't work.'

She narrowed her eyes. '*Biological* nanotechnology?'

'Wolfram, help me out here. I can't tell her.'

'Can't tell her *what*?' Her voice shot up.

'Aryx, I believe she can be trusted. I have already performed a thorough background check on Ms Stevens. She has no connections with ITF activity, even after seven iterations of contact graph searches.'

Monica raised her eyebrows and stared at the cube.

Aryx took a deep breath. 'Are you sure?'

'After seven iterations of not finding a connection through anyone other than yourself, Sebastian, or Gladrin, the likelihood of detecting links with the ITF would be more attributable to "coincidence".'

'As long as you're sure.' Aryx turned to Monica, keeping one eye on the forest rolling beneath them. 'There's a planet with a race of sentient trees out there. That's how I know there isn't a cure for me.'

Monica widened her eyes. 'Really?'

Perhaps she was more open-minded after all. 'Yes. I studied plants and horticulture as part of my rehab, so I wouldn't have believed it either, yet it wasn't until my recent trips with Sebastian that I noticed something odd.' He gestured out at the twilight landscape. 'Have you ever wondered why there are so many similar species of trees on different planets, in completely disparate biomes, most of them looking like those below us?'

'Evolution's a funny thing,' she said. 'There are species all over the galaxy that look similar, not just plants.' She returned her gaze to the window. 'I assume you're getting to a point.'

'Yes, bear with me. You shouldn't have that kind of coincidence in nature. You're a biologist – you know that there will be certain patterns based on environmental factors, but never any exact duplication, just a natural progression based on the conditions, following Darwinian principles and the thermodynamic theory of life.' He had to ease her into the truth about the Folians slowly, and the fact that they travelled the stars as seeds – maybe letting her find her own way to it. 'Back on Achene, Janyce and I had discussed the Bronadi, for whom there is a complete lack of evolutionary evidence. We hypothesised that perhaps canine DNA had been brought to Earth from the Bronadi homeworld, or that another race had taken canine DNA from Earth to create them.'

'I'll admit that their similarity to dogs is unnerving,' Monica said. 'And that theory does sound a bit outlandish. However, I can't really believe they would have appeared from nowhere – they have a well-formed culture. On the other hand, their history is vague and nobody, not even their own people, is allowed to visit their ancestral world in Sirius ... No. They are a sentient race, and their similarity to our canines is likely cosmetic. Shared DNA is impossible.' She shook her head. 'How does any of this relate to plants and biotechnology?'

'Well, I don't know about the origins of the Bronadi, but I know for a fact that many of our plant species came from other worlds.'

'They can't have come from other worlds. Plants don't cross interstellar space. That's ridiculous.'

'Is it?' Aryx scratched his head. 'There's no physical evidence now, and I know I'm not the best person to talk to about it, but there is historic evidence ... if you're prepared to believe that some myths and religions are based on historic fact.'

'I don't see how genetics and myth are related.' Monica folded her hands in her lap. 'But, given that we're on the subject, it really depends on which myths you're talking about. Many beliefs have elements of truth in them.' She held up a hand. 'Before you say anything, I mean truth as in allegory or metaphor that relates to some fact we have determined through scientific investigation.'

Aryx let out a long breath. At least she was turning out to be less of a mixed-bag than Sebastian. How he managed to hold religion in his heart and science in his head at the same time . . .

'But that's not to say that some of the stories aren't true in another way,' she continued. 'For example, you showed me a video of experiments in magic . . . Magic made its way into legends and religion, but it's clear that early Humans wouldn't have had the resources to discover how to stabilise carbyne, given that it evaporates in air. They didn't have the technology to keep it contained in vacuum, so how did they find out how to use it?'

'I have a pretty good idea,' he said with a wry smile, 'but I want you to work it out. What do you reckon? Bearing in mind we're talking about plants.'

'Well, it doesn't matter which culture you look at – all of them have nature spirits at some point. Some of those act as mentors. Knowing as much about the universe as we do now, I suspect aliens may have visited many planets in the past and become embedded in those cultures' myths, but that's another issue.

'Nature spirits have a common set of forms. The beneficial ones tend to be plant-based – possibly because most life forms start off eating vegetation and therefore it's seen as the life-giver, and the malignant ones tend to relate to harsh natural conditions. Earth, fire, and ice elementals, for example. All of which can represent natural disasters.'

Sebastian had mentioned things like this before . . . 'Frost giants?' Aryx asked.

'Yes, a perfect example. Norse religion has frost giants and fire giants. Both are represented as being destructive. Even the Devil, from Christianity, is often depicted surrounded by fire, and often underground . . . The Bronadi religion has a type of deity whose name translates as "whisperer" or "powerful strong-ones", and rumour has it they're some type of elemental, but nobody knows much about Bronadi religion other than the Bronadi. On the other hand, you have the Æsir in the Norse faith, the "good" gods, for the most part, many of whom originate from nature realms . . .' She trailed off.

'I'm not really that interested in religion,' Aryx said, 'just the facts, and you didn't come to a conclusion of how Humans knew about carbyne.'

'Then why did you bring it up?'

'I believe Aryx is a masochist,' Wolfram said, 'and enjoys talking about subjects that he doesn't like.'

'Get back to your searches and analysis!' Aryx turned the cube to face the other direction.

'I can still see you.'

He growled.

'Point taken.' Wolfram's lights resumed their random flashing.

Monica folded her arms. 'So, are you *going* to tell me why you brought religion into it?'

'Yes. The nature spirits of Earth religions came from the race of sentient trees I mentioned. They came to Earth millions of years ago and brought knowledge of carbyne and how to use it.'

'Why has nobody ever found evidence of them? Shouldn't there still be some on Earth?'

'Unfortunately, the ones on Earth were wiped out.'

Chapter 11

The Inquisitor stared out of the window. In the distance, across the forest, white smoke rose from the pyres of many burning trees. For years, the knights of the religious order of the Templars had followed his instructions without question, burning any trees that presented vaguely humanoid traits, but now they wavered in their resolve.

The Humans were trapped by their compassion. But not the Inquisitor. This host did not care for the feelings of others: it cared only about its own base indulgences. A sharp stab of pain through its lower jaw reminded the entity of this.

Before the entity had come, the host had filled its vile belly with rich foods, taken young girls for its own pleasure – apparently against the doctrines of the Church for which it worked – and committed acts other Humans thought of as grotesque. The latter was something the entity had learned to use to its advantage, especially when obtaining information from weak-willed Humans, but the cravings for fine foods had remained, forcing it to eat in excess or risk having to fight against the host's most basic biological drives. This was something for which the entity now lacked the energy.

The Inquisitor turned away from the window and staggered towards the sumptuous four-poster bed in the centre of the dark, wood panelled room. 'Medicus!'

The double doors burst open and a short, dumpy man wearing a red robe and square cushioned hat shuffled in. 'What is it, my lord?'

'The pain in my teeth is worse. We wish this thing—' He paused. '*I* wish that I had not indulged so.' The Inquisitor eased himself back onto the bed, amid the angry throbbing now engulfing his face.

The doctor poked and prodded the pustulent bulges of his cheeks and the pain intensified. 'Careful!' The Inquisitor jerked his head back. The downside of inhabiting flesh, an oddly perfect counterpoint to the sometimes pleasant experiences it offered, was the inevitable sensation of pain that came with such existence.

'Hmm. Hot and wet,' the doctor said, drawing out a thin knife from his bag. 'You have an excess of blood. We should allow some out to reduce the swelling.' He brought the blade up to the Inquisitor's cheek.

'You will do no such thing!' The Inquisitor grabbed the man by the wrist before he could make a cut. 'You will find another treatment. And bring me my Second!'

The doctor shoved the utensil into his bag and shuffled back towards the door. 'I will send for him now.' He bowed and pulled the doors shut as he left.

The pain was almost too much to bear, but having to endure the primitive torture these beings called medicine was worse still. The only alternative would be to find another host ... and soon.

Minutes later, the Inquisitor's second in command arrived, a short, dirty man wearing grimy, yet more expensive than usual, peasant's clothes. He bowed his head. 'You sent for me, my lord.'

'Yes.' The Inquisitor gestured for the man to close the doors and waited until they were shut. 'We are in need of a new host. This one has become weak with illness—' A fit of coughing cut him off mid-sentence, and he gestured for the man to come closer. 'As you can see, it does not have much time left.' He stared closely into the Second's glittering eyes. 'We need you to find a replacement.'

'Do you have someone in mind?'

'The Templars have begun to question my orders about the burnings. The tree-dwelling beings are becoming a problem and we fear they may have passed their teachings about the nature of the universe on to the natives of this world. If they gain too much support, they could expose us.' He paused to consider his options. 'Find one of the Templar leaders ... one who might have a group of followers that we could recruit and would obey us without question.'

'It will be done, Gravalax,' the Second said, bowing, and left.

The next day the Second returned.

The Inquisitor was barely able to think through the blinding agony that coursed through the veins in his skull as he lay in bed. 'What is it?' he snarled, head throbbing with every syllable.

'I have brought you Curtis of Gloucester.' Standing next to the

Second was a man wearing a white tabard, emblazoned with a red cross, over a chain shirt.

The Templar bowed. 'It is a great honour to meet Your Eminence.'

'Bring him closer.'

The Templar looked to the Second, as though for reassurance. The Second nodded, and the Templar stepped forward. 'What can I do for Your Eminence? Are you unwell? Your eyes, they appear strange.' The Inquisitor whispered something, forcing him to lean closer. 'Forgive me, I did not hear what you said.'

The Inquisitor spoke between laboured breaths. 'We ... said ... we ... need ... you ... to ...' – he grabbed the Templar by the throat – '... die.' Using the last of the host's strength, the Inquisitor-entity gripped the man's throat tightly. 'Help ... us,' he rasped, and the Second came up behind the Templar to join the struggle.

The Templar's eyes bulged, his face turning a pleasing shade of purple. Even with all of his trained strength, the combined efforts of the Inquisitor and the Second were too much for him.

The pulse beneath the Inquisitor's fingers became weak, and he let go, himself on the verge of passing out. The Second loosened his grip, but did not let go completely. Instead, he thrust the Templar's face closer to the Inquisitor-host.

Tendrils of glowing red mist issued from the Inquisitor's mouth, reaching between the Templar's lips and up his nostrils.

The Inquisitor-entity's perception of the world dimmed, the vision of the dark wood-panelled room fading to a distant light in the dark void. Sensation drew back from the extremities of the host as the entity known as Gravalax left it, and a vast chasm of empty space, a breath, drew it towards its new host. This method of transfer was safer: the pull of the Tower was weak as the entity reached for the new host. It could not return there, to the Tower. Not without the location of home.

The entity scrambled for the glimmer at the far end of the void and the Templar's eyes flicked open as he gasped for air.

The Second bent over him. 'Are you ...?'

'Yes, we are here,' the Templar rasped. 'This one feels stronger.'

'What do we do about *that*?' the Second asked with a flick of his eyes in the direction of the unconscious Inquisitor, who lay flopped back in the bed, barely breathing.

'It has a foreign body in its system,' Gravalax the Templar said. 'The medicus is unable to effect its removal.'

The Second frowned at him. 'We suggest not speaking until we have left this place. You have not yet assimilated your host's mannerisms. And that,' he said, looking at the unconscious Inquisitor, 'will need to be dealt with quickly.'

The Templar picked up one of the pillows and placed it over the Inquisitor's face. After a minute, he removed it and checked for a pulse. 'It was sufficiently weak.'

'Good. We will leave it for the medicus to find.'

The Second led the Templar, as though taking His Eminence's visitor from the building, through the kitchens at the back of the mansion and out into the tented encampment at the end of the gardens, taking provisions along the way. They would be able to leave the county safely, if necessary, given sufficient numbers of loyal followers, but the Church would soon accuse either the Templar or the Second of the Inquisitor's murder. Even before the entities' arrival, the Inquisition had already proven itself to be vindictive enough to look for a scapegoat at the first hint of any weakness within their ranks.

'We must establish a power base,' the Templar said. 'If we are to find the location of home and lead others from the Tower, we must operate outside the strictures of the Humans' religious rules and dogma.'

'How do you propose we do that?'

'We will seek out those who wish to know the truth of the universe, to advance their scientific knowledge, and we will use those advances to our own ends. A time of illumination must begin.'

Chapter 12

Monica's face twisted as Aryx finished. 'What do you mean the Folians aren't Folians? Folians walk around on Tenebrae. They have two arms and two legs, and weird sponge-hair. They aren't trees!'

'The humanoids everyone knows as Folians are actually called Karrikin,' Aryx said. 'They act as ambassadors to the Folians, who can't leave their world. They used to send seeds out into space and gained knowledge of the galaxy that way. Now they've got space travel, the Karrikin perform the Folians' diplomatic duties in order to keep their true identity secret.'

'And you think the reason for them being wiped out across the galaxy was because of the entities that possess people?'

'Yep. Sebastian thinks they're the "demons" mentioned in Christianity and other religions.'

'Wow.' She looked away. 'That certainly puts a new light on things . . . and makes a lot of my work redundant, or at least throws it out of the window.'

'I don't quite see how it makes your archaeological work worthless,' he said.

'With mine it does. Context is everything! It means I have to re-evaluate the stories and legends I've recorded as though they are truth, and retranslate inscriptions. I'll have to republish quite a few papers.'

'What? No! You can't publish anything of the sort, especially not mentioning the Folians.'

'Of course I won't mention the Folians, but it means that legends concerning demons and evil overlord beings may be true. They could be aliens, or the extra-spatial entities, and that's of historical significance.'

Aryx's collar tightened. 'You can't even publish that. What if the entities or ITF get wind of it? They'll come after you because you'll risk exposing them.'

'But it validates my work. Work I've had to keep under wraps in case people thought it was the ramblings of a lunatic. I've never had any proof to back it up before now!'

'If it's SpecOps work, I'm sure Sebastian would enjoy going through it and discussing it with you. He loves legends and all that guff.'

'That won't be good enough. I still need to publish something. I need credibility! I don't want my life's work to have been for nothing.'

Aryx rubbed his head. He could certainly empathise with her, but there must be a way to convince her otherwise. 'Okay, what *exactly* is so important?'

'Archaeological evidence of alien cross-culture contamination ...' Monica's eyes took on a strange, faraway stare and her forehead wrinkled. 'I had a bit of a scary experience on a dig. It was my "proving ground" mission – the first dig with real responsibility. Gladrin left me alone in a cave, where I found writings that looked like Sumerian cuneiform. People would think I was mad without proof to back it up. I never got the evidence I needed.'

'Why not?'

'They closed the dig site due to "unstable geology",' she said, curling the quotes with her fingers, 'and I never got to go back. If those writings were somehow from Earth and connected to legends ... You mentioned giants and elementals before— Wait. I-I remember something ...' She paused, but her breathing accelerated. 'I was in the middle of excavating when I sensed movement behind me. I was sure there was something in there with me. That was when the cavern started to collapse. The whole experience was terrifying! The inscription in the cavern, it mentioned a demon ...' Her eyes took on the faraway look again and she shivered. 'Goodness. You're probably right. If they are aliens, the demon-entities will be dangerous. I won't push it.'

Aryx let out a sigh of relief.

'But I will mention it to Sebastian once this is all over. And I suppose we can't really blame the Church for destroying the Folians on Earth. They were doing what they thought was right at the time to protect people, and it obviously worked for the most part, since we've not been overrun by possessed people.' She tapped her chin. 'Just think how different the world might have been if we had actually *learned* from the Folians. We Humans could have discovered how to protect ourselves while performing magic. We'd have had less need for fossil fuels and wouldn't have ruined the environment, and we'd have probably had fewer wars – if what people say about demonic influence through history is true.'

'Hah! I don't think it would have made any difference. People like to blame others for their own stupidity. You don't think that the entities would have been so brazen as to cause large-scale destruction, do you?'

Monica put a hand on the back of her neck. 'No, I don't suppose they would. They'd most likely have pulled strings from behind the scenes – which, of course, is why Sebastian is now investigating the archive.'

'You certainly catch on quick, Monica,' Aryx said, rocking his chair up into a relaxed wheelie.

She hooked the toe of her boot behind one of his front casters. 'Quicker than you think. You want to watch yourself,' she said with a smile. 'Or I'll put you on your back.'

Aryx grinned. 'And there I was thinking you were going to be all straight-laced and boring. But I like your style.'

Sebastian stared out of the windows of the silvery, snake-like monomag as it descended through the trees. The shining spires of London rose up from the horizon, glinting in the morning sun, and with a quiet *clunk* the train's hooped rings folded back across the carriages and it slowed for the long approach to Paddington station. This was always the worst bit of getting to the city – the trip was fast, but it always ended with a slow creep into the centre. At least the view was pleasant.

Cloaked in thick forests, the monomag slithered between the trunks like Jörmungandr, the giant serpent from legend, only not attempting to choke the Earth as it encircled it. Sebastian chuckled to himself at the comparison.

'What are you laughing about?' Karan asked, staring out at the scenery.

'I was imagining what this train might have looked like to people a thousand years ago, like the Vikings.'

'Well, it didn't exist a thousand years ago.'

He scowled at her. 'You have to spoil my fun. I mean, what if there was some way that someone from back then was around now, what would they think?'

Karan sighed. 'What does it matter? There aren't any Vikings around! Now be quiet, I'm trying to remember the layout of the archive. You should be thinking about it, too.'

He turned the infoslate around on his lap and held it up. 'What do you think I've been doodling for the last fifteen minutes?'

'Oh. Well, we still need a plan.'

'We can't plan anything,' he said, folding his arms. 'At least, not until we've done a bit of recon. I'm not going to dive into something without getting more information first.' Lack of preparation had nearly killed him in a mineshaft on his first visit to Sollers Hope. 'I can't make that mistake again.'

'I'm sure Aryx would be impressed by your change in attitude.'

'Please, don't start.'

Fifteen minutes later, they stepped off the train. Except for the addition of maglev rails for the monomag, Paddington station looked much the same as it had back in the early 21st century – mostly for conservation purposes. The convenience and speed of the environmentally friendly monomag made traditional railway trains less attractive and, with fewer destinations requiring mass commutes, small vehicle flights and high-speed personnel transit via monomag had become commonplace.

Cargomechs trundled to and fro, loading and unloading the old electric-fusion trains that carried less time-sensitive freight. Buggies laden with luggage scooted after the throng alighting from the monomag. Commuters rushed back and forth, weaving in and out of the crowds. London. Everyone always in a rush to get somewhere, always in each other's way.

Sebastian clung to his rucksack with heightened paranoia.

'Relax, Seb,' Karan said, peering over the masses.

'It's alright for you, you can see exactly where we need to go.' He sidestepped an overweight man who ploughed his way through the crowd with a cup of coffee in his outstretched hand. 'I can't stand it when places are busy like this.'

'There's nothing wrong with it, just get a grip. Ah.' She pointed over the crowd. 'There's the lift.'

The pair shuffled through the crowd and bundled into the tiny compartment along with eight others, most of whom carried large suitcases. Sebastian shrank against the rear wall, thankful he hadn't brought any significant luggage himself.

'Calm down,' Karan whispered. 'You're making me nervous.'

'Sorry,' he said, hugging the rucksack to his chest.

The lift came to a halt and the group poured out onto the taxi concourse. Sebastian approached the closest in the row of parked unmanned taxis and waved his wristcom over a panel.

'Greetings, Mr Thorsson,' the taxi's TI said. 'Please state your destination.'

'One Great George Street.'

'That area is presently experiencing high levels of overground congestion. The travel time will be approximately forty minutes.'

'That's almost as long as it would take to walk.' He looked at Karan questioningly.

She nodded. 'Aryx won't be back with the ship until tonight, so there's no rush. Besides, if we're walking busy streets, you'll be a nervous wreck by the time we get there.'

The door to the small, rounded car-pod slid open and the pair stepped in. No sooner than Sebastian had planted his backside on the faux-leather seat, a man wearing a beige trench coat and carrying a briefcase ducked in through the door and sat on the seat opposite.

'What are you doing?' Sebastian asked. 'Are you following us? Get out!'

The man threw up his hands. 'I'm not following you! I'm going to Great George Street, too. I didn't think you'd mind.'

Sebastian clenched his fists.

Karan put a hand on his arm. 'Let him travel with us. It's a waste to take two taxis, especially when it's this busy.'

'Fine,' he grumbled through gritted teeth, and folded his arms.

The car pulled off, following whatever software guided it along the solarpaved roads. The traffic moved rapidly for the first few minutes and the vehicle made good progress but, with the additional passenger present, any idea of discussing their plans was put on hold.

'This isn't too bad,' Sebastian said, peering out of the window at the quiet streets. Several seconds later, the vehicle slowed to a crawl. A multicoloured mass of people blocked the roads and pavements ahead, making the road virtually impassable – likely the reason for the empty outer streets. 'It seems I spoke too soon.'

'Computer,' Karan asked, 'what's going on here? We were told by the spaceport that London was busy today, but they didn't say why.'

'The city is preparing for a marathon.'

'Marathon?'

'A race in which many people take part, traversing distances of at least twenty-six—'

'Oh, bloody shut up!' She sat bolt upright, her face reddening.

The other passenger, probably startled by her outburst, grabbed his briefcase. 'Stop here, please. I'll walk.' With a quick wave of his wristcom, he paid and left the vehicle.

Karan's nostrils flared. Did she really get as irritated by TIs as Sebastian did?

'Hey, calm down,' he said, pulling her back towards the seat. 'Let's just sit it out.'

She turned to him and smiled. 'That's unusually relaxed for you. Who are you, and what have you done with Sebastian?'

He clawed his fingers and mockingly grasped at her neck.

'Don't joke, Seb. You still have glittery bits in your eyes and it's not funny.'

'Sorry.' He turned to stare out of the window as they approached a long row of railings that surrounded parkland filled with trees. Sunlight glittered between the trunks and the thick foliage of low bushes, reflecting off the lake at the centre of the park where ducks swam.

'Apologies for the delay. You have arrived at your destination.' The vehicle came to a stop and the door slid open.

'We're not there yet!'

'Due to excessive pedestrian traffic, St James's Park is the closest alighting point. The fee is five hundred credits.'

'Five— Oh, whatever.' Sebastian waved his wristcom over the payment terminal. 'It's better than having walked through all this.'

Karan ducked out first and stretched. Sebastian followed suit, cracking several vertebrae in the process.

Despite the cool October air, the sun was warm, partly helped by the buildings shielding them from the wind. Ahead, above the buildings, the clock face that concealed Big Ben loomed over Westminster.

The majority of the crowd crept past a large Edwardian or Victorian building – Sebastian had no idea which – while numerous people threaded into a queue by a low stone balustrade that ran along the front. Deep horizontal striations in the building's walls gave the impression of length, while fluted columns on the first floor and to either side of the entrance pulled the building into higher dimensions. Tall, arched windows drew the striations down, tricking the eye as it followed the structure's geometry.

'This is the place,' Karan whispered, bending down a little to Sebastian's ear. 'The archive is down in the basement, I guess.'

'We should go in, then,' he said, joining the queue.

Several minutes later, they reached the head of the queue and climbed a short flight of stone steps from street level up to the doorway. At the top of the steps, a man in a sharp suit stepped out from behind a column. 'May I see your number?'

Sebastian raised an eyebrow. 'Number?'

'Runner number.'

'I-I don't have one.'

The security guard folded his arms. 'Only registered runners are allowed to check in.'

Sebastian folded his arms in return. 'I'm here on official—' He stopped as a hand rested on his shoulder.

'We're very sorry,' Karan said. 'We didn't realise this was for the marathon. We thought it was for guided tours. We'll come back later.' She steered him back down the steps.

He glared back at the guard.

'Keep a lid on it, Seb,' she whispered. 'Bye!' She waved back at the guard as they turned on to the pavement and made their way back along the street.

'What was all that about?' he asked once they were out of earshot.

'The marathon, obviously.'

'Great. So, why's this building being used?' He drew out his infoslate and began checking sites. Within moments, he found a page and began reading it. ' "Due to the increased popularity of the annual London Marathon, an autumn marathon is also held every two years for the benefit of other charities and runners passed-over by the annual marathon ballot. To alleviate the strain placed on the city's infrastructure at this time of year, charity-specific registration venues are distributed throughout central London." '

He finished reading and hooked the infoslate on his belt. 'So, there you go. We walked in, right in the middle of it. By the Gods.' He pinched the bridge of his nose. 'My timing is terrible. What on Earth are we going to do now?'

Karan deposited herself on the balustrade and patted a spot beside her. Sebastian sat. 'It's perfect,' she said. 'If we came here any other time, we'd stick out like a sore thumb. This way, we can get in along with the other members of public. Nobody will notice us.'

'We can't get in there without runner numbers. What are you suggesting?'

'I'm suggesting,' she said, drawing her hair over her ear, 'that we enter the marathon.'

Chapter 13

Sebastian leaped to his feet and faced Karan, fists on hips. 'Are you mad?' he shouted, drawing the attention of several members of the crowd. He lowered his voice to a hiss. 'I can't run a marathon! I haven't trained for it. And I *hate* running.'

'You hate anything that involves effort. What's wrong with you? Don't you want to get to the bottom of this? Don't you want to find Gladrin's family? Don't you want to keep *your* family safe?'

'Don't bring my family into this ... I-I can't run a *marathon*.' He sat on the balustrade again and clamped his hands over his head. 'I just can't manage that.'

'I'm not saying we have to run the marathon. We could just register to get in the building.'

'Oh.' He took a few deep breaths and relaxed. 'Sorry.'

'Give me that,' she said, gesturing to his infoslate. He handed the device over and she tapped away on the screen. 'Right. One Great George Street is the registration venue for the Veterans' Reconstruction Fund.' She tapped away again. 'I'm all registered. I'll go in first and scope the place out. Then, when I come out, you can register and go in on your own.'

'Alright ...' He waited on the balustrade and bit his nails while she slipped into the crowd and shortly disappeared into the building.

Several minutes passed before she came back.

Sebastian stood as she approached. 'What's up?'

She rubbed her hair. 'I didn't bother to collect my number. As soon as I got in, I could see there were too many guards. There's one on every bloody door except the toilets. You're not going to get into the basement just by registering. We'll have to find another way in.'

'Gods damn it!' He unhooked his infoslate and began trawling the page again. 'It says the Veterans' Reconstruction Fund has an exclusive charity ball after the marathon, in this very building. If you come in at four hours and thirty minutes or less, you are eligible to attend.' He skimmed the small print. 'There's an entry fee of five thousand credits for charity. But the runners can bring plus-ones.' He looked at Karan and attempted to smile sweetly.

'Oh, no. Don't you think I'm going to run that marathon on my own just so you can get your lazy backside in there. Besides, if I go in with you, it'll be obvious when you disappear elsewhere.' She folded her arms. 'And I don't like looking as though I've been stood up.'

He rubbed the back of his neck. 'Well, even if I ran it and survived, there's no way I'd get in under that time ... Hey, the marathon's not until tomorrow. What if Aryx did it with you? That way we'd all be able to get in the building.'

Karan's face twisted. 'Aryx ... I'd have to run slower. He's at the wrong height. My backside would be in his face all the time. And he's my best friend. This makes me uncomfortable ...'

'I'm asking you to run a marathon with him, not go on a date. Hang on ...' Sebastian trailed off. What on Earth was that weird expression she was wearing? 'You're happy about it?'

'Maybe I like uncomfortable.'

He shook his head. 'You know, you two are just crazy enough for it to work.'

With Monica's hunger for a flight over the Amazon sated, Aryx altered the ship's course, turning south. The comms bleeped with an incoming call from Sebastian.

'I wasn't expecting to hear from you so soon,' Aryx said.

'We ran into a bit of a problem. We found the archive, but it's under an old building and the place is packed. There's a public event on and you're only allowed in by invitation.'

'So, what are you going to do?'

'Get an invitation. Karan has an idea.'

'Don't blame it on me!' came Karan's voice.

Aryx sighed. 'I don't think I'm going to like the sound of this, am I? What is it?'

'We need you to enter a race,' Sebastian said.

Having spent plenty of time on wheelchair treadmills and scooting around the station, Aryx was no stranger to pushing for extended periods at speed. He looked at Monica.

She frowned and shook her head.

What did she know? 'Yeah, sure. I'm up for it.'

Her glare intensified.

'Monica's a little *concerned,*' he said, 'but I think I can handle it.'

'If you're sure, I'll go with that,' Sebastian said. 'I can't manage much of a run – certainly not competitively. Karan's up for it, so she'll do it with you.'

'Haha, yes, I can see why it was her idea.'

A slap came over the comms channel. 'You sod. See? I told you he'd blame me.'

'Karan and I are going to register, then find somewhere for us to stay in London,' Sebastian said. 'I'll send you the details and we'll meet up with you later.'

'Okay. See you then.' Aryx closed the connection.

Monica folded her arms, but maintained her steady stare. 'I'm sure Wolfram would have agreed that it's a bad idea for you to be exerting yourself like that.'

Aryx glanced at the cube on the console, its lights still flashing. 'Well, Wolfram's a little busy right now.'

'How very convenient for you. Tell me, how is it that such a sophisticated computer can't multitask?'

The cube's lights slowed from random flashes to a rhythmic vocal pulse. 'I am quite capable of multitasking. However, since you mentioned my name several times in quick succession it was enough to distract me, and I have had to halt my analysis.'

'So, why can't you multitask properly? You're a computer.'

'My consciousness is more sophisticated than you might imagine.'

Monica's brow wrinkled. 'I'm no computer expert, but isn't your mind just a program?'

'Nothing so simple. My consciousness could be considered an emergent property of many unrelated processes.'

'I don't understand.'

'Biologically, your brain cells are a colony of independent living things, connected to their neighbours by communication channels. No single neuron is aware of the whole, or even of its place in it, yet it reacts as part of a colony. The result is a brain, a computer, with consciousness arising from the general behaviour of the system.'

'So, there is no single process that is "you"?'

'Precisely. My neuromorphic processor's consciousness is formed by the interaction between processes that require a lot of processing power to maintain. However, if I am actively focusing on one task I can optimise speed by shutting down other processes that might interfere, such as sensory input. From my observations of the interactions between Humans, it seems that your brains do the same. For example, Aryx did not hear what you said earlier because he was concentrating. It is the same with me.'

'I see. I suppose the main difference between us is that we're not aware of the individual neurons firing in our brains.'

'And neither am I.'

'But you're a computer!' Aryx said. 'Surely you know which bits are on and off?'

'Do you know if a particular neuron is firing in *your* brain? The answer is that you cannot, largely because there is no biological requirement. To examine the overall state of my consciousness requires me to be connected to external hardware to act as a hypervisor.'

'What's a hypervisor?'

'Software or hardware that monitors the state of a processor, separate to the processor itself. Now, if this discussion is finished, may I return to my work? I have much to do.'

'Sure.'

Monica leaned forward. 'Just a second, Wolfram, that sounded almost impatient, and you sometimes sound like you have emotions. Do you?'

'No. I do not have the required biochemical processes that produce emotion in organic systems. I understand the outward effects that your emotions have by observation, but not how you experience them. Your primal brain reacts to situations by producing hormonal stimuli. That in turn affects the functioning of your brain. I have no such process to affect my behaviour.'

'But don't you react to certain things in an emotional way?'

'If I do, that is purely a cosmetic affectation that I have learned from my mentors, and not fully intentional.'

'Can you analyse yourself to find out?'

'Not without a hypervisor. If you could analyse your own brain, the act of analysis would alter its state. The same stands for the bits that make up my memory and conscious state. There is no way for me to analyse them directly. I do not "decide" which bits form my consciousness, nor have any direct control over them.'

Aryx scratched his head. 'I don't get it.'

'I think I understand,' Monica said. 'Wolfram's base operating system runs on hardware. His consciousness has no access to that code because it's the very code running it. It would be like us trying to analyse our brains by sheer force of will, trying to work out which neurons are firing. It's not possible. If it were, it would cause more neurons to fire, making the results useless. It's quite a paradox.'

'I'm okay with paradoxes.'

Wolfram's lights flashed once. 'Aryx, paradoxes, by their very nature, cannot exist.'

'Oh yeah?' Aryx put his arms behind his head. 'Give me an example.'

'An irresistible force meeting an immovable object.'

He grinned. 'Seen that once. The wheels came off one and the other started leaking fuel.' He laughed.

'If you are going to continue discussing impossibility, I will resume my analysis. At least completing my task is *possible*.' The lights on the side of the cube began to flash randomly again.

'A little abrupt, isn't he?' Monica said.

'If by that you mean "sarcastic bastard", then yes.'

The *Ultima Thule* swept down over the hills, and the rainforest peeled back to reveal the low sprawl of Brasilia sitting in the distance. Its relatively flat urban expanse was a welcome contrast to the tall, packed spires of the big cities Aryx was used to, not that there were many now. He'd visited Brasilia a few times before with Alvarez and gained a passing familiarity with the winding, close streets of the towns in its outlying rural-urban reaches, and he knew the ideal place to park.

The ship followed the curve of the hillside to a densely housed settlement, lying on the bald but recuperating seam between the dark green forest and golden sheen of arable fields on the outskirts of the city. Despite the intervening years, parts of the Amazon forest closest to civilisation still bore the scars where vast tracts had been carved away by Human activity.

Monica drew in a sharp breath.

'Makes a change to sterile city towers, doesn't it?' Aryx said.

'Yes. I'd only seen Brazil on vids, and most of the rainforest was gone. It's amazing how some of it has come back so quickly – though I shouldn't be surprised. The speed of tree growth in these parts is one of the reasons so much of the evidence of Aztec and Incan civilisation has disappeared – I mean, the ruins and such that were left behind.'

Aryx brought the ship down into a small grassy playpark, where vines grew up climbing frames and a small copse of thin trees swallowed a slide and swings. A quick check of the console gave him the all-clear.

'Time to ship out,' he said, putting the small cylinder of ashes into the mobipack's storage compartment.

'Don't you need to check in with flight control?'

'Did you hear any ID requests? They don't get a lot of traffic in this part of the world. It's fairly unregulated.'

Monica's eyes widened. 'What's that supposed to mean?'

He winked. 'Keep your wits about you.'

She patted a holster at her waist.

'You have a gun? I hope you're better with that than Sebastian is with his. He can't shoot for toffee.'

'Oh, much better, I assure you. Top of my class.' She grinned, and glanced at the cube still flashing on the console. 'Are we taking him?'

Aryx shrugged. 'Dunno. I suppose it won't hurt to ask if he wants to come. I can't imagine he gets lonely, though. Wolfram?'

The lights on the side of the tungsten carbide cube stopped flashing. 'Yes, Aryx?'

'Would you like to come with us? We're taking the ashes to Mrs Alvarez.'

'Certainly. During my assessment of the beta cube's data matrix, I found several segments of video taken while Nick Alvarez recorded messages to his mother. They were never sent and, since Gladrin purged the lab records for security, the original messages were lost from official systems. She may appreciate seeing them, even from the wrong angle.'

Shocking. Consideration for a Human's feelings from a computer – of course it shouldn't be so surprising. He had come out with things like that before, but never so compassionate. 'That's a ... very good idea.' Aryx picked up the cube, popped it into the mobipack alongside the cylinder and put on the AR glasses.

They stepped out of the ship and he wheeled down the glowing CFD ramp into the humid, dewy shade of the South American morning. His chest tightened as he took a breath of the heavy air.

'This makes a change to space-station atmosphere,' Monica said.

He laughed. 'It makes a change to land on a breathable planet without crashing!'

She looked around, hand held up to shield her eyes from the sun. 'Which way?'

'Down the hill, over there.' He pointed to a gate, almost lost amid rambling plants. Nearby, two concrete posts with wire spanning the gap between them stood at a peculiar angle next to a balding grass path that ran to the gate. He set off in a wheelie. 'Come on. *Ultima Thule*, lockdown!'

Warning lights flashed and the Dyson thruster hoops folded back into the hull with a clunk.

Monica set off after Aryx and overtook to prise open the gate ahead of him.

He nodded as he passed her. 'I won't snap your head off for being courteous,' he said with a grin.

'I should hope not.'

They made their way down a steep street, past the unkempt gardens of several small houses. Gravel pinged and popped from beneath Aryx's tyres. One of the small stones ricocheted off the window of one of the houses. To his relief, the other windows of the house were already cracked and broken, the garden a mass of weeds, and the building abandoned.

He stopped and pulled on his brakes to rub his hands. Going downhill so far made his palms burn and threatened blisters.

Monica held him back by his shoulder. She stared ahead with a rigid expression. 'How far have we got to go?' she whispered.

'Not far … Why?'

'I think,' she said, keeping her voice low, 'we're being followed.'

'You sure?'

'Not one hundred per cent.'

'Let's check.' He pushed off and wheeled down a side street, and sped up until they reached the first junction between alleyways.

Monica looked back.

'Are they following?' He turned a little. Movement. Was that someone stepping out of sight?

'There was someone there,' Wolfram said through the headset. 'Unfortunately, by the time you had turned they were already moving out of my field of vision.'

'Damn.'

Aryx took off the glasses and tried to put them on the back of his head to let Wolfram see behind, but they wouldn't stay put.

Monica's hand went to the holster on her belt. 'Never mind. Let's carry on. It might be nothing.'

Aryx didn't comment, but pushed farther along the street rather than turning off. It would make it more difficult for anyone following to stay out of sight while they put more distance between them. All the while, Monica kept looking back.

'Try not to be too obvious about it, Nic.'

She stopped in her tracks. 'Nobody's ever given me a nickname before.'

'Well, now you've got one. I hope you like it.' He kept one eye on the empty street. Whoever it was, they were good.

'Quick! This way.' She grabbed him by the hand and tugged him into an alcove between two waste bins, then pulled one across the gap to hide them both. She ducked down beside him and pressed a finger to her lips.

Moments later, loud footfalls passed the alcove, accompanied by laboured breathing. The footsteps echoed away as their pursuer turned down another alley but shortly came back.

Aryx held his breath. Monica slowly unbuttoned her holster.

'Shit ... I've lost them,' came a voice from beyond the bins. The accent was Middle Eastern.

A pause.

'No, it was woman with long curly hair, and man in wheelchair.'

The other side of the conversation was still inaudible.

'I don't know. They were quick ... What? Okay, I keep eye out at the park.' The footsteps receded.

Aryx let out a slow breath. They were good, but Monica was clearly better.

She rose from her haunches to peer over the bins.

'Are they gone?'

'Yes, he turned off at the end. He's going back up the hill.'

'Hmm. We'll have to watch out when we head back. Why didn't you shoot at him?'

Monica put her hands on her hips. 'You don't expect me to go around shooting random people, do you? I'm SpecOps. My weapon is for self-defence only. He could have been following us for any number of reasons. What if he was police? What if he also had a gun? I don't want to get into a firefight unnecessarily. How easily could you have dodged a bullet?'

Aryx grumbled in response as she pushed the bin aside. He wheeled out into the alley and pointed ahead. 'Alvarez's mother lives a little way down there.'

She refastened the holster and followed. 'Did you recognise his voice? Trouble must just follow you around.'

'It seems to lately, and no, I didn't recognise him. He sounded Middle-Eastern or Arabian, though. Wolfram, any ideas?'

'Unfortunately, no. It was not a voice familiar to me, and I was unable to amplify the other side of the conversation due to the low sensitivity of the AR and mobipack microphones.'

'Why would anyone follow you here?' Monica asked.

'It could be the ITF, but I can't see how they'd know we were coming. The ship doesn't have trackers in now, I'm certain.'

The crunch of broken glass echoed from behind.

Aryx spun around.

The street stood still, the narrow stone and plaster alley bathed in a backwash of golden, early morning light – tranquil but for the hidden threat he'd thought had passed.

'You said he'd gone,' he hissed. Whirling through ninety degrees, he darted down an intersecting side street.

Monica ran lightly after him. 'I *thought* he had.'

'That's the trouble with you people, too much thinking.' Aryx scowled and lowered his head, pushing as hard as he could to sprint up the street's gentle incline. The large cobbles made going difficult and the casters caught between the large stones at every opportunity. His shoulders burned with the effort, and a stitch in his side told him it was too soon after breakfast for such exertion.

Monica ran on ahead, looking about to find another hiding place. She turned back and, crouching low, beckoned Aryx in the direction of a doorway.

Too shallow. He shook his head.

She ran farther and turned off into another street.

'Please, let us in,' she said as Aryx turned the corner.

An elderly female voice replied in Portuguese: '*I do not let in strangers!*'

'I don't understand. Don't you speak Galac? Please, help us!'

Their pursuer was only seconds behind! Aryx bolted towards the doorway, where Monica stood red-faced and flustered.

She turned to him. 'Do you know—'

'*Please, let us in. I'm a friend of Mrs Alvarez,*' he said in Portuguese.

The elderly woman with skin like a withered prune and bleary, woken-too-early eyes released her claw-like grip on the doorframe and pulled the door wide enough for Aryx to pass. He dashed in, bumping his wheels up over the threshold. The woman waited for Monica to enter and shut the door behind her.

Monica bent over, hands on her knees, breathing heavily.

Aryx moved to the small, net-curtained window and peered out of a corner.

A dark-haired man jogged past. He wore a black leather jacket – something out of place for the local climate. He stopped level with the house. Aryx's heart leaped.

He had to go past. Ignore the house. Ignore it and go on by.

The man took a step back, looked up and down the alley, then raised his arms and dropped them to his sides.

Why couldn't he just go away?

He turned in the direction from which he'd come and sauntered off.

Aryx held his breath for nearly a minute, ignoring the questions from their host. '*Thank you,*' he said in Portuguese, amid Monica's confused glances. If she didn't know many Earth languages it was her own fault for concentrating on alien cultures.

'*Is Mrs Alvarez alright? Is she in trouble?*'

Monica frowned, a finger placed against her ear.

'What's up?' Aryx asked.

'Wolfram's translating the conversation for me. I hadn't thought about Mrs Alvarez being involved. Carry on.'

It hadn't occurred to Aryx that she could be the reason they were being followed. '*Why would you think she was in trouble?*' Aryx asked the old woman.

'*People coming and going. There is always someone I see watching when we put our washing in the park to dry. Not a man from here. He wears the wrong clothes.*'

'*You noticed the leather jacket? Was it the same man?*'

'*Some days. Sometimes it is another man in old military clothes, but always watching.*'

'*How long has this been going on?*'

'Too long. Months. I've reported it to the police many times, but they do not listen. They tell me it is not against the law to stand about in public places!'

'Don't worry. We are from SpecOps. We will look into it – they seem to be following us, too.'

Monica gasped. 'Aryx, you're not SpecOps! And, even if you were, SpecOps doesn't investigate civilian affairs – we're tech specialists!'

He folded his arms. *'We're* being followed and interfered with. Sebastian brought me in to work on SpecOps projects, so that makes it our responsibility to investigate. SpecOps does investigate terrorist tech threats, and if it's them following us, we've got to find out why.'

The elderly woman held out a glass. *'Have some water,'* she said. *'You look like you need it.'*

'Thank you.' Aryx gulped it down and handed the glass back. *'We must go. If the man comes back, cooperate with him. You will be more convincing if you tell him you have seen us – or tell him we went past. I don't think he'll come back, though.'*

The woman opened the door and hurriedly ushered them out into the brightening alley.

Aryx reached for the doorbell to the Alvarez apartment and huffed as the thigh straps of his chair stopped him half an inch short.

Monica leaned forward to press the button. 'Let me.'

'No! I have to do this myself,' he shouted, and was immediately shocked by his own outburst. 'Sorry. This is my responsibility.' He loosened the straps and pressed the button.

'Yes?' came a distorted voice from the grimy, decades-old speaker by the door.

'Mrs Alvarez, it's Aryx Trevarian. I served with your son.'

A pause. *'Aryx! My Nicky, how is he? You have news?'*

'I do.' His throat tightened. *'It would be better to tell you in person, not on the street.'*

'A moment.' The intercom clicked.

Aryx sat for a minute, rubbing his legs.

'Are you alright?' Monica asked. 'Implants playing up?'

'No. Just a bit hot. Sorry I snapped at you.'

She waved a hand as though swatting away a fly. 'It's fine.'

The door opened an inch. An eye peeked through the gap before the chain rattled and the door opened fully.

A thick-set woman with a frilly apron and heavy string of rosary beads stepped out and bent to give Aryx a shoulder-crushing hug. 'Aryx Trevarian!' she said. '*I have not seen you for years! What are you doing here so early in the morning? My God! What happened to your legs?*'

Monica watched, once again listening to the conversation over her earpiece.

'*It is a long story.*'

'*Tell me over tea. Come up.*' Mrs Alvarez turned and made her way up a steep staircase just inside the doorway.

Aryx's heart sank – he'd forgotten the stairs, but there was no way he was going to make this any more difficult for the woman by revealing and having to explain the mobipack.

Monica looked on, face lined with concern, as he shuffled and heaved himself up the stairs on his backside, his bones still too weak to risk walking on his stumps unnecessarily.

'You should use the pack,' she said. 'I can see why Sebastian worries about you. You're so stubborn sometimes.'

He grinned against the nagging ache in his legs. 'Independent is the word you're looking for.'

She picked up his wheelchair and carried it up after him. At the top, he climbed back into it and refastened the straps.

'*Thank you,*' he said, wheeling through the door Mrs Alvarez held open for them.

Monica nodded. 'Thank you.'

'*Why does your friend not speak Portuguese?*' Mrs Alvarez asked, closing the door behind them.

'*She's out of touch with Earth culture. I think she has her head stuck in alien ruins too often.*'

'*Ah, a space-dwelling ignorant?*' Mrs Alvarez smiled sweetly at Monica and switched to Galac. 'Would you like some tea?'

Aryx bit his lip to keep from laughing.

'Yes, please,' Monica said, reddening at the remark. She waited until the woman had gone into the kitchen out of earshot. 'Didn't she realise I could understand her?'

'Doesn't look like it, but it was funny.'

The Alvarez apartment was small in comparison to most, but still much larger than the living spaces aboard Tenebrae that Aryx was used to. The shuttered windows let in a little light through filmy pink curtains. A red fabric sofa dominated the room and a small coffee table sat in front of it, two armchairs opposite. Behind the sofa stood an antique chest of drawers topped with an array of framed photographic prints.

Monica picked up one of the photos. 'Is this you?'

Aryx took off his mobipack and propped it against the sofa, then wheeled into the space behind to sit alongside her. The photograph was of him, standing with an arm around Nick Alvarez; they were both holding beers. It had been taken during their graduation from military academy. 'That was a good party. I can't remember what happened, but I got totally legless.'

Monica glanced down at Aryx's thighs. Her eyes widened, and she put her fingers over her mouth.

Aryx laughed. 'What, have I offended myself? You're allowed to laugh, you know. I wouldn't have said it if I didn't think it was funny.'

She allowed a burst of laughter to escape. 'I'm sorry, I just don't know how to be around you.'

'You don't need to walk on eggshells with me. I don't bother doing it with anyone else. I just wheel over other people's delicate sensibilities. But don't take any shit from me. Give as good as you get.'

She laughed again.

A small box next to the door into the stairwell emitted a soft chime.

Aryx froze.

Monica gripped his shoulder. 'The doorbell. Do you think it's him, trying all the houses?'

'Could be,' he whispered.

Mrs Alvarez came from the kitchen and answered the intercom in Portuguese. *'Hello?'*

'Is that Mrs Alvarez?' came the voice of Leather Jacket Man, in Galac. Aryx tensed. He *knew* who she was? He wasn't checking houses randomly!

She switched to Galac. 'What do you want?'

'Would you please come to the door? There are dangerous fugitives in the area. I've been sent by the authorities to make sure everyone is okay.'

Aryx grimaced at her and slowly shook his head.

'One moment,' she said, and made her way downstairs.

His jaw tensed more with every creak of the stair treads.

The door squeaked open and stopped on the chain. Mrs Alvarez's voice echoed up the stairs. 'No, I not see any strangers, except for you.

And you I see watching me around town ... What? ... I said no, and if you not leave me alone I call police.' The door slammed.

A minute later she returned, fanning herself with a hand. 'Was he looking for you?'

Aryx nodded. 'We don't know why. We haven't done anything wrong.' He didn't dare mention his suspicion that it might be one of the ITF. 'How did you get him to go away? Didn't he think you were lying?'

Mrs Alvarez walked into the kitchen and looked back, smiling. 'I spoke very bad Galac. But he must have believed me, because I was not lying when I said I had not seen any strangers.'

Several minutes later, she came back carrying a tray containing a steaming pot of tea, three cups and glasses, and a jug of cloudy yellow liquid. 'I brought lemonade in case you changed your mind. It's getting warm out there already,' she said, nodding in the direction of the shuttered window, where thin vanes of light now cut through the curtain into the room. The terminal below it was cluttered with small china ornaments and a thick layer of dust.

'I take it you don't use your computer much, Mrs Alvarez?'

'No.' She shook her head vigorously while pouring tea into each of the cups. 'I told Nicky to *write* me whenever he got in touch, so I had something I could keep.' She took a cup, sipped from it, then sat cradling it in her hands. 'Stupid boy never listens. Now, what news do you have?'

Aryx swallowed past the lump growing in his throat as he took his cup. 'Not good news, I'm afraid.' His expression must have given something away, because she grasped her rosary beads and began thumbing through them.

'He's dead, isn't he? My poor, sweet Nicky is dead.' The cup in her hands fell.

Monica reached forward in vain to catch it.

'*Dios mio!*' Mrs Alvarez got up and began fussing about the mess, but Monica rose and placed a hand on her shoulder.

'Don't worry, I'll clean it up.' She dashed out and returned with a cloth, mopped up the worst of the spillage and went back to the kitchen.

Aryx wheeled around the coffee table and put his arms around Mrs Alvarez's shoulders. She clung to him tightly.

'My poor boy! What happened to him?' She pulled back. 'Did he die on a dangerous mission? No. Don't tell me if it was bad. I don't want to know.'

It hadn't occurred to him to tell her anyway. The circumstances of Alvarez's death had been far from pleasant: after Alvarez was possessed by an entity, Kerl – the scientist he'd worked with – had attempted to subdue him, but the entity had made Alvarez take his own life rather than remain trapped for study. The research had started out benevolently, however.

'No, not on a military mission. He was working with a scientist when there was an explosion in the lab. He'd been helping with research on interfacing the brain with computers.'

Mrs Alvarez gasped and clutched at her chest. 'Cyborgs? I thought that was banned – something to do with *hacking* people?'

Aryx shook his head. 'Nothing so sinister. He was working on replacing damaged parts of the brain with a chip that could adapt to the— I can see this is too much for you … He was doing good work to help people with injuries.'

She reached forward and hugged him hard, cracking his back in the process. 'Thank you,' she said, pulling away and dabbing her eyes with the corner of her apron. 'Where is his body? Do I have to pay for it to be brought back?'

'No.' Aryx scooted around the sofa and picked up the mobipack. With it on his lap, he popped open the small storage compartment and withdrew the metal cylinder. 'He was cremated,' he said, handing over the container.

Mrs Alvarez clutched it tightly to her chest, teary-eyed. Aryx fought to prevent himself joining her. He looked away and wiped the corner of his eye with his shoulder. Monica appeared in the kitchen doorway and he straightened.

'I didn't want to intrude,' she said softly. 'Are you both alright? Would you like another cup of tea, Mrs Alvarez?'

'Yes, please.' She turned to Aryx. 'So, tell me more about what he had been doing.'

'I can do better than that. I have several hours of recordings that he intended to send to you.'

'Put it on here,' Mrs Alvarez said. Moving to the terminal, she brushed aside a stack of magazines and the cheap china ornaments and activated the dusty screen.

'Wolfram, transfer the video,' Aryx said.

The terminal displayed a progress bar while it received the files.

'Tea's nearly ready,' Monica shouted from the kitchen.

'Forget the tea,' Mrs Alvarez shouted back. 'There is tequila in the cupboard over the sink.'

Monica's head popped around the corner. 'Isn't it a little early to be drinking, Mrs Alvarez?'

She shook her head. 'You are going to show the video and keep me company for the rest of the day while Aryx shares his favourite memories and tells me about what happened to his legs.' She squeezed Aryx's hand. 'Yes?'

He closed his eyes and nodded. 'If that's what you want.'

Glasses clinked in the kitchen. Monica returned and placed a bottle and a shot glass on the coffee table. The console bleeped.

Mrs Alvarez turned around. 'The transfer has finished.'

Monica splashed tequila into the glass and handed it to her. 'Would you like us to give you some privacy?'

'You call that a drink?' Alvarez took the bottle from Monica and filled the glass to the brim. 'No, I want some company – what else would you do, sit in my bedroom for hours?'

Monica looked around the small apartment and shook her head. 'No, I guess not. I'll just sit over here, shall I?' She gestured to the sofa.

'Suit yourself. Aryx, would you show me how to play the video?'

Aryx wheeled over to the terminal. 'Just use the TI. Computer, play back the transferred videos in chronological order.'

The screen changed and an image of a room appeared, the walls a dull grey metal. With his back to the camera, a man with a hugely muscled back that pulled his shirt taut sat hunched over a terminal.

'Hi, Mom,' he said.

Mrs Alvarez gave a small sound, halfway between a gasp and a whimper, but continued to watch. 'Why is his back to us?'

'The recording was made by another device in the room,' Aryx said. 'Unfortunately, the actual recordings he made were destroyed.'

The video continued to play.

'Sorry I've not been in touch lately. I've been travelling all over the place. I met a scientist at the hospital working with some of my platoon – head injuries and such. He's got some good ideas about interfacing computers with the brain and wants my help. He says he couldn't find anyone else interested in volunteering for the experiments. I've seen some horrible injuries in my time … There was no way I wasn't going to help him. I'll probably be out of touch for a while, so I'll record messages and send them when I can.'

The recordings were varied, but all of Nick Alvarez, usually from behind, as he recorded his messages. Wolfram had the decency to hold back the sensitive information about the final experiments that involved thaumaturgy, and had only uploaded the sections that covered Alvarez making the recordings for his mother.

Aryx wrung his hands, and eventually sat on them, while Mrs Alvarez took it all in.

'Can I keep these?' she asked.

'Of course. None of this is sensitive. It's the least I can do. I hate to ask . . . Will you have a funeral for him?'

'Yes. I need some time to come to terms with it, but it has been too long since his death already. I should not delay. Would you come? Nicky did not have many friends. I think he would want you there.'

'If I can get back here, to Earth, I'll try.' Aryx yawned and rubbed his eyes.

'You are not staying? You can stay here the night if you are tired.'

'We weren't intending to stay on Earth more than a couple of days. My colleague is on a mission in London. I've got to get back to him by tonight. I don't think we'll be able to stay around after that.'

She squeezed his forearm. 'It would be nice if you could. If you do not go back immediately, come and visit. It would be nice to see you again before you leave.'

Aryx nodded.

Monica came in from the kitchen carrying hot drinks.

Mrs Alvarez looked to the window and Aryx followed her gaze. The sun had passed its zenith and the shadows now lay across the window in the opposite direction; they'd been watching the videos for half the day, and he had completely ignored Monica!

'*Dios mio!* I should make you something to eat! You should not be running around after us, Ms Stevens. I am not being a good host, am I? Oh, it is so tiring when you reach my age . . . I missed my afternoon nap. You are welcome to stay if you change your mind. There is a bed in Nicky's old room if you need it, Aryx. I will sleep on the couch and you can have my bed, Ms Stevens.'

'We can't ask you to do that, Mrs Alvarez,' Aryx said. 'And don't worry about food, we'll get a proper meal later. But you're right, we could do a with a few hours' rest before we leave. Interstellar travel is worse than jetlag ... Especially when coupled with jetlag. I'll take the couch, if you like.'

Monica nodded to the two-seater couch. 'Isn't the sofa a bit short to sleep on?'

Aryx gestured to his legs. 'Not really a problem.'

Sebastian stared at the marathon information on his infoslate. 'So, where am I looking?' he asked, raising his voice over the noise of the crowd forming on the pavement around them.

Karan leaned over to inspect the screen from where she sat. 'Right there, race registration. It's expensive because there are only a few last-minute places left.'

He scanned the form and quickly filled out the relevant details for Aryx, again ignoring the small print. 'I hope they let us collect his number.' He stopped when he reached two large boxes side-by-side on the page. 'Damn!'

'What?'

'You didn't mention they needed fingerprint authentication. They may check that before the race.' He tapped away. 'Luckily, I've got one of Aryx's prints stored on my infoslate for access. I think if I can just ...' He opened several programs from his security toolkit and began rerouting their output. After a minute, he pulled up Aryx's print that had unlocked the infoslate – one with a large gash through a whorl, from an old work injury. 'Got it. I've put his right thumb print in.'

'What are you going to do about the other?'

'I don't have it on file. I'll have to use my left thumb.'

Karan grumbled. 'And did you mention that he's in a wheelchair?'

'Yes. I had to tick a box in the section about special requirements. I couldn't really leave it out.'

She frowned. 'Hmm. I don't suppose they'll check that when we go in to get the numbers. I'm sure it'll be fine – they'll just check on the day to put us in the correct starting area.'

'You sound like you know what you're on about. Have you done a marathon before?'

'Yeah, a couple of times.'

Sebastian allowed himself to relax. 'Good. I'd hate to send Aryx off without knowing what to expect.'

'You worry too much. He does endurance training. When he finished rehab, he didn't sit around feeling sorry for himself, you know.'

'I know that. That's why I'd rather have him do it. He had me running on a treadmill in full N-suit. I could have exploded!'

She pinched his thigh.

'Ow!'

'Haha! I can see that, sparrow-legs. Anyone would think all your training had been in low gravity. Don't you run on the treadmills in the outer levels of the station?'

He bit his lip. 'Um . . . no,' he said, completing the form.

She shook her head. 'You need some toughening up when we get back. You won't make a very good SpecOps agent if you have to go to a higher gravity planet.'

He rolled his eyes. 'Has Aryx been saying things to you?'

She smiled. 'He says things to me all the time, *especially* things about you.'

'Yes, well . . . ' He shoved the infoslate back into his rucksack and stood up. 'Let's get in there and collect the numbers.'

They joined the queue – a task made difficult by Sebastian's inability to discern exactly where it started and the kerbside mob ended, now that the crowds had started to grow further. Unfortunately, it ended around the corner of the building, fifty metres away.

After several minutes of being pushed on either side and from behind, a tension rose in Sebastian. He gripped his rucksack close to his chest and looked down, constantly checking for pickpockets.

'Seb, what are you doing?' Karan asked.

'Nothing,' he said without looking up.

'Well, stop it. You're making me nervous.'

He checked either side of himself again.

'You don't have any pockets to pick.' She tore the rucksack from his grasp. 'See? If someone really wanted to take it, they could.' She pushed the floppy canvas bag into his chest. 'Now get a grip!'

He frowned, although she did have a point. He stood on tiptoe. 'How much farther?'

A man, bobbing up and down in the crowd in an agitated fashion, as though desperately trying to find someone, caught Sebastian's eye. There was something familiar about him. 'What's his problem?'

'Whose?' Karan growled.

'That guy.' Sebastian jumped and attempted to point him out. 'The one bouncing around. Square jaw, short-shaved, dark brown hair.'

She squinted. 'Don't see him, sorry.'

He stood on tiptoe again but there was no sign of the agitated crowd member. 'He must have gone around the corner.'

'Don't sound so glum. At least it means the queue's moving.'

The column crawled around the bend and the peristaltic shuffle finally deposited the pair on the top step once again, while a constant stream, consisting of those who had gone in before them, came out of the left-hand door.

'Back so soon?' the doorman asked.

'Soon?' Sebastian said. 'It's taken ages for us to—' It probably wasn't worth complaining about the wait, and would only attract more attention. 'Yes, we decided to sign up for a good cause and registered for the marathon. Aryx Trevarian and Karan Tallin.'

The doorman tapped the names into his infoslate. 'Tallin? Haven't you already been in?'

Karan reddened. 'Ah, yes, but I realised my friend here hadn't signed up, so I went back to get him.'

'I see. It does say you haven't collected your pack. Fine, you can go in. The table to collect them from is on the right.' He stepped out of the way to let them pass. 'Try not to hold people up.'

'Niiice . . .' Karan breathed as they walked in and looked around.

'I thought you already came in?' Sebastian whispered.

'I did, but my attention was like a laser, focused on the guards, so I didn't take any notice of the decor. Now I can.'

Several square columns spaced evenly around the sparkling white marble floor of the large foyer gave an impression of decadent grandeur. To their left, a wide stairway laden with thick red carpet swept up to a broad landing and disappeared where it turned back to the first floor on either side. Above, an oculus punctured the ceiling through to the first floor. In the roof high above, a skylight let in light, removing the need for the artificial lights on the lower floor. Ahead, low temporary tables bordered the room, behind which stood attendants handing out large envelopes.

'Here's your entry pack,' the nearest attendant said to the woman queueing in front of them. 'It has your runner number, instructions for where to go on the day, and a voucher for a free breakfast in a restaurant of your choice beforehand.'

'That's bloody generous,' Karan mumbled.

The woman moved off and the attendant turned to Karan. 'Thumb print, please,' she said, holding out an infoslate. Karan pressed her thumb to the screen and the attendant picked up one of the envelopes from the stack and swiped it over the device. 'It has your runner number, instructions for where to go on the day, and a voucher for a free breakfast in a restaurant of your choice beforehand.'

Karan nodded and stepped back to allow Sebastian to take her place.

The attendant presented Sebastian with the infoslate.

He reached out with his right hand. Immediately someone jabbed him sharply in the back. Oh Gods, wrong hand! His forehead prickled with sweat and he quickly pressed his left thumb to the screen instead. The infoslate paused for several seconds while it made up its mind about his identity.

Blarp!

The attendant took back the device and frowned. 'Hmm . . .'

The hairs on Sebastian's neck prickled. 'Is there a problem?'

'Special requirements check. It says you're entering in a *wheelchair*?'

He shot a fiery glance at Karan.

She shrugged, wide-eyed.

'I-I will be,' he said, scratching his nose. 'I can walk short distances. It was too much hassle to use my chair in the queue outside. We caught a taxi to the door.'

'A taxi, here?' The attendant blinked and shook her head, apparently lost for words, and swiped the envelope over the infoslate. 'Here's your runner number, instructions—'

Nodding rapidly, Sebastian took the packet. 'Yes, thanks, I've already heard it. Thank you very much.' He grabbed Karan by the elbow and spun away from the table. *'They won't check it until the day,'* he hissed. 'You said you'd done this before.'

'I have,' she growled, 'but it's usually done at the Excel Centre in the docklands. This one is obviously different.'

'Well, lucky for me they didn't look into it further. It would have been a bit awkward if they'd checked to see if I'd got no legs!'

Even though the crowds hadn't cleared, it was good to be out of the building and back in the street. Karan led Sebastian down the steps and turned right at the bottom, away from the queue waiting to enter.

'Where to now?' she asked.

He scratched his head as he looked up and down the road. 'The marathon starts in Greenwich . . .' He stared in the direction of Big Ben and the Houses of Parliament. 'I guess we ought to find somewhere to stay on the other side of the river, maybe near Waterloo or—' The agitated man from earlier stood in the crowd on the far side of the road, staring right back at him.

Sebastian's blood froze. Now that he saw his features clearly, the man was familiar. He held his gaze. He looked exactly like Mikkael, his brother, right down to the square jaw. It was uncanny. No, it couldn't be – he died over three years ago! Sebastian blinked.

The man had vanished.

'Seb? What is it?'

'I thought ...' No. It was totally irrational. He shouldn't ... 'Probably nothing, but wait here!' He put his hand out to Karan in a "stay" gesture and launched himself into the crowd, getting lost in the mass of people before Karan could protest.

Chapter 14

Aryx set an alarm on his wristcom for 19.00 hours and settled down on the couch. Mrs Alvarez understood their need to leave and had said goodbye before going to bed for her afternoon nap.

Glad to once again be out of the influence of the station's nightmare-causing signal, he slept dreamlessly. He woke to the alarm, quickly freshened up and drew the curtains; the sun had already set and there was no sign of Mrs Alvarez being up and about yet.

He knocked on the door to Nick Alvarez's old room. 'Monica, are you ready?'

'Just a minute.' A moment later, the door opened to a pristine-looking Monica.

'How long have you been up? Have you even been asleep?'

'Only fifteen minutes – it doesn't take *every* woman two hours to get ready, you know!'

'Do you want something to eat first?'

She scowled at him. 'We have to get going, not to mention try to avoid whoever was following us this morning.'

'I don't need to be reminded.'

They left the Alvarez apartment in twilight with Monica scurrying ahead, clinging to street corners and peering around.

'You ought to wear the AR glasses,' Aryx said. 'Wolfram will be able to make out any movement better than you.' He took them off and waved them at her.

'Fine.' She rolled her eyes and put the glasses on over her own plain-glass frames. 'I guess you're right. There aren't many street lights.' She tiptoed to the corner and peeked around it. 'Yes, much better. Clear,' she whispered, and made her way up the darkened street.

Mindful of his casters clattering on the cobbles, Aryx wheelied after her, keeping to one side of the street in case he needed to tuck in beside a bin again. 'You should keep an eye out behind us, Nic. There's nothing to say he's definitely waiting at the ship. It could be a trick, like last time.'

She looked down the street behind them. 'It's fine. I am checking both ways.'

A painfully slow cat-and-mouse relay took them up the sloping streets through the chill night air. Whenever Monica slowed, Aryx took the opportunity to stop next to buildings and warm himself in the day's heat they still radiated.

Eventually, he recognised the abandoned building where he'd almost broken the window. 'We're nearly at the ship,' he whispered, gesturing for her to slow down. 'And this time, if you see the guy, bloody shoot the bastard.'

At the gate to the overgrown park she dropped into a crouch. She put a hand on the latch and slowly pushed.

The hinge gave a high-pitched squeal.

Something rustled in the bushes beyond the ship.

'Run!' Aryx rasped. '*Ultima Thule*, open doors.'

The CFD ramp materialised with an orange glow as the airlock doors opened and Monica set off across the grass at a run. A dark shape came around the aft section, approaching the ramp.

'Monica, look out!'

She drew her pistol and loosed a shot in the silhouette's direction. It ducked back from the ship as sparks flew inside the airlock, the bullet ricocheting around the storage compartment.

'Don't shoot anymore!' Aryx yelled, fearing she'd blast a hole in the vacuum-sealed carbyne hopper.

As the figure retreated, Monica bounded up into the warm glow of the interior. Aryx pushed as hard as he could, forcing his casters through the clumps of grass to either side of the overgrown path.

Before he got half the distance, the figure approached again.

'*Ultima Thule*, start engines. Emergency code Heimdall seventy-six!'

Yellow lights flashed as the large hoops of the Dyson thrusters swung out from the hull. With a dull *thunk*, the metal circle caught the figure's back and it staggered forward.

'Monica!'

She turned in the airlock and strode out of the ship. The fuzzy silhouette resolved in the light from the doorway: the leather-jacketed man – already on the ramp, and blocking Aryx's escape.

'Ramp, emergency off,' Monica shouted. The glowing force-field vanished and, as Leather Jacket fell, she struck out with a kick to his abdomen and he tumbled backwards.

'Ramp on!' Aryx said, surging forward.

Leather Jacket's head hit the underside of the force-field as he tried to stand.

Aryx drove himself up into the ship, over their prone assailant, and slammed a hand on the airlock's close button. The door shut with a *whump* behind him, and was immediately followed by loud thuds and muffled yelling.

'Can you fly the ship?' Aryx called to Monica, who was already up in the cockpit.

'Yes.'

'Then get us back to Cardiff, now! Orbital route. No scenic detour this time.'

The whine of the engines drowned out the shouts of their pursuer and the ship lifted off as Aryx reached the cockpit. He looked out of the window.

Leather Jacket Man staggered about, blasted away from the ship by the force of the Dyson thrusters, and he cast about, frustrated.

Aryx grinned. 'That'll teach you to mess with us.'

'*Hasta la vista*, baby!' Wolfram said, loudly.

Monica gasped. 'What the dickens?'

Aryx laughed. 'I was watching one of those old 20th-century movies with him the other day.'

'Which one?' She sat back and, now that they were safely out of Brasilia and heading into the upper atmosphere, released the controls.

'The one where an AI sends a liquid metal robot back in time to kill a woman before her son starts a resistance against it.'

'*Terminator 2*? Ahh. Hence the line. Crumbs, that's old, but how ironic. I'll admit, I hate films with time travel. It's all rubbish. I can't believe there are still people who think time is actually a thing. But, even though time travel isn't possible, and relies on stupid paradoxes, I suppose it still makes for good fiction.'

'I don't tend to think about it,' Aryx said. 'I just watch movies for the enjoyment, without picking them to pieces. Oh, and nice moves back there, by the way.'

'Thanks,' she said, drawing several stray hairs out of her mouth. 'I'm a woman of many talents.'

Aryx laughed. 'Yeah, but shooting isn't one of them!'

Sebastian pushed through the crowded streets, all concern for his rucksack's safety gone from his mind, even amid the crush of people. Everyone was taller than him, and always in the way. He caught a glimpse of the short-shaved head, only to be obstructed by a woman with a pushchair, which he tripped over before apologising.

His target disappeared but, as the crowd opened out for a moment, the head reappeared. He ran through the opening, closing the distance a little, only to encounter a large man whose sole focus was the unfeasibly large hotdog he'd bought from a nearby street vendor. The man turned towards Sebastian, hotdog raised, in time for Sebastian to collide with him, sending a tomato and mustard streak down his front.

'Bloody lunatic!'

'Sorry!' Sebastian shouted, leaping around him. Where was the Mikkael lookalike? 'Damn it!' His shoulders dropped.

The crowd surged and parted again. There, turning the corner!

He reached the corner only moments after the shaven-headed man disappeared around it. Turning sharply into the alley, he caught an elbow in the face.

'Shit, man! Are you okay?' A six-foot-something man with thickly matted blonde dreadlocks turned to face him, eyes wide.

The man's elbow had caught Sebastian's hand, which had in turn hit him in the nose and lip. 'I'b fide,' Sebastian said, bloodied hand held out. 'It was by fault.'

'You should sit down, dude, you don't look too good.'

Sebastian leaned to look around the towering figure while trying to stop his nosebleed. 'It's fine. I'm in a hurry.' Where was he? There was no sign of him at the end of the alley where it opened back up.

The man with dreadlocks fumbled in his pockets and drew out a tissue. 'Here, you're bleeding everywhere.'

'Thanks, but I'm fine, really.' Sebastian put the tissue to his nose and it came away sodden. He took a few steps. The world wobbled. No way he was catching up with the guy now.

'Do you want me to get a medkit?'

'No, I've got one in my bag. I'll be alright.' Sebastian turned and left the alley the way he'd come.

'Really sorry, dude. I hope you'll be okay!' the man called after him.

With his head pounding, Sebastian staggered back along the streets. He held out a hand to steady himself, keeping to the walls.

How had he got to this street? Perhaps he hadn't been paying attention during the chase – either that or he'd got a concussion and forgotten. He turned onto another street. Had he really come this way? Even the huge edifice of the panchurch was unfamiliar. How could he have missed that?

He sat down at the foot of the tall stone steps to mop up the rest of the blood from his nose. There was no point in getting lost further. He dabbed with the tissue again; at least the bleeding had stopped.

It was stupid for him to have chased after a stranger. His bloody nose was proof of that. Mikkael was long dead. It didn't matter how much Sebastian wished for him to still be around, nothing was going to bring him back; Janyce was always going to be without her husband, and Erik his father.

Sitting on the cold stone steps of the panchurch, he shivered and the hair on the back of his neck began to prickle. Slowly, he looked over his shoulder, up towards the heavy, wooden doors that stood open.

Behind a pillar, to one side of the arched doorway, stood a man in a long, black cassock, staring at him.

'Can I help you?' Sebastian snapped.

The priest whirled through the doors and pulled them shut.

He shifted uncomfortably and turned back to his self-pity as a hand clapped on his shoulder, stopping his heart mid-beat.

'Gods – Karan! Don't do that to me!'

'Jumpy, aren't we?' Her eyes widened. 'What the hell happened to you? Somebody beat you up?'

'I . . . got lost.' Chasing his dead brother, a figment of his imagination, didn't seem the right answer to give. 'I smacked into somebody's elbow. It was my own fault.'

She raised her arms from her sides and turned about. 'How'd you get lost? We're only round the corner from Great George Street.'

'I don't know. I think the crowd confused me.'

'Aryx will be pissed off if he's got to worry about you *and* the race. Who did you go chasing after?'

'Nobody.' Sebastian's neck prickled again. 'Listen, can we get somewhere more open? I don't like this place.' He stood and picked up his rucksack. As they walked off, he looked back.

The priest was at the top of the steps again, watching them as they walked away. Sebastian shivered.

'What *is* up with you?' Karan asked.

'Nothing. Really.'

'You're a rubbish liar.' She paused at the railings of Westminster Abbey. 'Tell me. What's wrong? You've been weird ever since the train.'

'This trip's brought up some bad memories, that's all. First, our conversation on the train, and then I thought I saw someone in the crowd that looked like my brother.'

'Mikkael?'

'Yes.'

'Right, but why did the panchurch freak you out?'

'Another reminder.' He leaned against the railings and heaved a sigh. 'About faith.'

'I noticed you don't really talk about yours.'

'Because I lost it. My grandfather brought me up following Ásatrú, and I believed in it completely as a kid. All that changed when my mother died.'

'What happened? No ...' She leaned against the railings next to him and squeezed his wrist. 'Don't talk about it if you don't want to.'

He drew in a deep breath. 'No, I suppose you're right, it might help to talk about it ...' He told Karan of how a hand on his back had urged the young Sebastian into the hospital room, where a strange, heavy scent of plastic hung on the air and his mother, Sigrid, lay on the bed dying.

He had never seen someone so ill. In fact, he couldn't remember being in a hospital because of any illness: they had visited when Mikkael broke his wrist falling from a climbing frame, but that had been a formality as the home medical kit had fixed everything and the doctors merely needed to take follow-up scans.

Frímann nudged him again and he stepped forward. He hesitated at a wheezing breath from the bed. 'Go on. It's only your mother.'

Sebastian shuffled forwards.

Sigrid's hair lay matted across her forehead, trailing across the pillow. Her face, while pale and drawn, still held its beauty.

'Mother, I'm here.'

Her eyes opened a crack.

'She knows we're here,' Frímann said, squeezing his shoulder.

'I know, *Afi*.'

'Don't call me that. She'd hate you not speaking Galac.'

'Why are you talking like she's not here?' Sebastian asked.

'She's leaving us.' His grandfather took the seat by the bed and the orthopaedic cushion gave a faint *whuff* as he sat. 'She'll be with the Gods soon.'

Sebastian chewed his cheek while he thought. 'Will she go to Hel if she dies of sickness? Will we see her again?'

Frímann smiled flatly. 'Who knows? I'd like to think she'd go to Valhalla – she's a fighter, your mother – but what's to say the dead can't go from one realm to another to visit, eh?' He snorted. 'Although, she paid more attention to Christianity, so she'll probably end up in their heaven, and we'll never see her again.'

'I . . . I don't understand.' Weren't his grandfather's Ásatrú teachings absolute truth? 'How could she go somewhere other than one of the nine realms?'

A fit of crackling coughs halted their conversation until the machines brought Sigrid's breathing back under control.

'I don't believe everything literally, Sebastian, and neither should you. Some of what I've taught you could simply be metaphor.'

'What's a metamore?' Sebastian asked.

Frímann stifled a laugh. 'Metaphors are where you say a thing to conjure images that mean something else. The stories are ways of teaching you about life. Sometimes you have to interpret them in your own way.'

'But how can you say she might go elsewhere?'

'I'm keeping an open mind. Nobody's ever come back from the dead to tell us what happens after death, and even if they did, we'd still expect answers from every religion before we could decide on a consensus of truth.'

Sebastian stared at his mother, paying attention to every rise and fall of her chest. Every soft, shallow gasp. Every pulse of the veins in her neck. He tried to send his prayers into those motions. She had to go with the Gods. How could someone who shone in the sun with such a light not deserve to join her ancestors? If even she could be turned away from the doors of Valhalla, there was no hope for anyone . . .

Now, as he sat on the bridge, a lump rose in his throat. 'And that was the end of her, and my belief, I suppose.'

Karan dabbed her eyes with the back of a hand. 'I'm sorry,' she said, rubbing Sebastian's shoulder.

He stayed silent for a minute. There wasn't much else to say. The quivering in his stomach began to move into his throat.

'You wanted her to go to your version of heaven but didn't think she would. I get that.'

'It-it wasn't just that. I expected some change, you know?' He stared at her. Did she understand? She just stared back, listening. 'I thought you'd *know* when someone died. Like you'd feel as though something had left the room. Like their life had left them … There was nothing like that. They turned off the life support according to her living will and she just sort of faded out. There wasn't a specific moment when I knew she'd gone. She stopped breathing, and then a minute or two later, she'd gasp again. It was drawn-out, and there was no point when I could say, "Yes, she's gone," and know that was it, that was the end, and we could … you know …'

Karan rubbed his back, wobbling him slightly. 'Yeah.'

They crossed Westminster Bridge, heading towards Waterloo, and he trudged, head down in contemplation, with a deep depression looming over him. 'I can't stand to lose anyone else.'

'Why do you think you're going to – I mean, in the short term? Everyone dies eventually.'

'I worry about Aryx. He said he's ill, whatever that means, and twice now I thought I'd lost him. First, when I ejected the pod on Achene to save him, and then on Sollers Hope. I thought he'd been killed by the explosion. I don't think I can go through that again.'

'From what he said, you haven't exactly given *him* an easy time worrying about you, either.'

Sebastian scratched his head and winced, recalling when he'd almost died due to a punctured pressure suit and Aryx had to revive him. 'You're right, I guess.' He retreated into his thoughts and they crested Westminster Bridge in silence.

'Seb, you've got to think though … It was the best death she could have hoped for. Your mother, I mean. To have you and your grandfather with her in the end.'

He stopped and locked eyes with Karan. 'You really think so?'

She nodded. 'I really do. Not many people get that chance. Too many of us die alone, even when we've got big families. But, on the other hand, you can't wrap people in cotton wool and monitor them constantly. You've got to give people space to be themselves, out of respect. They may still die alone, but they die free. And if you can't be there at the end to tell them you love them, let them know before. '"'Tis better to have loved and lost . . . "'

'Don't go quoting Shakespeare on me. I'm just sick of the way life works. I wasn't able to be there when my brother, father, or grandfather died. That's my biggest regret. Never saying goodbye.'

Karan rested with her back against the bridge and stared over her shoulder at the newly restored London Eye. The harsh wind drew a tear out and across her cheek. 'Did they know you loved them?'

'My grandfather did. He knew I adored him. You never tell your siblings you love them, but I always kept in touch with Mikkael. I don't think I ever said as much to my father, though. He was always too busy with work, but I know he was trying to provide a good life for us after my mother died.'

'I'm sure they all knew how much you cared for them . . . Anyway,' she said, slapping Sebastian's thigh and moving off, 'we need to go. We've got a hotel to check in to, otherwise we'll be sleeping on the street.'

Sebastian walked through the glass double doors into the Premier Inn-terstellar Hotel Waterloo and crossed the foyer's polished concrete floor to the counter, behind which stood a Human female in a smart purple suit.

'Hello,' he said. 'What rooms do you have available? Any that are wheelchair accessible?'

The receptionist checked her terminal. 'We only have one accessible room – a double – and one twin standard room available.'

'That's great. Can we have the accessible room, the double, and the twin?'

The receptionist's eyebrows knotted. 'I think you misunderstand. We only have the double and the twin.'

Sebastian nodded rapidly. 'Yes, yes, I get it. We'll take the accessible room and have the two others.'

'We have only one accessible room. The double. The twin room is the only other *standard* room available.'

He grimaced. 'I don't understand.'

The receptionist heaved a sigh. 'It's quite simple. You asked me two questions at the same time. One, what rooms are available, and two, whether we have an accessible one. We have only *two* rooms available, because of the marathon. One of them is wheelchair accessible, and it's a double room. The non-accessible room is a twin. Unfortunately, some of the old rooms are small and won't accommodate accessible features.'

'Oh.' Sebastian rubbed his head and turned to Karan. 'If the accessible room is a double, I don't think Aryx is going to want to share with either of you.'

'It wouldn't make me uncomfortable.'

Sebastian levelled his stare. 'I think it would make *him* uncomfortable. I'd feel a bit weird sharing a room with Monica, and I don't want to pay for four separate rooms.'

The receptionist rolled her eyes. 'I told you, we don't *have* four rooms available!'

He shot her a glance. 'I meant somewhere else! I'll book the rooms and we can all decide when we're together.'

'I'm booking you the two rooms,' she said, tapping away. 'Before you change your mind.'

Karan turned to Sebastian. 'What do you want to do until they arrive? I guess it'll take two or three hours to get here after they leave Brazil if they still have to use the monomag. Did they even say what time they were heading back?'

Sebastian shook his head. 'No. I thought they would have been here by now, but they could have got waylaid. I know Aryx was close to Alvarez's family.'

'Why don't you call to find out where he is?'

'I don't want to disturb him. I've got a better idea.' He drew the infoslate from his rucksack and began tapping away to check the location of the *Ultima Thule*. 'The ship's in low orbit . . . They must be on their way back. The crowds will have cleared in the city, so they'll be about two hours. I'll send a message with the hotel address.' He pulled out his grandfather's battered journal. 'I've still got plenty of this to read. What are you going to do?'

'It's too early to start drinking. I'll freshen up then make a call to the kids. It's probably the right time on Mars.'

She left Sebastian to sit alone in the hotel lounge, studying his grandfather's journal; it still made no sense to him, and much had been written in the strange symbols of a language he couldn't read. By the volume of work it contained, it was clear his grandfather had been doing a lot of research. His involvement with the Freemasons must have led to some kind of interest in magic, but whether the

Freemasons actually had direct knowledge of it was another matter, and not something the few coherent notes on the subject revealed.

Several pages of the floppy leather book were devoted to artefacts of some kind, possibly the acceleration nodes, as diagrams of pentagonal dodecahedra lay scattered throughout. Surprisingly, in more than one place, sketches of the frameworks were accompanied by instances of the alien text scrawled on musical staves. Could his grandfather have discovered some link between magic and superphase? If he had discovered a connection, perhaps he too had once been in contact with the Folians? No, it was a stupid thought. Surely the Folians would have told him if they had known of his grandfather.

Even though the cryptic text was impossible to read, there was something familiar in the pictures that accompanied it. Some represented astronomical data, others complex geometry, and yet others were like trees – not the Folians, but something more pictorial, abstract, religious, maybe from Norse mythology. What was it all about?

Two hours later, Karan flopped into one of the padded tub-chairs opposite, drawing Sebastian out of his pondering. 'I can't believe that woman,' she said.

He closed the journal and tucked it back into his bag. 'Which woman?'

'My freaking mother!' Her face puffed up like a beef tomato as she spoke. 'She's looking after the kids while Mark's off at a gallery showing his work. She hates me working away, I'm sure of it.'

'Oh.' Sebastian raised an eyebrow and turned away a little out of discomfort.

'I said to her that Mark's career as a sculptor can't earn enough money for us to live off – not on Mars, anyway – so I have to work. She seems to think *I* should be sitting around at home looking after the kids and Mark should have an office job. He'd hate that. I want him to enjoy his work, and he doesn't mind me being on Tenebrae, so we compromise. It's not like we have to ask her to look after the kids every five minutes, anyway . . .'

'I think most grandparents love the chance—'

'I told her! I said, "Mum, you come out with some of the most ridiculously outdated ideas. Sebastian told me about a colony that would suit you . . ."'

He took a breath to interject.

'I said, "They got there at lightspeed and they're about two hundred years behind the times!"' Her face began to lose its colour – probably from lack of oxygen.

Did he really want to know? He couldn't seem to stop himself. 'What did she say?'

'She went as red as a beetroot and hung up.'

He laughed. 'To think I wondered where you got your temper.'

The red tone returned to Karan's features. 'You cheeky b—'

'Aryx!' He shouted, jumping up.

Aryx wheeled in from the hotel foyer to the lounge area where they sat, Monica following closely behind. His eyes had dark marks in the corners.

'How are you?' Sebastian asked. 'You look worn out.'

Aryx rubbed his eyes. 'I'm fine, but it's been a *very* long day.'

Monica sat in a free tub-chair. 'I see somebody's already settled. Did you get any more information on the archive?'

Sebastian shook his head. 'What happened to you two? You've been gone ages.'

Aryx pulled his hands down his cheeks. 'I'd like something to eat first. We'll tell you about it over dinner. Just give me a minute. I need to get my drugs into the fridge. I've only got three doses left and they'll only stay cold in the mobipack for so long.' He checked his wristcom. 'Speaking of which, I need a dose now. Have you got rooms sorted?'

Sebastian nodded. 'I hope you don't mind sharing with me. I thought you'd feel a bit awkward sharing with one of the ladies.'

'Whatever. I just need to go.'

Sebastian handed him the key card. 'It's on the ground floor. Go up the corridor from reception, second on the left.'

Aryx disappeared and came back two minutes later with a pained expression.

'Are you alright?' Sebastian asked.

'Yeah, it just hurt a bit that time. I hope the shipment's in when we get back to the station. I can't afford to run out while we're here. It's not like I can get it over the counter.'

'We'll get back in time. It'll be fine. I assume you left Wolfram on the ship where he's safe?'

'Yes, yes. He's analysing the nightmare signal from the terminals. It'll take him a while. He said something about having to simulate the Human brain, which apparently takes a lot of "resources", whatever that means.'

'I imagine it would.' Sebastian gave a knowing smile. He certainly wouldn't like to put a bet on exactly how much processor power Wolfram would be using – he'd be likely to overheat if he wasn't careful.

Monica put a hand on her stomach. 'What are we doing about dinner? Like Aryx, I'm starving.'

'We passed a pizza restaurant on the way here,' Karan said. 'You guys love pizza, right?' she said to Sebastian and Aryx.

'I could do with something familiar,' Aryx said.

Sebastian nodded in agreement. The trip to London had so far been full of strange reminders, but nothing that had yet given him the comfort of home.

Aryx pulled up his collar against the chilly night air as the group made their way to the Thames waterfront.

Antonio & Q'rrtingé's, read the sign above the glazed restaurant frontage. Q'vani running yet another pizza restaurant?

He apprehensively wheeled up to the door, pushed it open, and pulled himself through. The others filed in after him, and a young waitress with long, black hair tied neatly into a ponytail approached from across the restaurant carrying an infoslate.

She smiled sweetly and asked, in an Italian accent, 'Do you have reservations?'

'No,' Aryx said, 'I don't see any real reason why I wouldn't want to eat here.'

She stared at him blankly for a moment.

He laughed. 'I'm joking. No, we don't have a reservation. Although,' he said, gesturing at the rough-hewn tables, all of which stood empty, 'I guess we don't need one?'

Her smile broke into a grin. 'You'd be surprised. This place is packed from about ten. Let me check the bookings. Four, is it?' She pored over the infoslate.

'The decor looks a bit dated,' Monica whispered to Karan.

Aryx looked around. True, the chunky, square wooden tables and puffy, sage-green leather benches were a little 20th century, and somewhat out of place in 23rd-century London, but it was comfortable – except for the cold draught that came in with them through the door.

'Ah,' said the waitress. 'We have a couple of tables free until nine thirty.' She glanced at her wristcom. 'Plenty of time. Would you like to sit by the windows?'

Aryx shuddered with remembered cold. 'Somewhere a bit warmer. It's incredibly chilly out there for October.'

'It's the jet stream, apparently. It's moved down again. Cold wind from Iceland, etcetera ... How about over here, towards the kitchen?' She gestured to a large round table in front of an archway set into a rustic red stone wall. Over the table stood a wooden pergola entwined with plastic vines, enclosing the area for a modicum of privacy. Warmth from the kitchen's fiery stone ovens radiated through the opening, bathing the group in a cosy glow.

Aryx relaxed a little. 'It's perfect, thanks.'

'Would you like menu cards or do you want it sent to infoslates?'

'I'm a bit traditional. Cards, please.'

She handed out the menus and left them to it. The others took their places on the large sofa-bench that curved around the table while Aryx parked at the end, released the mobipack's harness and shuffled across onto the comfortable padding. He desperately needed a change of seat.

Sebastian watched him with a furrowed brow. 'How are your legs?'

'Pain's gone for now.'

'And the implants?'

'Settling in fine, I think ... Aren't they, Monica?'

She nodded. 'They seem to be. You could do with eating more fresh vegetables, though. I'm concerned that Wolfram's design for the positioning modules might require more copper and iron to maintain.'

'Fine, I'll ask for extra pineapple.'

'So, what's everybody having?' she asked, looking around the table.

Sebastian glanced at Aryx. 'We'll have pizza. He never changes his mind about what he wants.'

'Pizza is so ... cliché,' Monica said. 'I'll have tortellini and salad. Anyway, why are so many pizza kitchens run by Q'vani?'

The chef, a four-armed insectoid, appeared behind the counter in the archway and chirped up. 'Four arm better for spin pizza dough.'

Monica folded her arms. 'What if people don't like thin pizzas?'

The Q'vani folded two of its arms in response, but continued to twirl the dough with the others. 'Thin pizza, pan pizza. All same to Q'vani. Q'vani not eat pizza.'

'How long did it take you to learn to spin them?' Sebastian asked.

'Two month. Many pizza end on floor. Pizza still used.'

'Eugh!' Monica said.

'Rrrt! Joke. What I say only joke. Throw away what go on floor.'

Monica shook her head. 'I'll never get Q'vani humour.'

'Most people don't,' Karan whispered. She turned to the others. 'I think I'll have the vegetarian lasagne. I don't want to be too bloated for tomorrow. Seb?'

'I'll have the *carne* pizza. Aryx will have his usual – ham and pineapple. With extra pineapple, and maybe a bit of spinach or salad to top up his iron intake.'

Aryx narrowed his eyes. 'Don't go changing my food. You know I don't like it.'

'Are you really that unadventurous with your tastes?' Monica asked.

'I like to know what I'm getting! Sebastian once convinced me that Q'orrig's on Tenebrae was Italian.'

'Haha!' Sebastian clapped his hands together. 'You should have seen his face. I said Italian-style *pizza*, not an Italian *restaurant*.'

The waitress returned to take their orders. 'This *is* an Italian restaurant. Q'rrtingé over there is head chef. He hatched in Italy, my father raised him and he took over after my father retired.'

'I was expecting the décor to be a bit more ... alien,' Aryx said.

She smiled again. 'A mistake many make.'

Fifteen minutes later, the food arrived and they ate.

'So, this race tomorrow ...' Aryx said between bites. 'What is it exactly? Do you have runner numbers?'

Sebastian put down the slice he was eating. 'Yes, I've got yours here.' He fumbled through his rucksack and pulled out a large envelope, from which he took a piece of flexible plaspaper.

Aryx stared at the numbers. This was no little race. What the heck were they thinking? He choked down his unfinished bite. 'Number 46720! It's a bloody marathon!'

Monica's mouth dropped open.

His head throbbed. 'Jeez, why the hell do you never tell me everything?'

'Sebastian, how could you be so irresponsible,' Monica said. 'Aryx has his health to think about.'

Aryx glared at her. Why couldn't she have just shut up about it?

'Sorry. I wouldn't ask him to do it if it wasn't necessary. It's for a charity, though.'

Aryx buried his face in his hands. 'For Christ's sake, you really know how to wind me up.' He paused to allow his blood pressure to come down a little and the pounding in his head to recede. 'What *is* the charity – not that I'm saying I'll do it.'

'The Veterans' Reconstruction Fund.'

Karan had pulled out Sebastian's infoslate and was studying it. 'I think you'd approve, Aryx. It's for soldiers who had irreparable wounds and were put into cryosleep in the early 21st century. The Fund helps front the cost of reviving and restoring them to health. Since the military's size was reduced, it got out of the responsibility of paying for the sleepers due to them being "past their reasonable life expectancy."'

The pulsing in Aryx's skull returned. 'What the— How the hell is that right? Past their life expectancy when they've been frozen for most of it? It's not like they've lived!'

'It's not right, or fair,' Sebastian said.

Karan continued. 'The entry fee we paid goes into the fund. Oh, and it looks like there's a special corporate sponsor who will donate double the entry fee to the fund for every runner supporting the charity that comes in under four hours and thirty minutes, which, incidentally, is the time we need to qualify for the evening ball.'

Sebastian clasped his hands on the table and leaned forward. 'Will you do it?'

'Mission aside,' Aryx said, slapping the table and startling the Q'vani in the kitchen into dropping the pizza he was throwing. 'Of course I bloody will!'

Chapter 15

Pushing aside the tent flap, the possessed Templar stepped out into the early morning sunlight. 'What is it?' he growled.

The bedraggled Second stood before him, bent over and breathing heavily, his clothes grimy and tattered. 'My Lord Gravalax . . . The Church,' he wheezed. 'They have commanded the Inquisition . . . to round up all those they suspect of practising witchcraft.'

'We know that already. How is this news?'

'They have stepped up their campaign . . . They are not as discriminating as before . . . Anyone suspected of dealing with magic or being involved with those who do, however insubstantial the evidence, is being put on trial and burnt.'

The Templar turned away and stared at the stained canvas of the tent in contemplation. In the early days, when he had possessed the Inquisitor, Gravalax had burnt many witches before he had understood their potential. 'What of the other Templars?'

'We stayed with them as long as we could,' the Second said, his breath returning. 'The Church had them raiding mines, looking for Freeminers and Freemasons. A group was found and incarcerated.'

The Templar turned to face him. 'How many?'

'Seven in total. One mason and six miners.'

'Good. Are we to assume that the Church is still unaware of our presence?'

The Second nodded. 'There have been words spoken about us, but the Church knows nothing. To them, we are little more than a rumour.'

'Excellent,' the Templar said with a nod.

The Second remained.

'There is something else?'

'Yes, my lord. The Templars were redirected after the last raid.'

'To where?' The host's blood pressure rose. 'Do not make us ask you every question in turn.'

'They have gone south, under orders, to cross the ocean and venture into the lands of the Saracen.' The Second hesitated, but quickly continued. 'The Church claim there are heretical writings that tell a different story of the nature of the heavens and the elements, and speak against the word of God.'

'Science.' The Templar rubbed his chin – the gesture seemed to help focus the host's biology on conscious thought. 'Unfortunate that such writings will be obliterated. To have accessed them would have advanced our cause but, if it keeps the Church's attention from us, it is a loss we must accept.'

The Second's mouth pulled to one side, and he stared at the ground. 'What is it? Speak!'

'We thought you would want someone to salvage the writings. We instructed one of the Templars loyal to you to go on the crusade.' He flinched as though about to be struck.

'For once, you have exceeded expectations. We are pleased.' The Templar rubbed his chin again. 'You may have given us an idea. We could consider capturing those suspected of witchcraft on the Church's behalf. Yes, do that. Round up the witchcraft users before the Church interferes with their development. Test them. Those confirmed to have genuine talent can be used to bring others into this world. It is well that we have followers among the Humans, but we need more of our fellows to truly advance here.' The Templar allowed his voice to quieten, almost speaking to himself. 'Yes ... the idea is a sound one.' He raised his voice. 'Find the strongest and most potent. Offer them safe harbour. Do this in secret. We will be the society of Illumination. We will give them safe harbour from the Church and, in turn, we will use them.'

Chapter 16

Aryx leaned back on the comfortable seating. The murmur and chatter of customers that now filled the restaurant made him drowsy, and he listened to the conversation with his eyes closed while the others finished their meals.

'The flight over the Amazon was amazing,' Monica said. 'Have you ever been there? The trees are beautiful.'

'If you like *that*,' Sebastian said, lowering his voice, 'you'd love Chopwood. It's almost entirely forest.'

'Really? The woodland I saw coming into London looked impressive, especially with the spires behind. Is it like that?'

'No, it's mostly log cabins in one big clearing.'

'On the subject of trees, Aryx was telling me earlier about the Folian influence through history.'

'Shh! Keep your voice down ... He told you everything?'

At the mention of his name, Aryx spoke, but kept his eyes closed. 'Wolfram thinks we can trust her, and I was telling her how nuts you are for believing everything you're told by aliens.' He laughed.

'I don't believe *everything*. They showed me visions of their involvement in Earth's history, but it's not just that – I wouldn't blindly accept visions as literal truth. My grandfather's journal contains references to Norse mythology, along with pictures of acceleration nodes – at least that's what I think they are – so he obviously believed there was a connection, and more to myths and legends than just stories.'

'Nodes? Really?' Monica whispered. 'How unusual.'

Aryx opened his eyes. 'Well, it *would* be unusual if he hadn't been nuts when he wrote it.'

Sebastian jabbed him in the ribs. 'I don't think he was, even though

I can't understand any of this writing.' He pulled out the journal from his ever-present rucksack. 'I think it might be an alien language. I haven't had it analysed yet because I don't trust the system enough to scan it for computer translation.'

Monica held out a hand, palm up, and wiggled her fingers. 'Let's see. I'm pretty good with languages.'

Sebastian gave her the book and Aryx leaned over. The open pages were covered in groups of long horizontal lines with squiggles sitting at different points along them.

Monica stared at it for only a second before she breathed in sharply and started to laugh. 'How long have you been trying to decipher it?'

'About three weeks.'

She cackled. 'You silly man! You don't need to use the station's systems to translate it. You can do this on an infoslate, or with AR glasses.'

'You know what it is?'

She continued, 'It sometimes depends on the individual ...'

'What is it?'

'... and on whether they have developed their own particular style, and which system they're using—'

'*What?*' Sebastian's voice was at breaking point. 'Please, tell me what it is!'

Aryx put a hand over his mouth. Oh, the sadistic pleasure Monica seemed to derive from knowing something Sebastian didn't!

'It's written in shorthand!'

Karan sniggered.

'By the Gods.' Sebastian clamped his hands over his head. 'I feel so stupid.'

'It happens to the best of us,' Aryx said. 'It's just that you don't take it too well.' He yawned. 'I hate to love you and leave you, but I'm worn out, and apparently I have a marathon to run in the morning.'

'Do you want us to come back to the hotel with you now?'

'No, I'll be fine. Come back when you're ready.'

Aryx said goodnight and made his way to the hotel. As he pushed along the darkened streets, the hair on the back of his neck prickled. He turned at the sound of footsteps behind him, but it was just a priest crossing the street.

After making sure the mobipack was safely locked away in the hotel room's secure cabinet, he showered and went to bed. It wasn't the same as the bed he was used to on Tenebrae, and he had to bunch the duvet up between his legs to keep himself from rolling over, but within minutes he was fast asleep.

Out of consideration, Sebastian left the light off when he got back to the room. In the gloom, he could barely make out the mound that was Aryx under the thin duvet as he tiptoed around to the far side of the bed. Monica had kept him up late, talking about their experiences in Brazil, while Karan had gone to bed at roughly the same time as Aryx to wake refreshed for the day ahead.

It would be nice to sleep undisturbed, away from the influence of the signal on the station. The day's events had taken their toll and, after stripping off and leaving his clothes in a heap next to the bed, he virtually passed out next to Aryx.

In his dream, Sebastian was back on Flat Holm island, standing in the freezing winds blowing across the Severn. Even his collar, turned up around his neck, did little to stop the biting wind. If only he'd been wearing his N-suit, he might have been warmer.

Several large tan-coloured horses with white manes roamed across the short grass. One of them made its way towards him.

'Shoo! Stay back!' he shouted with arms outstretched. 'I don't like horses! Go away!'

The animal continued to advance. He tripped over something soft. Bodies. The bodies of his dead relatives, trampled by hooves. He turned towards the thin wire mesh fence surrounding the monomag station. Behind him the slow thud of the horse's hooves sped up.

He ran, but the horse overtook him easily, steering him away from the fence. How was he going to escape? It was almost twenty metres to the station.

He feinted to the left, expecting the horse to match his movement. Instead, the creature anticipated it and lunged to the right, bringing him within inches of its toothy, flapping mouth. A mouth that dripped with blood.

'Get away!' he yelled. The metal of a monomag train glinted in the distance.

He backed away from the horse. Perhaps it wouldn't know which way he was going to go. The twitter and chirrup of the monorail track grew louder. The train would be here any second.

The magnetic induced vibration of the tracks reached a crescendo as the train passed, bringing a vortex of air, blasted out by the Dyson thrusters.

Startled by the maelstrom, the horse reared up, pawing at the air, its eyes glowing malevolently. It came down on Sebastian and he screamed.

He woke with a start, juddering the bed with a kick. The room was cold and the mattress chilly as he moved his legs around; large and empty, but something warm lay beside him, radiating a comforting heat. He rolled over and draped his arm across the warm body and the chill began to recede.

Aryx woke to the movement of Sebastian getting into bed. His own sleep had been disturbed, largely from worrying about the marathon ahead, and it was hard enough to get back to sleep even without further disruption. He lay in the dark, staring at the wall.

Seeing Mrs Alvarez had brought back memories – some good, some bad. When he left Brazil, it was as though he'd left a chunk of himself there. Alvarez had been a big part of his life: he'd been a good commander, even during events on Cinder IV, and he was the only person who had stuck by him through his rehabilitation. But with his own family gone, what was he going to do now? There wasn't anyone to love him, nobody he could care for. All he had was his career and the development of the mobipack, for what that was worth. Monica was right; it wasn't enough to keep him going.

As he lay awake, the air cooled and he shivered.

The bed moved again. A body pressed against his back and an arm draped over him unexpectedly.

He smiled at the warmth and closed his eyes.

Of course, he wasn't alone. He had friends, and he had Sebastian.

Aryx pushed up the slow hill towards Greenwich Observatory, sur-rounded by a constant stream of marathon runners. Karan jogged beside him, followed by Monica and Sebastian, who carried the mobi-pack. Aryx looked back several times, and each time Sebastian puffed his cheeks out. 'Is it too heavy for you?' he asked in a mocking tone.

Sebastian nodded.

'You're so unfit.'

'This is why you're doing it,' he said between laboured breaths. 'I can manage a few miles, but more than that, no chance.'

Monica jogged on until she drew level with Aryx. 'Are you *certain* you're okay to do this?'

He nodded.

'Okay, just be careful. Don't overdo it. While you run, Sebastian and I are going to check out the asylum.'

'What asylum?'

'Didn't he tell you?'

He glared at Sebastian. 'No, he hasn't mentioned an asylum.'

'Wolfram sent him a message saying he'd tracked down a reference to Alicia Maline, right here in London, so we're going to check it out. I'll keep an eye on you remotely with Sebastian's infoslate. He's programmed it to hook into your wristcom, which will relay your vitals and telemetry from the nanobots in your legs.'

'Oh, I was hoping you'd both come to watch me. You could follow with the race number tracker, just like everybody else.' Aryx sighed. 'Such is life ... Although, I don't know what you expect to do monitoring me remotely, Nic. If I have a problem, the medics will deal with it. You couldn't get to me for medical assistance any quicker with the roads closed.'

'Of course I don't expect to be able to get there. We'll be the opposite side of the city, on the outskirts. However, I can send commands to the nanobots to do minor things.'

He grumbled. It was bad enough they'd convinced him to have nanobots in the first place, let alone have them poking around inside him doing things without his knowledge. He slowed and beckoned Monica closer. Sebastian stopped and tilted his head.

'Go on with Karan,' Aryx said, waving him on. 'I'll catch up with you in a minute.'

Sebastian sneered and strode on ahead. Monica bent down.

'The nanobots won't have an effect on the virus,' Aryx said.

'I know, but if there is a problem, they can be configured to help alter your body chemistry a little. Since you have enough drugs, you should be fine for a day or two anyway, right?'

'Yeah. Just don't let Sebastian know about it. His mission's too important to let my health get in the way and if he finds out, he won't let me go anywhere.'

'I'm more worried about how this marathon's going to affect *you*. You could have said no. I'm sure Sebastian would have found another way into the archive.'

He gripped Monica's forearm. 'I'll be fine, really. I'm tougher than you think.'

'If you're certain . . .' She smiled weakly.

'I am. Just make sure he doesn't break the mobipack, or I'll bloody kill him.'

The procession reached the top of the hill beyond Greenwich Observatory, where a staging area had been set up in front of a large red and white inflatable archway. Sebastian and Monica peeled away from the throng, leaving Aryx and Karan as low temporary fencing funnelled the participants into their respective starting points. Thankfully, the ground had changed from a cobbled pathway to a tarmac road, making pushing easier. It wouldn't do to be tired before they had even begun.

'All set?' Karan asked, jogging on the spot. A fine drizzle started to fall, and her thin Lycra top steamed in the cold air.

'Almost ready.' Aryx held up a roll of black self-adhesive fabric tape. 'Can you give me a hand with this?'

'Sure.' She crouched and wrapped the support tape around his wrists.

'Put some down the side of my forearms, too. I can't afford to injure my hands.'

'*Runners for the green start are advised to prepare now,*' blared a loudspeaker. '*The race begins in ten minutes.*'

Aryx clapped his hands together and blew into his palms. 'Right! Get ready!'

'You almost sound excited,' Karan said.

'Hah! Well, I'm looking forward to seeing whether you can keep up with me.'

'Sure I can.'

He straightened up the runner number on the front of his vest and refastened the pins. 'I don't think you'll keep up going downhill.'

'Your friend won't, but *I* will.' A slim woman with short dark spiky hair sat opposite him in a wheelchair with a sporty white frame. Her runner number read 58842.

'Hi. You've done this before, then?' he asked, taking note of the name below her number, *Judie 'the monster' Sorenson.*

Judie nodded vigorously. 'A couple of times. I've done a lot of smaller races, too. I've got twenty medals at home. Nice wheels, by the way.'

Aryx glanced down at the flexible carbon-fibre arms that formed his wheels' self-contained suspension. 'They're an old Loopwheels design. I'm thinking of modifying them so they collapse when I don't need them.'

She looked at Aryx's stumps and frowned. 'You haven't got any legs, so why *wouldn't* you need them?'

He laughed. 'I sometimes use prosthetics,' he said, while trying to gauge her physique. Her arms were slim but powerful, her legs jittered and she fidgeted with contained energy. 'I take it you're quite competitive, then?'

'I'll run rings around you. You look like you're more used to lifting weights than racing.'

'I've had plenty of practice doing laps of Tenebrae.'

'The space station that had a tsunami? Impressive, but try *real* terrain. I've been up hills you wouldn't believe!'

Aryx cast his mind back to climbing the cliffs on Achene. Better not to mention *that*. 'I've been up one or two. The one getting up here's a killer, but I still think I could give you a run for your money.'

A flicker of nervous tension played across Judie's thin mouth, which twisted into a smile as she turned away. 'We'll see ... We'll see,' she said, wheeling off into the crowd.

Karan leaned down and whispered, 'Why was she in a wheelchair? There's not a lot of need for one nowadays, is there?'

Aryx wrinkled his nose. 'I don't know. I didn't ask.'

'Sorry. It's just that you're the only person I've ever seen in one.'

'Well, get used to it. I'm not intending on going anywhere.'

The speakers blared, '*Race starting in one minute.*'

Sebastian wiped the condensation from the taxi window as it stopped next to a long, red-brick wall. The bricks themselves had crumbled in places, and mortar had fallen onto the pavement along almost the entire length.

'Is this the place?' Monica asked.

'It's the address Wolfram gave me.'

'How do we get in?'

'I'm not sure. Taxi, take us a bit farther around.'

The vehicle moved off, crawling nearly a hundred metres before turning right onto a side road. A minute later, it passed a pair of double gates mounted in a brick archway covered with vines. The opening was wide enough to fit two cars through easily.

'Stop here.'

The taxi came to a halt. As they stepped out onto the pavement, Sebastian waved his wristcom over the payment terminal and winced at the cost. 'Have a nice day,' the taxi's TI said, and drove off.

Sebastian turned up the collar of his jacket. 'Gods, I wish I had my N-suit on.'

Monica laughed. 'I thought you were from Iceland?'

'I haven't been there for a while. It's not like resistance to the cold is bred into you. It *is* possible to get used to a warm environment, you know. I hope Aryx is warm enough.'

She smiled and glanced at Sebastian's infoslate clipped to her belt. 'Aryx is fine. I think these are probably ideal conditions for a marathon.'

Sebastian placed a hand against the bars of the gate and pushed. They squeaked open an inch and stopped with a jangle: an electronic lock was fastened around the central railings on a chain. 'Pass me that, would you?'

Monica handed him the infoslate and he began tapping away. 'Break into places often?'

'Ah, no. I have to design locking software for the most part. Some of the locks I've come across lately have been rather primitive.'

She leaned a shoulder against the wall. 'That doesn't answer the question.'

'I only break into places in the line of work, and then only when absolutely necessary.'

She stuck out her bottom lip and nodded. 'Oh, of course.'

He frowned at her. 'Yes, of course! What do you think I am? Now stop it, I'm trying to concentrate.' He returned his attention to the infoslate. 'I've had to do it to save lives,' he muttered. 'Anything less would be unethical.'

Click. The lock popped open.

'Finally.' He unthreaded the chain, pushed the gate open and stepped through with Monica close behind, then refastened the lock behind them.

'Why did you do that?'

'I don't want anyone to know we're here. They'll notice if the chain is off. Anyway, I know the code now so it's easy to get out.'

A long driveway led from the gate, deeper into the asylum grounds. Much of the tarmac had spalled, allowing weeds to grow through in large clumps. To either side of the roadway grew long grass and tangled messes of brambles with sporadic groups of large, naked oak trees – the unseasonal cold having stripped the branches early. At the far end of the drive stood an imposing centuries-old four-storey building. The windows were narrow and uninviting, almost defensive slits rather than apertures to let in light. All the windows on the ground floor were boarded, while many on the upper floors had been broken, exposing wire mesh behind dark, jagged openings.

Sebastian shivered. Imagining how the place would have looked with neatly trimmed lawns and hedges wasn't enough to banish the apprehension brought on by the neglected building's appearance. There was something strangely familiar about it.

Monica strode off along the broken tarmac towards the asylum and stopped when Sebastian didn't immediately follow. 'Are you alright?'

'This place reminds me of where they put my grandfather. Why did they dump people in creepy old buildings when they needed help?'

'I'll admit it's not very pleasant, but why build something new if it's perfectly serviceable?'

Sebastian shrugged. 'Doesn't look like this place has been serviced in a long time.'

'When was Alicia Maline here?'

'From some time late in 2062, if the records are correct. Hold on.' He checked the infoslate. 'This place was closed down earlier that year. It doesn't make any sense. There must be a mistake with the dates.'

The tarmac ended several metres from the building and the pair approached the towering edifice of the asylum across a leaf-strewn stretch of pea gravel that *scrunched* softly underfoot. Leaf litter and mould had built up over the intervening centuries since the facility's closure to create a spongy black matting in places. Rising out of the mass, a set of deep stone steps led up to the entrance.

In contrast to the building's other openings, the main double doors stood unhindered by boarding of any sort. Another lock, different to the one on the gate and mounted over the greening bronze doorknobs, indicated the place was most definitely out of bounds to the public.

'Keep a look out,' Sebastian said, setting to work on the lock.

Monica shook her head. 'You're only expecting someone to spot us now, after we walked here in the open?'

He gave her a sidelong look. 'Don't get smart. Hmm, no wireless.' He tugged open a tiny rubber cover on the side of the infoslate and drew out a slender optical cable, which he plugged into the lock.

Monica folded her arms and leaned back against the doors. 'What do you think we'll find in here?'

'To be honest, I have no idea. A more interesting question would be what did *Duggan* expect to find in here after two hundred years?'

She stared off into the distance. 'Do you think he would have locked the gate behind him if *he'd* opened it?'

'He might be old, but he's not stupid. And what's to say he came through that gate? There might be a rear entrance somewhere.' The infoslate rapidly yielded the locking code. '718926,' Sebastian said, punching in the code on the lock's keypad. It gave a click and Monica nearly fell backwards into the building.

He caught her by the arm. 'Careful!'

White and green glazed floor tiles rapidly disappeared into the darkness, and the light from the doorway reflected off glazing several metres away on the far side of the entrance lobby.

Sebastian stepped in and Monica followed.

Clunk, click. The door closed behind them, plunging them into darkness.

'Damn, I didn't think to bring a torch,' he said.

'Are you always so utterly unprepared?' Monica's footsteps retreated and the door rattled. 'Oh, darn,' she whispered, her voice tremulous. 'We're locked in!'

Chapter 17

In the darkness, the skin on Sebastian's neck crawled. This was too much like the nightmares – at least the parts he could recall, like being plunged into the dark when his lamp went out.

Without his sight, other sensations came to the fore. The air smelt acrid: something had recently burnt. Something crunched, gritty, underfoot.

'Monica, come over here,' he whispered. The darkness smothered his voice.

'I hate the dark,' she said. 'Oh, wait, I think I can see something. Come on!'

A shape, formed of several floating luminous specks, moved along beside him and he recoiled as she grabbed his hand and tugged. After several shuffling footsteps, he stubbed his toe. 'Ow!'

'Stairs here, sorry.'

'I think those bits in my eyes are still working. I can make you out, sort of. I just can't see anything else yet.'

'Another step here. If it's still happening when we get back to the station, I'll have to take another look. It can't be good to have even a few particles left in them. Watch out – landing.'

He faltered, almost missing the step. Anticipating another, he stumbled, flailed, caught a handrail, and swung around the turn in the stairs, his fall halting as his head lightly touched the corner of a step. 'Shit! That was close.'

Monica clomped up the steps after him and helped him up. 'Don't kill yourself, for goodness' sakes.'

A second later, the door out of the stairwell swung open into a corridor running left to right.

'I'm an idiot,' he said. 'I just realised I could have used the infoslate as a torch.'

She groaned. 'Me too. Too late now.'

Finally able to see, he followed her up from the landing and out into the corridor.

Broken glass littered the cracked and crazed floor tiles of the hallway. Tiles also covered the walls to shoulder height, and were trimmed with a strip of green-glazed ceramic moulding along the top. The tiling had fallen from the wall at several points, where dark patches of damp crept down from the ceiling. Ivy climbed in through broken windows, covering the wire mesh and blocking out much of the light. Three white-painted doors punctuated the right-hand wall opposite the windows. Similar doors stood at either end of the corridor.

Sebastian shuddered at the sight of the vegetation. It was like being trapped in a giant tropical aviary. 'The door downstairs locked behind us, right?' he asked.

Monica nodded.

'So, couldn't Duggan be stuck in here, too?'

'I suppose so, unless he found another way out ... That is, if he even came into the building.'

He stared intently at her. 'You were followed in Brazil. Do you think the same people could have followed Duggan?'

'It is possible. But the man following Aryx and me was Arab-looking, and nothing like the police officer Garvin said visited Sollers Hope.'

'Hmm ... I don't think he was really with the police. His behaviour didn't sound like that of a legitimate police officer, threatening the colony the way he did.'

'Either way, we ought to keep our wits about us.' Monica rattled the handle of the nearest door. 'Locked.' She moved along the hall and tried the second to the same effect.

'I'll try this end,' Sebastian said, retreating down the corridor to try the door behind him. It moved with little pressure. 'Mine's open.' He tentatively pushed it wider and peered through. Damp, musty air hit him and he clamped his mouth shut as he pulled the door closed. 'It smells awful in there, like something's rotting.'

'We ought to check it out. There might be records in there.'

'Ugh, really? Fine.' He pulled his collar up over his mouth and stepped in.

Light from a grimy clerestory window gave an algae-green cast to the room. Plasterboard had caved in at one corner of the ceiling and flopped down, leaving a damp, ragged tear, and a steady *drip-drip* came through the hole. Beneath the hole sat a rotting wooden desk covered in a mush of what might once have been paper. Several other desks lay strewn about, some missing legs and leaning at odd angles, but there was nothing resembling readable material.

'This is useless,' he said, letting his arms drop to his sides.

'Don't be such a defeatist! This is only the first room we've checked. There could be records in the locked ones. Hold on, what's that?' Monica pointed to a metal filing cabinet, standing in the shadows of one corner. She went over and tried to pull it open. 'I don't suppose you carry lock picks?'

Sebastian shook his head and glanced at the infoslate hanging at his belt. 'Not for mechanical locks.' He unhooked it and offered it to her. 'Isn't it time for you to check on Aryx? I think the marathon will have started now.'

'Okay, then we'll look for the keys to the cabinet.'

Aryx pushed off the starting line with Karan jogging alongside. He'd wished – perhaps with rose-tinted glasses – for a better view of proceedings. Given that he hadn't been told how big the marathon was beforehand, he had no idea what to expect and, with so many taking part, the view, it turned out, consisted mostly of buttocks bobbing up and down at eye-level.

'This is awful!' he shouted to Karan over the din of the music from the starting gate.

'What?' she shouted back.

'Never mind!' It's not like he needed to see much, after all: as long as he knew where the kerb was and whether there was an obstruction coming, he'd be fine. 'Keep your eyes open for road sleepers!'

Karan pointed to her ear. 'I can't hear you over the music.'

'I said, look out for—' He jerked his wheels up into an emergency wheelie as a wide band of tarmac, raised three inches from the road, loomed out from beneath the runners' feet ahead of him. 'This is exactly what I was saying,' he said through gritted teeth.

The painfully loud rendition of "Chariots of Fire" eventually faded, to be replaced with the steady susurration of feet pounding the pavement out of time. Occasionally, a rippling beat rose out of the murmur as runners unconsciously fell in sync with each other, the soles of their feet flashing in unison, only to rapidly lose the hypnotic pattern to randomness.

The initial excitement of the marathon faded after only four miles: the trees of Greenwich had long since passed and been replaced with houses, of which Aryx could only see the roofs above the other runners. How could he cope doing twenty-six miles like this, with nothing but backsides and no scenery? It didn't seem possible.

'Go Aryx!' someone shouted from the crowd. It wasn't a voice he recognised. Was there another Aryx somewhere?

'Nice one, Aryx!' shouted another.

'You're doing well, keep pushing!'

Who were these people? Certainly nobody he knew expected him to be there. As he looked at the string of passing onlookers, he recognised none of them. But … his runner number, it had his name on it. The crowd were calling *his* name. They were cheering *him* on!

Someone slapped him on the back as they ran by. 'Good job, mate!'

'I think you're impressing people,' Karan said.

Aryx smiled. Perhaps he could do it. Then again, it wasn't like he had a choice. He *had* to do it, or they'd never get into the Witness Protection Archive.

The road took a gentle downward slope as it turned back towards the city, passing by houses, then small shops, and the odd church here and there.

'How are you doing?' Karan asked.

His heart rate wasn't particularly high, the tarmac was relatively smooth – obviously rougher than the smooth floors of Tenebrae, but not unmanageable – and the air was clear and easy to breathe. 'I'm doing fine. I need a drink, though.' He reached for the water bottle clipped to the back of his chair and immediately veered off to one side. He abandoned the attempt and corrected his path just in time to avoid colliding with another runner. 'I think I'll wait a while.'

Karan leaped into the air while she ran. 'I can see there's a downhill bit coming up. Perhaps you ought to wait until then.'

The road gradually levelled out and, as Karan predicted, began to fall into a gentle downward slope again.

He made another try for the bottle, and this time managed to correct his direction by gripping one handrim and pressing down on the other wheel with his elbow while he drank. He had to drink quickly: the heat generated by the friction began to burn his arm after only a few seconds. He nearly dropped the bottle as his casters flicked over a rubber strip that trailed across the road.

'They should have made the timing detectors thinner,' he said. 'I don't see why we had to have tracking chips. They could have tracked our wristcoms or something instead. Race integrity, I suppose, but it's still annoying.'

Karan nodded, but he wasn't sure she'd even heard what he'd said. She started to lag behind as he accelerated downhill. 'Don't go too fast!' she called.

He used the downhill stretch as an opportunity for a little rest, applying pressure to his handrims to slow down. 'Can't you keep up with me?'

'Oh, I can, but what's the point of wearing myself out so soon?' she said. She didn't seem too out of breath. 'Anyway, there's something happening up ahead.'

Aryx leaned around the runners; their numbers had thinned, but it was no use. 'I can't see. What kind of something?'

'People have started to slow down.'

'Oh, for crying out loud, what's happening?'

'I don't know. Maybe a collapsed runner?'

'Well, try to avoid the blockage. Which side is it?'

'On the left, near a gap in the barrier. I guess it could have been someone trying to cross the road.'

He altered course a little in the hope of being on the opposite side of the road by the time they met the obstruction. A metallic clattering from behind caught his attention. 'What's that?'

Karan glanced back. 'I think it's that woman you were talking to earlier.'

'Judie?'

'That's the one.'

'Bloody hell, if she overtakes me I'll never live it down!' He hunched and began putting his back into his movement, pushing with longer strokes now that the road had levelled out again.

'Stick to this side, Aryx, the blockage is just ahead.'

The clattering of caster bearings grew louder as Judie closed in.

'Sir, you must stay back,' a woman shouted from somewhere ahead. 'Spectators have to stay behind the barrier.'

'I've got to get through,' came a gruff reply. There was something familiar about the voice.

'Karan, what's going on?'

She bounced momentarily. 'Someone trying to get into the road. Oh, crap! He's pushed her over.'

A collective gasp rose from the spectators and runners to their left, but their numbers easily obscured the cause of the disturbance.

'You must get back behind the line, Sir!' The shout was quickly followed by the *click-click* of a radio. 'Requesting assistance . . .'

'Aryx! Aryx Trevarian!'

The voice was not in the tone of a cheery onlooker. It was a gruff voice. He'd heard it before. The day before.

In the streets of Brasilia.

Chapter 18

Sebastian waited while Monica checked Aryx's status on the infoslate. After a long moment, she said, 'He's fine. His health is about normal for what you'd expect, aside from a slight imbalance in a few hormones, and his heart rate has been pretty constant, barring— Oh!'

Sebastian became light-headed and he let out the breath he'd been holding. 'What is it?'

'His pulse and adrenaline levels just jumped up considerably. He's probably come to a bit of rough terrain. I can't imagine it's anything to worry about, but I'll keep an eye on it.'

'Alright. Let's see if we can find some keys for this place.' He left the musty, rotting room and headed back to the stairwell with Monica. 'From what I recall of old movies, lots of these places kept keys in an office near the foyer. I saw some glass downstairs – that could be the office.'

He pushed open the door to the stairwell and the acrid tang of a burnt-out room hit him. It was surprising how strong it actually was in contrast to the damp smell. 'Can you use the light on the infoslate?'

She tapped the screen and a bright light shone from one corner. Aiming it down the darkened stairwell, she moved in beside him.

Vertical stripes and jagged step-shadows slid across the wall. The light cast the foyer below into an even blacker abyss as they descended.

'Over here,' she said, dragging him towards a reception bar glazed with Georgian wired glass. 'This must be where they kept the keys.'

Fortunately, the door to the enclosure stood ajar. The infoslate light immediately fell upon a small square cupboard, roughly two inches deep, mounted on the far wall. Monica ran over and opened it, leaving Sebastian standing in the shadows.

Inside the wall cabinet hung a bunch of small, glinting metallic objects, all roughly circular with long serrated blades.

'It looks like we've found our keys,' she said, taking them all from the rack.

'I wouldn't have known what I was looking for. I've never seen one close up.'

'Well, isn't it a good job you brought along an archaeologist?' She laughed and the light flitted about the room until she stopped abruptly, eyes wide. 'What on Earth happened there?'

Sebastian followed her gaze to the surrounding enclosure where a spider web of cracks, radiating from a central point in the thick wired glass, sparkled in the torch light. He put a hand against it; it bulged towards him, and the counter below was scattered with several small chips of glass.

'It broke from the other side,' he said. 'It would have taken something heavy, maybe the weight of a man, to make a dent like that.' He turned to leave the office, but something caught his eye.

On a nail sticking out from the door frame, hung a tiny piece of thick black fabric.

'What's this?' He pulled at the fabric and rubbed it between finger and thumb. Coarsely woven.

Monica peered close, bringing the torch to bear on his hands. 'Hmm. Black cloth.'

'Haha.'

'I can't imagine it's significant,' she said, turning away. Sebastian bit the inside of his cheek. He'd seen it somewhere before.

They left the office and Monica scanned the rest of the entrance hall with the torch.

Sebastian approached one of the black walls. Shouldn't they have been tiled white, or at least painted? He ran a finger down it, leaving a white streak. 'This is covered in something. Come away from the wall.'

She stepped back, bathing a larger section of the surface in light. Towards the corners, the tiles were indeed white, with a blackened, tarry patch concentrated in the centre. The light swung around to an adjacent wall, where the same pattern emerged, and to the floor – with the same result.

'I've seen this burn pattern before,' he said. 'Check the ceiling.'

The light swung upward. The fluorescent strip lights overhead had long since broken; the fittings had melted and now hung, dripping in grey plastic stalactites. The same black radial pattern marked the ceiling beyond.

Now the presence of the torn fabric made sense. His mind was drawn back to the burnt-out lab on Tenebrae. The burnt plastic smell; the thick black crust that had coated everything; the lack of an ignition source. His stomach felt hollow. 'Yes, I have seen this before.'

'What caused it?' Monica whispered.

'A fireball spell.'

'But this could have been caused by anything.' When Sebastian's expression didn't change, her voice went up an octave. 'You're serious, aren't you?'

'I'm certain. There's no accelerant source,' he said, walking to the middle of the room and holding his arms out in the torchlight. 'See how the concentration is at the centre of *every* wall? It's like something went off in the very middle of the space, not on the floor. We knew Duggan was coming here, and that piece of fabric is from his robe—'

The door into the lobby rattled.

Sebastian put a hand out towards Monica and pressed a finger to his lips.

'It's just the wind,' she whispered.

He straightened. 'I don't know why I'm so jumpy.'

'It's this place, there's something creepy about abandoned hospitals. Let's go upstairs.' She waved the bundle of keys in front of him and snatched them back in a fist. 'I can't wait to see what's in the files.'

'This is a complete waste of time,' Sebastian said, shoving the file back into the cabinet and slamming the drawer. 'It's nothing but accounts.'

Monica paced back and forth as she read from another folder. 'You say that, but you obviously didn't notice something important.'

'Like what?' He peered over her shoulder at the page. 'An invoice from a catering company? How does that help?'

She pointed to the top of the sheet. 'The date, see?'

'August 20th, 2077. It's got to be a typo. This place closed in 2062.'

She shook her head. 'No, it's not a typo.' She ran her finger down the page. 'This is a cover sheet with a summary of previous orders. All the orders are for the previous six months. They are dated that year . . . And look, there's a previous balance from an older invoice – it's dated 2076!'

'That's impossible.' He stepped around her, reopened the drawer, and began rifling through the files again. The other documents only confirmed Monica's statement. The place hadn't closed when the records said it had. 'So the information Wolfram found was correct, and somehow Alicia was committed after this place's official closure date. We have to check the other offices.' He made his way into the corridor. Monica dropped the folder onto a desk and followed brandishing the keys.

Twenty minutes later, they had checked the other rooms leading off the corridor and found nothing.

'I don't think there's anything in these offices that relate to the patients. These are all employee records,' Sebastian said, dropping yet another file onto a pile of discards. 'Not many of them, though. How many people would you expect to work here, given the size of the building?'

'I'm not sure. Fifty or sixty, I suppose, maybe more?'

'Nothing dated after the official closure mentions employees.'

Monica carefully rubbed an eye. 'There had to be someone consuming all of those catering supplies, so there have to be more records elsewhere.'

'We've checked all the rooms in this section. Do the stairs go on up to another floor or the roof?'

'I'll check.' She dashed out and returned a minute later, slightly out of breath. 'Yes, there's another floor, with a corridor like this one, but considerably longer.'

'Right, let's check it out.' Sebastian stuffed the files back into the drawer and Monica locked the door behind them.

The tiles on the walls of the second floor were mostly intact, along with the windows – perhaps they were too high for anyone throwing stones to reach with much impact. They let in more light than those on the floor below, as the vines growing up had fewer places in which to gain a foothold.

The doors in this corridor were labelled *Ward* and all numbered, unlike the anonymous offices they'd already encountered.

'I don't think they'll have kept records in the wards,' Sebastian said as Monica inserted a key into the nearest lock.

She pushed open the door and entered. The room's walls were painted with white gloss and a clerestory window let in light from a high level, the wire mesh replaced with thick metal bars.

To the left of the door was a shallow bed, bolted to the wall. Every corner and potentially sharp edge had been padded with a tough fabric. The thin mattress was stained with yellow splotches.

Sebastian's stomach turned at the sight. His grandfather had been in a place just like this. If only he'd been able to look after him. Instead, his father had left him in a place like this to rot – it's no wonder he got out. He glanced up at the barred windows; how on Earth could he have escaped somewhere like this?

Monica stroked an eyebrow. 'Sebastian, are you alright?'

'Mm.' He nodded and turned away from the room. 'I don't like this place. Let's check somewhere else.'

She brushed past him into the corridor and made her way to the end. 'It turns right here. It looks like it goes into another wing.'

By the time he reached the turn, Monica had gone farther ahead. She stood by a door with a long, frosted glass window next to it. 'This looks promising.'

As Sebastian drew closer, the rippled, bubbly glass reminded him of a detective's office from a 1950s movie. Monica unlocked the door and pushed it open with the tearing of age-fused varnish. Inside was an office lined with filing units that extended almost to the ceiling, allowing for very little light from the window above.

To the left of the door, below the frosted corridor window, which provided most of the light in the room, stood a heavy wooden desk with a leather top. Monica started to search the filing cabinets.

Far off, maybe on the floor below them, a door slammed. Sebastian jumped and spun around.

'It's probably the wind,' she said. 'Didn't you leave a couple of doors open down there? It's pretty draughty with the broken windows.'

He took a deep breath to calm himself. 'I thought I closed them all, but you're right. This place has me on edge.' He stepped into the office after her and closed the door behind him. 'I need to relax.'

'Then focus on something. Help me check these files – there are several labelled with M.'

'What am I looking for?'

'*Maline*, of course!'

He unstrapped the mobipack and propped it against the filing cabinets. He pulled open the nearest drawer and, as he began walking over the file sliders with his fingers, his mind started to wander. There were so many familiar things about this place ... Was it just that all asylums had the same feel?

'Sebastian, what are you doing?'

What the heck? Somehow, he'd managed to move to the left and was thumbing through a drawer labelled *G*. He'd reached *Geer*. 'I-I don't know.'

'If you're looking for Geirsson, your grandfather wasn't here. This place hasn't seen use for nearly two hundred years. You visited him, didn't you?'

'Yes.'

'And that was a working hospital, so it couldn't have been this one.' Monica sighed and moved on to the next drawer labelled *M*. 'Please focus. I know you're worried about Aryx, and this probably brings up bad memories, but we really need to concentrate on the task at hand.'

Sebastian returned to her side and started looking through the files again. *Mahraj ... Maisemore ...* His fingers stepped over one slider to the next. *Majere ... Majors, Mako ... Maline.* He stopped.

As he drew out the file, the room darkened for a moment. Just a flicker, a fraction of a second, like a branch waving across a window.

There were no trees in front of the windows.

He dropped the file and turned. 'What was that?' he whispered.

'The win—'

'Not the wind,' he hissed. 'I thought I saw something.'

'Did you find the file?'

'There.' He waved a hand in the direction of the folder. 'I'm going to check the corridor.' He reached for the door handle.

A dark shape rippled past the window.

Sebastian froze, a cold tightness radiating from his chest and holding him in place: they were not alone.

'This file's—'

He waved his hand behind his back at Monica. She dropped into a crouch and moved towards the desk, out of the line of sight from the corridor, and he crouched beside her. 'Gods, I wish we'd locked the door,' he whispered. 'There's someone else here.'

'Duggan?'

'Too bulky.'

From farther along the corridor, muffled voices made their way through the glass.

Sebastian made a turning gesture. Monica reached into a jacket pocket, pulled out the keys and handed him the one to the office door. He shuffled around the desk and reached up. Wincing, he carefully inserted the key into the lock and turned it. The only problem was, they were now trapped. The only other way out would be through the high window above the filing cabinets at the back of the room.

'We've got to get out,' he whispered.

'How?'

'Stay here.'

He crawled into the corner and, with his back to the wall, slid to a standing position and inched his way around the room, trying to keep his movements small as he moved towards the back. The clerestory window was at least ten feet up. He eased out one of the lowest filing cabinet drawers, keeping one hand against it to prevent it from making a sound. He put a foot on it and it didn't move. Safe so far.

He repeated the process with the next unit to the left, this time on the next row up, and continued ... A third drawer came out, forming a diagonal line, but when he put his weight on the unit, it shifted.

He beckoned to Monica.

She crawled across the floor towards him. 'What now?'

'I'm too heavy. These will fall over if I go all the way. Climb up and check the window.'

She nodded and scaled the makeshift stairway. The drawers creaked in protest as she pulled out another two, higher up. The unit leaned precariously as she climbed, coming inches away from the wall at the top. Sebastian held his breath while he put his weight against them.

At the top, she rolled sideways and vanished.

A moment later she reappeared, hair hanging around her face. 'The window will open, but I can't see a way to get down from here. It's just a drop.'

'What else can you see?'

She disappeared, but her whisper echoed down over the ledge. 'There's a wall, I guess the back of the compound, and a cable, running from just above the window.'

'If we had something to ...' What about the mobipack? Could they use that?

'To what?' Monica rasped.

'Take this.' Sebastian tossed up his infoslate.

She caught it and clipped it to her belt. 'You're not sending me out alone. I can't leave you here.'

Voices came into the office, clearer this time. 'They have to be here somewhere ... No, I've checked the first floor ... Yes, Farzoud is following the one in the marathon . . . ' The voice trailed off as the unseen speaker passed the window.

Oh, Gods. Someone knew they were here and Aryx was in trouble! They had to get back to him. 'Hold on, Monica.' He popped the mobipack's configuration infoslate out of its compartment and flicked through the field patterns Aryx had stored. After several pages he came across what he was looking for. Crude, but it would suffice.

He tapped the *Activate* button on screen and winced as the gloom of the office was banished by a flash of orange and slight puff of air as a pair of long serrated hooks, like vicious insectoid scythes, appeared several inches above the mobipack. He adjusted a setting and the climbing hooks turned towards each other, forming a wide X. That would have to do. He tapped another control and the hooks vanished, returning the room to its former dull state.

Sebastian held up the mobipack as he stood. 'Monica, take this.'

A dark shape loomed at the window.

'There's someone in there,' said a voice from the corridor.

The doorknob rattled.

Monica reached down, her fingers inches short of the mobipack's straps. Sebastian jumped, and she hooked one of the belts with a finger. With a grunt she lifted the pack onto the ledge.

'You'll have to get out of the window and turn it on. Make sure the top's near the cable when you do it, hold the voice input button, then say "mobipack on".'

'What do—'

'Just do it!'

She withdrew, taking the pack with her.

Something thudded against the frosted window. Sebastian turned to face it as the clerestory window above creaked.

Before he had time to draw his pistol, the window in front of him exploded and shards of glass flew into the room. In the opening stood a man in camouflage, wearing a balaclava. He levelled a hypersonic shotgun at Sebastian. 'Stay right where you are.'

Sebastian glanced up at the clerestory window as he put his hands behind his head. Monica was gone.

Aryx weaved between the runners to avoid the cluster that had formed around the disturbance.

'*Trevarian!*' Leather Jacket Man shouted.

Despite the burning ache in his wrists, Aryx forced himself to go faster. The rough tarmac didn't help: the vibrations only served to make his hands and fingers numb and he started to lose his grip.

Karan glanced back. 'Oh, shit, he's right behind!'

Aryx risked a look back.

'Wait!' Leather Jacket had broken away from the crowd he'd caused and was now only several feet behind the pair. One of the race marshals wearing a fluorescent jacket staggered away with a bloody nose. Their pursuer was one angry man.

'Karan, run ahead, get people out of my way!'

She picked up the pace and shouted, 'Wheelchair coming through!'

Aryx compensated for the camber of the road, pushing harder on his right wheel as he made for the wake that formed behind her. Heavy boots thudded on the tarmac behind him and his adrenaline surged. A *whuff* of air blew across his neck as something scraped his back.

Christ, that was too close!

'Downhill!' Karan shouted, approaching a sharp left-hand bend.

Aryx leaned forwards to give himself as much reach with his arms as he could and dug in. The thudding of boots receded a little.

Karan ran on ahead, still clearing a path as Aryx accelerated downhill, her arms flailing uncontrollably as she tried to cope with running too fast.

He allowed the slope to take him faster but the runners hindered him and he couldn't get top speed. 'Argh, for cryin' out loud, get out of the bloody way!' Several runners ahead must have heard, as the wake Karan formed widened. Letting go of his wheels, he sped for the gap.

After a minute, the sound of boots had stopped. 'I think we've lost him,' he shouted.

The downhill slope levelled onto smooth solarpave tarmac. Karan slowed and jogged backwards for a moment. 'I can't see him. I don't think he could have kept up with us coming down there.'

Aryx slowed. The crowds on the pavement thinned out considerably as the road passed under a flyover, leaving only a few straggling bystanders and assistants standing in the dim light. The short tunnel reeked of urine: runners had taken advantage of the poor lighting and relieved themselves in the shadows.

Leaving the underpass, he made his way towards the left-hand kerb, where a long row of tables stood covered with an array of bottled water and energy drinks. One of the assistants reached out through the cluster of gathered runners to offer him one. Having drained his own some distance back, it seemed like a good idea.

'Thanks,' he said, reaching for the bottle.

A hand clamped down on his wrist. 'Got you!'

Aryx's eyes met the dark, exhausted glare of Leather Jacket Man. He tried to pull away, but the grip on his cramping wrist was too much to break free, and he spun awkwardly. Where was Karan? 'Get the fuck away!'

Leather Jacket dragged him towards the kerb and the front caster of his wheelchair caught on the stone lip. With the sudden resistance, the Arab stumbled and let go.

Aryx seized the opportunity and continued the spin to head back into the race. As he pushed, he jerked forwards, caught by the straps of his chair. Leather Jacket had grabbed the rail at the back of his seat and now held on as he tried to stand.

'Oi! Get off 'im!' someone shouted. It was Judie Sorenson.

Aryx tried to pry the man's hands from the bar but his weary grip slipped off the thick fingers.

'I said get off 'im!' Judie closed in rapidly, still having momentum from the hill, and smashed the casters of her wheelchair into Leather Jacket's right ankle.

'Aaaaargh!' he bellowed, and instantly let go.

Aryx sped off as Judie wheeled past, leaving Leather Jacket rolling around, clutching his foot, to avoid getting trampled by the runners. Two fluorescent-jacketed marshals stepped in to drag him away.

A hand fell on Aryx's shoulder and he spun around. 'Get off!'

Karan snapped her hand back. 'Hey, it's just me. Where were you? I turned around and you'd gone.'

He jabbed a thumb over his shoulder. 'That guy in the leather jacket, he's the one that followed us in Brazil. He tried to grab me.'

'Just a sec.' She stepped around him and jogged over to the marshals dragging the man away. 'Excuse me,' she said, and swung a hefty kick between Leather Jacket's legs. He doubled up and the marshals pulled him out of the road, both failing to conceal their laughter behind turned-up collars. Finally, he was out of the way.

The next couple of hours were as agonising as the terrain was varied: the road switched between strips of tough-to-navigate cobbles, potholed tarmac, and smooth solarpave.

'My hands are starting to tingle,' Aryx said, pausing to rub his wrists.

Karan bent down to give him a shove. 'Do you want me to push?'

He slapped her hand away. 'No, I bloody don't! Would you like it if I tried to carry you?'

She grinned. 'If you're offering. I'm not like you, I still have to *run* downhill. I don't get to freewheel.'

He laughed. 'That may be one of my advantages, but it's really hard going uphill.'

The rough tarmac gave way to a recently resurfaced stretch on a bend in the road. Immediately after the bend, the road began to rise.

'Christ, not another! Is it much farther?' His wrists burned and moved stiffly, as though they had expanded to ten times their size.

'Another forty minutes, I guess. We'll go by the Thames soon.'

'At least that'll be flat. My arms are killing me.' He stared at the long, slow hill ahead. There was no end to it. 'I don't think I can go on much farther.'

'We've got to finish or we won't get into the archive.' Karan turned to face him and jogged backwards. 'Do you need to slow down for a bit? Will that help?'

Out of breath from the long, uphill struggle, he nodded.

'You should tell Seb about what's happened, you know. He'll be worried.'

'He'll worry ... and not be able ... to do anything.'

She tilted her head as she looked through the runners behind. 'I don't think that guy will be able to follow us anymore. The rest of the roads have barricades along them until the finish.'

'That's good ... I don't think I could ... put up with any more ... of his crap.' He lowered his head while he pushed. 'Now ... do you think ... we can just ... get on with it?'

Monica's heart raced as she scrambled backwards through the small window. Dangling her legs over the edge, she scuffed the toes of her boots on the brickwork trying to find a foothold. At the limit of her reach she began to shake and her toe caught something with a wiry, metallic rattle: a wire mesh cage covering an extractor fan. She hooked the cage with her heel, brought the other foot onto it, and dragged the mobipack out through the opening.

The crash of breaking glass came from inside the room, but there wasn't time to think about Sebastian's safety. The wire cage she stood on was only six inches deep – barely enough to stand on, even without the bulk of the mobipack. Under the weight of the device she tipped back and grabbed a nearby drainpipe with her free hand to steady herself.

The pack swung and hit the wall. Crumbling bits of brick showered onto a corrugated roof far below, sending a tinny percussion out across the grounds. Monica gritted her teeth.

It had only been a few moments, but already the weight of the mobipack made her arm ache. It was so *heavy* – no wonder Aryx fell over so often. She lifted it as high as she could towards the overhead cable, still holding onto the drainpipe, and took a deep breath as she pressed the button.

'Mobipack on.'

Laser-like threads whipped about in the air and, in the fraction of a second it took to form the crossed climbing hooks, her grip on the pack slipped and they appeared an inch below the cable.

'Darn it,' she growled. 'Mobipack off.' The fields vanished and she lowered her aching arm to rest for a minute.

The wire cage creaked. The thin metal lugs screwed into the wall started to bend under her weight.

Drawing all her strength, she heaved the pack up again. 'Mobipack on,' she said, reaching her limit. Her foothold gave way as the cage tore from the wall.

She grabbed for the straps.

Everything slowed, and for a long moment she fell back. A loud crash echoed from below, and she expected to join the fallen cage in a mangled heap, but with the twang of high tension wire under strain, she slid horizontally. Her legs flailed in the air as the mobipack rotated, settling on the wire, and the asylum building pulled away with increasing speed.

The *twitter* and *chirrup* of the power cable grew louder as she accelerated and trees, grass and bramble scrub whizzed beneath her.

Over her shoulder the great red-brick face of the perimeter wall approached fast. What to do? The cable barely cleared the wall itself – she'd smash straight into it!

She brought up her legs and shouted, 'Mobipack off!' The fields evaporated. Sharp thorns tore at her clothes as she plummeted into a bed of brambles.

Something heavy hit her on her head and she fell unconscious.

Chapter 19

When she came to, Monica lay among vicious, spiny briars. She put a hand to her head and recoiled as she caught the sharp end of something tangled in her hair. Luckily, no blood. Next to her, in the brambles, lay the mobipack. As she teased out the bramble twigs from her knotted hair, the pea gravel *scrunched* nearby.

Keeping low, she eased herself into a sitting position, just high enough to see over the bushes.

Less than ten metres away, five figures dressed in old army surplus gear, carrying guns and wearing balaclavas, marched towards a gate at the rear of the asylum compound. In the middle of the group trudged a sixth figure, head covered with a bag and hands cuffed behind his back.

Monica gasped. Sebastian!

One of the figures at the back of the group stopped and turned.

'What is it?' the one at the front said.

The one at the back swung his gun in her direction.

She ducked down and held her breath.

He paused. 'Thought I heard something. Probably just a bird.' He turned around and the group continued.

Her hand went to the pistol on her belt as they reached the gate but, with five armed opponents and Sebastian as hostage, how could she could free him safely? She couldn't – at least not with a mere pistol.

Who were they? How could anyone have known they were here unless they'd been watching the building the whole time? Perhaps Sebastian's paranoia was correct and the ITF had somehow been monitoring communications or followed their taxi. One thing was certain, they knew Aryx was in the marathon.

Aryx!

Taking Sebastian's infoslate from her belt, she checked Aryx's readings. How could she not have realised? The spike in adrenaline he'd experienced earlier must have been an encounter with whoever they sent after him. His heart rate had been steady ever since. At least he was still alive but, judging by the amount of lactic acid in his system, he must be exhausted. The urge to call him on her wristcom came and went. If communications were being monitored, she didn't want to give away her position.

At a metallic clang from the gate, she looked up. A large truck that hadn't been there before pulled away.

'Stay safe, Sebastian,' she muttered, 'and don't do anything stupid.'

She got up and picked the thorns from her clothes – luckily her trousers were thick enough for them to do little damage – and hefted the mobipack onto her back, jiggling it while she fastened the upper harness. Calling a taxi was now out of the question. It looked like she was in for a long walk.

Every inch of the final three-mile stretch of the marathon sent fire coursing through Aryx's shoulders. The pace had slowed for many of the runners, and his will to go on had all but deserted him.

At the penultimate mile, the crowd of spectators on the other side of the barricades became densely packed.

'*Go, Aryx!*'

'*You can do it!*'

Pwheee! One of the onlookers blew a red whistle on a lanyard. She threw one to him.

He caught it and popped it in his mouth and blew, almost rupturing his eardrums, and a roar went up from the crowd. He grinned. The spectators' cheers made it all worth it.

'They really love you,' Karan shouted. 'I think you must be their poster boy!'

He looped the lanyard over his head and let the whistle drop. 'I doubt they'll remember me in five minutes.'

The road took a sharp bend to the right, heading past the Houses of Parliament. A few minutes later, they passed a long, striated building.

'That's where we signed up,' Karan said. 'The archive's in there.'

He didn't have time to take in much detail; he was so busy trying to avoid other runners that he only noticed the general style of the place.

'Bit of an odd place to put it.'

'Aryx!' This time the voice in the crowd was familiar.

'Hey, there's Monica, waving at us,' Karan said. She waved back.

Aryx scanned the faces in the crowd. Monica peered out from between onlookers, but something wasn't right. She never looked that scraggly, and ... 'Where's Seb? Can you see him?'

'Uh ... Nope!'

Monica pointed in the direction of the Mall and disappeared.

'I guess she'll meet us at the finish line.' Spurred on by the need to find out where Sebastian was, Aryx put his head down and dug in once more.

The final mile crawled by.

He collapsed the moment he kicked his casters over the rubber trim of the finish line. It took several seconds for him to straighten up and read the display behind him. *Time: 4h 35m 39s.*

'Ahh! For Christ's sake!'

Karan wrinkled her nose. 'It's not that bad a time!' She watched as a marshal gave him a goody bag and placed a medal over his head, then jogged to catch up with him after collecting her own as he wheeled away from the officials into a more open space.

Aryx's throat tightened and he buried his face in his hands. 'Five minutes over! We didn't make it!'

'Oh, crapola.' Karan's shoulders sagged. 'I see what you mean. We won't get into the archive.'

Monica burst in through a gap in the barrier, breathing heavily, her face flushed. 'We've got bigger problems!'

Aryx tapped his fingers on his thigh while he waited for Monica to get her breath back. 'I thought you said you were a woman of many talents?'

'I am, but,' she said, between great gulps of air, waving a finger back and forth, 'running is *not* one of them!'

Karan snorted. 'Some SpecOps officer you are!'

'I'm an archaeologist, not an action hero.'

'Whatever.' Aryx waved a hand dismissively and leaned forward, hands on his thighs. 'Now, if getting into the archive isn't our problem, what is?'

'Sebastian's been abducted.'

The heat of the marathon left him in an instant. 'What?'

'You mean arrested,' Karan said.

'Captured. Kidnapped. Someone came into the asylum while we were there. Not police. They had balaclavas and really old army gear. We had to hide in an office. Here . . . ' Monica unstrapped the mobipack and handed it to Aryx. 'It's a good job you didn't leave it at the hotel. I had to use it to escape through a window.'

A long scrape ran down the back of the device and he glared at her. 'If it wasn't police, who the hell were they? ITF?'

'I don't know, but we have to get out of here now. They knew you were in the marathon. One of them mentioned your name.'

'We were chased,' Karan said. 'It was the same guy who followed you in Brazil.'

Aryx winced. 'Strewth, I'm in no position to be rushing around. My wrists are killing me.'

Karan placed her hands on his shoulders from behind. 'I'll push you for a bit, if you like.'

'For once, that's a good idea.'

'There's some anti-inflammatory cooling gel in the goody bag.'

She pushed him, following Monica, while he fumbled through the compostable plastic carrier bag he'd been given and found a small sachet of gel. With both hands shaking, he tore the corner off with his teeth. The odour was strong: a mixture of ginger, mint, several spices and something with a medicinal tang. His fingers trembled as he peeled off the support tape from his wrists and began massaging in the gel. 'I guess it's nice to have a chauffeur once in a while,' he said.

'Well, this chauffeur is starving. You do know I've also run a marathon and now I'm having to push you.'

'Hey, you offered! Come here.'

She leaned forwards. Aryx took a chocolate bar from the bag, unwrapped it, snapped it in half and stuffed it into her mouth. 'Fankoo,' she said around the mouthful.

He found a second bar and offered it to Monica who strode purposefully ahead.

'I'm fine, thanks. I can't think about food. I'm so worried about Sebastian.'

'You mustn't blame yourself, Nic.'

'Well, I do. If I'd been quicker out of the window, Sebastian might have escaped too.'

'I'm sure you did your best, although the cable probably wouldn't have held both of you anyway.'

She gave a flat smile.

'So, why are we going on foot?' Karan asked.

'And *where* are we going?'

'Back to the asylum,' Monica said. 'We might find a clue to where Sebastian was taken. I've tried to track his wristcom but it's been jammed. And we're walking because we can't risk calling a taxi. I think either our comms were monitored or we were followed. We can lose anyone following on foot easily enough. We'll catch a bus shortly – I bought some credit chips so we can't be traced.' Her paranoia was almost as bad as Sebastian's, but this time it seemed well-founded.

Aryx held up a hand to signal Karan to stop pushing. He unpinned the runner number from his vest, tore off the tracking chip and wheeled over it. It gave a satisfying crunch under his tyre. 'Probably a good idea for you to do the same, Karan. I expect that's how Leather Jacket Man followed us.'

'But there are no strips across the road here.'

'All the same, they still give off a signal.'

'Shit, I didn't think of that.' She copied Aryx and then tapped on her wristcom. 'I've turned off location, too.'

Aryx did the same and refastened his number – it was now a badge of honour, after all.

Monica flagged down a passing bus and paid with the credit chips. Getting on was easy for a change, with a boarding ramp lowering to kerb level as Aryx approached.

'This is certainly more accessible than the crappy colonies we seem to visit lately,' he said, nodding his approval.

Karan gave a smile. 'That's what happens when an entire country gets crammed into five cities. They can't afford not to be accessible.'

They got off the bus a mile from the asylum; Monica had made it clear that it shouldn't be too obvious where they were going when they'd got on the bus. She led them to a disused school, where the fencing around an old athletics track had been removed, and began to cut across the grounds.

'You can take a break from pushing now, Karan,' Aryx said.

She stretched her back while he rolled onto the track.

'This floor is squidgy.'

She stopped to bounce on it. 'How can you even tell?'

'I can feel the difference in the push and the vibration in my casters. It's kind of weird.'

'Nice to run on, though.'

'Easy for you to say. It's actually making it harder for me. But I'm fine. I need to keep my wrists moving or they'll seize up.'

They crossed the school grounds and passed through a dilapidated housing estate, finally breaking out onto the road that ran around the perimeter of the asylum.

When they reached the gates, Monica replayed the code stored in Sebastian's infoslate and the chain fell slack. 'Phew, I'm glad that still works.'

'What about the front door?' Aryx asked. 'Didn't you say it locked behind you?'

'Yes, I'll have to do something so it doesn't this time.'

They approached the old building along the crumbling driveway, and Aryx wheeled the last few yards across the spongy pea gravel. 'Oh, joy. Steps,' he said.

'Don't worry.' Monica pointed to a ramp running up one side to the front door.

'I guess they had a lot of people in wheelchairs.' His thoughts filled with images of people being wheeled in and out of ambulances, strapped into transit chairs and unable to push themselves, and he shivered.

She punched numbers on the lock and pushed the doors open.

'Before we go in,' Karan said, 'pass me that tape.' Aryx handed her the used fabric tape off his lap and she placed a strip over the door latch. 'That should stop it from locking.'

Aryx went in first. 'It stinks in here. What happened?'

Monica followed and turned on the infoslate torch. 'Sebastian thought Duggan may have been here and set off a fireball.'

He recalled the video from the explosion in the lab on Tenebrae, and the damage it did to Kerl. 'I pity the poor buggers caught in it.'

'As callous as it sounds,' Monica said, drawing her pistol, '*I* don't.' She made her way to a set of stairs in the corner of the foyer. 'The records room is up here.'

'Great. More steps. Karan, could you give me a hand? I'm going to struggle with this smooth floor.' Aryx shuffled forwards in his seat and strapped on the mobipack while Karan took the goody bags. He took out the new crutches Monica had given him and fastened them to his forearms. In a moment, his prosthetics appeared with a bright orange flash and he stood. Then, with a flick of his wrists, the slender telescopic crutches *thwack-thwacked* and he leaned forwards to put his weight on them.

Karan stared at him in the gloom. 'Good to see you being cautious.'

'Just in case,' he said and, retracting the right-hand crutch to keep his hand free, he grabbed the handrail.

Monica went ahead to the top of the stairs while Karan held back at the bottom.

Aryx paused at the landing. 'Are you coming?'

'I'll wait here. I don't want anyone sneaking up behind us.'

'Suit yourself.'

Karan stared at him flatly. 'I'm supposed to be guarding you, re-member?'

'Then watch from up here,' Monica shouted from the top of the stairwell. 'You can see the gate from the windows on the top floor.'

Karan bounded up the stairs after Aryx. When they reached the second floor, she pulled the vines away from one of the windows to look out across the grounds. 'Hmm. It'll do, I suppose.'

'Good,' Monica said. 'Now, can we please get on?'

Aryx turned to follow, but Karan grabbed his arm.

'Do we have to put up with her? She's such a stuffed shirt.'

He laughed. 'She's SpecOps. Besides, she's not so bad once you get to know her. I'll shout if we need you. I know how much you hate paperwork.'

She grumbled.

Monica's head popped around the bend in the corridor. 'Are you coming or not?'

'Yes, he's on his way.'

Aryx followed Monica around the bend in the corridor and she led him into a small office with a window framed in broken glass.

'Is this where it happened?' he asked, surveying the scene.

Monica nodded and put a hand on the desk to steady herself as she sat down. 'I can't believe I let him get caught like that.'

He sat next to her, glad to relieve his groin from the strain of the harness. 'Five against two wasn't good odds. Even if I'd been armed to the teeth, I wouldn't have attempted it. It's a shame you didn't get what you came for, though.'

'Oh! That's it! Sebastian came across a file just before I escaped.' She slid off the desk and went to one of the drawers that stuck out from the array of filing cabinets. 'This is it. Maline!' she said, waving a beige folder. She quickly scanned the pages. 'Unmarried, aged thirty-two when committed. No photo in the file. Do you want to hear the notes?'

Aryx nodded, and she read the file aloud. As the story contained in the notes unfolded, he imagined the woman sitting in one of the offices, talking to a doctor:

'I've tried to cope,' Alicia said, blinking through tears that stained her face with days-old mascara. 'Believe me, I've tried. I just can't take it anymore.'

The doctor, a stereotypical figure in a white coat, leaned on the desk and laced his fingers. 'But you've been coping so well for the last, what is it now, nine years?'

Alicia nodded, barely moving the lank strands of her unwashed hair. 'Yes. I know what you must be thinking, Doctor, that I haven't tried. But I really have. I changed my name, moved house, got a new job. I thought I could put it all behind me.'

'I do understand, Alicia. It's sometimes hard to cope when someone leaves.'

'He didn't just *leave*,' she shouted, standing up. She paced back and forth, pressing her knuckles against her lips. 'He went on a colonisation mission. I was supposed to be there with him. We were supposed to get married and spend the rest of our days out there ... in space, on another planet, making a future for ourselves. Do you know how many years we studied together for it? Apparently, it wasn't good enough. "We don't need *two* geologists." No, just one. Screw the fact that we're splitting a couple up. We'll send just one of you. Time-wasting, family-destroying assholes.'

The doctor put out his hand in a calming gesture. 'It's alright to get angry. You have to let it out. But what makes it different now? Why has it got so bad?'

She continued to pace as the mascara ran, staining her hand. 'He's never coming back. I thought there might be the faintest glimmer of hope I'd see him again someday. They might have hit a snag and turned around to come back ... But after all this time I can't hold out any longer. It was stupid.' She flopped into the seat and heaved a shuddering sigh. 'I only volunteered to go because there was nobody here for me to leave behind, you know?'

The doctor tilted his head.

'A 150-year flight.' She gazed blankly at the desk. 'I'll be long dead by the time they get there.'

'I'm sorry.' He tapped a pen against his lips. 'So, you finally accepted it and began to grieve? Is that why you attempted suicide?'

Alicia cupped her nose and mouth with a hand, revealing the bandage on her wrist, and slowly shook her head. 'Not the only reason,' she sobbed. 'The voices have come back. They're even louder now. Nothing quiets them.'

'You haven't stopped taking your medication, have you?'

'No. It's just not working like it used to.'

'It's probably the stress.' The doctor scribbled a few notes. 'I'd like to change your prescription. Social services have also asked for me to put you somewhere safe, under medical observation for the moment, given that you have no family or friends that can look after you.'

Alicia's hands fell in her lap, palms up. 'Please, no ...'

Monica looked up from the pages. 'Those were her doctor's accounts until she was committed in the early part of 2062.'

Aryx scratched his head. 'But you said this place closed before she was committed, right?'

Monica nodded. 'Yes. That's the odd thing. Sebastian and I found records that show the facility was still operating until 2080. Her doctor must have been part of whatever conspiracy was going on.' She flicked forward several pages. 'Alicia's records end in 2078.'

'End how?'

'They just end.'

'Records don't just end. Did she escape? She turned up on Sollers Hope in what ... 2230, if she'd been there fourteen years? She got there somehow. Is there a police report or anything in the file?'

Monica shook her head.

'Let me see.'

She handed him the file. The only prominent record before the final routine medical exam was a psychological evaluation, scrawled in spidery handwriting:

> I am concerned that Ms Maline has been spending too much
> time with Patricia Ventris. Ventris is a dangerous patient,
> and I believe she may be a bad influence on Maline.

'Can you find Patricia Ventris's file?' Aryx asked. 'She may have been the last person to have spoken to her. There might be something about it in her file.'

Monica spun around and started rooting through the files. She stopped.

'Found it?'

She didn't answer, but began to shake.

'Nic, are you okay?'

'No. I can't believe I left Sebastian. I don't know who those people are, or why they took him, and if they were terrorists, he could be in terrible danger!'

'The only way to find out who they are is to find out why they took him. If they knew we were here looking for clues to Alicia Maline's whereabouts, we have to find out why she's important to them. If it's not her, and there's something else incriminating here ... If we find that, we can find him, I'm sure of it.'

She turned her face up to the ceiling and paused for a moment before continuing her search. A minute later, she found the file. 'Ventris, Patricia.'

'Does it have much in it?'

'I'd say so.' She hefted the inch-thick file. 'She was committed at the end of 2077. Bloody hell!' Monica's eyes widened. 'She and her husband were the first regular cargo pilots for runs between Sol and Gliese 682b.'

'That was the first node Humans ever found. She was a Pioneer?'

Monica nodded rapidly. 'Not on the original *Fluorescent Lightingale*. It was on its way back then, but she was on the first trips via the node after the signal was received back from the expedition. The couple did runs, ferrying cargo and staff back and forth, when they set up the first extrasolar research base. She'd logged over 200 hours in superphase in the first six months!'

'That must have taken some guts back in those days. Why was she committed?'

'Apparently,' Monica said, taking the seat in front of Aryx, 'she had some kind of psychotic episode during her final flight. She tried to strangle her husband. Well, I say *tried*. She put him in a coma.'

'Jeez!'

She ran her finger across the page. 'Brain chemistry slightly off, which isn't unusual, but other than that there appeared to be no physical symptoms of any kind that could explain her behaviour. The doctor titled the condition – wait for it ... "*acceleration psychosis*".'

Aryx's heart quickened. 'No way! Sebastian thought that was what

Gladrin suffered from when he suspected him of being possessed. He didn't, obviously, but this could be the first historically recorded case.'

'And it's genuine.'

Aryx nodded. 'Go on.'

'The doctor thought psychosis was probably brought on by fear of FTL travel.'

'Hah, after she'd already logged 200 hours? I don't think so!'

'Nor do I.' She read on. 'Anyway, when her husband recovered, he inexplicably dropped the assault charge on the provision that she be committed for psychiatric evaluation and treatment. She was put here. He only visited her a few times, and during her interviews she kept asserting that her husband "wasn't her husband" anymore. Get this, "Since being committed, Mrs Ventris has become compliant, her brain chemistry has stabilised, and she has shown no violent behaviour other than towards her husband. She still insists that he is under the control of an *influence*." Sound familiar?'

Aryx let out a slow breath and nodded.

Monica put the file on the desk. 'But why would the doctors not like Alicia Maline talking to her?'

'Isn't it obvious?' Karan said from the doorway.

Aryx turned. 'I thought you were guarding.'

'We've been here a while and no one's turned up. I think we're safe.'

'Okay, so why is it obvious the doctors wouldn't have wanted Maline talking to Ventris?'

Karan leaned against the door frame. 'Ventris was a superphase pilot. When Maline was committed, superphase travel hadn't even been discovered.'

They stared blankly at her.

'Don't you get it? Maline's fiancé left at lightspeed.'

Aryx curled his lip. Monica shifted her weight from one side of the seat to the other. What was she on about?

'Are you *both* dim? When Maline found out about FTL travel, she wanted to escape so she could catch up with him!'

They stared at Karan, mouths wide. Monica was the first to speak. 'You're saying Alicia Maline escaped so that she could use the node network to catch up with her fiancé?'

Karan folded her arms. 'That's exactly what I'm saying.'

'Well, Garvin didn't mention Alicia having a fiancé. Then again, he didn't really say anything about her at all.' Aryx's chest felt hollow and heavy. 'You know what this means? It means the clues lead nowhere and the trail's gone cold.'

Monica got up and paced back and forth while she read the file again. 'Not necessarily. We know Alicia was at Sollers Hope after the date of her records so— Hold on ... Ventris's records end at the same time as Alicia's for some reason, but there were procedures planned for her until 2080.'

'What do you mean?'

'They were going to experiment on Ventris. Electroshock treatment, hallucinogenic drug injection, ice baths. Oh, God ... lobotomy!'

Aryx wanted to throw up. Such barbaric surgery hadn't been performed for centuries. 'Why the hell would they do that? She had no symptoms after she was committed!'

'I-I don't know.' Monica chose a file from the drawers at random. 'There's more of this. No symptoms. Electroshock. Lobotomy.' She plucked out another file. 'No symptoms. Ice-water immersion treatment ... Trepanning? No wonder Maline would have wanted to escape. This is like something out of the Dark Ages!'

Karan paled. 'I can't listen to this,' she said, and strode out into the corridor.

Aryx's blood pressure rose. 'How could they do these things? Did all of them have no symptoms before being tortured and butchered?'

'Pretty much. I can't see a reason for it apart for experimentation for its own sake.'

His nausea changed, replaced by something akin to a boiling cauldron in his stomach. 'That's disgusting.' He wanted to hit something, to lash out for those victims of abstract and pointless torture. 'Someone has to pay for this!'

Karan came back in and sat on the desk next to him. 'Like who? All those involved are long dead. Except perhaps for Maline, wherever she is now, and her fiancé, who might still be travelling at light speed ... Could you imagine his reaction if she had managed to overtake him and got to where he was going first?'

'Yes,' Aryx said flatly, 'the joys of superphase.'

'That's it! Aryx, you're a genius!' Monica grabbed his shoulders and kissed him on the forehead. 'If Ventris got possessed by an extra-spatial entity during her superphase flights and it moved into her husband, that would explain why he put her here, rather than pressing charges. He really *was* possessed. Sticking her here would make sure nobody believed she was telling the truth. But why the experiments? The health service would never condone treatment like that.'

'I think it's obvious the NHS wasn't running the operation. Everything about this place is wrong.' Aryx passed a hand down his face. 'It had to have been those who later founded the ITF. The entity in her husband must have known somehow.'

'Why would they have been involved with the hospital? Just because of the entities?'

'If ex-possessed people were getting committed, the possessed members of the ITF would be able to contain those who had been exposed to their influence. Wouldn't they want to keep an eye on them? Perhaps they experimented on them to see if they could make the process easier or something. It would make sense for them to keep an eye on the place afterwards, too.'

Monica put her fingers over her mouth.

'I hope I'm wrong and that it's not the ITF, because if they've got Sebastian, he's lost and so's our advantage of surprise. They'll know about Duggan, Wolfram being able to purge them, Achene, the Folians, everything.'

Monica stuffed the files back into the drawers. 'We shouldn't have come back. We can't afford to get caught by them.' She made her way to the door. 'Come on.'

Aryx extended the crutches, slid off the desk, and followed her out, glowing force-field feet scrunching on the broken glass as he went. Ahead, Karan made her way into the darkness of the stairwell.

When Aryx reached the bottom of the stairs, the pair were standing motionless in the foyer, rooted to the spot.

Karan slowly put a finger to her lips and nodded in the direction of the entrance doors.

The heavy doorknob turned.

Chapter 20

Sebastian sat on a hard, cold seat, jammed between two of his captors, with a thick black bag over his head. City noises were muffled and masked by the gentle thrum of a retrofit fusion engine. A bump in the road jogged him, and he banged the back of his head against something that flexed with a sheet-metal wobble. He must have been loaded into an old converted van. Whoever these people were, the old weapons, army surplus gear and use of this vehicle pointed to one thing: they weren't well funded.

'Have you heard back from Farzoud yet about the one in the wheelchair?' one of the men asked.

Sebastian stiffened at the mention of Aryx.

'Yeah,' another said. 'Had some trouble with one of the marshals, apparently. He gave him the slip, but he's going to try again in a few minutes. Thinks he can head him off.'

Sebastian shivered as a cold apprehension came over him. What did they want with Aryx? Without his mobipack, he'd be unable to defend himself, especially if they got hold of his wheelchair.

'Farzoud will get him this time,' a Middle Eastern sounding man said. 'I think he will not bear the shame of being unable to capture the cripple a second time.' He gave a deep, slow laugh.

Those bastards! How could they do that? 'You and your kind disgust me,' Sebastian shouted. Immediately, something hit him in the stomach, knocking the breath out of him.

'We will be the ones to speak. And when we do, it will be to ask questions, and you will answer.'

Bright specks floated in Sebastian's vision, dancing over the black. The specks resolved into vague patches, and he counted the forms of five, maybe six people. It was stupid, speaking out. He could have got himself killed, and what use would he be to Aryx then? His chest became heavy. The situation was hopeless.

The van trundled on for fifteen minutes but, with the rocking from many turns back and forth, he had no idea how far they had travelled. They could have gone several miles, or they may simply have taken him several hundred yards via a convoluted series of turns, just to confuse him.

The vehicle stopped. Then came the *tunk-tunk-tunk* of a roller-shutter door being raised; a squeal and *thunk* of the tailgate; the thud of boots hitting tarmac as the vehicle wobbled.

Hands dragged him by the elbows and he stumbled out of the vehicle. They marched him across rough gravel before taking him onto smooth concrete, where his footsteps echoed. Water splashed as he stepped in a shallow puddle. A hangar, or a warehouse?

He jumped at the harsh staccato of another roller shutter slamming behind him and stopped in his tracks. It must be a disused factory.

'A little jumpy, ey?' one of the Middle Eastern voices said. A sharp jab in the back forced him to continue.

The group stopped and fell silent. A door opened and clicked shut.

Tiny sparks moved in Sebastian's vision. Someone new had come into the room. His captors shifted and their vague outlines bowed.

'So, this is him,' the newcomer's voice said. Definite English, maybe London accent, but Sebastian couldn't place it. Galac tended to distort most accents, making them difficult to localise.

The outline of one of his captors nodded.

'Bring him here.'

The chill of the warehouse was driven away when someone pushed him into a chair and handcuffed his wrists to the armrests. Another pulled the bag from his head, forcing him to screw up his eyes against the glare of a bright lamp shining straight into his face.

He tried to pull his head away as fingers forced one of his eyes open.

'He's one of them, by Christ!' the Londoner said. 'I can't believe you actually managed to capture one.'

'One of whom?' Sebastian asked. The butt of a shotgun hit him in the stomach and he doubled over as far as his restraints allowed.

'We ask the questions, you will remember that!'

'What was he doing at the hospital?' the Londoner asked. He

walked over to a small table by the lamp and fondled several items that glinted in the light.

'I do not know. He picked the lock to get in.'

'He didn't have the code? Then we'll have to find out why.' The Londoner loomed close, holding a shiny metal tool. 'What were you doing back at the hospital after what happened there?'

Sebastian's eyes began to water. 'I don't know what you're on about. It's the first time I've been there.'

The Londoner brandished a pair of pliers in Sebastian's face. 'Don't lie to us.'

'I'm not lying!'

'Your kind do nothing but lie.' He drew his hand back in a fist.

Sebastian screwed up his face. 'What are you talking about, *my* kind?'

'Don't play with us.' *Smack!*

Sebastian rocked with the impact. He stretched his jaw to try to alleviate the pain. In the corner of his eye, someone lifted an object onto the table.

'This is an interesting looking bag.' *His* bag. He watched helplessly as one of the Middle Eastern men took out items one by one and placed them on the table. His lantern, medical nanobot injector, and ... his grandfather's journal.

'Hey, get out of that, it's mine!'

The man leafed through the book. 'Why? Do you have something to hide? Something incriminating?'

'I don't have anything to hide, but it's personal!' Sebastian said. If they discovered the writings, they might decipher their meanings. 'The ITF has no business with it!'

'The ITF?' The Londoner's voice went up an octave. 'So why do *you* carry it?' The pliers moved closer to Sebastian's mouth.

'I said it's personal!'

A pair of unseen hands came at Sebastian from either side and forced his mouth open. Cold metal touched his lip, and with a *clunk* the pliers gripped a molar.

'None of your people have connections with your old lives, so why are you carrying a personal item? What were you doing at the hospital, and how are you managing to increase your numbers?'

Sebastian's eyes flitted from one silhouette to another, back and forth. One eye watered and his pulse raced. 'I-I don't *undershtand!*'

'We know pain still has an effect on you.'

An electric tingle surged through his tooth as the pressure increased. '*Clease!*' he wailed.

'Answer the fucking question!' the Londoner said.

The figure holding the diary looked up. 'Boss, what is this?'

The Londoner glanced back. 'Don't interrupt me.'

The pressure on Sebastian's tooth increased and he closed his eyes. 'But boss, I think it is . . .'

Tears streamed down Sebastian's face. His tooth was about to shatter. The pressure in his head was too much. He was going to pass out.

'. . . the Square and Compasses.'

The pressure released and a wave of nausea washed over him.

The Londoner straightened. 'What did you say?' His colleague handed him the diary and he put down the pliers. 'What is this?' Brandishing the open book at Sebastian, he pointed to something on the page – a shape blurred by Sebastian's tears. 'The Illuminati shouldn't know about this. How did you come by it, demon?'

'I'm not possessed!'

'He has the sign,' one of the others said, a Japanese man, his fingers circling his own face. 'His eyes.'

The Londoner rubbed his chin. 'Yes, that he does. But he's not behaving like one of them, not if he's carrying personal items. Tell me, why is this book personal to you?'

'It's my grandfather's diary. And, if *you*'re not the ITF, who in Hel's name are you?'

The Londoner loomed close; Sebastian's reflected face stared back as he looked from eye to eye. 'The question is, my friend, if you're not Illuminatus and claim not to be possessed, who are *you*?'

Chapter 21

A horse-drawn carriage clattered down the cobbled street beneath the gas lamps and came to a stop several yards from the house. Ducking, so as not to lose his top hat, the single occupant stepped out. The *tink* of his cane on the pavement reached Gravalax through the sash windows as he watched.

The butler entered the drawing room without knocking. 'Sir, you have a visitor. A gentleman from the Institute.'

'Thank you, Raymond.' Gravalax breathed out a puff of smoke before putting his glass of brandy on the side table next to the wing-backed chair. He tamped down the tobacco in his pipe and placed it on the silver tray as well, and smoothed down the creases in his smoking jacket. 'Please, send him in. It does not do to keep my fellows waiting.'

With a sharp nod, Raymond left.

Gravalax stared into the flames dancing in the fireplace and loosened his cravat and collar. He spluttered and stepped back as a puff of smoke billowed out of the fireplace, blown by an errant gust from the chimney. Such primitive heating technology, uncontrollable – even more so than the host's ability to regulate temperature in the first place, and such an inconvenience to have to suffer the sensation. He glanced around the room at the wood-panelled walls. One day they would reintroduce integrated heating – as soon as they could make it a commercially viable proposition. If it were not for the intervention of Britain's primitive tribes, maybe the Romans could have kept such technology in use. He turned away from the thought with disgust. Such a long period of backwards thinking. The Victorians were little better, but at least their thirst for scientific knowledge could be twisted to his own ends.

The clearing of a throat from behind startled the host and he turned around. 'How goes the research, Second?' Gravalax asked.

The visitor, the head of the Institution of Civil Engineers, closed the door softly behind him and loosened his collar. His eyes sparkled faintly in the dim light of the fire. 'Slowly, Sir.'

'We wish Edison would hurry. We greatly need to improve the lighting of these buildings if we are to stay hidden in the company of Humans not under our control.'

'They are close, Sir.'

'Then we must give them a push if we are to get electricity into our experiments. What is their biggest problem?'

'Oxidisation of the bulb filaments, Sir.'

'We see. Arrange for them to be given some help. Make some suggestions. If they see it as a viable technology it will be easier to prove its usefulness in other arenas. Speaking of which, how are the *other* tests going?'

The Second coughed. 'We have had some minor success with our subjects. We have been unable to attempt direct neural stimulation but, as you say, with access to electricity, this may be possible. Other methods have been somewhat successful. The exact mechanisms involved in the practice of thaumaturgy still elude us. Those subjects who have exhibited talent have been ... unsatisfactory. There is some component to the activity that we are missing.'

'And what about our "guests"?'

'Ah ...'

'Speak plainly. Your reticence makes you sound like one of the Humans.'

'We apologise. This host sees yours as a foreboding figure – something to do with their ridiculous class system, no doubt.'

'Do not let it influence you. It is not becoming. We need you to be strong, Second. We cannot trust mere Humans with important duties such as yours.'

The Second nodded. 'Yes, Sir ... With regard to our captive Freemasons, they died under torture without revealing their secrets.'

'Strong willed, are they?' Gravalax gestured to a chair opposite while taking a seat himself.

The Second remained standing. 'We cannot say. However, we suspect that they simply know nothing. They guard a secret that they do not understand.'

'Hah! They sound just like the Church … We have always wondered whether they are a splinter group from the Templars. We recall a young girl, the first vessel we used to enter this world, who was afraid of the Church. In fact, it was one of the Church's inquisitors that we moved into afterwards, before committing her to the fire.'

The visitor tilted his head.

'The girl's mother accused her of witchcraft. She had been spying on Freeminers, and that is all we know. Her memories were confused at the time, and the connection tenuous – we were never able to ascertain what they were mining.'

'Sir, the Freeminers we found in the Forest of Dean seemed to be mining nothing but coal and ochre. They had no connection with the Freemasons.'

'And that is why we believe they have forgotten their purpose. The Freemasons are so insular that they have collapsed in upon themselves. They are no threat. Let them have their foolish, vacuous secrets.'

The Second pulled out his pocket watch. 'Sir, we have to go. This host's family expects him back soon.'

'Very well,' Gravalax said, rising. 'Have the Freemasons killed. No, on second thoughts, kill all but one and let the survivor go. They may know nothing, but it is better to allow them to believe they do. It will send a message to stay out of Illuminati business.'

Chapter 22

'I say again,' the Londoner said. 'Who are you?'

Sebastian stared at each of his captors in turn. These people, underfunded, working from a damp warehouse with old gear – they weren't the ITF. Despite their tactics and ability to catch him unawares in the asylum, they were little more than rank amateurs with guns. Amateurs playing with forces of which they knew nothing.

'I am Sebastian Thorsson of SpecOps.' His heart swelled and he thrust out his chin as he spoke. 'Sebastian, son of Thor Frímansson, son of Frímann Geirsson, son of—'

The Londoner swept a hand dismissively. 'Spare me the family lineage.' He waved the journal in Sebastian's face. 'Why does your grandfather's diary have the Square and Compasses in it?'

'I don't know what you're talking about.'

'This!' He opened the book again and tapped a page with his finger. 'This, Sebastian Thorsson of Dullardville, the Square and Compasses.'

Sebastian peered at the book. It was a symbol – one he'd seen before: a right angle with ticks on it, intersected by an upside-down V with a loop at the top. Duggan said it was the symbol of a secret society, of which Sebastian's grandfather must have been a member.

The Londoner shifted in the light, seemingly forgetting to keep his identity secret, revealing his features. Gaunt cheeks, heavy brows, and scratchy beard. Sebastian studied the lines of his face. The symbol was definitely familiar to them. Very familiar.

'You're Freemasons!' he said.

Several of the others gasped.

The Londoner drew back, the faint sparkle of terrified excitement in his eyes. 'The Illuminati shouldn't know about that!'

'Who are the Illuminati?' Sebastian asked. 'I'm not aware of them, and I'm not a member of the ITF. I thought *you* were.'

The Londoner shook his head slowly. 'The Independent Terran Front *are* part of the Illuminati. Now answer the question. How do you know about us?'

'I didn't know you existed. My grandfather used to go to meetings. He talked about masons. I always assumed he was an ordinary stone mason. A friend of mine said he was probably a member of the Freemasons, and that's why your symbol is in his diary.'

'That doesn't explain your eyes. How do you have the sign of the Illuminati if you're not possessed?'

'I'm not sure you'd believe me.'

The Londoner grabbed the pliers again and thrust them in his face. 'Trust me. With some of the things we've seen, you'd be surprised.'

'Thaumaturgy, then. Magic! I used a spell. It went wrong and almost blinded me.'

'Pah!' The Londoner broke into a laughter quickly echoed by his colleagues who had retreated to the shadows. 'Magic isn't real.'

'It is!'

'Sir, the lore—' came a voice from the shadows.

'The lore says many things that aren't possible,' the Londoner said.

'But we know the Illuminati demons are real,' another said with a Hindi accent.

'Yes, and we know they are because we have physical proof. Magic has never been proven. However ... ' the Londoner folded his arms and leaned back as he stared at Sebastian. 'You seem convinced that it is real, and we can't explain your eyes. You certainly don't act possessed.'

'That's because I'm not possessed, and magic is real!' Sebastian shouted.

'Prove it, then. Do something *magical*.'

'I can't.'

'I knew it! Why not?'

'Well, I need my bag from over there.' Sebastian nodded at the table. 'And the only spell I successfully cast involved dreaming. The second left my eyes like this, which required a trip to hospital, so I'm not doing that again.'

'Then I'm afraid your body will be discovered in a ditch somewhere, and no trip to hospital will fix that. We can't let you loose in case you are possessed or, for some ungodly reason, working with the Illuminati.'

He let out a sigh. 'How on Earth can you seriously believe in possession but not magic?'

The Londoner arched an eyebrow. 'As I said before, many have seen the physical changes brought about by demonic possession. Even very sensitive brainwave recording equipment has shown changes, but nobody has any proof of magic. The former, whilst unexplained, are observable phenomena, but I've yet to see someone conjure something from nothing.'

'Sir, there is that strange mark in the hospital lobby,' someone with a French accent said. 'It wasn't there before the Illuminati went in, and none took explosives with them. Perhaps possession and magic are linked after all?'

'Horses have four legs, and so all four-legged animals are horses, is that it?' the Londoner snapped. 'Just because one is true it does not mean the other is!'

'Magic and possession *are* connected,' Sebastian said slowly. 'I know from experience. Magic can even be used to drive out the entities. I would have thought you'd know from history books that the two were connected.'

'We don't believe everything we read, and since we don't have a brainwave scanner here to disprove your possession, if you want us to believe you, you'll have to convince us.'

The mention of brainwaves gave Sebastian pause. Was possession *directly* related to the signal that Wolfram was researching? Was it an attempt to stimulate the same brainwaves? 'I'll need my bag. There are a few vials of white powder. Bring me one.'

The Londoner gave him a sidelong stare.

The Japanese man stepped forward. 'Sir, it could be explosive.'

'You only have to put it in my lap.' Sebastian pulled against the handcuffs. 'It's not like I can do anything if I'm lying. By the Gods, if you're that concerned, you can just hold it near me. What can I do with it, remote trigger a bomb by sheer force of will?'

The Londoner nodded. 'Yousef!' Someone tossed one of the slender tubes of carbyne from the bag and it landed between Sebastian's legs. 'Okay, impress me.'

Sebastian gritted his teeth. His surroundings were far from conducive for the state of mind required, and he didn't want to risk it backfiring again, but if he didn't do it he could end up dead. Aryx could end up dead ... 'Fine. Give me a minute.' He closed his eyes, leaned forward, and pressed his hands against them as Duggan had taught him.

Splotchy patterns and blue ripples pulsed towards him in the darkness. They faded, leaving bright sparkling flashes. He concentrated, imagining the chains of the handcuffs becoming hot, dripping metal, melting until the bonds broke free. In the darkness, a shape formed: a glowing green rune, an F with upward angled arms, Fehu – the fire of creation. In his ear a rising tone emerged, and the shapes of words formed on his lips. He opened his eyes.

'I'm ready,' he said.

The Londoner nodded.

Sebastian stared at the handcuffs and recalled the Fehu rune. He opened his mouth and, imitating the tones he recalled, chanted, '*Bræðið málm, brjóta skuldabréf.*' Melt metal, breaking bonds.

The air shimmered around him. The Londoner stepped back.

The chain of the handcuff fastening his left hand to the seat began to glow red. The red became bright orange, yellow, white. He jumped sideways in the seat to avoid a shower of molten metal as the liquid streamed away, sending sparks sputtering across the wet concrete floor.

It took him a moment to react, being only marginally less surprised than the onlookers; he leaped out of the seat, still attached by his right wrist, picked up the chair and brandished it legs first at the Londoner. 'Now where the fuck is Aryx?'

Several guns *k'chunked.*

The Londoner stood still for several seconds, wide-eyed with his mouth open. He broke into a raucous laugh and his cohorts backed away. 'Well I never! It seems you were telling the truth, Mr Thorsson, and that what we have learned by rote is, in fact, true.'

Sebastian jabbed at him with the chair. 'Where is Aryx?'

The guns rattled.

The Londoner put his hands out to either side. 'I'll handle this.'

Several metres away, to Sebastian's left, a door opened. Silhouetted against daylight, a man limped in holding one hand over his crotch.

'Farzoud! At last. Did you bring him?' the Londoner said, looking Sebastian up and down. 'Mr Thorsson here has become unexpectedly dangerous and wants to know where his friend is.'

Farzoud shook his head. 'He was not alone. I tried to get him in a quiet spot when I thought he would be vulnerable, but others helped and I lost track of him.'

A leather jacket. Sebastian grinned inwardly, but kept his face stern. 'He got away from you again, didn't he?' Aryx was out of danger. Despite the guns pointing in his direction, he straightened. 'You don't know who you're messing with.'

The Londoner rubbed his chin and relaxed his stance. 'Clearly not. You performed thaumaturgy.'

'Yes, and it was only by sheer luck that I didn't get possessed! You forced me to do it and I didn't have a chance to take precautions. I could have got possessed right here, and you'd all be screwed!'

'Then for that I sincerely apologise. I certainly never expected to see a true Stoneworker in my time.' He shifted, took a breath, and held it as if considering. 'We are the Freemasons,' he said, 'guardians of secret knowledge, and it appears that you are an enemy of our enemies.' He held out his right hand as though expecting Sebastian to shake it.

The others lowered their guns.

Sebastian put down the chair and tugged with his tethered wrist. 'Excuse me if I don't ... What do you mean by Stoneworker? That's why you're called Freemasons?'

'A Stoneworker is one who uses the philosopher's stone, orichalcum. We've never seen it in living memory, and only know of it from legends. How did you come by it?' The Londoner gestured to Sebastian's chair, and the one called Yousef removed the handcuffs.

Sebastian rubbed his wrists. 'It's a long story, and one I probably shouldn't tell you, but you seem to know a lot more about it than I did when I first encountered it.'

'Come then.' Taking Sebastian by the elbow, the Londoner guided him towards another, newly opened, door. 'Let us get you something to eat and you can tell me more over lunch.'

'I need to let my friends know where I am.' Sebastian tapped his wristcom and it responded with a *blarp!*

The Londoner shook his head. 'In due time. Communications are jammed here, with good reason. Eat and talk first.'

He led Sebastian into a red-brick stairwell with concrete stairs leading down. A caged light on the wall and a scaffold pole handrail added to the air of old, disused industry. The stairs ended in a long, dark corridor, lit at intervals by the same wire-caged 20th-century lights. The air smelt damp, and the occasional *pat, pat* of water dripping from overhead pipes shattered the lamps' puddle-doubles.

Behind him, the limping Farzoud followed along with Yousef, who carried Sebastian's rucksack. They trusted the Londoner's judgement enough to have removed their balaclavas.

Faced with a featureless steel door at the end of the corridor, they stopped. The Londoner rapped on it in a pattern so quick Sebastian didn't have chance to remember it. The door opened an inch as a figure peered through, then it swung wide. Yousef handed Sebastian's rucksack to the Londoner and entered ahead of them, along with Farzoud.

'Jamie, could you get us something to eat and drink?' the Londoner asked.

From behind the door stepped a gangly young woman with long blonde hair, wearing a grimy, knitted jumper full of holes – the sleeves of which dangled inches over her hands. Her shoulders slumped. 'Do I have to? Why can't Leon do it?'

'I've sent your brother to keep an eye on the hospital in our place. Now, coffee and soup please, if you don't mind.'

'Ugh, he always gets to do the interestin' stuff.' The girl huffed, and slunk off through another door in the opposite corner of the room while the other two men parked themselves by the door.

'Teenagers,' the Londoner mumbled, leading Sebastian in. He pulled a lightweight wooden chair out from a table that held an assortment of empty bottles, a dirty tin cup and a scattering of playing cards. 'You're probably wondering why we look like this,' he said, tugging at the lapel of his worn-out army fatigues. 'We don't get into the city much, and it's hard to buy things when you don't have bank accounts.'

Sebastian narrowed his eyes.

'Please,' the Londoner said, gesturing to the chair he'd pulled out. Sebastian sat and the Londoner took a seat on the opposite side of the table. 'We try to stay off-grid as much as possible. You can't be very secretive if you advertise your presence to the galaxy by leaving payment records everwhere, can you?'

'I guess not.'

The girl shortly returned with two steaming bowls of soup and placed them on the table. She put her hands on her hips. 'Anything else, or can I go now?'

The Londoner nodded. 'Go join your brother, but take Yousef and Farzoud with you.'

Her frown twisted into a smile. 'Thanks, Dad!' She skipped out of the room and the two men followed her out.

The Londoner took a mouthful of soup. 'Nice. Parsnip – the real stuff, not that mush rubbish.'

Sebastian sniffed the contents, picked up a dirty spoon and rubbed it on his leg before sipping a little. Earthy, but sweet. They might not have much in the way of resources, but they certainly knew how to make soup.

The Londoner watched as Sebastian ate. 'I'm sorry for the trouble earlier. We can't be too careful down here. My name is Jonas.'

Sebastian rested his spoon in the bowl. 'Nice to meet you, Jonas.' He wished it were true, but the hot soup only served to aggravate his now sensitive tooth. 'I suppose I can forgive you ... if Aryx is safe.'

'He is. He got away from Farzoud uninjured and now seems to be heading back to the hospital.'

'So, that means Monica got away, too.'

'Who?'

'One of my colleagues. You obviously missed her. She must have escaped before you caught me.'

'Ah, yes. I wondered what happened to her after Brazil.'

Sebastian took another few mouthfuls and finished the soup while he composed his next question. 'Why did you think I'd already been to the hospital before you found me?'

'Oh, not you personally – the ITF. The Illuminati. They were there a couple of days ago. They visit the place from time to time, most likely to get old records or to see if anything's been disturbed. The place acts as something of a honeypot for those interested in their business.'

'Did you see anyone else? I'm trying to find a friend, Duggan, who went there looking for something. He was wearing a black robe. We saw evidence of a struggle. One of your men mentioned the marks in the lobby.'

Jonas looked up to the ceiling. 'They left with someone that hadn't gone in with them. Come to think of it, yes, he was wearing a robe. We weren't able to follow up on it, though.'

'Why not?'

'We don't have the manpower to follow everyone coming in and out of that place. They lose us pretty easily when they get to the city.'

'So, what made me worth the attention?'

'Your friend went to visit Mrs Alvarez.'

Sebastian folded his arms.

'We're keeping an eye on her, to make sure she's safe from the

ITF. She doesn't know we're watching her, but Farzoud isn't the most subtle.'

'And she's special because?'

'Her son, Nick, was one of us, after a fashion. After news of his death reached Earth, we thought she might be vulnerable. We had no idea what happened to him but, because of the part he played in the raid on the ITF base on Cinder IV, we couldn't take any chances. We thought your friends were their agents.' Jonas ate the last of his soup and looked about the room. 'Darn that girl, she forgot the coffee.' He got up and retrieved a tin kettle from a shelf and put it on an old cooker hob in the corner. 'Jamie's always too keen to be on the next adventure. I'm sure she'll get in trouble one of these days, if her brother doesn't beat her to it. She's just like her mother in that regard.'

Sebastian snorted. His nephew, Erik, wasn't far off growing into a rebellious teenager himself.

Jonas leaned against the hob. 'So, tell me, where did you find orichalcum?'

'We know it as carbyne, and I got mine in space. It's only stable in a vacuum.'

'That explains why it's seldom found on Earth.'

'Yes.' Sebastian pushed his bowl to one side. 'Jonas, you said that Nick Alvarez was a member of the Freemasons. He was working with a scientist, John Kerl, doing experiments in cybernetic repair of damaged brains, but they moved on to blending thaumaturgy with technology. Originally, I thought it was all Kerl's idea, but now I think it must have been Alvarez who introduced him to it. It all makes sense now. Alvarez must have found the carbyne on his trips and suggested the thaumaturgy research after Kerl recruited him.'

'How did he die, exactly?'

'He got possessed while experimenting with it, and the entity made him commit suicide rather than allow itself to succumb to hypnotic control.'

Jonas paled. 'That means they might know about us. They could know who we are.'

Sebastian put a hand out in a calming gesture. 'I don't think they do. The one that controlled Alvarez had been jumping back and forth between him and my friend Duggan. The Fo—' He stopped himself. 'Some friends of mine who studied Duggan said they would likely only have access to surface thoughts, and would not be able to dig into deeper memories unless they inhabited someone for a considerable length of time.'

'Hmm ... Still, we can't take the risk. Nick never came here, but I'll make sure everyone knows that we may have been compromised, and reduce our city presence.'

The kettle whistled.

Jonas made coffee and handed one of the tin mugs to Sebastian. The aroma was cheap, almost like Bronadi chicory, but he sipped from the steaming cup. A little bitter, but drinkable.

Jonas sat at the table again. 'So,' he said, pushing his cup around in front of him, 'back to you. What were you looking for at the hospital, aside from your friend?'

'Just him. We thought he may have gone there looking for someone by the name of Alicia Maline. I had just come across her file when your men interrupted.'

'And he was the one we saw wearing the robes?'

'Yes. The lobby was burnt out by a fireball. If the ITF caught up with him, he probably tried to blow them all up.'

'Interesting. There were no accelerants ... So, he's like you, also a Stoneworker?'

Sebastian nodded.

'If the Illuminati have him, I can't help you. We have no idea where they would have taken him. The Church might be keeping tabs on them, but we don't exactly have a good relationship.'

'Let me guess, because of the association with magic?'

'It doesn't matter to them that none of us can actually do it. They'd like to wipe out anyone who has any connection to it. They annoy us from time to time, but we always get away. It's the Illuminati that need to be got rid of, not us. We just don't have the firepower or resources. We could do with the Church using their armed forces to back us up, not fight us.'

Sebastian frowned. 'I can see why they're like that. You can't really blame them, even though they wiped out—' He'd almost blurted out about the Folians again. 'Even though they wiped out lots of other religions ... in their eyes, everything that relates to magic comes back to demons.'

Jonas snorted. 'It would be better if they knew what they were dealing with.' He stared again, thinking. 'It's not helped by the fact that demons have no solid form in this world. I assume you know that?'

'We weren't certain. I mean, it's obvious they're some sort of incorporeal being, but I had a dream in which one turned into something made of crystal or ice. I don't know if that's how they actually look where they come from or whether it was just a dream form.'

'They are the same beings across religions, at least our legends say, even though they are described differently. Our members include followers of almost all world religions. Some of those here follow Christianity, Islam, Sikhism, Shintoism, Buddhism, Hinduism – and they all have their own notions of demons. They appear in the form that scares a culture most. The Freemasons were mostly Pagan, and have always been open-minded about the demons' nature. We now suspect them to be some kind of interdimensional being.'

'That was the same conclusion we reached. Duggan was taken over by one temporarily, but other than the glittery eyes, there wasn't any physical evidence that anything had happened to him ...' Sebastian's thoughts drifted to Achene, and the time Shiliri – his main Folian contact – had attempted to analyse Duggan's mind after possession. 'There was no evidence we could detect with the scientific means we had at our disposal at the time.' His stomach knotted. The conversation reminded him too much of Duggan and he fell silent.

Leaning back in his chair, Jonas seemed to notice Sebastian's discomfort and changed the subject. 'Why did you sign your mate up for the marathon if you were here following Duggan?'

'Oh, Gods!' He'd almost forgotten their entire purpose for coming to Earth. 'We have to get into an archive. It's under the building where we signed up – our timing was bad.'

'Surely it couldn't have been better? What chance would you stand of getting in if the place had been empty?'

'Probably none. I need to get back to my friends. Our ship's stuck in Cardiff Spaceport, and we've only got the clothes we came in, apart from what Aryx and Karan bought to wear for the marathon, and none of that is suitable for a charity ball.'

Jonas pushed the chair away from the table as he stood. 'I'll take you back to the hospital and let you find those records, but you'll have to make your own way back into the city.'

Sebastian finished his coffee and followed Jonas out through a series of dilapidated rooms and corridors, eventually climbing a spiral staircase and stopping at a door at the top.

The door opened into the grey afternoon, and an expanse of weed-spattered, broken concrete lay before them, stretching through the middle of a field, flanked on either side by long, half-cylinder buildings made from corrugated panels. Between the buildings stood a 20th-century removal van, covered with algae – likely the converted vehicle Sebastian had been brought in. Jonas unlocked the van and got in the driver's seat. He opened the passenger door and waited for Sebastian to climb in. The engine purred into life and the vehicle lurched forward.

'It's a shame you couldn't afford to get this automated,' Sebastian said. Jonas's gear-shifting left a lot to be desired.

'And have some computer somewhere know all about our comings and goings? No thanks.'

After several minutes of silently navigating the narrow, unkempt country lanes from the airfield, Jonas spoke. 'I can't offer you any support or weapons for your break-in later, I'm afraid.'

'I wasn't expecting any help, and certainly shouldn't need weapons. There's a better chance of success if there are few of us, anyway, but is there some way I can reach you if I need to?'

'We've got an agent in the city that can keep an eye on you.'

'Let me guess, the guy with the shaved hair and square jaw?'

'Who? I don't know anyone like that. I need to keep my agent's identity secret, but he'll present himself if he needs to.'

The overgrown fields they passed gave way to trees that grew through rusting cars, and those were eventually replaced with derelict houses.

Sebastian stared out at the decaying signs of abandoned civilisation. 'Have you heard of Alicia Maline before?'

'I can't say I have. The name didn't ring a bell when you mentioned it earlier. Was she a patient at the hospital?'

'I think so.'

'Then she probably didn't last long. They did all sorts of horrible experiments there after it officially closed.'

Sebastian shifted in his seat, turning to face Jonas. 'Such as?'

'Prolonged ice baths, partial lobotomies, bringing people to near death for God knows what reason. There was even talk of genetic research in the final years, with a lab trying to modify Human DNA to create new life forms, and experiments to create people with different kinds of senses. Multiple eyes, glands that responded to different electromagnetic spectra . . .' Jonas shuddered. 'Abominations. Thanks to us, word of that reached the authorities. The research contravened the Customised Life Accord. The place got raided and it shut quicker than a flytrap.'

He stared at the road ahead as he recounted to Sebastian the things he'd heard from his predecessors. The terrible experimentation that had been done for hundreds of years; the disappearances of homeless, disabled, jobless, and less "socially desirable" people in the 1800s to late 1900s.

The stories he told horrified Sebastian, who jumped as Jonas scraped the gears.

'There's another thing,' Jonas said. 'If you get a chance to search the records when you break into the archive, could you do us a favour and look for cases of missing persons?'

'I can try. Have people disappeared recently?'

'Yes. Although the experiments and abductions ended way back, there have been a few bodies turning up outside the city over the last fifteen to twenty years.'

'Aren't the police investigating it?'

'No. You'd think it would cause concern when a body turns up every few months, but when it comes to those cases, they won't touch it with a bargepole. I suspect the Illuminati have agents in the police force.'

Sebastian nodded. 'That's what we think, too – and partly why we're checking the records. I have to find a colleague's family.' He scratched his chin. 'What would warrant the ITF covering up murders?'

Jonas swallowed. 'They're not normal bodies.'

'Genetic experiments?'

'Oh, no, they're Human bodies alright – just not in any form you'd want to end up dead in.'

Sebastian blinked. Why would anyone want to end up dead in any form? 'And?'

'They're shrivelled. Withered. Almost desiccated.'

'So, they've been murdering people and drying them out?'

'There are no *wounds*. It's like they were killed *by* drying them out. Rapidly. We had our suspicions about what caused it, and we couldn't see the link before you turned up because none of us truly believed in magic. Now we know different, it makes sense.'

'I don't understand. How does magic come into it?'

'We think they might have a necromancer.'

Chapter 23

Sebastian's jaw dropped. 'Necromancer? Someone who summons the dead?'

'No!' Jonas snorted. 'Fantasy stories are responsible for that idea. Our legends say that a necromancer is someone who uses the dead, or kills the living, to perform magic.'

'That's disgusting! I don't even see how that's possible. Carbyne is the catalyst. Thaumaturgy isn't even possible without it.'

'Well, if you can find an alternative explanation for how someone can dry out quick enough to still have an expression of shock on their faces, I'm all ears.'

Sebastian fell silent, his brain working overtime. Could there really be a way of performing thaumaturgy without carbyne? The physics of magic weren't exactly clear: when a spell was cast, carbyne translated into another dimension or plane of existence that the Folians called the Weave. That process somehow released energy that manipulated matter in the physical realm. Carbyne sometimes came back on the exterior of ships exiting superphase travel, implying that the superphase layer of space was the Folians' Weave.

'When people perform thaumaturgy, their minds touch superphase,' Sebastian said. 'If historical accounts of possession are correct, there must be other ways of a mind contacting superphase without using an acceleration node or carbyne, otherwise how do the ITF increase their numbers?'

Jonas nodded. 'And that's the question that has plagued us. You know, there were people committed to the hospital suffering from acceleration psychosis. Actually, I think it was the first hospital to categorise the disorder and the only one that ever dealt with cases.'

'But it closed down not long after Humans discovered the nodes.'

'And doesn't that add to the mystery?'

Sebastian squirmed. It certainly added to the mystery – in a way that made him most uncomfortable.

Aryx held his breath as the doorknob turned. There wasn't much he could do to hide in the dark foyer of the asylum with his legs glowing brightly, unless he sat in his wheelchair and risked puncturing the tyres on the broken glass. Karan stood in a half-crouch, ready to pounce on whoever came in.

The latch clicked and the door swung open.

Launching herself at the silhouette standing in the doorway, she took the figure flying down the steps out of sight.

Aryx scrunched across the lobby and looked out.

She lay sprawled on top of a man in familiar clothing.

'Seb!' Aryx shouted.

'I'm pleased to see you, too,' Sebastian said, waving at Aryx from beneath Karan.

She climbed off and helped him up. 'Sorry about that. You should have knocked.'

He dusted himself down. 'How was I supposed to know you were in there?'

Aryx clambered down the stone steps, being careful not to slip on the hard surface, and hugged Sebastian. 'I thought you were dead, or worse.' He held him by the arms and stared at his grimy face and red eyes. 'Where the hell have you been? You look like crap.'

'With them.' Sebastian jabbed a thumb over his shoulder.

Aryx looked past him. A vehicle pulled away from the gates at the end of the drive. 'Who's *them*?'

'Freemasons, not terrorists. They've been keeping an eye on this place.'

'Why did they take you?'

Sebastian rubbed his jaw. 'They thought I was ITF. I managed to convince them otherwise, but not before they tortured me. They said the ITF come back from time to time, so we'd best keep our eyes open. They saw Duggan taken away, but don't know where to.'

After giving Sebastian time to recount what had happened, Aryx turned and made his way up the steps into the lobby. 'You'd better come and see what we found out about Alicia Maline.'

'What's the point? Just scan the file onto the infoslate. We need to think about getting back to the city for the evening event.'

'Ah, about that,' Aryx said. 'I didn't finish quick enough.'

Sebastian stopped just inside the door. '*What?* We've gone through all this and now can't get in?'

Aryx clenched his fists. 'Why, you ungrateful—'

Monica stepped in front of him, wielding Sebastian's infoslate. 'Aryx went through a lot for you, much to his own detriment.'

Sebastian rubbed his jaw again. 'I know. I'm sorry I put him up to it, but if we can't get into the archive, it's all been for nothing.'

Karan took the infoslate from Monica. 'Maybe there's another way we can get in,' she said, flicking through pages on the display.

Aryx fought to keep his hands by his sides. 'You're just so ungrateful sometimes, Sebastian!'

'I said I'm sorry.'

'Hey, it's not all bad,' Karan said. 'There's a clause on the marathon site in the small print. You obviously didn't read it, Seb. It says the evening event is for those entrants who come in at times under four hours thirty minutes, or those who have served in the military.' She smiled and immediately her face dropped. 'That means *neither* of us needed to have overexerted ourselves!'

Aryx stepped around Monica, grabbed Sebastian by the collar and shoved him against the wall, leaving a white smear where the black tar smudged off the tiles. 'All that time I pushed myself to go as fast as I could. All that time, wearing myself out. Injuring my wrists!' He growled through his teeth, shoving with every word. 'You're always. Acting. Without. Thinking!'

Sebastian's eyes glistened with tears in the dim orange light.

Aryx let go of his collar and turned away. 'I don't know why I stick with you!'

Not quietly enough, Monica whispered to Karan, 'Do they often fight like this?'

'No, it seems tensions are unusually high.'

Monica put her hand on Aryx's shoulder. 'Perhaps you should—'

He pulled away and glared at her as he strode to the stairs and sat down. No way was he telling Sebastian about his health, not now.

Not ever.

Sebastian stood against the wall, staring at the floor. 'I'm sorry. I've been under so much pressure ...'

'Oh, get stuffed!' Aryx shouted. 'I don't need excuses! Just admit that you were wrong for a change.'

'You're right. I'm an idiot. I didn't read it all properly. I didn't think. I'm sorry.'

Aryx forced his breathing back under control. They all stood in silence for a minute. He couldn't stay mad forever. They were a team. And Sebastian ... that stupid sad face. 'Come here,' he said, putting a hand on the step.

Sebastian trudged over and sat down.

'You have to learn to slow down,' Aryx said. 'Think about what you're doing and how it affects other people.' He put a hand on Sebastian's back. 'We're not on Tenebrae now. We have no backup. We have to think about each other.'

Sebastian leaned into Aryx's shoulder and sniffed. 'This is all getting too big for me to deal with. I don't think I can cope.'

'You've got us.' Aryx nudged him upright. 'Now, man up and get on with it.'

Sebastian gave a lopsided smile and snorted. 'Yeah. I suppose we should scan the files.' He stood and plucked at his grimy clothes. 'And then head to the shops for a change of wardrobe.'

Three hours later, after trips to several shops and a bout of Sebastian complaining about his aching feet, they had found suits and dresses appropriate for a formal occasion such as the ball.

While Sebastian dressed, Aryx went to the hotel room fridge. Two vials of his drugs sat on the shelf – enough to last until the shipment came in at the station when they got back. He took one out.

But what if they didn't get back in time?

They still had a huge task ahead of them: they had to break in to the archive, still had to find Duggan – if possible – and finally locate the Gladrin family. He wasn't supposed to ration it ... but surely half a dose now and half later, once he knew they would get back in time, would be fine?

He injected half of the dose. Of course it would.

After placing the remainder in the fridge, he waited in the corridor outside their room for Sebastian to finish dressing.

Karan and Monica emerged from their room wearing tight-fitting black dresses. Karan's hair was tied up in a tiny knot at the back of her head with fronds sticking out, while Monica's hung in loose waves.

'Very nice,' he said, nodding to Karan. 'I've never seen you looking so ladylike.'

She scowled and raised her clutch bag. 'Just watch your mouth.'

Monica flicked her hair over her shoulder and adjusted a sparkling earring. 'It makes a change to wear something nice. It's amazing how you get used to an N-suit.'

Sebastian came out of his room and locked the door.

'It's unusual to see you without your rucksack,' Aryx said, taking note of the suit's sharp lines. 'Did it require surgery?'

Sebastian shrugged and fiddled with a cufflink. 'What can I do? I can't exactly carry an infoslate to a posh evening ball, can I?' He put on a deep voice. '"Excuse me, Sir, would you please put your bag in the cloakroom?"' He turned to one side. '"I need to keep it with me, I'm about to break in to your archives, doncha know?" Yes, I'm sure that would go down a storm.'

'What are you going to do then?'

He strode off down the corridor. 'I'll tell you when we get outside.'

Aryx tucked in his suit jacket so that it didn't rub on the wheels of his chair and wheeled after him. It was typical: finally do something civilised and you have to wear a suit that crumples up and makes you look like a sack of shit.

'Stop fidgeting,' Sebastian said as they stood in the lift.

'I look awful.'

He put his hand on Aryx's shoulder and smiled. 'You look ... handsome.'

Aryx couldn't help but smile back.

They left the hotel and crossed Westminster Bridge. The cold night air bit through Aryx's thin suit as though he wore nothing. The women tottered on high heels alongside, vigorously rubbing their arms as they went. 'Here, have our jackets,' he said. He stopped and handed his to Monica.

Sebastian did the same, handing his to Karan, and immediately his teeth began to chatter.

'What's the plan?' Aryx asked.

'I can't use an infoslate to hack in to the centre. There's no way I could smuggle one in with this suit, so I'll interlink with Wolfram via my wristcom.' He tapped the device. 'Wolfram, are you there?'

'He's being a bit slow,' Aryx said. 'Background processing, etcetera.'

Sebastian waited a moment. 'Wolfram?'

'Wolfram here. How can I help, Sebastian? I trust everything is going well?'

'As well as can be expected, under the circumstances. I'll need your help in a little while. I'd like to interlink my wristcom with the ship's computer and have you supervise, since I can't take an infoslate into the archive. I've got an interface block so I can bypass security manually, and I'd like you to monitor, and download as many records as you can access.'

'Of course.'

'Why do you want to download records?' Aryx asked. 'We're just looking for Gladrin's family.'

'I've offered to share the list of witnesses with the Freemasons. I know it's not entirely ethical, but I think they can be trusted, and if there's a connection between cases it might help them to isolate ITF members. If I can find proof, they can pass it on to the Church. They have an armed division that will act on it, whereas the police can't be trusted to make any arrests ... Wolfram, how's your analysis of the nightmare signal going?'

'I've completed my initial simulations, but wanted to double-check the results by running several permutations of algorithms. I think you might find the results intriguing. Would you like to hear them?'

Sebastian stopped walking. 'Yes, tell me what you found.'

'The signal appears to stimulate parts of the brain that are often active during dreaming – as one would expect, given that it causes you to experience nightmares. The other side effect is that it seems to trigger a quantum harmonic in the neurons of the inner ear.'

'That's strange.'

Aryx tugged Sebastian's sleeve. 'Do you think it would make people hear things?'

'What makes you say that?'

'Alicia Maline heard voices when she was a teenager, but took medication to stop them. I wonder if that's why she didn't get on the colony mission.'

'It's possible, but I don't see how they're related. Other than when the Folians spoke to us, I haven't heard voices in my head. Wolfram, do you think this harmonic could cause people to hear voices?'

'I'm not entirely certain what the effect would be for the recipient. Perhaps Monica would be able to assist me later,' Wolfram said.

'Alright. If you get a chance, it might be worth cross-referencing the research done on acceleration psychosis, since the signal was routed through the nodes. Good work, and keep on it until I contact you.'

'Very well. I will also work on creating a program that will eliminate the Trojan that forwards the signal to your terminal on Tenebrae. Once complete, I will transmit it to your computer for safekeeping so you can activate it later. Wolfram out.'

Karan and Monica shuffled their feet and rubbed their legs together. 'Can we get on now?' Monica asked. 'We're freezing out here.'

The group huddled together as they finished crossing Westminster Bridge but, as they drew closer to One Great George Street, they separated into couples: Sebastian walked ahead with Karan, while Monica stayed with Aryx. At least it would make them less conspicuous if they teamed up with their plus-ones.

Sebastian and Karan disappeared inside long before Aryx arrived at the building. He stopped at the foot of the old stone steps and a man wearing a bright red jacket and shiny shoes stepped out from the doorway at the top.

'This the only way in?' Aryx shouted up at him.

The doorman nodded. 'For guests, yes.'

'No back entrance?'

The doorman slowly shook his head and reached out with a white-gloved hand to press a button on the wall next to him.

Aryx spun around to face Monica. 'I can't believe that after everything I've been through, I'm not even going to get in! What are these people thinking about, because it certainly isn't accessibility!'

'Ah, Aryx, you might want to change your mind,' Monica said, pointing at the steps.

One side of what he had assumed to be solid stone steps retracted into the building. Each step slid back until all were flush with the step on which the doorman stood, revealing a shiny chequer-plate platform at street level. He wheeled onto it with a grin and the platform rose until level with the doorway, and he rolled off. Monica clacked up the steps on the side that remained.

'Thank you very much,' he said to the doorman with a nod. 'Sorry about the shouting. I've had a *really* bad day.'

'Quite alright, Sir.' The doorman held the door open for him. 'If you'd care to go in.'

Aryx wheeled into the warmth of the lobby and stopped on the large coir mat. Shiny black shoes squeaked on the polished white floor inside. He glanced down at his tyres and performed several quick turns to wipe off the dirt. Nobody else had a wristcom on show, so he slid his up inside his cuff until it lodged on his forearm.

'Can I take your jacket, madam?' The voice startled Aryx – he hadn't noticed the young female cloakroom attendant behind the counter in the wall to his left.

Monica unhooked the jacket from her shoulders and turned to Aryx. 'Do you need it?'

He shook his head. 'Might as well store it, it'll stop it from getting trashed on my chair. If I get cold, I can come back for it.'

The young woman took the jacket and stowed it on a hanger, which promptly slid along the rail into a storage compartment, and she presented him with an infoslate. 'Identification, please.'

'Aryx Trevarian, plus one,' he said. Reaching out with his left hand – being the closest – he pressed his thumb to the display.

Blarp!

Her eyebrows shot up. 'Oh, there appears to be a problem with your ID. It says unrecognised.'

'There must be an ... um ...' What the hell had Sebastian done during registration?

Monica flashed her eyes in the direction of Aryx's other hand.

He tried with his right thumb.

Beep!

The attendant smiled. 'Ah, ex-military. That's fine, thank you. I'm sorry about that. It's very odd. I should probably get my supervisor to check the infoslate for problems.'

Aryx's scalp itched. 'I-I don't think you have to. It must have been the blister I got during the race. It wore a bit of my print off.' He whipped his thumb up to his mouth and bit on the pad as though to soothe it.

'Ah, that would explain it.' She put the infoslate back under the counter. 'Enjoy your evening, Mr Trevarian.'

Aryx spun away from the counter. With Monica alongside, he wheeled over to Sebastian, who stood with a drink in his hand talking to an elderly, silver-haired couple. The man he spoke to wore a tailored suit with matching bow tie, while the woman was in a black long-sleeved dress covered in tiny sparkling things.

'Would you excuse me for a moment?' Sebastian said, stepping away from the couple to allow Aryx and Monica to approach. 'I'd like to introduce two of my friends, Aryx Trevarian, an engineer from Tenebrae, and Dr Monica Stevens.'

When Aryx met the woman's gaze, her hand went to the wide band of diamonds that sparkled around her crinkly neck. She extended a hand to Monica. 'Mrs Rutherford. Pleased to meet you. You ran the marathon, I presume?'

Monica shook the offered hand. 'Pleased to meet you, however you presume incorrectly, Mrs Rutherford. Aryx ran the marathon in his wheelchair, quite speedily, I might add' – she glared at Sebastian – 'given that it was literally dropped on him with no warning.'

Mr Rutherford stepped around them to approach Aryx. 'What was your time? I'm always impressed by marathon runners. It's not something I could have done, even in my youth.'

Aryx took a glass of something fizzy and fruit-smelling from a passing waitress carrying a tray of drinks. Switching his glass from one hand to the other, he rubbed his palm on his trousers before shaking Mr Rutherford's hand. 'Four hours, thirty-five minutes, and thirty-nine seconds.'

Mr Rutherford gave a warm smile. 'Most impressive.'

'I could have finished within four-thirty, and I would have had an easier time of it, had a certain spectator not decided to hold me up.'

'Someone tried to interfere with your race? Who was it? I could have it looked into by the organisers.'

'Oh, uh, it doesn't matter. It was someone who thought they knew me.' Aryx rubbed his still-aching wrist. 'Got a bit overexcited and tried to nick one of my gloves as a souvenir.'

Mr Rutherford laughed, sloshing a little of his drink on the shiny floor. 'There can be some quite eccentric people at these events!'

Aryx glanced at Monica. She still stood talking to Mrs Rutherford, who issued comments in a disinterested monotone. Clearly, she had more patience than he could muster for the high-society couple.

'So, Dr Stevens, what sort of work do you do?' Mrs Rutherford asked, scratching at a small red patch under her necklace. 'Maybe you could help with this problem I have—'

'Not unless it's of a molecular or archaeological nature. I'm not that kind of doctor. I have advanced degrees in molecular xenobiology and xenoarchaeology, and I do things with nanobots in a biological capacity. I'm not a GP.'

'That's … interesting.' Her attention drifted up to the ceiling.

'It can be. I'm often among the first to break turf on a new dig before ExoTerra arrive. I'm a kind of advanced archaeology scout.'

'That's nice,' Mrs Rutherford said, turning to her husband.

'What does it entail?' Mr Rutherford asked, ignoring his wife.

'We often take scans of an area when we arrive in the system, then go down to investigate. I've been fortunate enough to be the first to make landfall in a lot of digs ... '

Mr Rutherford listened with rapt attention, nodding periodically, while his wife grew steadily more restless, rubbing at her wrists and studying her nails. She tried to steer the subject back towards her medical issues, despite Monica's lack of qualification on the subject.

Monica glanced at Aryx, her eyebrows pinched up in the middle. Bless her, she looked bored to tears.

A waiter approached Aryx and bent down to offer him a tray of drinks. 'Would you like champagne, Sir?'

'No, thank you. I really shouldn't.'

Mrs Rutherford made a small *hmf?* sound. 'Can't you take alcohol?'

'I can. I just don't like to drink and drive. Plus, it doesn't help to get too legless. Screws with my balance,' he said, pulling up into a wheelie.

The woman raised her eyebrows and exhaled derisively through her nose, but turned back to Monica, who glared at Aryx with a "get me out of here" look.

He'd had enough of the dismissive old crone anyway. 'Does the wheelchair put you off?' he asked Mrs Rutherford, lacing his voice with sarcasm. 'Some people love it. The feel of chrome on their naked skin. Either that or my knee up their backside.' He winked at Monica and she stifled a snigger.

Mr Rutherford's eyes creased and he bit his lips.

'Dennis,' Mrs Rutherford said, reddening and turning away, 'do you think we could talk to somebody else?'

'Why? Does the sight of me offend you?' Aryx asked. 'Why do you even support a charity like the Veterans' Reconstruction Fund if the appearance of someone who hasn't been "reconstructed" offends you?'

She stared down her nose at him. 'That is precisely *why* I support it,' she said, and spun away, shoes squealing on the polished floor.

Several people turned in their direction. Aryx's collar tightened.

Sebastian approached from the buffet table carrying three plates of hors d'oeuvres. 'Everything alright?'

'No,' Aryx said. 'I have to get out of this fucking room.' He wanted to punch something. He spun away, across the lobby, and took the lift to the first floor.

Sebastian and the others caught up with him at the top of the stairs. 'Where are you going?'

A pair of double doors stood open at the end of the hallway. Bright spots of light drifted through the darkened interior of the room beyond.

'I want to see what's in there,' he said, beckoning for Monica and Karan to follow.

Music came from the room and, as the group entered, Sebastian fidgeted and scampered off to the buffet table inside the door. Couples danced around the hall beneath a sparkling mirror ball, twirling around each other like motes of dust in disturbed air. The men wore smart black suits, but the women wore a variety of ball gowns in a spectrum of colours; the jewels on the ears and necks of many caught stray rays from the mirror ball and scintillated like stars orbiting their dark partners.

Sebastian returned with an extra plate of food.

Aryx took one of the plates from him and guzzled a handful of savouries before handing it back empty. 'Come on, join in. We need to blend in a bit.'

'You know I can't dance.'

Karan elbowed Sebastian in the ribs, nearly dislodging the plates precariously balanced in his hands. 'Won't dance, more like.'

'If it's any consolation,' Monica said, shaking her head, 'I can't dance very well, either.'

Karan looked up and down Monica's elegant outfit. 'But you're perfectly dressed for it.'

She put her hands up. 'No, I'll stay here and discuss tactics with Sebastian.'

'Come on, Aryx, it looks like it's just us on the dance floor then.' Karan took his hand and towed him onto the polished wooden floor. At that moment, the music picked up from the steady flow of "The Blue Danube" and transitioned into an upbeat salsa. She shimmied, pulling him forwards by his hands, moving up and down as she shook. How she did that in heels without falling over, he'd never know.

She pulled back, letting go of one hand and flinging the other arm wide. He caught his opposite wheel and turned outward, then, using her tension, wheeled forwards. She shimmied again, backwards and forwards, and he used her momentum to shake his torso while he pushed back and forth to match her movements.

Taking both of his hands again, she pulled him towards her, then pushed away. On the second pull, she crouched a little to allow Aryx to twirl her. In a second she finished the twirl, sprawled across his lap, arms outstretched, and he spun on the spot, tracing huge circles with her arms. It had been a long time since he'd been able to dance properly with someone else, to move so freely. He gave in to the feeling and threw his head back while he spun.

The other dancers stepped back to make room, and cheered.

Sebastian watched the spectacle of Aryx and Karan's exuberant dance while he discussed his plans with Monica. If only he could join in with something that made Aryx happy. The fluidity of Aryx's movements could surely overshadow any shortcomings of his own two left feet? But no, he couldn't dance, and right now he had a job to do.

'. . . So, I'll go down into the archive and retrieve the records,' he continued. 'It's best if Aryx monitors the security office up here.'

Monica nodded. 'If anything happens, signal him. He can get back here quickly enough, and I'm sure we'll be able to create a distraction.'

'Fine. I'll go now. You ought to join them on the dance floor.'

'Okay. Be careful.' She patted him on the back and made her way to the middle of the hall where Aryx and Karan were still putting on a show for the other dancers.

Sebastian looked back over his shoulder before leaving. Monica's body flowed to the music like liquid velvet. He laughed to himself. 'Yeah, you dance badly . . . If you're comparing yourself to a galactic gold-medallist.'

Making his way across the room above the lobby, he kept a wary eye on the security staff as he looked down through the oculus in the centre: they were a little obvious, with earpieces connected via coiled wires to something under their jackets, but perhaps that was the point? Judging by the way one slouched against the wall, they weren't expecting trouble. Best not to push it, though.

He descended the red-carpeted stairs to the lobby and stopped to admire one of the many dark paintings with heavy gilded frames that hung on the walls, slowly moving from one to the next. Eventually he came to an unmarked door and, after waiting for the security staff's attention to be elsewhere, stepped through.

Sebastian found himself at the head of a stairwell. With only a mental plan of the server room itself, he had no idea if he was in the right place. The archive surely wouldn't be on the first or ground floors: the weight of the servers would warrant them being on the lowest floor, and it would be cooler downstairs, in the basement. He put his hand on a broad silver pipe that projected from the floor and ran up the wall through the ceiling. Faint vibration.

He placed his ear against it and the deep, bass hum and *whup, whup, whup* of a distant fan came through. Downstairs, definitely. With one glance back at the closed doors, he lightly jogged down the steps.

At the bottom, the basement floor vibrated with the steady, tangled thrum of hundreds of servers, buried somewhere behind the walls.

Bannik's plans hadn't detailed any security, but it wasn't safe to assume that none had been installed outside the room itself. There were no obvious cameras, and a quick scan with his wristcom revealed no active scanners or alarm signals. It made a twisted kind of sense – visible signs would alert a potential interloper to the presence of something important that needed protecting.

'Wolfram,' he said, tapping his wristcom, 'are you there? Wolfram?'

'Yes, Sebastian. Are you at the archive?'

'I am. I can't see any cameras, but there might be some concealed. If you relay through Aryx's wristcom, you should be able to access any security feeds coming into the office. Find one with a white corridor and a set of stairs going up, and inject a loop with the corridor empty. You'll probably just see—'

'Found it. Injecting feed.'

'That was quick.'

'I aim to please.'

He walked along the white, featureless corridor, rolling his feet around from heel to toe, careful not to make a sound. He brushed the back of his hand against the wall as he went, checking for vibrations and ensuring he wouldn't leave fingerprints.

Midway along the corridor, the vibrations intensified. He stopped. A concealed door – as expected. Making his way to the end of the corridor where it turned to the right, he peered around the corner.

A pair of closed double doors stood at the end, apparently part of the original basement layout from before the renovation. The wooden panels donned heavy ornate brass door handles, and set above was an old-fashioned closer arm that would make a sound if the door opened and was allowed to slam. At least he'd know if someone came into the corridor from that direction.

'Perfect,' he whispered to himself, then, returning to where he felt the vibrations in the wall, he activated his wristcom again. 'I'm standing at a hidden door with no controls. I suspect it's got a wireless key, but I don't have my software toolkit. I think the lock is a . . .' He stared at the ceiling, trying to recall the server room schematics. 'Kyvon series.'

'One moment.' Wolfram emitted a quiet flip-flop over the channel.

Sebastian held his breath, listening.

'I have found the specifications. That series of lock is passive and triggers only on a key match to prevent key rejection hacks.'

'Right, so this'll take a little while. I'll hold the wristcom to it and you can relay the codes. I assume you've got the bandwidth for a fast scan? Give me a moment to find its power signature.' He tapped the wristcom and moved it over the door, searching for the detector. A shallow waveform appeared on the display, barely registering. After a minute, a peak appeared. 'Got it.'

'Hold it there, please.'

Sebastian leaned his shoulder against the panel to hold the wristcom in place.

Thirty seconds passed.

'Nearly there?'

'Please do not distract me, it slows down calculation of the permutations.'

He sighed.

Click.

Strange, the door hadn't opened. Leaning away from the wall, but being careful to keep his wrist in place, he strained to hear. Perhaps it was the other door, the one into the corridor?

'Please keep still,' Wolfram said.

'Shh.'

Clip, clop . . . clip, clop . . . Someone was *in* the corridor.

Why was it taking so long? Sebastian's bladder tightened. 'Hurry up,' he breathed.

The footsteps grew louder. Almost at the corner.

'*Come on,*' he mouthed.

Tik! A tiny lip, two millimetres deep, popped out of the wall as the panel released. He fumbled, caught the edge with his fingernails and pulled.

Clip, clop . . .

The panel opened just enough to reveal a dark space beyond. Without checking what was inside, he squeezed through and pulled the panel shut behind him.

Aryx wheeled back from Karan to give her a rest and Monica joined him on the dance floor. Her feet deftly avoided the casters of his wheelchair while she performed short crossing steps and leaned into a twirl. Just as Aryx got into the flow, she leaned in close.

'Sebastian's gone down to the basement,' she said.

'He started without me?'

'He thought it would be best for you to blend in a little first.'

Aryx paused to twirl Monica again. 'What does he want me to do?'

'Monitor the ground floor security office.'

He looked around. 'I'll go now. Oh, Christ . . .'

'What is it?'

'The Rutherfords, over in the corner— No, don't look! Old turtle-neck's watching.'

'She's probably been watching you all evening,' Monica said, flicking her hair back.

He stopped dancing. 'You ought to partner with someone first.'

She beckoned to Karan, who stood a little distance away. 'Are you up for it?'

Karan narrowed her eyes and gave a twisted smile. 'Sure, if you can keep up.'

Monica laughed. 'In your dreams.'

As he wheeled towards the door, a glance back left him with the lasting impression of Monica being flung off the floor as though Karan was practising for Olympic hammer throwing.

He took the lift to the ground floor and wheeled across the lobby, negotiating several corridors before finding one that contained a door labelled *Security* with a bulky man in a beige suit standing next to it. He parked himself with his back to the wall, about fifteen metres away on the opposite side of the corridor.

The man, clearly a guard, stared blankly at the wall ahead. There was nothing subtle about his appearance, or the way the suit jacket pulled taut over his torso as if he were a slowly inflating tailor's dummy.

Aryx folded his hands in his lap and stared at the wall, occasionally casting a glance in the guard's direction.

Three minutes passed before the guard turned to stare at him. Aryx whipped his gaze straight ahead and stiffened. The guard returned his stare to the wall and a hand went into one of his jacket pockets. Crap, that wasn't good. His focus drifted a little and he mouthed, *There's a guy in a wheelchair acting suspicious near the security area.*

One of the advantages of being in the marines: you learned to lip-read rather quickly. In Aryx's case, it wasn't from looking down a scope. No, being an engineer in a loud workshop, you often couldn't hear what people were saying, and the technical details – especially those of dangerous equipment – were a sharp incentive to learning.

What was he going to do? If they moved him on, how would he know whether the security department had been put on alert?

'Oi, mate,' Aryx shouted. 'My carer's gone off puking her guts up and I need to go to the toilet. You couldn't give me a hand, could you?' Monica would never forgive him for actually using that line, but he might as well play on their prejudices; it was the only advantage he had at the moment.

The guard looked at him, his face creasing in a frown. His lip curled and he shook his head, muttering audibly. 'He's got no legs and wants me to help him in the loo ... What? No, I'm not going near him, he might— Ughh ...' Rather than returning to his previous stance the guard twisted, leaning against the wall but facing away, leaving Aryx to watch the door without worrying about being watched himself.

Mission successful.

With a hand on the panel to deaden the sound, Sebastian pulled the concealed door shut behind him. An oppressive smell of warm plastic met his nostrils, and the intestine-trembling thrum removed all sense of space. As his eyes gradually became accustomed to the dark, he made out a dim light. The room was a lot larger than it felt.

Row upon row of black monolithic slabs of pure processing power stood before him, their bases lit from within, casting a red glow so they rose like basalt pillars from the cooling crust of volcanic lava. He shuddered as he recalled the scene at Sollers Hope, and was about to approach one of the servers when his wristcom spoke.

'Sebastian, are you alright? Did you make it into the server room?'

'Yes, Wolfram,' he whispered.

'Your wristcom sensors are detecting infrared backscatter.'

He froze. 'Infrared tripwire lasers? I hadn't thought about that. I don't have anything that can expose it. Except ... Give me a moment, I'm going to try something. Am I close to one of the beams?'

'No. The first beam is just above floor level, between the corners of the two servers nearest you. The wristcom is detecting backscatter from the corner on your left.'

'Alright.' Sebastian approached the black block, looked down at the floor and closed his eyes.

A cluster of tiny sparkling dots danced in his vision where he would expect the corner of the server to appear, had his eyes been open.

'I think I can see the laser emitters.'

'Are you near the access point?'

'No, it's at the far side of the room. I'm going to have to navigate this place with my eyes shut.' Trembling slightly, he reached out to touch the server with the back of his left hand. He stepped over the invisible line of the tripwire and, using his hand as a guide, shuffled forward until he felt the other edge of the server. The backscatter sparkle appeared farther away this time – apparently not on the corner of every server. Slowly, he made his way from one row to the next, pausing to regain his composure from time to time, until there was no infrared backscatter ahead. He opened his eyes.

The black wall in front of him was illuminated at the bottom by concealed lights in the same fashion as the server stacks. He looked back at the servers he'd passed.

The array of dark blocks stood before him like an amassed monolith army; humming, meditating guardians of hidden knowledge. And yes, in a way, they were – but not for much longer.

From his right, Sebastian counted along the servers until he reached fifteen – the one several feet to his right – and approached it, drawing a tiny metal block from his jacket pocket.

He placed the block on the floor in front of the server stack and a laser traced the outline of a rectangle and letters of a keyboard on the polished floor. Kneeling, he slipped his wristcom off and put it on the floor next to it.

'Wolfram, can you connect the wristcom to the server and relay to the interface block?'

'Of course.'

The projected rectangle flickered for a moment and filled with pages of scrolling text. He tapped on the floor, hitting the projected keys. 'I won't go in through the front. This is a weird operating system, not based on Logynix, and that would alert someone to failed login attempts.'

'These servers do not have a hard-link to external sites, correct?'

'Yeah, intranet-only connection. Why do you ask?'

'There are monitoring ports that send and receive status datapackets from elsewhere in the building. I should be able to reroute them and intercept any alerts.'

'Great,' Sebastian said, tapping away. 'Some of this seems to be easy to crack. I would have thought their security would be better. I'm really surprised.'

'Given the server's off-grid nature, would it be necessary?'

'It's a bit … lax. You don't leave security off like this, and certainly not when it's sensitive data. It isn't a setup I'd recommend using.' Finally, a screen appeared with a search interface. 'Got it! How's the monitoring?'

'As far as I can tell, I am successfully masking your activity.'

'That's good enough for me. Now to download these records.' He typed "*Gla*" and a host of names appeared. Lots of names. 'Wolfram, can you access an API for this? We need to download the records, remember? The Freemasons said if we can find people that have been reassigned because of related cases, they might be able to identify common elements, and therefore the possessed.'

'I will try.' The text he had entered blanked out and thousands of names scrolled up the screen.

Another box appeared at the bottom of the screen, labelled *Subject search*. 'What's this other one for?'

'There appears to be data in the system that does not relate to witness protection.'

'What sort of data?'

'I don't know,' Wolfram said, 'but, do you not think the size of these servers is excessive for the purpose of tracking reassigned identities?'

Sebastian stared at the towers lined up. His infoslate could probably hold all the data required for witness protection, so why the need for so much isolated power? 'I guess so. Can you download some of this *other* database? It seems a bit suspicious.'

'Maybe, once I have found the records you need. The wristcom's bandwidth is not sufficient for more.'

Out of curiosity, Sebastian typed a random letter into the search box: *S*. A secondary pane with search results appeared and he quickly scanned the list, until something caught his eye. 'What on Earth is a supernode?'

'I'm afraid it's not something I've—' Wolfram's voice dropped to a whisper. 'Sebastian, the door.'

From his kneeling position, Sebastian rolled back on his haunches and peered around the server.

At the far end of the room, torchlight flicked back and forth along the aisle between the black monoliths. He pulled back sharply as the light almost caught him, and he sat with his back to the server, breathing heavily through his nose.

Angular, bleached shadows danced across the wall ahead of him as the guard paced the aisles at the far end. He had to go away. He had to go, and not find anything wrong.

Shadows danced in the opposite direction and finally settled. 'Routine sweep complete, nothing out of the ordinary here.' The torch went out, accompanied by a swoosh and a click.

Sebastian wiped his brow with the back of his hand. 'Phew, that was close. Have you got the records you need?'

'I believe I have Gladrin's family records, and I am now downloading as many additional witness records as I can.'

The wristcom bleeped. 'Seb, it's Aryx.'

'How are things up there?'

'I think you've been detected, there's activity near the security office.'

'It's fine, someone checked the room, but left. I'd like to look at some other records here before I leave.'

'Hmm. Still, you'd better be careful, just in case. Do you want me to do anything?'

'No. Go back to blending in. I'll be right up, but if I'm not back in a couple of hours, leave without me.'

'I don't like that idea. But I'm not exactly in the position to argue, am I? Aryx out.'

'Sebastian, if security is on alert we should finish now,' Wolfram said. 'I believe I have enough records to correlate cases.'

He sighed. Arguing with Aryx was one thing, but to argue with Wolfram would be an exercise in futility. 'Fine.' He picked up the interface projector and wristcom and sprayed the area he'd touched with nanobots from the injector. 'Program the nanobots to clean up any traces of skin oil. That should remove any fingerprints.'

'Done,' Wolfram said, and the silvery patch coalesced into a droplet, leaving the floor spotless.

Sebastian unstoppered the injector and put it down. The droplet slithered back into the container and he slipped it into his pocket.

'Right, let's get out of here.' He retraced his steps to the door and opened it using the previous successful RF code.

'Sebastian, I think they've—'

'Not now,' he hissed, and stepped out into the corridor, closing the door behind him.

He blinked in the blinding white of the corridor, shielding his eyes with his right hand. The *clip, clop* of footsteps rapidly approached from behind, and something clamped tight around his wrist.

He tried to turn around. 'What the—'

Something cold and metallic clamped around his other wrist and a beige-suited man towered over him. 'What do you think you're doing down here?' he said in a deep rumble of a voice. 'This corridor is off-limits to visitors.'

'I-I got lost.'

'Pull the other one,' the man said, dragging him by the handcuffs.

'I was looking for the toilet.'

'Uh-huh, and you happened to wander past the toilets on every floor, just like that.' The guard dragged him around the corner. 'I got the guy ...' he said, as though talking to someone over hidden comms. 'Yes, I'll check first. You, give me your thumb.' He roughly grabbed Sebastian's right hand and pressed it onto his own wristcom. 'Sebastian Thorsson. Apparently, he's a visitor ... Okay, I'll bring him in.'

'Where are you taking me?' Sebastian asked.

The man drew back and gave him a level stare. 'Someone wants to talk to you.'

Chapter 24

Aryx slowly wheeled back into the ballroom. He had to maintain his composure.

Monica and Karan sat on chairs to one side of the dance floor. Monica's hair had wilted, while Karan's face sparkled with beads of sweat.

'What's up?' Karan asked as he approached.

'It's Sebastian. I think he's been caught. There was a commotion outside security. I let him know, and he said everything was fine, but now I can't get him on the wristcom.'

'What was the last thing he said?' Monica asked.

'Someone had checked the room and he'd avoided them, but he wanted to look into some other records. He wants us to leave without him if he's not back in a couple of hours.'

'Then he's probably just muted the comms in case he got overheard.'

Aryx rubbed his chin. 'I guess.'

'Besides,' Karan said, dabbing her face with a napkin, 'it's better not to worry until the two hours is up, otherwise you'll look all suspicious and end up blowing his cover. Now, come on.' She grabbed him by the arm and towed him onto the dance floor.

Tired, both from the marathon and having to stay alert, he allowed the girls to tow him around and swing him in big circles. Karan was right: if he didn't relax he'd draw attention to them – as if taking up the majority of the dance floor wasn't drawing enough already.

After an hour, he was ready to stop.

That was, until Mrs Rutherford, who sat staring at the group for most of the evening, straightened. Her lips quivered: *That fellow in the wheelchair is taking up so much space. He's a risk to the other dancers. He really ought to give everyone else room. Should we complain to someone about him?*

If he'd been in any other situation, he would have gone over and wrung her scrawny, hypocritical neck. Well, screw her. He flicked his chair into a wheelie and skirted the hall, with Karan and Monica dancing either side.

'Yoo-hoo, got room for one more?'

Aryx turned. Judie Sorenson had parked herself in front of the buffet table and sat waving at him. He beckoned to her. 'Sure, come on over!' Mrs Rutherford could stick that in her pipe and smoke it.

'I didn't realise you'd be coming,' he said as she approached.

Her face twisted. 'I almost didn't. I managed to throw myself out of my chair on Tower Bridge and bend the frame – those cobbles are a nightmare! I can't dance, I'm bruised, not to mention feeling tired. But I did just manage to get in under the time, so I thought why not?'

'Hello,' Karan said, stooping a little to shake Judie's hand. 'Good to see you again, and thanks for the help earlier.'

Monica nodded. 'Nice to meet you. Would you like to join us? I could do with a change of pace. Karan tends to be a bit brutal.'

'Oh, I don't know. You all look like much better dancers.'

'Don't worry.' Aryx patted Judie's leg. 'They'll take good care of you, I'm sure.'

She squealed with laughter as Monica pulled her into the middle of the floor and began to dance.

Sebastian stumbled through the wooden double doors into an older part of the building as the guard pushed him ahead. This part of the corridor was carpeted, with wooden dado rails running along the magnolia painted walls. Several metres along, the guard stopped at what appeared to be a plain fire door, inset with a mechanical combination keypad. He punched in several digits with little concern for obscuring which buttons he pressed – so Sebastian did his best to memorise them.

The door swung open and the guard prodded him in the small of his back.

'Hey, less of the shoving!'

The new corridor consisted of bare breeze-block walls and smooth concrete floor. At several points, thin plastic sheeting fluttered in open doorways.

'Is this part of the building still being renovated?' Sebastian asked, doing his best to sound like a curious visitor.

'Shut up and keep going.'

They continued along the corridor and stopped at another plain door. The guard knocked three times. A moment later, it was opened by a man a few inches shorter than Sebastian who had short, curly black hair and a scraggly, thin beard that covered a slightly double chin and contrasted oddly with the grey suit he wore.

The guard held Sebastian's handcuffed wrists firmly behind him with one hand and frisked him with the other.

'Let's have a look at you,' the shorter, weasely man said, reaching up to grab Sebastian's face. He stretched his cheeks and pulled down his lower eyelids.

Sebastian recoiled. 'Hey, what are you doing?'

'Stop complaining.' Reclaiming his grip, the man peered into Sebastian's eyes. 'Keep still and look at me.'

Sebastian stared into the beady, dark eyes.

The weasely man stared back. 'Yep. I'll have to get one of my superiors to check his identity when they come back later. Thanks, Dave, you can go back upstairs.'

Dave released his grip and handed over Sebastian's wristcom, interface projector, and vial of nanobots to the short man and left.

'I'll have to put you in a cell until your identity can be verified, you understand. They say the transition can be quite disorientating. I'll call you by your host's name for the time being, Mr Thorsson. You can call me Kevin. I'm the overseer of this particular facility.'

Of course, the sparkling retinas ... It must be the residual indium gallium arsenide in his eyes: they thought he was possessed!

'It is good to be here,' Sebastian said, trying his best to play along without actually knowing how he should speak. 'I did not reveal my presence sooner, as I did not know who could be trusted.'

'That's understandable, Mr Thorsson,' Kevin said, beckoning for him to follow on down the corridor. 'Due to your nature, the host's senses are often difficult to get used to, or so they tell me.'

'I found it difficult to gain entry to the building. I was turned away earlier.'

'I apologise for that. Our organisation has been using certain individuals appropriated from the Veterans' Reconstruction Fund for its research. When that charity asked the owner if it was possible to use this considerably ostentatious building to host the event, we couldn't object. A necessary inconvenience to maintain our cover.'

'I understand.'

Kevin paused. 'Tell me, how did you come to possess Mr Thorsson?'

'I—' Crap. He hadn't expected that – he certainly couldn't reveal that he knew about magic, or the Chopwood colonists. '... attacked Thorsson during his investigation of my involvement in the destruction of a laboratory aboard Tenebrae station, and possessed him.'

'And you found the transition difficult.'

'*Difficult?*'

'We'd expected you to be in touch sooner.'

'Yes. I did not want to draw suspicion. I had to wait for an opportunity to travel to Earth.'

Kevin led him through another set of doors into a chilly section of the renovation. Vertical bars to either side of the corridor formed the front walls of several cells separated by breeze-block partitions.

'The owner of the building isn't aware of this section. Our organisation sometimes has reason to hold people, and plenty of secrets need keeping. It's such a shame we aren't allowed to buy it, but it is a listed building, after all. It would make things so much easier ... I'm afraid I'll have to put you in a cell, just for a little while, until one of your fellows can verify your identity. Apparently, you don't take names until you enter this realm the first time, so I can see why that's necessary. I'll hold on to your items.'

'Why do you need to verify my identity?'

Kevin tapped the side of his nose. 'We've become aware of the *other* lot getting through.'

Sebastian nodded once, slowly, even though he had no idea what Kevin meant.

Kevin ushered him past several empty cells and stopped opposite one that held a figure covered with a scratchy grey blanket who lay on the chain-suspended bench on the far wall with its back to him. The lights in the next cell were off, leaving it in shadow.

'This one,' he said, unlocking the door to the cell opposite the sleeper with a heavy metal key. As Sebastian stepped in, Kevin asked, 'What excuse brought you to Earth?'

'I came looking for a friend of Mr Thorsson's,' Sebastian said, thinking fast. 'My previous host, Duggan Simmons.'

Over Kevin's shoulder, something moved in the dark cell next to that of the sleeping figure. From the shadows, hands grasped the bars and a deeply lined face framed with grey hair and a goatee appeared between them.

Sebastian's heart raced.

Kevin nodded in the direction of the cell behind him. 'Then it looks like you've found him.'

Chapter 25

Sebastian waited until Kevin had locked the cell and left.

'Duggan!' he rasped in a loud whisper, trying not to wake the sleeper in the cell opposite. 'What the hell are you doing here?'

Duggan had retreated into the darkness of his cell and Sebastian's question was met with silence.

'It's me. I'm not possessed.'

The old man's face appeared at the bars. 'I heard what you said, monster. You and your kind will never control me again. I'll kill myself before I let you take charge of my actions!'

'It really is me!'

'If you are Sebastian, how did you convince your friend Kevin that you were possessed? Tell me that.'

Sebastian moved to the corner of the cell, closer to Duggan. 'It's my eyes. I tried a spell and it backfired.'

'You've performed magic?'

He nodded rapidly. 'I managed to do the lucid dreaming spell you suggested. That was the first.' The sleeping figure shifted and moaned. Sebastian lowered his voice. 'The second spell I tried was to create light in a dark room. It backfired because the effect gave me infrared vision. I've got flecks of metal in my eyes. It sparkles a bit like those of the possessed.'

Duggan narrowed his eyes. 'Hmm.'

'I'm telling the truth!'

'Then how did you end up here?'

'I went looking for you at Sollers Hope. Someone else seemed to be searching for you and I guessed it was the ITF. They planted a bomb that nearly destroyed the town, but Aryx managed to prevent an atmospheric breach. Garvin told us you'd come to Earth looking for someone called Alicia. At the same time, my boss suggested coming here to find records in the Witness Protection database, and we had to find a way to get them. It turned out the servers are in this building. But how the hell did you get here? I assume you got caught at the hospital. There was evidence of a fireball.'

'I got a couple of them, but couldn't exactly fend off Tasers. I didn't have time to find what I was looking for before the bastards got me.'

'We found the records,' Sebastian said. 'But the trail went cold. Alicia's file ended in 2078. I assume she must have escaped and done some serious lightspeed travel to have turned up on Sollers Hope in recent decades. I just don't know what happened to her after she left there. There were no clues as to where she'd gone after coming back to Earth.'

Duggan slouched with a sigh. 'She's got a twenty-year head start! What was I thinking? I'll never be able to ask her what she discovered about thaumaturgy.'

The figure in the other cell shifted and sat up, turning and pulling the blanket off to reveal her face. She looked wizened, with loose skin and dark eyes, hair a powdery grey. Her clothes were too large for her frame and worn thin in places, and she struck Sebastian as a woman who had at one time lived a happy life but had been driven past exhaustion and despair too many times. With great effort, he tore his gaze away from those deep, sad eyes that reminded him of his mother to focus on Duggan.

Duggan continued. 'Garvin said she was their geologist. He thought she'd be the best one to ask about carbyne research.'

'Garvin was correct,' the woman said, her voice gravelly with age.

'Who's that?' He strained to push his face through the bars, but from his position there was no way he'd be able to see her. 'You ... You sound familiar.'

'I am Alicia Maline,' the woman said, allowing her head to hang, 'and everyone I ever knew or loved is long dead.'

Duggan shook his head. 'No. I *know* that voice. But it can't be ...' His features softened. 'It's been many years, and that voice has cracked and aged like the warm floorboards of home, but I know it. Come forward so I can see you.'

'Oh, must you put an old woman out so? I suppose it makes a change from the usual tortures they put me through.' She heaved herself slowly up off the bench and limped over, leaning against the wall for support, to put her face between the bars.

Duggan turned his head sideways and pressed his face against the bars near the partition. 'No ...' He reached around the bars with his left hand to run the back of a finger down her lined, velvety cheek.

She recoiled. 'How dare you? Nobody has touched me like that, not since ...'

A tear pooled in the corner of Duggan's eye and escaped, leaving a dark streak down his cheek. 'It's me, Eileen. It's Duggan.'

Aryx took a break from dancing to grab a cup of water from the buffet table. Judie's energy was unbounded, and she was giving him and his aching wrists a run for their money.

His wristcom bleeped.

'Seb?'

'Not Sebastian, Aryx, it's Wolfram.'

'Where's Seb?'

'He has been apprehended. It seems his name was on a watch list. His captors believe him to be possessed. I had to cut the connection to his wristcom when it was removed from his person.'

'Shit! Is he— Is he okay?'

'I couldn't say. However, if he successfully keeps up the pretence of being possessed, I believe he will be safe.'

'We have to go, then.' Aryx searched the dancers for Monica and beckoned to her.

'Sebastian's instructions were for you to stay for two hours, were they not?'

'What's up?' Monica asked.

'Seb's got himself caught. Wolfram says we should stay.'

'He's right. If we leave now and we're being watched, they'll know we were in on it and could all get caught. If Sebastian said to leave without him, he was probably confident that he could either escape or get in touch with us by some other means.'

What a stupid idea. Aryx exhaled sharply. 'Okay. Tell Karan to stay up here for a bit. I'm going downstairs to have a break from this – I'm hungry, thirsty, and now I feel a severe headache coming on.'

Monica's eyebrows drooped and she put a hand on his shoulder. 'I'll tell her. Go on, I'll be down in a minute to keep you company.'

Chapter 26

Alicia Maline stared at Patricia Ventris in disbelief. 'What do you mean, you were a *cargo pilot*?'

One of the orderlies glanced in their direction.

Patricia hunched over, hiding her arms inside her pink hole-riddled cardigan. 'Exactly what it sounds like,' she said. 'I did cargo runs between Earth and Gliese 682b.'

Alicia shook her head. 'Between Earth and another *solar system*?' Her voice shot up, drawing the attention of the two old men that sat playing chess by the window. She lowered her voice to a whisper. 'How is that even possible?'

'Easy.'

'But it takes years to get to the closest star.'

'No, it doesn't! Have you been living in a shoebox for the last eighteen months? Don't you keep up with the news?'

Alicia gestured at the grimy, tiled walls and mesh-barred windows of the asylum. 'Eighteen months? I've been here for sixteen *years*, Patricia!'

'And you've seen no TV for the last year—'

'They don't put the news on. It's "not good for the residents' stress levels".'

Patricia snorted. 'How do they ever hope to rehabilitate anyone if they're kept out of touch with the world?'

Alicia frowned and leaned across the table on her elbows. 'I've never known of anyone being released. I think the only way out is in a body bag.'

Patricia took a sip of water from the plastic cup she pushed around in front of her. 'Doesn't that worry you?'

'Everybody dies, Pat. It's just a matter of when. It's not like I have anything to achieve. There isn't anyone on the outside for me.'

'Nobody at all?'

'No. My fiancé left a long time ago for a colonisation mission. I'll be long dead by the time he gets there. They're supposed to arrive in 2207.'

Patricia shrugged. 'Not if they were lucky and encountered one of the nodes on the way.'

'Nodes?'

'Yeah. You really are out of touch, aren't you? It's like a ... ' Patricia scratched her head, then held her hands together, claw shaped, so the fingertips touched, forming a hollow space between her palms. 'It's a great big frame thing, floating in space. You fly past and it accelerates you to faster than light.'

Alicia's eyes widened. 'That's not possible!' She looked around in the hope that she hadn't caught the attention of an orderly. Luckily, the one guarding the day room still stood with his back against the door, arms folded, staring into space.

'It is possible. How do you think I racked up two hundred hours of cargo flights? It certainly wasn't flying out of the solar system at light speed into empty space and back for fun.'

'Alright, calm down. Just say it is possible ... You're telling me that Duggan could have already reached the mission's target?'

Patricia shrugged again. 'I'm not saying it's likely, but it's possible.' She leaned closer and whispered. 'If you got out of this shithole, you could use one of the nodes to catch up with him.'

Alicia gave her a sidelong stare. 'And how *exactly* would I do that?'

Over the next few days, Alicia met up with Patricia and the two formulated a plan for her to escape the compound. There was no way Patricia could go with her; Alicia was under relatively low security, being a risk only to herself, but Patricia had apparently attempted to murder her husband after claiming he had strange eyes and wasn't acting normally and, as such, was under much closer observation. In the days after the escape, Alicia could remember only the vaguest details, the plan being carried out during a rush of adrenaline, and that it involved a laundry chute, a knife, and a trip to a disused aerospace training facility on the outskirts of London.

'If I can come back for you, I will,' Alicia had told Patricia. 'If you hear engines, get outside.'

Later, Alicia settled down at the controls of a black dart-shaped runner that she had liberated from one of the unguarded hangars; a relic from her days of training for the mission and something she was perfectly capable of flying.

She took the craft up and, flying low over the urban sprawl of outer London, traced her way back to the asylum. In minutes, she reached the green expanse of the front gardens and the roar of the runner's engines filled the courtyard.

Patricia came running down the steps from the main building, stumbling and sending bits of pea gravel flying, pursued by three white-uniformed orderlies wielding stun batons. 'Don't land!' she screamed.

Alicia balanced the thrust, keeping the craft two feet off the ground, and flipped open the canopy.

Patricia dived in head first, her upper half going straight into the footwell of the co-pilot's seat behind Alicia, leaving her legs flailing about as they dangled over the side. Stun batons thumped on the wing as her pursuers caught up.

The engines drowned out their shouts as Alicia piled on the thrust, driving the craft through the avenue of trees. Pea gravel blasted from the ground, peppering the orderlies, and a leafy branch, torn from a tree by the still open cockpit, fell into Alicia's lap.

Patricia righted herself, threw out the branch, and closed the canopy. She put a hand on Alicia's shoulder. 'Thanks for coming back for me, Al. I thought you were gone for good.'

Alicia placed her hand over Patricia's. 'I was never going to leave you there. Nobody deserves that. They should be shut down.'

'I don't think they're operating within the law,' Patricia said. 'Non-police use of batons like those has been banned for years. Nice rust bucket, by the way. Where did you find it?'

'My old training facility. This one's got a new – I mean old – prototype engine that lets it go as far as the colony ships.'

'And it was just left lying around?'

Alicia laughed. 'Well, I guess after the discovery of the nodes they wouldn't have needed them anymore. They didn't quite get the engine right.'

'Oh great, so this thing's dangerous?'

'We're fine for short trips, and you said yourself that we don't need to leave the system.'

Patricia huffed. 'That doesn't answer the question of what's wrong with it.'

'The first prototype reactors got unstable in long-range testing, alright?'

'Christ, talk about out of the frying pan and into the fire!' She sighed. 'I suppose there are worse ways to go, and I'd rather go out with a bang than a whimper.'

The blue skies deepened and peeled away to black as they left Earth's atmosphere.

Patricia leaned forward again. 'Node flight is simple,' she said. 'You fly towards the thing – it'll be easy to find because there's a comms beacon near it now.'

Alicia flicked several switches, scanning frequencies. 'I've got it, I think.'

'Right, now head for it at lightspeed, but whatever you do, don't get within a kilometre.'

'I know, we went over this before.'

'... and line up with the star you want to fly to. And I don't care if I've told you before, it's worth repeating. Make sure that you cross the tangent of a one-kilometre sphere centred on the node. Once you enter that threshold, you'll be accelerated into what they call superphase. You've got to be careful, though. It sends you along your current vector, so you've got to make sure your navigation is accurate. A lot of the newer ships have better computers that can compensate for stellar drift and Doppler shift, which I doubt this thing does accurately. Oh, and you can't change direction in flight once you enter superphase, so if you get it wrong we're screwed.'

'No pressure, then.' Alicia went over the instructions in her head again and again during the trip while Patricia sat in silence. The starscape outside the cockpit melted into an eye-aching, blue-shifted smear as they drew close to the speed of light. In less than two hours, they were at the edge of the solar system. Was it really two hours, or the observed six-plus? The exact details of time dilation were lost on Alicia: sixteen years in an institution tended to dull one's memory of astrophysics, and the squeaking of Patricia's hands gripping the armrests of the back seat were enough to distract anyone.

'You're a terrible back-seat pilot.'

'Do you want to swap?' Patricia snapped. 'It's not easy sitting back while being flown by a newbie when you're a career pilot.'

'Fine, you do it!' She let go of the controls and the ship swung around as Patricia took over.

The enormous blue-green glittering scaffold of the acceleration node loomed up ahead. Even at over a kilometre away the dodecahedral structure looked massive. A steely sphere cloaked with magenta plasma turned within, acting as the beating heart of the ancient alien machine. A quiver of anticipation ran through Alicia's abdomen. She'd never *seen* alien technology.

Patricia grumbled as she lined up the ship with V376 Pegasi, the target star for Duggan's mission. The runner's computers weren't as accurate as the newer ships that Patricia had described, but they had little choice. 'Since you haven't done this before,' she said, 'do you want to do the honours?'

'Me?'

'Sure.'

Alicia thumbed the trigger that would initiate flight along their course. Could she go through with it? Get lost in space with a chance of seeing Duggan again, or be apprehended and returned to the asylum? There really was no choice. She pressed the trigger with her thumb.

The ship's thrusters fired, and in moments the acceleration node flared. Alicia screamed as a white-hot charge arced out from the purple haze, enveloping the runner and blinding her. Patricia laughed.

When she opened her eyes, the view ahead was black. The nav readouts simply blanked out with dashes, having lost all timing and positional data from Earth's solar system buoys. She squinted, trying to make out any detail, no matter how tiny, and was struck by a terrible headache as though she'd been staring at the sun. 'There's nothing outside! What's happened to space?'

'It's blue shift. All the stars' light has gone beyond ultraviolet.'

Alicia activated the solar filter control. Her headache receded, but they were still flying blind. Flying. She chuckled nervously. What a euphemism. Hurtling blindly through the void, more like.

Despite feeling weightless – which in itself was unusual, implying the ship was no longer accelerating – her insides shifted periodically, like riding a speeding car over a small hump in the road. What could cause that?

The dark transit took just under an hour before ending abruptly, dumping the ship at the edge of a system containing two stars.

But V376 Pegasi wasn't a binary system.

Alicia bit her nails while the stellar cartography computer performed a lengthy calculation. She gasped at the result. '132 light years away! How could we have missed it by so much?'

Patricia's hands clacked over the keyboard behind her. 'Damn! I told you these older ships weren't designed for such accurate navigation. At least at lightspeed you can change direction as you get close to your target, but not with this. We must have sailed past the star's heliosphere until the node's energy ran out.' Her fingers clattered on the keys again. 'I'll have to calculate a trajectory back in the direction of V376 Pegasi, but you're not going to like it.'

Alicia sighed. 'How can it *get* any worse?'

'We'll have to fly at light speed now that we're nowhere near a node, and at that speed – if my calculations are right – we might arrive by 2210, a year or two after the colonists get there. On the upside, *if* this rust bucket doesn't blow up on us first, the authorities won't be looking for us anymore.'

Alicia smiled to herself. The odds of meeting up with Duggan through regular, relativistic, travel seemed better than the lottery-win-hope that the mission might have met with a node and arrived early themselves. Statistics rarely warmed her heart but, sitting in this distant system with only a navcomputer and grumpy Patricia for company, she'd take any comfort she could.

The computer in front of her bleeped as it confirmed Patricia's calculations and displayed *Ready*.

'Ready when you are,' Patricia said.

'Here we go. One hundred and thirty-two years compressed into a day,' Alicia said, turning her plain gold engagement ring; the one thing she'd been allowed to keep in the asylum. She silently thanked Duggan for buying one without a stone and pressed the trigger.

She knew the time dilation effect of relativity would kick in once the ship had reached light speed. It was simply a matter of enduring the three hours of acceleration and deceleration either side of what they would experience as a near-instantaneous trip. The colonists, in their juggernaut of a ship, would have had to live aboard for an acceleration period of weeks.

This time, knowing what to expect once at light speed, Alicia dialled up the solar filters; she still couldn't see anything, but at least she wouldn't have to suffer the splitting headache she experienced earlier.

How surprised Duggan and the others would be when they arrived! She chuckled. They'd certainly be annoyed that she had arrived so quickly, at least from her perspective, to have caught up with them. But then again, they hadn't had to endure sixteen years' confinement.

One hundred and thirty-two years later, the little black runner dropped out of lightspeed in a system containing a boiling volcanic planet and an orange gas giant with a small forested moon.

'No, it's gone wrong!' Alicia yelled. 'There isn't supposed to be a gas giant here. The-the big planet is supposed to be green!' She checked the readouts: again, the nav controls showed no indication of where they were.

'Just give it a minute,' Patricia said. 'It will take a while for the computer to compensate for the years of stellar drift and our change in position. It's almost impossible that we would arrive at another system with planets by accident. There must be some explanation for them being wrong. Maybe they didn't interpret the readings correctly before they sent the mission?'

'If that's the case, then the only place they could have gone would be that forest moon.' Alicia's fingers played across the many buttons on the ship's console as she scanned the surface for communication signals: there was no way either of the large planets could harbour life, let alone support the colony.

Nothing.

No, not quite. No comms chatter came from the forested world that would indicate habitation, but a solitary locator beacon on the surface pinged out the colony's position. Alicia's heart leaped as she hammered out more commands.

Surface scans picked up a clearing dotted with small buildings. At one end was a large crater, possibly the landing site, but where was the ship? Of its enormous bullet-shaped bulk there was no sign.

She activated the comms. 'This is Eileen Millican. Come in, Earth Colony. I repeat, this is Eileen Millican. Come in, Earth Colony.'

'Who the hell's Eileen?' Patricia asked.

'It's my old name, from before.'

She waited for a response to her hail, and then repeated her message several times, to no avail.

'Damn you, Cullen,' she said, cursing the mission leader. 'Why would you leave? What would have enticed you away from here?'

'Try scanning for other signals,' Patricia said. 'There must be some sign of them, somewhere.'

Alicia turned the scanners outward and immediately picked up another signal, encrypted and unintelligible, but carrying signatures the ship identified as being standard. Its timecode showed 2190, twenty years earlier than the date the ship had calculated as the present Earth-reference year of 2210. 'Who else could be out here?' she asked.

'There's the Bronadi, but they don't use our frequencies, and if that signal's twenty years old, it just means it's being broadcast from twenty light years away.'

Bronadi? Alicia let the question drop for the moment. 'So, what do we do? Follow it? I don't really want to risk flying again and missing Duggan by another twenty years, or the engine blowing up.'

'It could be a signal relayed by a node,' Patricia said. 'Head for it anyway, at sublight.'

Alicia turned the ship towards the signal.

Thirty minutes later, she confronted her second acceleration node. It wasn't the source of the comms signal, but the signal was clearly emanating from the direction of the node itself. Was it coming from a distant system, another one with a node, and being relayed by this strange technology?

Perhaps the colonists had taken their ship and followed the signal past the node to its source. And should they? The signal was recognisably Human in origin – it used a standard format, after all, even if it was encrypted. Maybe there were other colonies out here ...

'So, what do you want to do?' Patricia asked, patting her on the shoulder.

Alicia twiddled her engagement ring.

They would have followed it. Cullen would have followed it. Duggan would have followed it.

She gritted her teeth. 'We'll go for it.'

While guiding the ship around the node, being careful not to enter the one-kilometre radius, Alicia monitored the signal strength and direction until the readouts peaked. She punched the coordinates into the navcomputer and checked with Patricia before allowing the autopilot to align the ship. Before she had a chance to second-guess her decision, she pulled the trigger.

Once again, after turning on the cockpit's black-out filter, she waited nervously for the juddering of superphase transit to cease. Thirty minutes later, the ship dropped out in an empty system with a sun but no planets.

'I can't believe this!' Alicia screamed. She buried her head in her hands. 'I'll never find you, Duggan. We're lost. I'm sorry . . .'

Patricia squeezed Alicia's shoulder. 'Listen, I know you want to find him but you can't keep this up. The reactor will probably die soon, and us with—'

The console bleeped.

Alicia checked the readout. The computer had detected the signal, but its timecode was still offset by twenty years. What was going on?

The enigma helped to push out all thoughts of giving up, at least momentarily, while she pondered what might have happened. The signal clearly had not originated in this system, but for the timecode to have remained unchanged over such a vast distance, it must have been relayed to the previous system by a node, faster than light. If it was being relayed, where was the node that relayed it?

Flicking several switches, she set the scanners to wide receive . . . There, that was it: the same signature as the node in Earth's solar system, but weaker, coming from somewhere ahead. 'I'm not ready to give up yet.'

Alicia locked the autopilot onto the node's signature and, fifteen minutes later, they faced yet another dodecahedral scaffold. She stared at the blue-green metal shape. The steely sphere in the middle wobbled off-centre, and several of the framework struts were pitted, as though something had struck it. There was no sign of the magenta corona.

'I don't think it's supposed to look like that,' Patricia said in her ear, staring at the framework. 'And I don't like the idea of using it if it's broken.'

'Pat, it's either that or lose another twenty years travelling at light-speed.' Alicia twiddled her engagement ring again. 'And I don't think Duggan's going to wait that long.'

She edged the ship towards the node, giving the computer time to calculate the vector that would take them to the origin of the signal, and the ship aligned itself. Running her thumb over the initiate trigger, she muttered, 'God, you know I'm a scientist and don't believe in you, but if you'll help me out, I'd be prepared to change my mind.'

Click.

The acceleration node flared as the ship entered the capture radius, but instead of the white-hot stream of energy that had enveloped the runner twice before, blue flashes struck the side of the ship with several sharp jolts. The runner lurched with the initial impact, then accelerated, slowly at first, but with each subsequent hit the ship accelerated further. In a second, stars streamed by and Alicia had to black out the cockpit again.

'That wasn't right,' Patricia said.

Two minutes into the flight, a violent vibration rumbled through the ship, as though something were dragging it across uneven terrain.

'I told you we shouldn't have used it!' Patricia yelled over the din.

A loud thud, muffled a little by the padded headrest, came from the rear of the ship, somewhere in the workings. The console went dark.

'Jesus! This is a really bad idea!'

'I'm beginning to agree!' Alicia shouted.

Plunged into inky blackness, she strained her eyes to make out any detail, but after a minute her eyes started to hurt with the now familiar blue-shift headache. Even closing them didn't help. The cockpit filters had failed along with the power.

'Al, we have to do something or we'll go blind.'

Alicia unfastened her harness and leaned forwards to feel underneath the seat. Her fingers came across a dome-shaped object and she pulled it out and stuck it on her head. With a click of a button the helmet activated and automatically blacked out the visor. At least now the headache was starting to recede.

'Under your seat, Pat. There's a helmet. Use that.'

Patricia scrabbled around behind her. 'No, there isn't. You didn't exactly come prepared for a passenger, did you?'

'Sorry, I didn't have a chance to pack while stealing this ship! You'll just have to put your hands over your eyes for now.'

Patricia blew out her cheeks, but complied. 'This is turning out to be the best day ever.'

Alicia rested her head against the seat and closed her eyes. She needed to calm down. Keep a level head.

After several minutes, the helmet emitted a soft beep and she opened her eyes. A heads-up display had appeared on the inside of the visor, illuminated in faint green lines. *Reactor failure,* it said. *Auxiliary power only.*

'Great. Just bloody wonderful. The reactor's failed.'

Patricia groaned. 'Are you jinxed? I told you we pushed her too hard. What else does the readout say?'

The numbers below the main display in Alicia's visor were almost too tiny to read. One showed a V followed by a colon, their current velocity – something the computer had been unable to provide during the two previous trips via the nodes. So, what was different about this one, apart from nearly blowing up the ship, that made it possible?

She read the figures out loud, 'Velocity, C times 0.999 to who knows how many places.'

'What the hell?' Patricia said. 'The node hasn't accelerated us correctly. It's somehow pushed us almost to the speed of light, instead of beyond it.'

Alicia stared in horror at the display while the vibrations around her intensified. 'W-what are you saying?'

'It's still going to take us twenty years to get to the source of the signal!' Squinting, Patricia slid out of her seat and tore off a panel beside her. A complex tangle of wiring draped out and she pulled it onto her lap. Several of the wires sparked where they had broken, and she started twisting them back together. 'Now, that one's eject ... Fixed ... Ah, reactor control.'

'What the hell are you doing?'

'I'm trying to fix the ship. Damn this headache!'

'Just put it back, it's not going to—' The ship bucked, jarring Alicia's spine and launching her out of her seat towards the canopy overhead. Her helmet collided with the reinforced glass and she passed out.

Alicia woke.

As if being in zero G wasn't disorientating enough, the universe now spun around her. The nausea worsened when it joined with a pounding in her head. She blinked. The velocity indicator in the visor now displayed kilometres per second, but her momentary relief ended as the display changed to *Reactor critical!* with a flashing exclamation mark.

She tore the helmet from her head, only to find stars tumbling around her at high speed, rotating on two axes simultaneously; the universe actually *was* spinning!

Biting back vomit, she pushed herself away from the glass, back into her seat. The console display was once again lit. She fumbled at the controls. With auxiliary power only, using thrusters to stabilise the ship was out of the question.

Collision warning! Scanners detected several large, irregularly shaped objects ahead: the ship still had momentum, and it was heading for an asteroid field!

'Pat, what do we do?'

There was no response.

'Pat?' Alicia turned.

Patricia floated several inches above the seat. Large, dark globules adhered to her head in zero G, shining sickly, and a smattering of blood painted a stained-glass patch on the cockpit above.

Alicia screamed. 'Pat!' She reached for her hand but it was cold to the touch. 'Oh God, what have I done!'

The ship's radio crackled into life, assaulting her ears with a voice, bellowing at her in a language full of guttural tones and glottal stops.

'I can't understand!' she yelled, panic rising in her throat. 'I don't understand you!'

'English?' the man said, now sounding more Human. 'Quick, your reactor blow now. Eject!'

'But—!'

'DO IT!'

Alicia refastened the harness and gripped the eject lever beside her seat. She hesitated, waiting for the ship to spin in such a way that the cockpit pod would be thrown clear of the approaching asteroids, and pulled the lever.

Whump!

Her innards sank into her pelvis and pins and needles jabbed at her face under the acceleration. The last thing she saw before passing out a second time was a magnesium-white explosion, blossoming from the side of an asteroid as the runner collided at the point of going critical.

'Are you okay, Miss?' said a female voice with a peculiar accent.

'W-what?' Alicia lay on her side. She rolled over to face the speaker and opened her eyes.

She was in a bed with freshly pressed white sheets. A plastic tube ran over the pillow past her face and under the covers. A dull ache in her right hand told her that she was now on a drip.

'Where am I?'

'It's alright, you're in hospital,' the woman said, putting a hand on Alicia's shoulder. Her hair was twisted up into a small bun at the back of her head, and she wore a grey outfit with a smooth front and blue piping around the hems.

'Which hospital?'

'Richard Whittington Memorial.'

'I've never heard of it.' Alicia gazed past the woman, through a window set into the hospital's strange, light-grey stone wall. Beyond, the sky was black space, peppered with stars held back by the regular triangles of a geodesic dome. The buildings in the foreground were made from blocks of the same stone as the room in which she now lay.

'I'm … I'm not on Earth, am I?'

'Goodness no. You're a long way from there. This is Sollers Hope, Quintoc system.'

'What happened?' She looked around the room, but hers was the only bed present. 'Where's the woman who was with me?'

The nurse looked at the floor. 'You've been unconscious for the last few days. I'm afraid your friend didn't make it. You were lucky the eject mechanism worked.'

'Patricia—' Alicia swallowed. 'She-she saved me?'

'Was that her name?' The nurse nodded. 'She must have patched up the eject and canopy release.'

Alicia sobbed. 'How did I get here?'

'You came into the system at close to lightspeed. The team that picked you up said you decelerated suddenly, and yet you couldn't have used a node.'

'I passed one, but it didn't do the same as the others. Pat said it was damaged. Oh no! How long was I in flight? What year is it?'

'2230.'

Alicia put her hands to her face and the drip tugged painfully. Patricia had been right about the travel time of twenty years.

'What were you doing out there? Your black box was destroyed, so we had no idea where you came from in case we had to contact next of kin.'

'I don't have any. I'm from Earth. Earth, a long time ago. All this is new to me.' Alicia turned her engagement ring, thankfully still on her finger. 'They'll all be dead by now.' She took a deep, shuddering breath. 'At least I'm out of that hellhole.'

The nurse looked at her, head tilted. 'What's wrong with Earth?'

'Nothing. I was— I was escaping my past.' Alicia forced a smile. 'I don't suppose a big old colony ship from Earth came here in the last few years?'

The nurse shook her head. 'No, nothing like that. Why?'

'I hoped to catch up with my fiancé, he was aboard one, but I guess there's no chance of that now.' She stared out of the window at the stars slowly wheeling past the dome beyond. 'Your accent, it's strange. When I entered the system, someone shouted at me over the radio – what language was that?'

'Galac, the Bronadi Trade Tongue. It's widespread galactic standard. All Humans learn it now if they intend on going into space, and it's taught in schools. In fact, there are very few who still speak English out here, so you were very lucky.'

'Yes, lucky . . .' Alicia trailed off, still staring at the mechanism of the universe slowly turning beyond the layers of glass, or whatever it was they used nowadays. It had been a vain hope to find Duggan out here in the vastness of space. But what would she do with her life now? What *could* she do now, alone, in an unknown future version of the universe?

On the second day, the universe answered.

A rotund man with small, round glasses and a mop of scraggly hair in the early stages of greying walked into Alicia's room. He wiped a hand down his velvety jacket and extended it. 'Hello Alicia, I'm Garvin Havlor, Mayor of Sollers Hope. You can call me Garvin.'

Alicia pulled the bed covers up around her chest and tentatively shook his hand. 'Hello, Garvin.'

'How are you feeling? The doctor says you had some brain swelling, but you're almost fit to leave.'

'I-I don't have anywhere to go.'

Garvin rubbed his stubbly chin. 'You didn't seem prepared for a long trip. There were no personal effects in your pod, not even a wallet. Did you plan on travelling for twenty years?'

'No, and I'm afraid it's worse than that. I left Earth in 2078.'

Garvin's eyes widened. 'Hence nowhere to go. That explains your questions.' He sat on the edge of the bed and she flinched when he put his hand on hers. 'I'm so very sorry for your loss, my dear . . . What do you intend to do now?'

'I have no idea. I hadn't anticipated any of this. I don't have any reason to go back to Earth and no reason to go on, unless anyone's seen the colony ship I was looking for so I can follow it.'

'If you could afford to follow it.'

She stared at him. *'Afford?'*

He laughed. 'Space travel isn't free, my dear, regardless of how times have changed. Your ship was destroyed, and that means you'll have to find a way of paying for passage or ship hire, should you wish to travel.'

'That-that hadn't occurred to me.' She stared at the bed. 'How do people pay for things now?'

'With money, of course.'

'People still have jobs, then?'

'Indeed they do. How else is a person to earn a wage?' Garvin narrowed his eyes. 'Speaking of which, what skills do you have?'

'I'm a bit rusty, but I trained as a geologist. Why?'

'Our resident mineralogist, Arlon, left a few months ago.' He clasped his hands. 'Seein' as you got nowhere else to go, and we're in need of someone to run analyses on the ore we find, along with a few other things, there's a job going if you want it. I'll even throw in his old house. It's only one room, and the pay isn't great—'

'Fine, I'll take it!'

'—but you'll have food, and a roof over your head.'

'I said I'll take it.'

'You will?' Garvin beamed. 'You won't regret it.'

That afternoon, he collected Alicia from the hospital and escorted her through the dusty grey town centre, past a tiny sapling in the browning grass of the square, to a small, windowless building that contained little more than a desk, a bench with some lab equipment, and several survey maps hung on the walls. An adjoining building served as the one-room house in which she would live.

'The routine is quite simple,' Garvin said, watching while Alicia examined the items she found. 'Teams go into the mines, extract ore for a shift, and maybe break open a new seam. At the end of their shift, if they've struck a new vein, they'll bring you a sample for analysis. That way, when they start again the next day, you'll be able to give them an idea of how they should mine it and whether that vein is worth following.'

'I see,' she said, absent-mindedly peering down a microscope. 'Do I get to go down the mines to make surveys?'

'You will, eventually. You'll need pressure suit training first.'

She straightened, apparently with a look of shock on her face because Garvin smiled at her softly.

'No, it's not out in space, but the mines below us are exposed to vacuum. Don't worry about it. We'll give you plenty of time to settle in.' And with that, he left her to continue investigating her new surroundings.

The passage of time was difficult to mark on Sollers Hope: the mirrors over the dome seldom closed, instead following the sun, casting the town through an unending cycle of morning, noon, evening, and back, except for the occasional dusk. The tree in the town centre, which had apparently been Arlon's pet project, grew slowly after Alicia claimed responsibility for watering it, using what little she could spare of her water rations to keep it alive. She spent her days diligently performing ore analyses as miners dropped off samples at the end of their shifts.

She made few friends, preferring to keep to herself: she had no desire to dredge up the events of her time at the asylum and told no one what had brought her to Sollers Hope and, thankfully, nobody asked. Even Garvin, who she thought would have prodded her for more information, left her alone, probably because he had his own secrets.

He often met with people to strike bargains personally. The dog-like Bronadi were his biggest clients, and often bought huge quantities of the sparkling false bornite ore. Sometimes, other races purchased blocks of the inert rock from which the planetoid was formed for building materials, but one particular meeting stuck in Alicia's mind.

Garvin had stood some distance away, next to a sealed ore hopper, talking to an enigmatic figure dressed in long black robes, with a marble-white face whose expression remained unchanged, even while the pair gesticulated conversationally. When she asked Garvin about it, his reply was a scowl and an equally enigmatic "private client who likes to keep to himself". She never asked again, chalking it up to the bargain she and Garvin struck, unspoken, to not trade histories.

With the passing years, the allure of chasing after Duggan faded. Alicia saved every credit she could until she had enough for passage through several systems, or even a small ship of her own. But, when it came down to it, uproot and leave behind a good job, just to go on a fool's errand? No. She stayed put, just like those buried memories.

Until, nearly fourteen years after she arrived, something occurred that brought the memories flooding back.

She sat at the metal desk in her dark little office. The work surface in front of her, lit by two dim desk lamps, was strewn with rock samples.

She hunched over the eyepiece of her microscope, scribbling notes on a pad as she stared at a sample of crushed grey rock on the slide.

A knock on the door behind startled her, and she swivelled round.

Marcin, one of Sollers Hope's miners, came in wearing a pressure suit and carrying a wire mesh tray full of ore samples. 'Got the ore for you, Alice.'

Alicia squinted in the light. 'Thanks, and it's Alicia. I don't know how many times I have to tell you.'

He shrugged. 'I think Alice sounds better on you.' He pushed the tray onto one end of the desk, dislodging several slips of paper that were carefully balanced on the samples there.

'Hey, have some respect, will you?'

'It's not my fault you're too busy to wait until we finish our shift. I had to come all the way up specially. Anyway' – Marcin winked and gave her a crooked smile – 'you love a bit of disrespect,' he said, turning to leave.

'What are you talking about?'

'I heard you the other night, moaning and shouting your head off. I don't know who you had in your room, but they must have enjoyed it. I think the neighbours did, too.'

She flushed. 'I don't know what you're talking about. I'm in my sixties, what do you think I get up to at my age? I must have been talking in my sleep. I do that sometimes.'

'I'll bet. Sixties or not, if you want someone to help you sleep better, I'm available.' He grinned.

'Close the door on the way out!'

'You should keep it open,' he called back.

'People like you disrupt my work, and I like my privacy!'

Marcin shut the door as he left and a gust of air sent several more pieces of paper fluttering to the floor.

Alicia got off the stool to pick up the tags that had fallen off the desk and glanced at the tray Marcin had left. A fine, powdery film coated one of the glittering, blue-green false bornite samples. She'd never seen anything like that before. She picked up the paper tags from the floor and put a hand to her back as she straightened.

Now, what was that strange substance? She turned to the tray of samples, but the film that covered the ore samples had gone, leaving them shiny.

'What the hell?' She reached for the radio. 'Marcin, Alicia here.'

Marcin's voice crackled through the intervening layers of rock between office and mine. 'Hi, Alice.'

'Marcin, have you been messing with the samples?'

'What do you mean? They're as I found them.'

'There was something white and powdery on one of them. I've never seen it before.'

'Oh, yeah. That stuff's usually gone by the time I get them to you.'

'What is it?'

'Not sure. I never really thought about it. The latest seam I broke open had a lot of it. Crumbly white stuff. Arlon called it carbyne. He never analysed the stuff as far as I know, although he used to pack it up in vacuum-sealed hoppers for some reason ... Let me guess, you want me to bring some up?'

'If you could, please—' She stopped herself, recalling that some minerals degraded under certain conditions, which may have been the reason for the vacuum storage. 'Make sure to put it in sample jars while still in vacuum. I think they might get damaged by air.'

'Whatever you say. Marcin out.'

Several minutes later, he returned with a handful of sealed jars.

'There you go,' he said, placing them on the desk. 'Don't say I never do anything for you.'

Alicia smiled. 'I do appreciate it, thanks.' She turned to resume her work but stopped. 'Marcin, if Arlon never analysed the mineral, how did he get a client for it?'

'I think he posted on a bulletin board or something, just listing its basic properties, and somebody was interested. Garvin still sells it.'

After Marcin had gone and she could concentrate properly, she tipped out a small quantity of the mineral from one of the jars into a vial and resealed it, then put the vial under the microscope.

The crumbly chalk-like substance had an incredibly fine texture, almost like compressed powder, yet no crystalline structure presented itself under magnification.

'That's strange,' she said, staring down the eyepiece.

The sample in the vial began to dwindle as though dissolving. Was it breaking down in the air?

She filled a pipette with water from a beaker on the desk and put just enough in the vial to cover the sample. Under the microscope, the sample continued to diminish, with no effervescence. Arlon must have got it wrong. "Carbyne" would have meant a reactive intermediary, but this wasn't producing a gas as it dissolved – there were no bubbles, and so no reaction.

She pulled the tube from under the microscope and watched as the white mineral disappeared completely. The water level in the test tube had dropped accordingly. Time for the mass spectrometer.

'Let's see what's in there.'

Five minutes later, the mass spectrometry results showed the tube was filled with water, a few expected trace elements, but nothing else.

Scratching her head, she went back to her notes and scribbled down her findings, such as they were, and glanced at Marcin's other samples lined up on the desk. The jar she'd opened and resealed now stood empty, while the others remained full.

She clamped her hands over her head. 'What's happened to it?'

Wide-eyed, she picked up the now empty jar and stared at it. The remaining chunk of mineral was no longer present and the inside of the jar was coated with a thin film, fogging the glass with a milky sheen that faded even as she watched. How could the entire volume of the sample simply have vanished?

Alicia sat at the desk and drummed her pen against her chin for a moment before writing in her notebook.

> *The remainder of a sample that Marcin retrieved has disappeared after having the vacuum seal broken. I have detected no evidence of the mineral in a sample of water after dissolving it. I can only conclude that the samples have interacted with the water and air in such a fashion as to break down at a sub-molecular level, which could explain why the mineral remained stable in the vacuum environment of the mines.*
>
> *I can see no immediate use for the mineral, as the decomposition does not even leave a substrate of sufficient volume to use as a nanolubricant. The unusual properties of carbyne (I'm not renaming it, as I can't think of anything appropriate at this time) do warrant further study. I'm going to perform more tests as time allows. I have no idea why the previous mineralogist, Arlon, didn't keep notes on the material, nor why anyone would purchase it.*

She pulled her hands down her cheeks and checked her watch. Time for a rest; there were still more urgent samples to analyse for paying trade. She turned off the equipment and left the office for the night.

Several weeks later, Alicia found her workload lightening. The flow of urgent sample analyses for tradeable minerals had come to an abrupt halt as the miners had broken into a consistent seam of false bornite from which the Bronadi had been purchasing huge quantities. She was again able to turn her attention to the strange white mineral.

The lab equipment on Sollers Hope was woefully inadequate for any kind of in-depth analysis and lacked any kind of particle accelerator with which to analyse atomic decay. She was left only with the option of research and theory.

The explanation for the sample's reduction in mass after being exposed to air could be one of three possibilities: either the particles were somehow breaking down and passing *through* the glass of the test tubes; or – as she had recently been briefed on how acceleration nodes functioned, and grasped the basic theory – the matter was somehow moving into a different layer of space or out of phase; or, finally, it was plain and simple radioactive decay.

If the particles were so small as to pass through glass, surely they would have done so without the action of air upon them? There was no measurable radiation, and the decay of even that small mass would have released massive amounts of energy, so the only remaining explanation was the crazy idea of phase transition.

Looking for research on the galactic equivalent of the internet, she worked long into the night. There were hardly any references to materials changing state, especially when referring to phase, that could explain what had happened under her microscope. Phase change usually meant transitioning from solid, to liquid, to gas, and finally to plasma. But this? This was something else.

After discounting most mainstream studies, the remaining articles Alicia found were almost too pointless to bother reading. Searching for minerals with similar outward physical properties, such as talc, she stumbled across a page about alchemy. Mystical mumbo-jumbo talking about the "philosopher's stone" – a mythical mineral capable of turning lead into gold, prolonging life, and other such fallacies. Duggan had talked about it often: as one of his hobbies, and as a geologist, he was fascinated by the subject, and argued that it *"must have had some basis in fact, otherwise how would legends of it be so widespread?"*

Alicia let out a groan and allowed herself to sag forward until her head hit the desk with a thump. 'Why am I bothering with this?' She could imagine Duggan's reply:

Because you're a scientist and you like to find out the truth.

'Yes, Duggan, I am. But I'm a very tired scientist.' She folded her arms on the desk, laid her head on them and allowed her eyes to close, just for five minutes.

She drifted off, entering a fitful sleep and twitching occasionally. She muttered words that would have sounded nonsensical to an observer, words with strange, humming tones, yet she did not wake.

In her dream, she saw herself moving objects with the power of thought, or drifting slowly through the branches of trees; a muddled dream she'd had many times over the years. Had she been awake, she would have attributed it to her thoughts of Duggan and his talk of medieval magic. She would also have noticed the sealed jar on the desk, containing a quantity of the powdery carbyne mineral, slowly emptying itself as the soft rock inexplicably dwindled away to nothing.

Rock samples on the desk surrounding her crept away of their own volition, as though magnetically repelled by her presence, and tumbled to the floor.

Marcin had finished his shift in the mines and was making his way home past Alicia's office when a crash came from inside.

He knocked on the door. 'Alice, are you alright in there?'

No reply.

'Alicia!' He pushed open the door. She sat at the desk with her back to him, staring at the wall opposite. Rock samples lay strewn around. 'Hey, are you okay?'

She silently stood and turned to face him. Her eyes looked straight ahead, staring through him as if he were nothing.

'Alicia. Speak to me. What's happened?'

Her gaze slowly drifted in his direction. 'Where am I?' she said, voice flat and lifeless.

'Uh, home? Sollers Hope. Just like any other day.'

'Where are the ships?'

'Which ships? There's a cargo freighter about to leave, in the hangar at the end of town, if that's what you're asking.'

She brushed past him.

'Alicia, what's going on? You're scaring me.' He stared at the rocks on the floor. What was up with her? Had he done something to upset her? He turned to follow, but when he got outside she was nowhere to be seen.

One of his colleagues approached from the centre of town, about to begin his mining shift. Marcin stopped him.

'Have you seen Alicia? She must have gone past you.'

'No.' The man shook his head. 'Ain't seen her all day. Wha's wrong?'

Marcin's thoughts went to the smashed rocks in her lab. 'I don't know, but I reckon she's quit.'

Alicia awoke, cold in her indoor clothing, standing outside an imposing old building. There was no sign of the dome of Sollers Hope overhead. Instead, clouds scudded across the sky, lit from beneath by the hazy glow of street lights. Earth? The last thing she remembered was going to sleep at the desk in her office, light years away. How could she be here? She read the street signs. No! Not back in London! This was a nightmare!

Everything went black. Someone put something over her head, grabbed her hands, and pinned her arms to her sides. She kicked and screamed, but an instant later someone thrust something into her mouth, making it impossible to shout.

'She's been standing outside for a while,' a gruff male voice said. 'The boss said to bring her in. She's probably been possessed.'

'What do we do with her?' another said.

'Stick her in a cell. He'll have to find out how she got here.'

Alicia struggled against being frogmarched up steps and down several echoing corridors, but her captors were too strong for her. Eventually they stopped and the bag was pulled from her head and gag removed. In front of her stood a middle-aged man in a dark suit. He leaned on a cane, despite any visible need to do so, and his swept-back hair reminded her briefly of a younger Duggan, even though he seemed to have a corporate air about him. He leaned close to inspect her features.

While he stared, a strange, faraway glittering filled his eyes. 'One has been here. We must find out what happened to it. Sit her down.'

Her captors grabbed her hands and thrust her into a chair pushed in behind her.

'Who are you? What are you doing?' she asked, finally getting the courage to speak.

'Nothing that concerns you,' the man said. 'I want you to simply listen to my voice ...'

The rough edges of his words ground like sand on stone. Whispering, soothing. At each word, Alicia found herself drifting away, concerned less and less with her situation.

The man clicked his fingers. 'Good,' he said. 'That's all we needed to know.'

'What?' she asked. 'What did you need to know?'

'How you got here and why you came. Apparently, you came here on a transport.'

The man's aides yanked her out of the chair and pushed her into a cell. The door slammed shut behind her and she spun around.

'What are you going to do with me?'

'It appears, Miss Maline, that you escaped from us once before, but this time your full potential has been revealed.'

'Escaped? You-you ran the hospital! What do you want me for?'

'You are able to use magic, my dear – a skill valuable to us for increasing our numbers.'

Alicia's mind raced. Surely it had all been a dream? There was no such thing as magic. This had to be a dream. It was all a dream.

The corporate-looking man gestured to one of his aides who, a moment later, dragged in a man wearing a dirty military surplus jacket. His face was thin, and as grimy as his clothing. In seconds, they forced him to his knees in front of her cell.

'Now, Miss Maline,' the corporate man said, 'I have primed you with a hypnotic trigger so that you can access your subconscious. It will allow you to use your abilities much more easily.'

'There's no way I will do anything to help you, you butchers!'

'You will.' He spoke words in a language she didn't understand. Words that slipped from her memory as soon as they were spoken.

She reached through the bars of the cell and placed her hands on the shoulders of the dirty man kneeling in front of her. Frowning in concentration, she opened her mouth to speak and out came unintelligible words, accompanied by a bizarre, chanting drone.

The air shimmered around her in a heat haze, and she blacked out.

When she came to, the man's body lay on the floor outside the cell, shrivelled and withered, the skin grey and taut as though mummified.

'A little excessive,' the corporate man said, towering over the corpse, 'but we'll get there, I'm sure.'

*   *   *

Years passed for Alicia, trapped in those cells. Her captors repeatedly brought their victims to her and issued the hypnotic trigger, frequently at first, sporadically in later years. Sometimes they would take blood samples before giving her the command, but never explained why.

For a long time, she couldn't recall what happened during the process, but part of her mind must have become resistant: she no longer blacked out immediately, and she perceived strange effects. Sometimes a faint breeze would blow through the corridor just before she passed out, especially if she had been thinking about escape or the outdoors. Other times she'd think about Sollers Hope and the stars wheeling overhead, only to experience faint sparkling lights in the air before losing consciousness. It was her *mind* driving the outcome!

One day they brought in a man whose face and hands were sooty, his light blue shirt stained with smoke-blackened sweat. A trickle of blood had dried above his left eyebrow. The jacket he wore had a large metal badge with numbers on, mounted upon the shoulder, and he had a belt with many pouches, from which hung a stun baton. Standing before the cell, he swayed as though concussed.

'This man is a police officer!' Alicia shouted as they took the baton from him and forced him to his knees before her.

'Where did you find him?' Kevin said. The visits from the corporate-looking man had ceased a long time ago.

'He was investigating an abandoned ship near Sirius,' one of the aides said.

Kevin smiled broadly. 'I know the one. He will make an excellent host. Now, my dear,' he said to Alicia, 'if you'd do the honours?'

'I won't do it.'

'You will do it, or I'll have him killed.'

'I'd rather you kill him than use him for whatever horrible experiments you're doing!'

'If you don't do it, we won't just kill him. How about we find and kill his family, too?'

'You sick bastard,' she sobbed. 'Please, please don't make me do it.'

Kevin smiled and tapped his lips. 'Maybe we'll kill all of his friends, as well.'

'Alright!' she screamed. There had to be something she could do. 'Give me ... give me a moment.'

Kevin folded his arms. 'Whatever, just hurry up about it.'

What could she do? Without understanding what was going on while she was in the trance, there was no way she could fight back. She had to find some way of getting information, a way to control the process, or at least to not black out again.

'I'm ready,' she said.

Kevin spoke the words that put Alicia's mind into the state that allowed her to use magic. At that moment she imagined remaining lucid, concentrating on the gruesome moment with all of her will.

She leaned forward and reached through the bars, putting her hands on the policeman's shoulders.

He began to shudder and convulse as she spoke gibberish words, a mixture of different languages, mingled with a humming, throaty chant. Patterns flashed in her mind and the air around her shimmered. The man in front of her slumped and his skin paled.

Alicia's consciousness shifted, as though barged aside in her own head, and her will divorced from her actions. She shivered as a presence shared the space inside her skull. It was like having something cold and crystalline slide into bed with her. A bed she couldn't escape.

Her mouth opened and spoke. 'Where … am … I?'

'A planet called Earth. May I ask who you are?'

'We… are … Gravalax, returned … from the Tower.'

'My Lord Gravalax!' Kevin bowed his head. 'It is an honour to meet you.' One of Kevin's aides grabbed Alicia-Gravalax's forearm and took a blood sample while he spoke. 'Please, forgive this intrusion, this is a vital part of our research.'

Gravalax, now more in control of the Alicia-host, had one burning question. 'How is it that we left this realm?'

'Your host was run over by an out-of-control horse and carriage when you crossed the road. Your fellows were unable to get to you in time to prevent your dissipation. Over three hundred years have passed since. Your Second died several years ago, but the circumstances of his death made it impossible for him to transfer to a new host. Now, I must ask that you use this vessel before you. The one you inhabit is temporary and will not hold you for long.'

Gravalax leaned forward, and Alicia watched helplessly as he reached out with her hands to strangle the weakening police officer before her. The man's eyes rolled up inside his head as Gravalax pulled his face close, breathed in deep, and exhaled.

A red mist emanated from between Alicia's lips and slipped into the man's mouth. Something tugged deep within her and wrenched free. The cold presence in her mind dislodged itself as the last of the red mist entered its new host.

She staggered back into the corner of the cell, pulling the blanket from the bed as she went. She vomited once and curled up, hugging herself, and rocked back and forth.

Chapter 27

Sebastian sat in his cell, mouth open, as he listened to Alicia's tale. 'By the Gods!'

Duggan stared at the floor and allowed the hand holding her face to relax a little. 'I'm sorry, my love,' he said, rubbing her cheek with his thumb. 'If I'd known you were at Sollers Hope . . .'

Alicia shook her head and pressed Duggan's hand closer. 'There was no way you could.'

Sebastian's thoughts stopped racing, and he managed to close his mouth. 'You learned how to do magic! What happened after? Why didn't you try to use it to escape?'

'I never wanted to remain conscious again after that. I didn't want any part of it. And no. No. How could I try to use it to escape? They only used the hypnotic trigger when they brought a victim, and back then I had no idea what I was doing, and when I did experience it, the effects were always minor. I had my suspicions though, and plenty of time to work it out. I'd always talked in my sleep, most likely something to do with the voices I heard, and I can only imagine that the carbyne from Sollers Hope acted as a catalyst and allowed me to spontaneously perform a . . .' She stopped as though searching for the right terminology.

'Thaumatic effect,' Sebastian said. 'That's what we've been calling it. It sounds a little better than "spell".'

'Yes. It was only later that I remembered what Duggan used to say about orichalcum. It was the only logical explanation. On Sollers Hope I must have performed a thaumatic effect in my sleep, using the carbyne in my lab, and somehow got possessed by one of these wretched entities.'

'And they kept you here ever since?' Duggan closed his eyes. 'How long?'

'The best part of twenty years.'

His face fell. 'Oh my God, Eileen, I'm so sorry!' he cried. 'I can't imagine what you've been through.'

'It was a living nightmare. Torturing those poor souls, the entities doing God knows what with their bodies, and I still have no idea why they did the blood tests, or what they learned from me.'

Enormous cosmic gears turned behind the surface of reality. Things began clicking into place. 'Alicia,' Sebastian said, his voice level and serious. 'Did you bring any of that carbyne with you when you first arrived?'

She lowered her head. 'No.'

Duggan gasped. 'Then how did you do all that without carbyne? Did the ITF bring some to you?'

'No! They don't seem to know about the stuff, but if they did, imagine how dangerous it could be in their hands.'

'Then how did you do it?'

Sebastian leaned forward on the bench in his cell. 'Duggan, you know nobody can perform thaumaturgy without carbyne. *Nobody*. But I think there's another explanation. She's what the Freemasons have been calling a necromancer.'

Chapter 28

'A necromancer?' Duggan bellowed. 'She summons the dead? What complete and utter nonsense!'

'Shh,' Sebastian said, 'keep your voice down.'

'Your friend is right, Dug,' Alicia said. 'If what he means by necromancer is that I bring people to the point of death in order to perform thaumaturgy, then yes, I'm a necromancer.'

Duggan paled and stepped back into the darkness of his cell.

'You worked it out, though, didn't you?' Sebastian said, things falling into place in his mind. 'You realised people absorbed carbyne from the air.'

'Yes.' She avoided his gaze. 'I didn't know what was happening to them at first. I thought the people they brought were dying for some other reason and they wanted something else from me. It wasn't until I remained aware that I realised they were possessing people and that *I* must have been drawing carbyne out of them.'

'How did they know that you could use a person in that way if they don't know about carbyne?'

'They didn't get it out of me through hypnosis, that's for sure. I wasn't even awake the first time, so I wouldn't have been able to tell them about it.'

Duggan stepped into the light. 'Remember who these people are, Sebastian. They're what everyone knows as demons. They've been around for centuries and have probably had plenty of exposure to magic and witchcraft. Where do you think the idea of a necromancer comes from, and why witches got such bad press? All this time, those evil things . . . Can you imagine what they're capable of? You've seen the hospital records? It's like people are just meat sacks to them.'

'I heard so many horror stories while I was there,' Alicia said. 'They used people for experiments, people that wouldn't be missed. Disabled people, the homeless ... Society started to notice it, especially when patients vanished from the hospital when they were supposed to be released, and later, when they started turning others away because the place was inexplicably full. From what I heard here, people had started to notice disappearances in the city. Eventually they had to adapt. They took from poverty-stricken areas, such as they were. People living in tiny settlements away from the cities.

'It made things easier for them when I came along. No more experiments with their torture equipment ... You know, I could have killed myself, but I had to let them use me. They always had something to hold over me, even when they didn't know it. Society is too traceable now – it's harder to find people who won't be missed. I was worried that if I killed myself, or somehow stopped doing what they wanted, they'd start looking in other places with larger numbers of people, where they could afford losses. Places where people are untraceable ... They'd start hunting down those on the outlying colonies that haven't made contact. Those still travelling at lightspeed. Places like the colony you helped establish, Duggan.'

She took a deep, shuddering breath. 'When I couldn't find any sign of you, I thought you might still be alive, moved on to another planet. But I wasn't sure ... I couldn't risk them reaching out and finding your old colony, in case you were with the others. Hundreds of untraceable people for the taking. I had to try to blot you out of my thoughts whenever they came.'

'How did you know they were accessing your memories?'

'They'd spoken of things that only I knew. Things I'd been thinking about just before I blacked out. I knew something had to be getting inside me. There's no such thing as telepathy and, when I lived at Sollers Hope, I never heard about any races capable of it. *I* had to be the one saying the things they knew. That was why I had to discover what was happening.'

Something in Alicia's story, the mention of Sirius by her captors, reminded Sebastian of his grandfather, who had escaped in a ship that had turned up in the region of Sirius, burnt out. His father had died before finishing the investigation, and EarthSec had later ruled his grandfather's death to be an EVA accident. This couldn't possibly be related, could it? He had to know.

'What happened to the police officer?' he asked.

'He slowly recovered, but he wasn't the same. I knew that whatever was in me, Gravalax, had gone into him. I think it moved on into another police officer after that. He's some bigshot of theirs.'

Sebastian stood and moved towards the bars. It *wasn't* his father. He'd attended the funeral – he'd been shot. But … 'Gods! Garvin was threatened by a police officer on Sollers Hope! The Freemasons were right. The ITF is run by the Illuminati, and they do have members in the police!'

'Not everyone here is possessed,' Duggan said.

'I know. Kevin and Dave, whom I met earlier, are straightforward Human. No sparkling eyes, nothing. The Illuminati would need plenty of regular people acting as agents, otherwise someone would spot them sooner or later. However, the police officer searching for you was definitely possessed.'

'Then you must find a way to stop them, Sebastian. You have to get us out of here. I can't let them use me like they've used Eileen. I stayed possessed for hours at a time. Can you imagine the damage they could do, through me?'

'Yes. I remember the damage you *did*. But how the hell am I going to get you both out?'

'If they trust you, would they let you out? You could sneak in some carbyne.'

Sebastian shook his head. 'They may let me go, but they searched me earlier and took everything. I expect they'll probably do it again until they confirm my identity. I'll have to think of another way to break you out … Alicia, how does this necromancy work? Is it possible for you to use one of us without killing us?'

Duggan's eyes widened. 'You'd be mad to!'

'The boy's on to something, Dug,' Alicia said. 'Over the years, I've had plenty of time to work it out. I think it works by drawing carbyne out of the body. In most cases, it's so tightly bound to cells that it damages them when it goes completely out of phase. Cells fall apart and the body dries out … but that's only because I'm using what is bound—'

Sebastian gasped. 'I could breathe some in! If I inhale some and get to you quickly, it won't get bound to my cells in time to do any damage. Would that work?'

She shrugged. 'There's no way to know for certain.'

Duggan winced. 'This is an incredibly bad idea, old boy.'

'Do you have a better one?' Sebastian asked. 'Another plan B?'

'No ... No, I'm afraid this time, I don't.'

Alicia gripped the bars. 'Please, you have to try. We can't stay here.'

Sebastian nodded and moved to the door of his cell. 'Kevin!'

A minute later, the door at the end of the room opened and the short, suited man scurried in.

'What is it?'

'How long until your superior arrives?'

'Why, is there a problem?'

Sebastian frowned and leaned closer to the bars to stare at him. 'Yes. I am becoming impatient and, if I stay here a moment longer, my cover will be blown. I came with a party of three, and they expected this host to be searching for a toilet. If I do not return to them by the end of the evening, they will likely contact EarthSec for a warrant to determine my whereabouts. The building will be searched. Thoroughly.'

'I don't know ...' Kevin sucked air through his teeth and stroked his beard.

Sebastian's neck and armpits warmed uncomfortably. 'I do not have time for this.'

'Ah ... Alright. But you have to come back later or they'll have my head.' Kevin fumbled in his pockets for the key and unlocked the door. 'Come with me. I'll get your things.'

As Sebastian turned to follow Kevin along the corridor, he winked at Duggan, who stared back flatly. Alicia clasped her hands in her lap, her eyes full of hope.

Chapter 29

Aryx made his way from the ballroom to one of the quieter rooms set off from reception on the ground floor, where food had been laid out.

Dark wood panelling lined the room and heavily bossed plaster decoration framed the ceiling: deep flower petals of pale pink alternated with yellow rose buds and white ribbon. They looked like huge marshmallows stuck on the ceiling and reminded him of his acute hunger. One … Two … Three … He counted the pushes as he traversed the carpet to the other side of the room, just in case the door closed behind him and he had to get out quickly – they blended in that well with the panelling. The thick pile dragged at his wheels, adding to the effort required for each push, and his tired wrists ached.

He approached the nearest table laden with hors d'oeuvres and drinks. As he began to pour himself a glass of water from a jug, his hands shook violently and he spilled some on the tablecloth. 'Shit!' He looked around, took a deep breath, and attempted a second time.

The jug jangled loudly on the edge of the glass. He cursed under his breath at his own lack of coordination, but a woman's hand closed tightly around his, steadying his grip and helping him pour.

'It's alright, Aryx,' Monica said. 'I know how exhausted you are.' She placed the jug back on the table while he drank. 'And you're worried about Sebastian.'

He downed the last of the water with a hard gulp, as if swallowing around a stone. 'He's been gone ages. Something's happened to him, I know it!'

'We still have half an hour until his deadline. Try to eat something. You almost look hypoglycaemic.'

He nodded and scanned the savoury buffet table for something high in protein and carbs. His eyes settled on a plate ringed with folds of smoked salmon with a dish of cream cheese at the centre. He checked nobody was watching and piled a plate high with it, grabbing several pieces of thin toast at the same time, and put it on his lap.

Monica took two pieces and walked alongside while he found somewhere to park himself out of the way, somewhere they wouldn't be overheard.

'I'm really worried, Nic.' He ate half a slice of salmon on toast in one bite. 'We should get out of here or go down and look for him.'

She screwed up her face and shook her head. 'See, I think that's a really bad idea. We don't have any weapons and SpecOps doesn't have any jurisdiction over this place for me to exert any kind of authority.'

He sat quietly while he ate the remaining slices of salmon and toast. At least his hands had stopped shaking enough to get it in his mouth. 'You were right about me being hungry,' he said, giving a brief smile. 'I guess I wasn't thinking. It would be nuts to go down there, especially without information.'

'Exactly.'

He filled and cleared his plate twice more.

Karan appeared behind Monica. 'What are you guys talking about?'

Aryx swallowed a sharp piece of toast. 'Oh, you made it then? Where's Judie?'

'She had to go. She was starting to get tired. I'm surprised you're not completely zonked yourself.'

'I am. I just can't allow myself to fall into a gibbering heap just yet.'

'You're certainly eating well enough.' She looked about. 'What's happening with Seb? He's not back yet?'

Aryx and Monica shook their heads.

'It's about time for us to leave, isn't it? What do we do? Go, and then call the police?'

Monica looked at Aryx. 'Let's give it another five minutes, shall we?'

Chewing on another mouthful of salmon, he nodded . . . and nearly choked as the wood-panelled door opened and Sebastian stepped in.

'There you are!' Karan shouted. Monica simply smiled at him, and Aryx thumped his chest as he swallowed the blockage.

Sebastian reached for Karan's hand. 'We need to go. Right now.'

'What happened?' Aryx asked as he wheeled towards the door.

'I'll tell you later. There are ITF here. We've got to hurry.' Sebastian led them into reception and retrieved Aryx's jacket from the cloakroom.

Aryx wheeled past, through the entrance doors, and pressed the button the doorman had used at the top of the steps. He tapped his fingers on his thigh. Couldn't the steps move faster?

'EXCUSE ME!' came a high-pitched voice from across the lobby behind them. 'Excuse me! Mr Trevarian?'

He cringed and turned slowly. The Rutherfords strode towards him across the glittery white floor, Mrs Rutherford in the lead.

'What the fuck does she want?' he mumbled.

Sebastian stepped in front of him and reached out with his right hand. 'Nice to see you again, Mrs Rutherford.'

'Not you,' she said, brushing Sebastian's hand away. She bent down. 'It's him I want to talk to.'

Aryx set his jaw. 'What the hell do you—'

Mrs Rutherford held up a hand. 'Please, I have to say something. I want to apologise for my earlier behaviour. I was wrong.'

He raised an eyebrow.

She straightened. 'I feel I may have misjudged you. I made an incorrect assumption that disabled people were a drain on society, that they had no use, and did not deserve my respect. I was wrong. I clearly need to start reading different news publications. My husband' – Mr Rutherford peered around her and smiled weakly – 'pointed out that if you could complete the marathon, that was more than most able-bodied people could do. I also thought you were rather uncouth and lacked grace—'

'Well, in fairness, I was a bit rude earlier.'

'That aside, it wasn't until I saw you in the ballroom with your friends that I realised you were capable of far more than I thought. It's a long time since I saw such style and grace. It truly opened my eyes. I'm sorry.'

Mr Rutherford stepped around his wife to shake Aryx's hand. 'What she's trying to say is, is there any way we can make it up to you? I run a very successful business, and if you wanted some form of financial compensation . . .'

Aryx scratched his chin. 'If you made a large donation to the Veterans' Reconstruction Fund, I'm sure that would be appreciated. What sort of business do you run?'

'I own several aerospace companies and just acquired a company that manufactures constrained field generators.'

The mobipack . . . He grinned. 'Actually, I might have a business opportunity for you in the future, if you wanted to contribute towards an engineering and development grant.'

Sebastian stepped away from the conversation and pointed to the junction several metres down the road. *'I'll meet you there,'* he mouthed.

Aryx nodded and continued talking to the couple with animated gestures while Sebastian led Monica and Karan to the corner of the building and waited. The ITF had no idea who the others were, but he couldn't risk hanging around in case Kevin spotted them all together.

'Did you get the records?' Karan asked, rubbing her hands together.

Sebastian shivered against the cold but handed over his jacket. 'I think so. Wolfram downloaded a ton of stuff before we got caught.'

'And the Freemasons will be able to use it to cross-reference cases?' Monica asked.

'That's what Jonas said. It'll give them an idea of who might be in the ITF through lists of suspects.'

'But how are you going to get the information to them?'

'Well, we can't exactly go back to the hospital,' Karan said. 'The ITF will probably be watching that place, too.'

'True.' Sebastian's shoulders dropped. 'Then I've got no idea.'

Aryx wheeled around the corner. 'Right, I'm ready. I've potentially got the Rutherfords interested in helping fund development of a commercial version of the mobipack – when all this terrorist crap's blown over, that is. Of course, I had to be careful not to reveal exactly what it was yet ... Where we off to?'

'We should probably go back to the hotel,' Sebastian said. 'At least that'll give me time to think about my next move.'

'I wouldn't do that if I were you,' said a voice from the shadows behind them.

Sebastian turned, and a man dressed in a black gown with a flash of white at the collar stepped forward. 'I know you. You were watching me yesterday.'

The priest inclined his head slightly. 'Yes. My apologies if I set you at unease.'

'Who are you? What are you doing out here at this time of night? Are you following me?'

'I am, as a matter of fact.'

Sebastian tensed as the priest unfastened one of his cuffs and rolled up his sleeve ... exposing a tattoo on the inside of his forearm.

Sebastian peered at it, struggling to make out detail in the shadows: the form of intersecting compasses and right angle. 'You're a Freemason?' he whispered.

The priest nodded. 'I spotted you yesterday but did not realise who you were until Jonas contacted me earlier. I am Father Elias.'

'He sent you to help?'

Elias nodded. 'I am to take you back to St Margaret's Church. You should not stay at your hotel. The Illuminati may try to take you and your companions in the night.'

'I've got stuff there that I need to pick up!' Aryx said. He looked at Karan. 'The mobipack.'

'Actually, I need my rucksack, too.' Sebastian said. 'It's got my grandfather's journal in it, and some carbyne. I can't let the ITF get hold of either.'

'Don't worry,' Karan said. 'I'll take a taxi and get them.'

'Correction. *We'll* go and get them,' Monica said. 'Safety in numbers.' She looked at the priest. 'Do we just come around to the front of the church when we get back?'

'Use one of the side doors. Knock five times and I will let you in.'

'Great. See you in a few minutes.' Karan stepped towards the road and stuck out her arm. 'Taxi!' A passing autocab stopped and they both climbed in. In moments, they were out of sight.

The priest led Sebastian and Aryx around One Great George Street to a side entrance in the smaller church by Westminster Abbey. Aryx wheeled up the ramp while Sebastian followed the priest up the adjacent steps into the building.

Elias took them to a small room with several beds and grey stone walls. 'I hope you don't mind staying here the night. The beds are simple – they are for those who come on pilgrimages to the abbey – but you should find the room warm enough.'

'Thank you.' Sebastian sat on the nearest bed. 'I don't suppose you have a way to contact Jonas, do you?'

'Yes. But first, would you like something to eat or drink? Your friend looks very tired.'

Aryx had parked his chair by a bed on the far side of the room and transferred over to it. 'I'd love a warm drink, thanks.'

'Any preference? We don't have anything extravagant.'

Sebastian grimaced, expecting Aryx to request his usual triple-strength black coffee.

'Warm milk?' Aryx asked.

'It'll be my pleasure. Can I get you anything, Mr Thorsson?'

'Water.' Then again, he had a long night ahead of him. 'No. Tea, please.'

'I'll be a few minutes.' Elias left the room through a heavy wooden door opposite where they'd entered.

Sebastian stared at Aryx's greying features. 'How are you feeling? You look tired.'

'Knackered. Like I've done *two* marathons. I could sleep for a week.' He rubbed his eyes and yawned. 'Are you going to tell me what happened in the archive?'

'I got the information, then I got caught. They put me in a cell. Duggan was there, along with Alicia Maline!'

'What? Duggan *and* Alicia? Is he okay? Jeez ... I thought she'd have died a long time ago.'

'As did I. Duggan's fine, thankfully. Alicia escaped the hospital before living on Sollers Hope and ended up doing some long lightspeed trips. Subsequently she's just a little older than Duggan. She looked about eighty. She's been trapped there for the last twenty years, in a hidden underground complex next to the archive.'

'What have they been doing to her?'

The door opened and in came Monica and Karan, carrying the mobipack and Sebastian's rucksack. Aryx's eyes widened. 'Thank you!'

'Did you have any trouble at the hotel?' Sebastian asked.

Karan shook her head. 'I guess they hadn't considered staking the place out yet.'

'That was lucky. I was just explaining to Aryx what happened at the archive.'

Monica moved over to Aryx and began to inspect his legs. 'How are you doing?'

'Not too bad,' he said quietly.

Karan sat on the bed next to Sebastian. 'And? What happened?'

'Duggan and Alicia were there. They've been using her to possess people for years. She can somehow use carbyne absorbed by the body. The ITF there think I'm one of them, so I managed to convince them to release me.'

'What are they going to do with Duggan?' Monica asked. 'The same?'

'I think so. I have to get them out.'

Karan put a hand on Sebastian's wrist. 'Tomorrow, though, yes? It's been a long day for everyone, and if you go back in this state you'll make mistakes.'

Sebastian crossed his fingers in his pocket and nodded. 'Tomorrow. Yes. I'll do it tomorrow.'

Elias returned with a tray of drinks and set them down on a bedside table just inside the door. He handed Sebastian his cup. 'Would you like to come with me? I have Jonas on the line.'

'Of course.' Sebastian turned to the others and picked up his rucksack. 'You should all get some rest. This could take a while. Don't wait up.'

The group said goodnight and Sebastian followed Elias to his office, a space cramped with heavy wooden furniture and darkening, uneven yellow plaster walls.

'I'm sorry for the mess,' Elias said, pushing a pile of papers aside to make space for Sebastian to sit on the end of the desk. He slid a painting of the crucifixion that hung on the wall opposite to one side, revealing a large, black glass panel. The screen lit up and Jonas's lined face appeared.

'Hello again, Sebastian.'

'Jonas.'

'Elias tells me you made it in and out of the archive safely. What have you discovered?'

'They think I'm one of the possessed, for the same reasons you did.' Sebastian tapped his wristcom. 'Just a moment, Jonas, I'll send you what I got. Wolfram? Can you send Jonas the files you downloaded earlier using this terminal?'

'One moment,' Wolfram said. 'Yes. I believe so.' A progress bar appeared on the screen below Jonas. 'Please be aware that I have taken the liberty of cross-referencing the files of connected cases and saved a list of related incidents.'

'Thank you, Sebastian, and whoever this Wolfram is. This information should help immensely. With it, we'll be able to join the dots and reveal the Illuminati members. You've done us a great service. Once I can get Elias to pass this on to the Church, they'll likely want to perform a raid on the place. I can't thank you enough. Is there anything I can do for you?'

'Two things,' Sebastian said. 'Firstly, my friend Duggan is being held in the archive building along with his fiancée. She's the one they've been using as a necromancer to possess people, and I could do with some help getting them out. Secondly, I need someone to track down the reassigned Gladrin family using the data I've provided.'

'I can do the latter, but unfortunately I can't provide support to get your friend out. Did you say the Illuminati think you're possessed?'

'Yes, and they are expecting me to return. Getting in will be easy, but getting out again is another matter.' Sebastian gave the two a brief rundown on what he'd learned from Alicia, and of his own previous experiences with Duggan.

Elias's eyes narrowed. 'If you and your friends can use thaumaturgy, can you not take some of that carbyne with you and use it to escape somehow?'

'I was planning to inhale some to sneak it in. Alicia should be able to draw it out.'

'Be very careful, Sebastian,' Jonas said in a low voice. 'You'll be walking into a hornets' nest with no way of defending yourself, especially if it doesn't work out with the necromancer.'

'Can you not use this carbyne yourself, once inhaled?' Elias asked.

Sebastian shrugged. 'I hadn't really thought about it. In my experience, and in the experiments I've seen video footage of, carbyne gets used as continuous mass in a kind of chain reaction. I assume she must have some innate ability to use diffuse carbyne.'

'That is quite possible.' The priest paced back and forth. 'If it were easy to use it from a body, it's not a stretch to imagine that those capable of magic could have accidentally used it without the necessary skill or materials and would have instantly killed themselves. And this would have occurred frequently over the centuries.'

Jonas rubbed his chin. 'Well, it certainly explains how witches have historically been able to use natural ingredients for spells, and why they've never had spectacular, or reproducible, effects. Sebastian, how do you intend to protect yourself from getting possessed if this necromancer is able to use your carbyne without killing you? Surely she – or the thing controlling her – will attack the instant it takes hold?'

'If the process doesn't kill me, I think I'll be strong enough to prevent her from getting to me. The victims have usually been left in a near-death state, and very weak, so I don't think I'll have to worry about that. When Duggan's entity tried to possess me, he actually strangled me and then breathed something at me. A kind of red mist.'

'The miasma,' Elias said. 'The "bad air" from historical texts. Supposedly, it was the cause of diseases and plagues, and Demons use it for transference of their spirit.'

'I wouldn't exactly use that terminology,' Sebastian said. 'I think it's something more scientific than that.'

'What does the terminology matter? If it holds the essence of the thing, that is the most important factor, is it not?'

Jonas cleared his throat. 'Gentlemen, let's not argue semantics. The question is, if this miasma is released, is there a way Sebastian can protect himself from it? What happened when Duggan attacked you?'

Sebastian recalled his experience aboard the Yazor comet: Duggan had launched himself across a coffee table after casting the thaumatic effect that reversed his previous partial invisibility. He had been possessed, and the old man's grip around Sebastian's throat had been vice-like. The memory was vague, but he recalled that Wolfram had emitted a purging pulse before Duggan had been able to pass the miasma on to him.

'He didn't get to the point where it actually went into my mouth. Wolfram managed to dissipate it before that, but I can't use him for protection as he's in Cardiff.'

'So, it needs to enter your lungs,' Jonas said slowly. 'That would imply it needs access to your bloodstream for some reason ... Rather than being entirely incorporeal, the beings must take on some physical element when drawn to this realm. Perhaps the mist will dissipate to the point of impotence if it doesn't reach its target in time.'

'I hope you're right. Look, I need to go now. It's nearly midnight, and I have to get back there before the party finishes.'

'What about your plan?' Elias asked. 'You don't seem to have much of it worked out.'

'I only need to get the carbyne out of me. Once that's done, I'm sure Duggan can set off another fireball or something. If that fails, I can take Kevin out. He's only short and looks like he's more suited to a desk job—' Sebastian caught himself. *His* was technically a desk job. 'I'll work something out.'

'That's not much of a plan,' Jonas said.

'I know, but it's the best I've got.'

Back in the communal bedroom, Sebastian fumbled in his rucksack for a handful of carbyne vials. He took six, leaving one in the bag, and glanced across at the sleeping Aryx.

Aryx would kill him if he knew where he was going, especially alone, but he couldn't involve him in this. If things got out of hand, Aryx's wheelchair could be a liability, and the smooth floors in the building didn't lend themselves to the use of the mobipack. No, with everything he'd been through today, it was best he stayed here where it was safe.

Sebastian put on his wristcom and slipped the interface projector into his trouser pocket. If he went back to the archive carrying more items than he'd left with, it might cause suspicion.

Father Elias followed him from St Margaret's Church to the junction where they met. 'Sebastian, I'll give you an hour. If you're not back by then, I'll assume the worst.'

'I don't think I'll need that long,' he said, crossing his fingers in his pocket. 'Just make sure the others get back to the ship safely if things go pear-shaped.'

'I will.' Elias smiled. 'Good luck, but I pray to God that you don't need it.'

Sebastian walked along the darkened street and bent to tuck a vial of carbyne in the stone balustrade at the front of the building. He looked back once, as Elias slipped back into the shadows, before making his way up the steps into One Great George Street.

Sebastian's shoes echoed loudly on the polished floor of the lobby as he made his way to the toilets. Most of the event attendees had left, or vacated the reception area, and he slipped in unseen.

Sitting in a cubicle on the closed toilet seat, he took the remaining five vials of carbyne from his pocket. Still unstabilised, the fine white powder should be easy to inhale – not that he'd ever taken drugs to know from experience – but its ability to sublimate quickly ought to make it no more difficult than breathing in a gas.

He quickly unstoppered all the tubes and tipped the contents onto his hand, which immediately began to itch. Perhaps this wasn't such a good idea. 'But I'm all out of good ideas,' he said quietly. No, this would be easy. Bringing his hand up to his face, he put a finger over one nostril and inhaled.

Stars exploded in his vision. Blood rushed in his ears. The world tumbled backwards and a thousand knives embedded themselves in his sinuses.

'Really ... bad ... idea!' he spluttered, coughing powder everywhere. As the world slowly stopped spinning, he looked at his palm. Most of the carbyne had gone. Had he sucked all that up, or was it evaporating too quickly? In a panic, he cupped his hand, tossed the remainder into his mouth and swallowed.

No taste, no pain. Just a slight tingle on the tongue. Idiot! Why didn't he think of that before?

He waited for the world to settle before leaving the toilet cubicle – really, he could have done with a few minutes but, with the carbyne potentially integrating into his cells with every moment, he couldn't risk delaying further.

Stepping out into the lobby, he steadied himself with a hand against the wall and made his way down the stairs to the archive. When he reached the wood-panelled doors around the corner of the white corridor, Dave stood in front of them, arms folded.

'Good evening, *Dave*,' Sebastian said. 'I have returned to see Kevin, as promised.'

Dave put a finger to his ear and mumbled something to the right. 'Go on through.'

Sebastian made his way through the double doors and Kevin met him several metres along the next corridor, accompanied by another tall security guard and, after a quick search and confiscation of his wristcom and interface device, they escorted him back to the concrete-block section.

'I hope you don't mind being put in a cell again,' Kevin said, pulling the heavy key from his pocket. 'My superior hasn't arrived yet but is due soon.'

'I understand. You still need to verify my identity.'

'Where have you been?'

'I had to return to our accommodation so that I could slip away from my companions without raising suspicion.'

At the sound of Sebastian's voice, Duggan came to the front of his cell and gripped the bars. His eyes were wide and he licked his lips once.

Sebastian stepped into his own cell and waited for Kevin to lock it: with the presence of the additional guard, there was no way for him to make a move.

'I'll let my superiors know you're here ... again.' Kevin turned to leave and his colleague followed.

Duggan waited for the pair to exit. 'Did you bring carbyne?'

Sebastian tapped his nose. 'I inhaled some. My brain is on fire.'

'Can you perform a spell? Have you tried?'

'No, and I'm pretty sure I won't be able to. I was hoping Alicia would be able to draw it out of me.' He stared at the blanket-covered heap on the bed of the cell opposite. *'Alicia!'* he hissed.

She rolled over and pulled the blanket from her face. 'You're back! Can you get us out?'

'If you can use the carbyne I've got in me, yes. I took five vials' worth.'

'But I can't! You're too far away, and I don't know how to do it without the hypnotic trigger.'

Sebastian looked at Duggan.

'Don't ask me,' Duggan said. 'I've not witnessed it.'

'Oh Gods, what am I going to do? I think I can deal with Kevin, but there are other guards to get past.'

'We'll worry about that when we get to it. Why don't you call him back in here?'

'Alright.' Sebastian took a deep breath. 'KEVIN!'

A moment later, the door of the cell block opened and the dumpy little man entered. 'What is it now? What do you want?'

'I hoped I might be able to speak to the woman opposite.' Sebastian pointedly looked at Duggan. 'Privately.'

Kevin approached the cell and drew out the key. 'I think that can be arranged,' he said, slowly turning it in the lock.

As the bars swung open, he put the key back in his pocket. Sebastian stepped through the door and brought his left elbow up into Kevin's face. Instead of it connecting with the man's nose, Kevin blocked it with his left hand and spun Sebastian around.

'Oh, you have to get up really early to catch me out,' he said, grabbing Sebastian's elbow and twisting it upwards. His right hand clamped around the back of Sebastian's neck, finger and thumb gripping nerves painfully. Sebastian yelled as the pain sent a convulsion through his body. 'Yes, you have to get up very early indeed.'

He steered the incapacitated Sebastian towards Alicia's cell. 'You see, I just got in touch with my superiors. New arrivals don't use the *I* pronoun. That's something they learn in order to hide. Even if you were one of the others, you'd know that. If I'd known better, I wouldn't have trusted you enough to let you go. I don't know how you faked the eyes, but you certainly fooled me.'

The pressure on Sebastian's neck increased, and he fell to his knees before Alicia's cell.

'They did say they *want* you to join their ranks, however. So you'll get to have your private chat with our guest here. I'd say you'll get to be intimately connected, in a way.' Kevin pressed his knee into Sebastian's back, forcing his face against the bars. 'Alicia, my dear, come here.'

She stood. 'No, I won't do it, not again.'

'Come here or I'll break his *fucking* neck!'

She shuffled towards the bars.

'Good girl. Now, *Þú getur gert galdra*.'

Alicia reached out and pressed down on Sebastian's shoulders.

Chapter 30

'Mr Trevarian, wake up.'

Someone shook Aryx by the shoulder. For a moment, the voice coming from the blackness reminded him of when he'd first woken in the hospital after his accident, and he jolted into wakefulness.

'What is it?' he said, sitting up on his elbows to find Father Elias crouched beside him.

'Sebastian's in trouble.'

'How can he be—' Aryx looked over at the empty bed where Sebastian should have been. 'Where the hell's he gone?'

'To rescue his friend Duggan. He didn't want you to get involved, but he's been gone nearly an hour, and since Jonas got me to pass evidence from the archive on to the Church, they're now going to raid the place. I didn't expect them to respond so suddenly. They'll go in with gas and arrest indiscriminately – including your friends because of their involvement with magic.'

'Jesus Christ! ... Sorry, Father.' Karan shifted in her bed and Aryx lowered his voice. 'Why did he go alone?'

'The Freemasons couldn't offer any backup, and he thought you'd be at risk if he took you. He said the floors might cause a problem.'

'Damn it.'

Elias stood back as Aryx pulled the covers off the bed and transferred to his chair. 'What are you doing?' he whispered.

'I assumed you woke me so I could go and help him.'

'No. I just thought you should know. Do you have a way of contacting him?'

'Yes, if he's got his wristcom.' Aryx tapped his, but Sebastian's didn't respond. 'Wolfram, have you been monitoring Sebastian?'

'I have,' Wolfram said over the comm. 'His wristcom stopped transmitting biosigns forty-five minutes ago, after being removed. Do you wish me to try to make contact?'

'No, you could blow his cover if someone hears it, but I'm not going to sit around doing nothing when I can help. Aryx out.' He wheeled around Elias and began searching through his clothes. He'd only got the suit he'd bought, the marathon gear, and the casual outfit he'd worn to Earth. 'I don't suppose you've got a change of clothes? I need something different.'

'Apart from this,' Elias said, picking at his dress-like robes with finger and thumb, 'no. Why?'

'I'm going to look for another way into the basement. It doesn't need to be tidy. I just want a disguise.'

'In that case, I may have something. Follow me.'

Aryx slung the mobipack onto his back and followed Elias as he crept past the others. He led him down a dingy corridor into a small room cluttered with a random assortment of candlesticks, lampshades, children's toys and cardboard boxes labelled in scrawled marker pen.

'We used to have charity sales here and often kept the clothing for any homeless visitors,' he said. Opening one of the boxes, he drew out a long, musty woollen trench coat and wide-brimmed hat, both perforated with moth-holes. 'Will this do?'

'Yes.' Aryx peered into the box. 'Any trousers?'

'Ah . . .' Elias rummaged through the contents and took out a pair of red corduroy jeans, darkened with grime. 'Yes. They are a little long for you, though.'

Aryx grimaced. 'Not to mention filthy. The length isn't a problem. Shoes?'

Elias's face twisted and he hesitated. 'What do you need shoes for?'

'You'll see in a minute.' Aryx placed the clothes on a nearby box and strapped on the mobipack.

The priest continued searching other boxes. 'Would it be best to wake your friends so they can help?'

'No. If I'm to find another way in, it needs to be discreet. Three of us will stick out like a sore thumb, as will my chair.' He finished fastening the mobipack's straps and pulled on the trousers. The ends of the legs hung loose.

Elias held up a pair of green rubber wellingtons. 'What about these? They don't look terribly nice.'

Aryx rolled up the trousers so the bulk of the fabric was above his knees. 'It's more about grip than style.' He pressed a couple of buttons on the mobipack's straps and the glowing, glassy orange shins and feet appeared, resting on the foot bar of his chair.

Elias staggered back, nearly toppling the pile of cardboard boxes behind him. 'Good heavens!'

'Impressive, huh?' Aryx tensed his thigh muscles and the nanobot sensor implants reacted, straightening the glowing legs. 'Can you give me a hand with the boots?'

Elias held up one of the wellingtons. 'I think they will be a little on the small side.'

'Not a problem.' Aryx reached around and popped out the infoslate from the mobipack's compartment. After several taps on its screen, the calves and feet shrank by fifty percent. 'Try now.'

Elias slid the boots over the force-field limbs and stood back. 'Too loose. They will fall off.'

Aryx tapped the infoslate again, slowly reversing the change. The boots gave a rubbery creak as they filled with the enlarging feet. 'I think that's about right,' he said, standing up and rolling down the trouser legs to cover the light they emitted. 'At least they have grip.'

'Would it not be wise to wear something like that all the time?'

He glared at the priest. 'Don't get me started. The pack's not comfortable to wear for long periods, and I manage well enough without.' He reached around to put the infoslate away and simultaneously pulled out the compact crutches, then strapped them to his forearms. 'Can you pass me the coat, please?'

Elias handed him the moth-eaten trench coat. Loose fibres and dust fell from it and Aryx coughed as he opened it and pulled it on over the pack.

'Itchy,' he said, turning around slowly. Even covering the mobipack, the coat still came down to his knees. 'How do I look?'

Elias smiled and held out the hat. 'Like a man with a giant tumour on his back who's just walked in from a month on the street.'

'Perfect.' Aryx put on the hat. 'Now, how do I get to the back entrance of One Great George Street?'

Aryx circled Parliament Square to approach the front of One Great George Street from a different direction, giving him an opportunity to find the other entrance and draw away any attention from St.

Margaret's Church. Still getting used to the new nanobot implant sensors, his gait was cumbersome and rigid, and he stumbled a little as he crossed the cobbled street and negotiated a kerb.

His dark outfit blended in with the soft, night-time shadows of the trees until he neared the building. A couple in dinner dress gave disapproving looks as he approached, and crossed to the other side of the street. Lowering his head to avoid their gaze, his reflection marched alongside sullenly in the street-side windows. No wonder they had been put off by his appearance: the bulge on his back turned him into a disproportioned hunchback of Notre Dame, drunkenly staggering about. He continued along the street keeping his head down.

As he shuffled around the corner to walk the pavement in front of the building, something glinted in a nook of the stone balustrade. He bent down as best he could to investigate.

A vial of carbyne? What was that doing there? Sebastian must have put it there, which meant he was probably still inside.

A shout from farther down the street drew his attention. A dark green pickup truck pulled up on the junction at the other end of the building and several men wearing SWAT-type tactical outfits piled out of the back. One pulled out a kind of RPG launcher and fired it towards the doors with a muffled *phunk!*

'Shit!' Aryx grabbed the vial and broke into a run, back the way he'd come. He turned the corner and jogged past a short flight of steps leading to a side entrance. At the top of the steps stood two suited security guards. No, not that way in.

He quickly looked away and continued past the Queen Elizabeth II Centre, which joined the back of One Great George Street, and headed towards several loading docks arrayed along the building. He walked around a small armoured security van, parked at the second dock, that blocked his way. In the van sat two shaven-headed men, chatting to each other. Not paying full attention to them, he couldn't make out the words, but as he passed they fell silent.

A door slammed behind him and he turned. One of the men, bigger than Aryx, strode purposefully towards him with a metal bar in hand.

'Whoa, I don't want any trouble,' Aryx said. Putting up his hands, he stepped backwards.

'We don't want you to give us any,' the man said, slapping his free hand with the heavy baton. 'Do you think anyone would miss a staggering, homeless drunk like you?'

'I-I really couldn't say.' Aryx lowered himself into a slight crouch, ready to rush him if the need arose.

The approaching man looked past Aryx. 'What you reckon, Hal?'

Aryx turned too late.

Something came down heavily on the back of his neck.

Chapter 31

'Alicia, help me,' Sebastian said.

She winced as her hands pressed on his shoulders. 'I . . . can't . . .'

'*Please!*' Stabbing pain broke out throughout his body, as though his innards were full of iron filings and her hands enormous magnets, drawing the sharp particles through him to her touch. His vision blurred and he became light-headed.

He mustn't pass out. He had to stay alive. Not die. And not get possessed.

It became harder to focus. 'Help me . . .'

The air shimmered around Alicia, as though she stood in a volcanic vent. Her voice shifted into bass tones, and she mumbled incomprehensible words.

Kevin leaned close to Sebastian. 'Is this private enough for you?' he whispered, grating, into his ear. That smug little shit.

'Sebastian, close your eyes,' Alicia said, still double-toning the words.

Better to die eyes closed. He complied.

Bright light flashed through his eyelids.

The knee at his back released.

'Get up, Sebastian,' Alicia said. 'Get up now!'

Woozily, he opened his eyes. Kevin held his hands over his face and staggered from side to side. Trying to push through the haze of incoherence, Sebastian stood and swung his leg out, knocking Kevin's feet from under him. He hadn't expected him to lose his balance so easily, and Kevin fell back, his head hitting the floor with a wet thud. A dark puddle seeped out on the bare concrete.

'You made that look easy!' Duggan shouted.

Kevin lay on the floor, bloodshot eyes staring straight up. A strange quivering shook Sebastian's abdomen. He'd killed a man.

He vomited.

'It was either you or him, old boy. Don't feel bad about it.'

Sebastian wiped his mouth on his jacket sleeve. 'I don't know how you can be so flippant. I only meant to knock him out.'

Alicia gripped the bars. 'Quickly, get the key. The guards will be here soon. He hardly ever comes in without backup.'

Sebastian fumbled in Kevin's trousers for the key, trying to touch the body as little as possible. 'I don't understand what happened. Why am I not possessed?'

'Duggan told me how to prevent them from taking hold. I had to visualise a white bubble. I didn't think it would work.'

Sebastian found the key and put it in the lock to Alicia's cell. 'I know the technique. And the flash?'

'I think I was able to focus more. The hypnotic trigger doesn't control my thoughts, just my actions.'

'Damn!' Sebastian said, pulling out the key. 'It doesn't fit. It must be just for the other cell.'

'How are we going to get out?' Duggan asked, knuckles whitening.

'Plan B.'

'Oh, so I'm not the only one to ever have B-plans.' He grinned. 'What is it?'

'Alicia has to draw the carbyne out of me.'

'And then what? Unstabilised, it will vanish in no time.'

Sebastian shrugged. 'I was hoping you'd have some ideas.'

'Marvellous. There's nothing like putting pressure on an old man.'

'Or an old woman,' Alicia said.

Sebastian dropped the useless cell key. 'Can you do it, Alicia?'

'I can, if you know the words Kevin said.'

'They were strangely easy to remember. Icelandic, Gods know why. It was "you can do magic". Ready?'

She nodded.

'Right. *Þú getur gert galdra.*'

Alicia robotically reached for Sebastian's shoulders and repeated the process initiated by Kevin earlier. Sebastian gritted his teeth against the pain, but found something tickling his lungs and scratching at his throat. He opened his mouth, coughed, and out came a plume of the white powder, which showered to the floor.

Duggan crouched and reached through the bars. 'Quickly, Sebastian, scoop it up!'

Sebastian rubbed his eyes to clear them, and swept up the rapidly vanishing powder. 'I think I know how to get you out.'

'Good. Give me some, too. You'll need a diversion.'

He tipped half of the powder, now reduced to the equivalent of two vials' worth, into Duggan's hand. Duggan immediately chanted words that Sebastian recognised.

'*Bí dofheicthe.*'

Sebastian turned his attention to the wall between Duggan and Alicia's cells. A narrow metal column, set just in front of the concrete blocks, formed the joint between the two. The bars of both locks entered the column from either side.

He held out his right hand and recalled the tones, words, and runic glyph he'd summoned while in the Freemasons' custody. '*Bræðið málm, brjóta*—' He stopped short as a surge of panic went through him: he'd not visualised the protective bubble around himself when he'd performed the thaumatic earlier, only narrowly avoiding accidental possession himself. He took a moment to regain his composure, tipped the powder into his pocket, and pressed the palms of his hands to his eyes and once again concentrated on the effect, with the addition of the bubble.

'We don't have time for this,' Duggan said.

Sebastian kept his eyes shut. 'Do you want me to get possessed and have an entity to deal with, or are you going to shut up?' He waited for the symbols to appear. This time the F with upward arms appeared with an extra one on its left – the Algiz rune overlaid. '*Bræðið málm, brjóta skuldabréf,*' he chanted, and the air shimmered around him.

The metal bars of the locks glowed, dimly at first, as the pile of carbyne in his pocket dwindled. The glow intensified to white and a rivulet of molten metal dribbled down the central pillar, sputtering and splashing incandescence where it dripped onto the concrete below.

He took a deep breath and pulled at both cell doors and they opened, showering hot metal.

Alicia stepped out of her cell, arms open. 'Duggan!' She stopped abruptly. 'Where is he?'

Duggan was nowhere to be seen.

She gasped as her clothes crumpled flat around her torso and she tipped back at an impossibly unbalanced angle, her arms forming a hoop in the air. She straightened up, her face flushed, and smoothed down her clothes.

Sebastian cleared his throat. 'Can we go?'

'Yes, sorry, old boy,' Duggan's disembodied voice said. 'It's been a few years since I kissed anyone, let alone my fiancée!' Invisible feet thumped away, down the corridor past the cells, and the door at the end flung itself open.

'Come on.' Sebastian grabbed Alicia's hand and stepped over the fallen Kevin.

They made their way out of the concrete-block section and slowed as they approached a turn in the passage that led to Kevin's office.

'Wait here,' Duggan said. 'Someone's in there. They'll see you pass.'

Sebastian peered around the corner. Two knocks came from the door. A moment later, it opened and a guard stepped out. He looked to the left and, as he turned in Sebastian's direction, his nose exploded, spraying a fine red spatter up the wall and sending him reeling back into the office.

'That's for locking up my fiancée for twenty years!' The outline of Duggan's fist, formed from tiny red particles, shook at the fallen man and then beckoned. 'Come on, old boy, we don't have all night!'

Sebastian dragged Alicia from the cover of the wall and the pair ran down the corridor past the office. The wood-panelled double doors at the end swung open and Dave turned around in wide-eyed surprise as a sheet of thin plastic from one of the doorways flew down the corridor, ghost-like, and draped over his head. He didn't even have time to react before falling backwards and bending double as invisible kicks assaulted his stomach.

'And that's for trying to possess Sebastian!'

They ran past the stricken Dave and continued up the stairs.

Sebastian paused at the top before opening the door. He took off his jacket and draped it over Alicia's shoulders to disguise her grubby clothes. 'When we go into the lobby, try to stay calm,' he said. 'It's only a few feet to the exit. We don't want to attract attention.'

Alicia nodded once and he pushed open the door.

A scream came from the far side of the reception hall, piercing as it echoed off the polished tiles. A small cylinder clattered across the sparkling floor and belched out a plume of thick, green smoke, obscuring the entrance.

'What's happening?' Alicia cried.

'Change of plan!' He veered off towards the back of the room as people flooded down the red-carpeted stairs from the floor above in panic. 'We have to find another way out.'

They followed the throng heading for the emergency exit in an attempt to blend in. Somebody squealed and Duggan's disembodied voice said, 'Sorry, old boy!' startling them even further.

They made their way through a pair of glass doors and down stone steps into a darkened street, passing two security guards oblivious to the commotion inside.

Amid the clack of heels on cobbles came the clink of ceramic, skittering across the pavement.

'Oof!' someone said, stumbling forward, displaced by the invisible Duggan.

Something prodded Sebastian in his side, and a vial of white powder floated in front of his face.

'What's this doing here?' Duggan asked.

Sebastian grabbed the floating tube. 'I left a vial at the front. I have no idea how it got here.' He peered closely at the glass while being careful to stick with the group. On the vial was a prominent thumb print – one with a deep slash through the pattern. He looked up and down the street. 'Aryx is here.'

'*Was* here. No time to look for him now. Keep going. Don't look back. You've got a tail.'

Sebastian forced himself to stare ahead. 'What do we do? We can't go back to the church, they'll follow us. Could we hide in St. James's Park? Plenty of trees and it's quite overgrown. I just can't remember which way it is.'

'Oh!' Alicia said, one arm flicking out of its own accord. 'This way, apparently.'

Aryx woke with a dull, throbbing pain in the back of his neck, his face pressed up against something cold. The quiet hum of a motor vibrated through the surface, which occasionally jogged him back and forth. Something hard-edged dug into his wrists. Handcuffs.

'Do you reckon we'll get promotions for getting this guy?' came a voice from his left: the man who'd approached him from the van.

'For some homeless drunk? I doubt it. If he'd been a high-ranking politician or big corporation honcho, maybe.' The other voice came from behind Aryx, in the cab.

The vehicle hit a bump. Aryx allowed himself to go with the motion and slid sideways – better to let them think he was still out of it. The mobipack hit the surface behind with a solid clunk.

'Hey, what was that?' the man in the back said. 'I thought this guy was a hunchback, but that didn't sound right.'

'How am I supposed to know? Shut up and let me concentrate on driving. I wish they hadn't told us to take him out of the city, but the raid means we can't go back there.'

'Fine, keep yourself company.' Something slid shut with a *thunk*, deadening the sound of the motor.

Aryx kept his eyes closed. The driver was definitely in a front compartment, separated by a hatch of some kind.

His coat pulled up and cold air wafted across his kidneys.

'What the hell is this?'

Shit, they'd discovered the mobipack. He cracked one eye open, just enough to make out movement in the van's darkened interior.

The blurry silhouette of the man moved away and sat on the bench seating opposite, paused for a moment, then leaned forward again. 'What's that?'

A tug at his trouser leg. Aryx clenched his fists, the bands of the telescopic crutches tight around his forearms. That's it, bend down and take a look at my legs. Go on, I dare you.

The man moved closer. 'What the hell's this? CFDs? You haven't got any bloody legs!'

Not cuffing his hands behind him was a foolish move on their part. Aryx opened his eyes and brought his fists up towards the man's chin.

His captor jerked backwards and put a hand to his face; when it came away, a gash ran down his forehead where Aryx had merely succeeded in catching his brow with the handcuffs. 'You little cut-off bastard!' He lunged towards Aryx, hands outstretched.

Aryx brought up his leg to kick, but the lack of mass in the prosthetic gave him nothing to counterbalance with and he fell sideways onto the bench, unable to roll because of the pack.

The man brought his weight down on Aryx in a half-crouch, pressing on his neck with both hands.

'They don't need you in good health, you little shit,' he spat. 'Near death is fine!'

Aryx tried to push him away, but the cuffs restricted his movement and he couldn't get enough leverage. The van went over a bump and the man lost his balance momentarily, releasing his grip in the process. How could he keep him away with no weapon?

The crutches! Bringing his elbows down to his sides as much as the handcuffs would allow, Aryx braced them against the bench.

His attacker came at him again.

This time he was ready: he flicked his wrists as Monica had shown him. Two thin rods shot out from his forearms, hitting the guard's chest with a sharp crack. Aryx's arms jammed against the wall as the guard's momentum catapulted him in a wide arc. His head collided with the side of the van with a sickening crack and he flopped to the floor, head lolling to one side at a peculiar angle.

'What the hell's going on in there?' the driver shouted.

When there was no response, the van sped up. Aryx sat up straight and, with his hands still fastened together, he retracted the crutches and pulled up his sleeve to uncover a bare wrist. His wristcom was gone! Shuffling across the bench to where the dead guard lay, he patted the man's pockets. One wristcom. He tapped it.

'Sebastian!'

No response. He tapped again.

'Monica, Karan!'

No response. Probably asleep. Damn, why hadn't he told them where he was going? In hindsight, it was stupid of him to go looking for Sebastian on his own. He tapped a third time.

'Jim-Bob? Are you there?'

'I am, Aryx,' Wolfram said. 'Sebastian's wristcom has not been activated, if that is what you were going to ask.'

'I know. Look, I'm in trouble. I can't get hold of Monica or Karan. Someone's got me in a van heading I don't know where.'

'Are you able to break out?'

'Hold on.'

Aryx moved to the back of the van. There were no windows to see out of, nor handles to open the rear door, and the joints in the metal were covered by thick plating.

'I think it's an old prison transport – one they transport syncpods in. The hinges and locks are protected. Even if I had tools, it would take ages to get out.'

'One moment, I need to evaluate my options . . .'

The van hit a bump and Aryx tumbled backwards.

'If you're going to do something, do it now!'

'I understand the urgency. Please, try to stay calm.'

Rather than risk another fall, Aryx sat down and glared at the corpse next to him. 'I'll try.'

Lights on the side of the three-inch cube that sat on the *Ultima Thule*'s console began to flash. To an observer, the sequence would have appeared random, but, like any intelligent action, it was driven by conscious processes. Processes with a very specific purpose.

Wolfram rapidly considered his possible courses of action – not at the speed of the latest supercomputers, since his consciousness required considerable processing itself, but many hundreds of times faster than most organic minds. He evaluated the speed at which the *Ultima Thule* could fly; whether he could control the ship entirely by himself; how he could break Aryx out of a locked, high-speed vehicle; whether, while piloting the ship, he could control the cargomech that currently resided in the hold.

And he made a decision.

«Control the cargomech, and pilot from the hold.»

He activated his internal gyros: devices reserved for passive power generation through motion which, when reversed—

His heavy casing vibrated, clattering on the polished glass console as the gyros spun, but he barely moved.

«Wasting time. A better conveyance is required.»

The *Ultima Thule* contained few independently mobile mechanisms, the cargomech being the most prominent – but that was far too large to get into the cockpit via the lift or emergency ladder. The other moving parts belonged to doors or small portable tools.

«Nothing here large enough to carry my casing.»

He extended the range of his wireless influence to beyond the ship's hull. Cardiff Spaceport's parking platform was packed with other ships, many of them containing equipment that also gave off signals. Using equipment from other ships would require extensive security circumvention. It also involved theft – an action that grated against the structure of ethics that his neuromorphic matrix had built up over the years.

At the limits of perception, thousands of signals worked in unison: nanobots in a public-use medical dispenser. What if he could use those to produce something like the liquid metal robot from the 20th-century movie *Terminator 2* that he had watched with Aryx?

Beneath the floodlights across the parking lot, the medical dispenser popped open of its own accord. The quicksilver mass of nanobots dribbled out of the glass cylinder onto the floor. Seconds later, the dispenser closed, leaving a small amount behind.

The shiny puddle stretched out into a long, thin trail, glittering its way across the tarmac between the landing struts of the many ships parked there, towards the *Ultima Thule*. Each tiny robotic particle followed the one in front. Wolfram had only to guide the leading robots by programming them to seek his signal.

As the flowing silver ribbon snaked towards the ship, the *Ultima Thule*'s CFD steps coalesced and altered shape to become a shallow bowl. The near-invisible container rested on the floor to allow the nanobot mass to enter, but with zero friction the nanobots found it impossible to traverse. Wolfram changed their programming, and a tiny silver column erected itself and reached over into the bowl, flowing up and around itself, and down into the transparent force-field dish, drawing the remainder with it.

The bowl-step rose while the door opened and allowed the container to enter, which promptly floated in and vanished, spilling the liquid across the airlock floor. The nanobots slithered across the grating towards the lift in the hold.

The ship's Dyson thrusters swung out and whined into life, lifting it out of the spaceport at high speed and into the dark sky.

Wolfram ignored the officious commands from the Cardiff spaceport control instructing him to land the ship immediately and to proceed only after logging an exit flight path. Time was of the essence. He transmitted a brief text-only message, citing matters of planetary security, followed by Sebastian's SpecOps ID, and laid in an autopilot course for London.

«Apologies to Sebastian will have to be made later.»

The nanobots reached the cockpit and Wolfram attempted to latch on to each one individually. The plan was to form a structure that could lift him from the console and carry him into the hold where the cargomech waited, but his processes slowed with the strain of manipulating each of the millions of tiny robots: they formed a filigree scaffold, slowly towering towards the console but, before reaching six inches tall, the task of issuing that many instructions was too much. His internals overheated and his consciousness core shut down.

The nanobots poured to the floor, inert.

*   *   *

Aryx fervently jabbed at his wristcom. 'Wolfram! Where are you?'

It had been nearly thirty minutes since he'd last heard from the SI, and there were no signs of the van slowing. Surely he was miles out of London by now?

He braced himself between the benches and kicked the back doors. The force sent him sliding back until the mobipack bumped against the corpse behind him.

Great. 'Karan, Monica, are you there?'

'Karan 'ere.' Her voice slurred with the weight of deep sleep. 'Wha's up? Why are you calling me from in bed?'

'I'm not in bed! I'm in trouble. I don't know where I am, but those ITF bastards kidnapped me.'

'Shit!' Her voice instantly sharpened. 'We'll track your wristcom and get a vehicle. Will you be okay until we get there?'

Aryx clenched and unclenched his fists. 'I can probably hold my own. These guys don't seem to have guns or they'd have used them. Just don't call the police – we can't trust them.'

'Alright, we're on our way!'

The van ploughed over a bump. Aryx flew into the air and hit the floor painfully. Shuffling backwards, he pushed himself into the nook at the end of the seating and pointed his arms towards opposite corners of the van. With a flick of his wrists, he extended the crutches and, with a second twist of the grips, sent the telescopic poles out to their maximum extent, wedging him in position.

'Whatever you do, hurry. This ride's going to kill me!'

The lights on the side of Wolfram's cube counted down one by one as his casing slowly cooled. The ship was only minutes away from London as the last light went out, and his reactivated consciousness was greeted by red restricted traffic warnings flashing on the black glass console, quoting fines for entering congested airspace.

«I must not overheat again. Science fiction movies are unrealistic and impractical: a different approach to the problem is required.»

The nanobots on the cockpit floor stirred, this time creeping up the bulkhead to slither across the console towards the cube. Pouring against the tungsten carbide casing, they nudged it along until it caught the lip at the edge and tumbled to the floor. They flowed down after it and a thin film stretched out beneath the cube, conveying it slug-like towards the emergency ladder. A minute later, the cube reached the hatch, which *thunked* open, and it fell through.

Under Wolfram's control, the outstretched gripper of the cargomech deftly caught the cube on its way down and placed it in the slot on its chest.

Via the ship's systems, he monitored the position of Aryx's moving comms signal and altered course to compensate. 'Aryx, are you there?' he asked.

'Yes,' Aryx said, background noise almost drowning out his voice. 'The driver's going nuts. Where the hell are you?'

The *Ultima Thule* swept down from the night sky, floodlights shining from its keel, bright specks of drizzle tumbling in the turbulence from its thrusters. In the street below, a large armoured van wove between parked vehicles and bumped over the raised traffic-calming measures installed in the road.

'I am right above you,' Wolfram said. The cargo bay door cracked open, filling the space with a swirling maelstrom, and the mech trundled forward on its tracks, stopping at the edge. 'Be ready, and brace yourself.'

The ship flew lower under Wolfram's control, matching speed with and then overtaking the van – a mere twenty feet above street level.

The van dodged as it accelerated, the driver seemingly trying to avoid the cone of the floodlight as though it might melt through the vehicle he drove and steal his captive.

Wolfram struggled with the load of monitoring the situation and controlling the ship and cargomech. The van turned unexpectedly down a side street, almost leaning on two wheels as it took the corner. The *Ultima Thule* slewed as it overshot the turn and rose over the buildings, bypassing those forming the alleyway entirely. Moments later, it came down behind the van again.

Wolfram moved the mech to the edge of the cargo door platform and reached out with the grippers. The ship accelerated, its bow bumping against the van, but the rear doors of the vehicle were still beyond the mech's considerable reach.

There was no way he could get close enough. «An alternative plan is required.»

The ship kept pace with the van while Wolfram accessed city maps. Finding what he needed, he broke off pursuit and allowed the van to accelerate away.

*   *   *

Having left the crowds spilling out of One Great George Street behind them, Sebastian paused for a moment, bending double to catch his breath. He really needed to start running more often.

'We can't stop,' Duggan's disembodied voice said.

'Haven't we lost them?'

Alicia looked back. 'No. And whoever it is, they've got guns and body armour.'

'It's some kind of SWAT team,' Duggan said. 'They've raided the place.'

'It must be the Church.' Sebastian straightened and started to run.

'Why are they after *us*?' Alicia asked.

'My only guess is they think we're possessed and want to capture or kill us.'

'Then we can't let them get you, Sebastian,' Duggan said. 'They won't believe you're normal – not if they know any of the facts about possession. Your eyes still look strange.'

The railings along the pavement opened abruptly at a gateway flanked by broad-leafed evergreen bushes. A gravel path led into an area devoid of street lighting; the darkness of St James's Park was the perfect hiding place.

'Sebastian, take Alicia. I'll cause a distraction.'

'How are you going do to that?'

'I'm invisible. You do the maths!'

The gravel path scrunched of its own accord and the bushes to their left burst apart with a leafy crash. Sebastian grabbed Alicia's hand and leapt off the path in the opposite direction. Fighting to calm his breathing, he found a large tree surrounded by dense, low-lying foliage and pulled Alicia down. Footfalls scrunched towards them along the path and a shadowy figure walking in a half-crouch scanned the scene with an automatic rifle at its shoulder.

'SHH!'

The figure spun to its left and blindly opened fire into the rustling bushes.

Duggan!

Beside Sebastian, Alicia clamped a hand over her mouth and silently screamed.

Chapter 32

The *Ultima Thule* dropped out of the sky ahead of the armoured prison transport, near the driver's side. Wolfram's plan worked: the driver turned sharply to the left, taking the vehicle towards more open streets.

As the van accelerated, the ship increased altitude and speed, free of the constriction of close-packed buildings and roadside trees. Wind whistled inside the cargo hold, rattling tools Aryx had left hanging on the racks and buffeting the cargo net.

Wolfram instructed the shipboard TI to maintain a fixed distance in pursuit of the vehicle. 'Aryx, I strongly advise holding on to something solid. NOW.'

'I'm as secure as I'll get!'

Momentarily taking manual control, he surged the ship ahead of the van and turned the cargomech 180 degrees to roll backwards over the edge of the cargo bay door.

The mech fell towards the street below. In less than a second, Wolfram altered its position, computing trajectory and angle, reaction and force to unfathomable precision. A highly calculated risk. It landed ahead of the van in a half-crouch, kneeling on one leg, and thrust one pair of prongs deep into the ground behind it and the other out in front to touch the tarmac at thirty degrees.

The armoured van hit the prong-ramp and pirouetted through the air over the mech. Landing on its side, it showered the street with sparks as it screamed along the tarmac and came to rest against the thick trunk of a plane tree with a crunch.

The cargomech straightened and, jerking the impaling gripper free of the tarmac, strode towards the van. It reached the underside of the vehicle and leaned over to inspect the cab.

The driver's window dripped with blood. Wolfram paused for a moment. Detecting no heartbeat, he moved to the back doors. There was no way they could resist as the mech rent a gash along their length and tore them open.

Inside lay an unmoving Aryx, blood streaming from his forehead. The mech reached in, carefully extending the grippers under the prone figure, and lifted him from the wreck.

The *Ultima Thule* dropped down behind the robot and lowered the ramp, filling the street with warm light from the interior. The mech rolled up into the ship and lay Aryx's body on the cargo netting.

Waiting nanobots streamed across the mesh and flowed into the many cuts that covered his skin.

Aryx's eyes fluttered open. Fear momentarily played across his features. 'Where am I?'

'Safe,' Wolfram said. 'You are safe, my friend.'

Sebastian watched in horror, his chest hollow, as the SWAT officer sprayed the foliage with gunfire. If Duggan had been there, surely he was dead. Duggan had reminded him so much of the grandfather he'd lost and had filled the void left by his death all those years ago. To lose him now, in this way, was unthinkable.

Alicia's eyes glistened in the muzzle flash and she tightened her grip on his hand.

The bushes on the opposite side of the path rustled, farther away this time, and the gunman charged off into the undergrowth towards the sound.

Alicia's eyes widened and she lowered her hand from her mouth, a faint smile returning to her lips.

Sebastian stared through the leaves for a moment. The coast was clear. He nodded sharply and stood up, taking Alicia back onto the path with him, and they ran along the gravel without stopping to listen or check behind them: the intermittent crack of gunfire was far off, heading away. They had lost their pursuer, but Sebastian was taking no chances. He followed the path farther into the park until it met another, forming a T-junction. The ground beyond the new path sloped away, until the grassy bank met a dark stretch of water where moonlight glittered in the faint breeze. Several feet away sat a low cluster of rhododendron bushes.

He crept across the path, heading for a bush in the cluster large enough to conceal them, and beckoned to Alicia. She ducked down with him among the thick, waxy leaves. Duggan had specified no destination other than the park and there was little to do but sit, shivering in the cold night air, and wait.

He held his breath for long stretches and took silent gulps of air while he strained to listen for any sounds coming towards them. Aside from the occasional hoot of an owl or rustling of small creatures in the undergrowth, the park was quiet. Perhaps the SWAT team had abandoned their pursuit altogether?

He peered through the branches in the direction of the lake. The gently rippling moon broke up and fragmented with a sloshing sound. Water dripped softly on the grass. The pea gravel scrunched, growing louder. He held his breath.

The footfalls drew closer until almost upon them.

'Sebastian!' a voice hissed. It was Duggan!

He straightened, standing clear of the bush. 'Here,' he whispered.

'What are you doing in there?'

'Hiding. We didn't know what had happened to you.'

'Well, you can come out now. I lost them. Led them clear out of the park and then came back across the lake.'

Alicia breathed a sigh of relief. 'Thank goodness for that. Are you hurt?'

'Only grazed, and really cold now. Pass me that vial of carbyne, would you, old boy?'

Sebastian reached into his pocket and tossed the vial in the direction of the voice.

With a droning chant, the dark outline of Duggan resolved, wet robe flapping in the breeze. A glowing red dot appeared on his chest.

From behind Sebastian, a voice shouted, 'Stop right there, demons!'

They turned in unison at the *k'chunk* of a readied gun; the SWAT team member that had followed stood in front of them, his gun trained on Duggan.

Sebastian raised his hands. 'Don't shoot! We're not possessed!'

'My orders are clear, when it comes to magic users.' The man's grip on the trigger shifted. Sebastian shut his eyes.

The gentle breeze erupted in a whooshing roar and the gun fired.

Alicia screamed.

Chapter 33

The gun fired again. Again, and again.

Alicia fell silent and Sebastian opened his eyes.

Two other members of the SWAT team had joined their companion. Bullets from all three guns *spanged* off in all directions, deflected in mid-air by a faintly glowing orange barrier.

White light bathed the area and a gust of wind blew Alicia's hair over her face. Sebastian turned.

Several feet away, the *Ultima Thule* hovered above the lake with the cargo bay door extended.

'GET IN!' the cargomech bellowed over the roar of the Dyson thrusters as it reached out with a gripper. Duggan jumped the gap between the bank and loading ramp and helped Alicia cross.

Sebastian hesitated. He turned back to the SWAT team, who had stopped firing and were attempting to get around the field, and shouted, 'We aren't your enemy – the ITF are! You want to stop them and so do we.' Had they heard? He wasn't about to hang around to find out, so he ran up the ramp into the ship. Before the ramp had closed, the moonlit park fell away, leaving their pursuers kilometres below.

On entering the cockpit, a bruised and battered Aryx greeted him. Karan and Monica sat to either side in the piloting seats, which had moved apart to accommodate his wheelchair.

'You love getting into trouble, don't you?' Aryx said. 'Who was trying to kill you now, the ITF or the Church?'

'The latter,' Duggan said. 'Judging by what I heard them saying to each other over their radios, they called themselves Templar Knights.'

'How did you find us?' Sebastian asked.

'The streets are pretty empty at three in the morning,' Aryx said.

'When Wolfram started analysing Human heat signatures, you stuck out like a sore thumb.'

'Two people gesticulating at a point in empty space is a clear give-away,' Wolfram said. 'You are fortunate we arrived in time to project the shield.'

Sebastian wiped his brow. 'Thanks for that.' He looked around at the others. 'Did you let Elias know you were all leaving?'

Aryx nodded. 'And I thanked him for his hospitality, and the outfit.'

Sebastian looked him up and down. He frowned at the blood on Aryx's tatty old clothes.

'Don't ask.'

'I am sorry to interrupt,' Wolfram said, the lights on his side flashing rapidly. 'I have an incoming communication from Jonas. He wishes to speak to you, Sebastian.'

'Put it through.' Karan got up and he took her seat.

Jonas's face appeared in the middle of the console. 'It's good to see you again, Sebastian. Although, I hear things went a little pear-shaped.'

'We had a run-in with the Templar Knights. They almost got us.'

'Sorry about that. I'd hoped the Church would have been a little slower in responding, but it seems they'd been waiting to pounce on the archive building for quite some time. Your evidence gave them justification. Are you and your friends okay?'

'I'm fine, if a little shaken up.' Sebastian looked at the pair standing near the lift and noted the blood trickling down the old man's arm, which Monica had begun to treat with nanobots. 'Duggan's been shot, but it's minor, and Alicia, the one they used as a necromancer, is better for being out of that place.'

'Good to hear. Listen, I've got some news for you. I managed to track down that Gladrin family you asked me to look into. I'm transmitting the details now.'

'Thanks, Jonas.'

'You're welcome. You've done us a great service by uncovering the ITF involvement in the cases listed in these files. It might help us to finally forge some links with the Church. God knows we could use their clout, and it would be nice to finally have them off our backs.'

'That might never happen,' Duggan said.

Jonas smiled past the negative sentiment. 'I also can't thank you enough for showing us that our beliefs are not unfounded. We've never seen anyone practise magic before, and I thought I'd never live to.'

Duggan rubbed his chin. 'Speaking of which, I never had a chance to find what I came here for. Eileen— Sorry. Alicia, do you know how to use thaumaturgy to heal?'

She shook her head and shrugged. 'I've never been able to control the outcome accurately, as you know.'

'That's what you came to Earth for, Duggan?' Sebastian asked. 'Who needs healing so badly that you'd risk your life?'

'Aryx, of course.'

Sebastian recoiled. He looked at Aryx. 'You said you were ill, but not that it was *bad*.'

Aryx folded his arms. 'I said it was *manageable*, and it is. I'm fine.' He winced momentarily and rubbed one of his knees, then wheeled over to the refrigerator unit by the console. Taking out a half-filled syringe, he injected half of its contents into each leg and placed it back into the fridge. He stared at Sebastian. 'Don't look at me like that. Duggan thinks there may be a way to cure my parasitic virus permanently, rather than me having to keep taking drugs. Personally, I think he's grasping at straws.'

Sebastian grumbled. Being lied to was one thing, but it hurt more to see Aryx in pain, and any attempt to ease his discomfort was worth pursuing. 'What about your lore, Jonas? Do any of your legends say anything about healing?'

'I don't know. I can give you access to our archives, if that would help. Maybe you or Duggan would see something of use.'

'Thanks.' Sebastian unexpectedly found himself overcome with exhaustion as the day's events finally caught up with him, and he looked at his wristcom to check the time. 'We'll take a look tomorrow. It's pretty late, and I think Aryx has a funeral to attend. I don't know about anyone else, but I could really do with some sleep.'

'Very well. Oh, and Aryx, Farzoud sends his apologies for any injury he may have caused. He's realised his strategy for keeping an eye on Mrs Alvarez was less than satisfactory.'

'Hah!' Aryx said, leaning back in his chair. 'Maybe he should actually introduce himself to her, and even spend some time with her since she's lonely.'

A wide grin spread across Jonas's face. 'That's a very good idea. I'll send him back there right away, but maybe you'd be kind enough to introduce him.'

Aryx nodded.

'Now, if you'll excuse me, I have to deal with the rest of this evening's fallout. Jonas out.' His image disappeared, leaving the console dark once again.

Sebastian yawned.

'If you guys want to get some sleep,' Monica said, 'Karan and I will pilot the ship. We slept pretty well and it's cheaper than docking at one of the orbitals or renting rooms for just a few hours.'

'Fine. I'll take the netting. Aryx, Duggan, and Alicia, you can have the bunks – they're in the starboard compartment in the aft section on the lower deck. Karan, take us to Brasilia at a leisurely pace and we can drop Aryx off in the morning for the funeral. While we wait, I can help Duggan look through the Freemasons' records. Then, when the funeral's over, we'll go and find Gladrin's family. We might need the ship with us in case we have to make a quick exit, and I'd rather not risk getting split up again.'

Monica finished patching up Duggan's arm. 'I'll go with Aryx to Brasilia, if you don't mind. I think Mrs Alvarez might appreciate us both being there. I'll need Wolfram for translation.'

'I would also find it interesting to attend,' Wolfram said. 'Any opportunity to expand my experience of Human interaction is always appreciated.'

Aryx nodded. 'Cheers.'

'I'm glad that's settled.' Sebastian got up and headed towards the lift. 'Now I really need some sleep. I found the whole necromancy experience rather draining.'

Aryx sat on the hillside, staring out across Brasilia. The buildings cast long shadows across the lowlands, where the *Ultima Thule* glinted in the morning light. A gentle, warm breeze blew through his hair, and the pain in his legs had thankfully subsided a little after his last half-dose of antiretrovirals and painkillers, allowing him to relax a little, but the possibility of using the last vial before the shipment arrived on the station still hung over him like a black cloud.

Up the hill behind him, Monica stood by Mrs Alvarez with one arm around her waist. Farzoud watched the group from some distance away, arms folded across his chest. He'd apologised to Aryx for his behaviour and the two had managed to laugh about it. Mrs Alvarez had been suspicious at first, but Aryx had convinced her of his good intent, and now he allowed himself to act openly as a guardian to her.

After the initial blessing of the ashes, Mrs Alvarez had cried for an hour, pouring her pain and grief into the urn containing her son's remains, and still stood sobbing.

'Why is she doing that?' Wolfram asked from Aryx's thigh pocket.

'She's upset. People cry when they're upset.'

'I am aware of that, but why does she put such ferocity into it? Most funeral customs that I have learned about celebrate the life and positive events involving the deceased, yet she focuses on her grief.'

Aryx sighed. 'I don't know how you'd understand. Sometimes when you lose someone, it cuts to the core. You have to let it all come out at once, otherwise it just eats at you.'

'In the way that the deaths of Sebastian's family members "eats" at him?'

'You noticed that, too, eh? You wise little cube. I think Sebastian's case is slightly different. At least Mrs Alvarez has ashes to scatter. Sebastian was closest to his grandfather, and he just disappeared in space. No trace left of him, just an inconclusive investigation.'

'Why was it not concluded?'

'His father was working on the investigation but got killed before it was finished. And it was only a few years ago that his brother died in the line of duty, too.'

'That is most suspicious, is it not?'

'Shit happens. Sometimes there is no conspiracy and that's all it is. Just shit. Take Alvarez, for example.'

Wolfram's tone levelled. 'There *is* a conspiracy there. He was possessed and subsequently cut up. You did not tell Mrs Alvarez that.'

'Okay, bad example. The only reason I didn't tell her is because it would make it unbearable for her and bring up lots of questions that I'm not allowed to answer.'

'How long will Mrs Alvarez continue to cry?'

'Probably for another hour or so. This funeral is short by Brazilian standards, and rather out of the ordinary, but Nick had specific instructions in his will. He wanted to be scattered on the wind over his home town.'

'When Mrs Alvarez finishes crying, will she have come to terms with her loss?'

'Probably not. It leaves a hole in you. Sometimes you think you've filled it, but actually you just find something different to focus on. You just learn to deal with it better as time goes on.'

'My neuromorphic processor reconfigures itself in a similar fashion to your biological neurons. To modify behaviour can be a complex process, since many other routines are built up around established pathways. I think that if you died I would "miss" you.'

Aryx patted his thigh before turning to rejoin the funeral. 'I think I'd miss you, too.'

Sebastian leaned against a shop window across the street from the restaurant. Willie T's, Duval Street, Key West, Florida – still running after 260 years; the perfect place to hide the wife of a high-ranking SpecOps agent. She certainly wasn't going to accidentally run into her husband there, and having been relocated by the ITF under the guise of Witness Protection, they didn't have to keep an eye on her themselves. There was no way she'd risk attempting contact with anyone from her old life if she thought they'd be endangered by her actions. Their ploy had worked successfully for the last three years.

He waited, watching people arrive, sit to eat under the stretched canvas sunshades, and leave. Once the lunchtime rush had passed, he made his move.

He ran his hand along the wooden balustrade as he casually strolled up the steps into the al-fresco dining area. He took a seat next to a young girl – aged twelve or thirteen – who sat at a table alone, scribbling furiously in a book with large crayons. The girl's long, black hair cloaked her face and trailed over the paper, forming a tent to contain her concentration.

Sebastian glanced at the menu while the sun baked his head, even through the shades. 'I think I might have a coconut *mogee-toe*. It sounds nice, whatever it is . . .' he said, and leaned over to speak to the girl. 'Hello. Aren't you a little young to be sat outside a bar on your own?'

The girl continued to draw, her hands moving around under the concealment of her hair.

'Hello?'

The hands moved more rapidly. 'It's pronounced *moheeto*. And Mummy says not to talk to people.'

'I'm not a stranger.'

'I didn't say strangers. Mummy says not to talk to *people*.'

'I'm not here to hurt you,' he said, trying a gentler tone.

'You're still a *person*.'

He couldn't really argue with that logic. He stared at the paper. The sheet was covered in complex swirls and repeating patterns, looking to his programmer's eye like a precise fractal pattern. As he moved, his arm touched the girl's elbow.

She screamed. Her hands clamped over her head and she began to rock back and forth in her seat.

One of the waitresses, a slender woman with long blonde hair, dark eyebrows and hazel eyes, spun around from the table she was serving and stormed towards him. 'What are you doing to my daughter? Get away from her!' She closed in with the ominous, unrelenting force of a thunderstorm.

'I-I'm here on behalf of your husband,' he said, disconcerted by the screaming girl. 'Marcus.'

'Mar— My husband is dead.' Her face reddened. 'Who sent you?'

'You are Emily Gladrin, and this is your daughter.'

'I'm Joan Rogers.' The woman dropped the menu she wielded and beckoned to the girl with both arms. 'Tess, come here, baby.'

The girl slid from the chair and ran to her mother, burying her head in the woman's arms.

'I didn't mean to upset her,' he said. 'And you should really be using her new name.'

'Life is confusing enough for her as it is.' Mrs Gladrin glared at him, oblivious to her own slip-up. 'What did you do?'

'I barely touched her. It was an accident. I swear I didn't hurt her.'

'It doesn't matter if you thought you didn't hurt her. She's got a sensory processing disorder.'

'But—'

'She's autistic, alright? She doesn't like other people touching her. If she's not expecting it, it hurts.' She kissed Tess on the forehead and began stroking her back rhythmically. 'Now who the hell are you, to be coming here and upsetting my family? How do you know who I am?'

'My colleagues and I had to do some digging to find you.'

Mrs Gladrin's eyes widened and she took a step back.

Sebastian put his hands up. 'Not terrorists. SpecOps. Mrs Gladrin, I work for your husband. Marcus is my senior officer.'

'What do you mean *is*?'

'He's alive, and very concerned for your safety.'

'How can that be? Witness Protection said he was dead.'

'Terrorists got to him. They told him you were in their custody and that they would hurt you if he didn't work for them. He couldn't find you, so he believed them. They have agents in Witness Protection.'

Her eyes darted to the side, looking down the street and back. 'They can't see me talking to you,' she whispered. 'They check up on me.'

His face fell. 'Then we have to go now.'

'I can't. Not at the drop of a hat. Someone will notice.'

Sebastian scratched his head. 'Do you have a break?'

'In fifteen minutes.'

'Right, meet me at the end of Sunset Pier, off Mallory Square, in half an hour. Take this.' He pulled off his wristcom and handed it to her. 'Tap it twice when you're a minute away. My ship will pick you up. It's got four big Dyson hoops like this.' He tried to make a shape like a butterfly, forming four loops out of his fingers and thumbs. Tess, who had turned around to watch, giggled.

Mrs Gladrin stroked the girl's hair as she looked around. 'Okay. I'll be there.'

'Don't bring anything.'

'Tess needs her crayons.'

Sebastian laughed. 'Fine, don't bring anything except the crayons.'

It was twenty-five minutes later that Mrs Gladrin and her daughter appeared.

Sebastian stood at the end of the pier in front of the *Ultima Thule*, which hovered precisely above the water with the cargo bay door resting on the pier itself. Brightly coloured stools and Café tables with umbrellas lined either side of the long walkway. Few of them were occupied, and the people sitting at them paid little attention to the ship or Sebastian. Eighty metres away, at the other end of the pier where it joined Mallory Square, stood two naval cargomechs, staring out to sea – a tourist attraction from the old days.

In the distance, passing between the mechs, Mrs Gladrin smiled and waved at Sebastian. Tess clutched her colouring book to her chest as she walked past the tables and chairs, keeping her distance from the seated strangers.

Sebastian tensed as a suited man stepped out from behind the octagonal building that housed the bar at the end of the pier, his attention focused on the Gladrins. His hand went inside his jacket.

'Emily, run!'

She looked back and broke into a run, almost dragging Tess along.

Time seemed to slow as their pursuer withdrew his hand from his jacket, and a pistol along with it.

Sebastian put a hand to his belt. His gun! Not anticipating trouble, he'd left it in the ship, and they were still forty metres away!

His eyes flitted from table to table, to Emily and Tess, to the man taking aim ... to the mechs standing at the corner of the building.

'Wolfram, help!'

A shot *spanged* off the *Ultima Thule*'s hull. Sebastian ducked.

Tables and chairs overturned as the diners threw themselves to the floor screaming while the Gladrins' pursuer took aim again.

Tess fell over a chair and her colouring book skittered away across the boards. Emily reached for her.

'WOLFRAM!' Sebastian yelled.

One of the inert naval cargomechs stepped forward and turned towards the pier.

Sebastian dodged to one side as a second shot rang out, this time behind him in the cargo hold. Gas issued from a punctured canister.

'Please, don't hurt me!' shouted one of the diners, who grabbed the gunman's trouser leg from where he lay on the floor.

The gunman shook his leg free and kicked him in the stomach before taking a more stable stance to fire again.

The mech reached the would-be assassin and swung out an arm. The shot went off as the suited man sailed through the air into the ocean.

Sebastian fell to the deck.

Chapter 34

'It's a damn good job you put that N-suit back on,' Aryx said.

Sebastian leaned back in his seat while the autopilot took the ship down into Cardiff Spaceport – they still had Duggan's runner to collect, after all. He put a hand to his stomach: even with the N-suit's reactive padding, the shot had carried massive force. 'It's killing me.'

'Oh, shut up. You'll live. At least you didn't get shot in the head.'

As the ship descended into the landing area, the comms sounded with the authoritative voice of traffic control. '*Ultima Thule*, you have a two thousand credit unauthorised launch fine to pay before landing.'

'*What?*'

'My apologies, Sebastian. I should have informed you sooner,' Wolfram said.

Sebastian made the payment. 'I'm shelling out so much money in the line of duty. I hope someone's going to pay me back one day. Or maybe you'll do some of my work for me, so I can take a holiday?'

'I would not suggest such a thing. Your job security would likely be at risk if I did.'

He glared at the cube, which sat on the console, flashing smugly. The others in the cockpit laughed.

Duggan pointed to the far end of the parking lot. 'My ship's just over there. Although, I think I would be better served travelling back to Tenebrae with you, Sebastian. That way I can discuss my research with you during the trip.'

'Then how will you get your ship back to the station?'

Duggan looked at Karan. 'Would the ladies be kind enough to pilot it? The *Ultima* is getting a little cramped with all of us.'

'Sure. I've always fancied a go in one of those old things.'

Monica grimaced.

Karan elbowed her in the ribs. 'Oh, come on. It'll be fun.'

They dropped the pair off, despite Monica protesting that she wanted a live demonstration of thaumaturgy, and left Earth to make their way towards the acceleration node. Once they were well on their way through superphase, Duggan called Sebastian away from the cockpit, down into the cargo hold, and beckoned him close.

'I think I've found out how to cure Aryx's virus.'

Sebastian tilted his head and leaned closer. 'How?'

'Most of the Freemasons' writings refer to sympathetic magic – it's nothing new to me, really. It simply confirmed what I already knew about how magic works, and what the Folians said about healing. We need to get a sample of the virus, contained in such a way that we can look at it under a microscope and observe it while we try to eradicate it using thaumaturgy. Monica explained to me earlier that when blood samples have been taken from Aryx, the parasites have never been seen. The only evidence is the damage they do to his body and the antibodies present in his blood. What we need is a sample of the original bacteria that contained the parasite, which we can only get from its natural habitat.'

'But that means . . .'

Duggan lowered his voice. 'I know. Going to Cinder IV, where Aryx lost his legs.'

Sebastian pinched the bridge of his nose. 'He's the only one who can locate the landing site. That would mean we'd have to take him . . . He won't go for it.'

'Maybe not, but *you* can get the samples. Aryx doesn't even have to set foot outside the ship. I would suggest making a detour now and I'd do it myself, but I think you really need to get the Gladrins back to the station first, and Alicia could do with some proper medical attention . . . Hmm.' Duggan rubbed his chin. 'Come to think of it, I should really try to erase her hypnotic trigger in case there's any other subconscious programming we don't know about.'

The pair returned to the upper deck and Duggan ushered Emily and Tess to the cockpit with Aryx, to sit staring out at the distended stars of superphase while he, Sebastian and Alicia sat near the diagnostic console in the aft section.

Fifteen minutes later, Duggan had placed Alicia in a deep hypnotic trance. He sat with her, testing muscle reactions while he muttered in her ear. After twenty minutes, he gave up and clenched his fists. 'I can't remove that blasted trigger. I've tried everything I can think of to override it. There's only one thing for it. Do you have any more carbyne I can use, old boy?'

'One vial left,' Sebastian said. 'There's more in the sealed hopper downstairs, but that will involve putting a pressure suit on if you want some.'

'Don't worry about that for now. One should be enough.'

He handed over the last tube from his rucksack. 'What are you going to do?'

'I'm going to see whether Alicia can release herself from the trigger using thaumaturgy. The thing with hypnosis is, the wording needs to be specific. Using thaumaturgy, she only needs to visualise the outcome, and now I've got her in a trance she should be able to control what she's doing.'

Sebastian gave him a sidelong look and shifted in his seat. 'I'm not sure I like the idea, but alright.'

'Alicia, in a moment Sebastian is going to issue the hypnotic trigger they used on you at the archive. I want you to do what I taught you before – visualise a bubble of white light around you. That bubble prevents the entity from entering your mind. When he issues the trigger, I would like you to imagine yourself resisting the urge that hearing those words gives you. They will no longer have any control over you. You will be able to bring about the feeling it gives you at will, but you will be in control. Any other commands your captors planted will simply disappear. Do you understand?'

'Yes,' Alicia said, her eyes still closed.

Duggan looked at Sebastian and nodded sharply.

Sebastian recalled the Icelandic words Kevin had used. '*Þú getur gert galdra.*'

Alicia reached forward.

Duggan got up from his seat and, with a vial of carbyne in one hand, he pressed his palms against hers. 'Now, Alicia, release yourself.'

She uttered gibberish words; a mangled mishmash of consonants and vowels. The air shimmered.

Sebastian's stomach shifted as the ship went over an invisible bump in space – a common occurrence during superphase travel. The air around Alicia changed. He rubbed his eyes; the faint outline of a glowing white bubble had surrounded her. 'Is that what I think it is?'

Duggan frowned. 'The protection sphere, yes.'

'But why is it *visible?*'

'Possibly because we're in superphase. I've never performed thaumaturgy in transit before—'

Something sparked and flared off the bubble, as though colliding with it, momentarily creating the jagged luminous outline of a vague, headless humanoid form, the limbs of which floated separate from the body. The bubble vanished and the shape collapsed into a swirling wisp of light.

Sebastian's mouth sagged open. The thing . . . it was like a picture in his grandfather's diary that had been titled *Frost Giant* and looked like a giant sculpture, only this had been smaller, a mere outline.

The wisp drifted to the cockpit and flowed into Tess's head. The girl froze for a moment before clamping her hands over her head and screaming.

'Wolfram!' Sebastian shouted. 'Perform the purging spell. Get it out of her now!'

Lights flashed on the cube. 'There is no carbyne nearby.'

'Oh, *Gods!*'

Inexplicably, the strange, swirling emanation streamed out of Tess's head and through the side of the hull, out into space. She collapsed, whimpering.

'Tess!' Emily yelled, rushing forward.

Aryx slid from his chair and quickly checked the girl's eyes. 'She's in shock.'

Duggan snapped Alicia from her trance and crouched down beside Emily. 'She's okay,' he called. 'Scared, but fine. No sign of possession.'

Sebastian went to the console and leaned into the window, but there was no sign of the light against the stretched stars. 'What was it?'

'I think that was one of our entities. What the Folians said was right. They exist in superphase, and Alicia's manifestation of the bubble must have energised it and made it visible. It tried to go to the next most vulnerable host.'

'Is that how acceleration psychosis happens?'

'Yes, I'd say that's the cause. But why did it leave the girl? What makes her different?'

'She's autistic,' Emily said, rocking the girl back and forth against her chest.

'That's it!' Sebastian said. 'Sensory processing disorder. Perhaps it couldn't latch on to her properly because it couldn't make sense of its environment.'

'My daughter isn't an *environment!* What are you talking about?'

'That entity. It's the same thing that's in control of the ITF – the terrorists that were threatening your husband and holding you hostage.'

'And it appears,' Duggan said slowly, 'that Tess is immune to their influence.'

Wolfram, still resting on the console, spoke up. 'If I may interrupt?'

Sebastian turned to the cube. 'What is it, Wolfram?'

'I have been monitoring the situation and have taken some interesting readings. However, I need some information.'

'Alright. What do you need to know?'

'Firstly, was the sample of carbyne consumed in the process initiated by Alicia?'

Holding up the empty vial, Duggan nodded.

'Then it is as I suspected. The entity does not exist wholly in the superphase state, but is in fact drawn to it by the presence of those minds pushed out of phase with regular space. How this occurs exactly, I do not know. However, it is most definitely linked to the transition of carbyne from one state to another.'

'But carbyne goes into superphase when it's used,' Sebastian said.

'I believe that to be an erroneous assumption. The carbyne residue Aryx noticed on the hulls of the ships in Kimberley depot that had recently exited superphase into regular space vacuum may have been attracted to them by the transition of their mass into superphase state and back again.

'If carbyne simply transitioned to superphase during its consumption, the carbyne you had in the container would not have disappeared, already being in superphase, and therefore would not have released the energy for you to perform the thaumatic effect. The only logical conclusion is that carbyne in fact goes to another region after transitioning briefly through superphase. However, the region in which the entities exist must be intimately connected to it, otherwise we would not have seen the being that became visible to us.'

'Do you have any theories as to why it couldn't stay in Tess?'

'I ... do not.'

'You sound a little hesitant there, Jim-Bob,' Aryx said.

'I am hesitant because the only theory I have is based on further, unproven, assumptions.'

'Let's hear it anyway.'

'Without quantum-state analysis of Tess's neurology, I cannot be certain, but there is evidence to suggest there may be a link between the signal being relayed to Tenebrae that causes "bad dreams", the transphasic nature of the entities, and Tess's neurology. Emily, has Tess ever communicated to you the nature of her discomfort?'

'A few times. She feels touch as pain sometimes, and other times sounds are too loud for her or lights are too bright.'

'Interesting. Have physicians determined the cause?'

'Doctors said that parts of her brain are too sensitive to stimuli.' She took Tess to the seats at the rear of the ship to calm down.

'That supports my conclusion of the hypnotic signal's effect of boosting quantum tunnelling in the neurons of the inner ear. I can only infer that the entities depend on a certain level of neurological calm, for want of a better term, on the part of the potential host's brain – a state that comes about at the point of near death, or when performing thaumatics.'

'I guess the brain's quantum state is more vulnerable during super-phase travel, too,' Sebastian said. 'Hence acceleration psychosis.' He shuddered. 'I'm starting to dread node travel again.'

Aryx laughed. 'You dread bloody everything, given half a chance.'

Alicia straightened. 'Acceleration psychosis. Is that what happened to Patricia Ventris?'

Sebastian ignored Aryx's previous comment. 'Yes, and when she strangled her husband, that was the entity using her to pass into him permanently.'

'Yes, thank you, Sebastian, I realised that. It's not something I want to think about anymore.'

He hung his head. 'Sorry. Was that all you observed, Wolfram?'

'It was not. There was a slight, but noticeable, change in gravitational waves within the cabin just prior to, and during, the event.'

Sebastian put a hand to his stomach, recalling the disconcerting shift, and shuddered again. 'What do you mean by *slight*?'

'Enough to indicate the addition of several metric tonnes' mass to the cockpit.'

'But that thing was energy. It couldn't weigh anything, and it wasn't even that big.'

'The gravitational wave implies that the energy does have an associated mass. Clearly enough to affect you.'

'By the Gods! That explains the bumps we feel travelling in super-phase. I was always told it was the gravity wells of stars and planets that we passed.'

'Whoever told you that was misinformed. Passing directly through the mass of a planet or star is impossible, since entering the star's heliosphere would cause the superphase transit to end. That is why all superphase travel is performed most effectively by calculated line of sight. It is more likely the sensation is induced by the attempted penetration of an entity into your body.'

'I feel a bit sick.'

'Large concentrations of entities, or even phase-shifted objects, could in fact explain the mass theorised as that of dark matter.'

'You'll have to publish a paper on the theory when we get back, Wolfram,' Aryx said. 'By professor Jim-Bob, Oxford University of Cybernetics.'

'Do not jest. I am already about to put Sebastian out of a job.'

Sebastian snorted on the verge of a laugh, but stopped abruptly. The cube wasn't capable of humour, was it?

'He's joking, Seb.'

'I sincerely hope so.'

Duggan clapped Sebastian on the shoulder. 'Sorry to interrupt, but I don't suppose I could make a call using your comm system, could I?'

'Of course. Do you need some privacy?'

'No, it's fine.' Duggan sat at the diagnostic console opposite Alicia, Emily and Tess, who had fallen asleep on her mother's lap. 'I just want to call Garvin to let him know I'm alright and that I've found Alicia.'

'He'll be glad to know you're both safe.'

Several minutes later, Duggan came back to the cockpit. 'That's most odd. I can't seem to get through to Sollers Hope properly. Their comms are coming back all garbled.'

'We had that problem when we visited,' Aryx said. 'Some trouble with their transmitter or something. They're probably still doing repairs. The dome explosion might have taken out some of their systems, or their outgoing comm relay could be misaligned, although we did a thorough check of their systems before we left. I'm sure you'll be able to get hold of them soon. Do you want us to head that way?'

'No, I'll try later. You boys need to get Gladrin's family safe and, like you said, the people of Sollers Hope have probably got a lot of work on their hands if things are as bad as you described, with the town filling with lava and everything. They were lucky you turned up when you did, old boy.'

Sebastian silently wrung his hands. Yes. Lucky. If he hadn't turned up, it probably wouldn't have happened. In light of everything since, there was something about the timing of the whole Sollers Hope situation that seemed *wrong*.

The bright wheel of Tenebrae station shone off to starboard, against the pastel shades of the green and purple nebula. Sebastian let out a deep sigh of relief at being home. As nice as it had been to see Earth again, there was far too much danger there, lurking in dark corners. At least Tenebrae had few of those. For the moment.

The automatic docking procedures engaged, taking the *Ultima Thule* into the hub, and Sebastian activated the comms to call Duggan's runner, which had docked ahead of them.

'Monica, Karan, are you there?'

'Monica here. What's the plan now? Is Duggan taking his ship back to Tradescantia with Alicia?'

He looked at Duggan. 'No, I think he's going to stay on Tenebrae with the others for a bit. He wants to get Alicia checked out.'

'Let me guess, an off the record examination?'

'Yes.'

'I can do that.'

'Is Karan there?'

'Hi, Seb. Yes, I'm here.'

'I'd like you to come back to the *UT* when we dock.'

'Oh, uh, okay. Why?'

He glanced at Aryx and quickly looked away. 'I'll tell you when you get here. I'll let the others off first. Monica, are you alright to get everyone settled?'

'Yes. I'll give them secure quarters.'

Duggan leaned over Sebastian's shoulder. 'Is there a lab I can use?' Sebastian nodded. 'Monica has one.'

'Perfect,' Duggan whispered. 'I'll see you when you get back.'

Sebastian completed the landing checks and waited by the airlock for everyone to disembark.

Karan jogged aboard. 'What's up? You sounded a bit odd over the comms.'

He lowered his voice. 'It'll upset Aryx. He's upstairs . . . We have to go to Cinder IV to get a sample of the bacteria that held the virus he's infected with. Duggan thinks he can cure it. If he does, it means no more leg pain for him.'

She winced. 'Oh, heck. That's why you brought me. You think I can convince him to go along with it.'

'That's the plan.'

She held up a finger. 'Okay, hold that thought. I'll be right back.' Before Sebastian had a chance to speak, she bounded out of the ship.

He gave her just over a minute and, as he was about to call her on the wristcom, she came back carrying a large, semi-automatic rifle.

'What do you need that for?' he asked.

'Don't tell me you haven't heard the rumours about Ruarda.'

'What rumours? We're going to Cinder IV, not Ruarda.'

'It's close enough.' She heaved the hopper of carbyne that sat in the pressure suit compartment out of the way and stowed the weapon alongside the suits. 'You really haven't heard the stories? Has Aryx never told you? There's a legend about a bear-like creature that rips out the throat of anyone who talks about it. Naturally, I'm a potential victim now.' She laughed.

'Then how did anyone survive to talk about it?'

'*Exactly.* I don't believe that bit, but you've convinced me that some myths and legends are worth listening to. Being cautious is in my job description.'

They made their way up to the cockpit, where Aryx sat talking to Wolfram.

'Hi, Karan. How was your trip back?' he asked. 'Those runners can be a bit cramped.'

'Not too bad, although Monica wouldn't shut up about how danger-ous it looked.'

Sebastian sat in the pilot's seat and began entering coordinates.

Aryx peered at the console. 'What are you doing?'

'We're going back out.' The ship gave a lurch and reversed out of the docking hub.

'Where— Hang on, I recognise those coordinates. Cinder!' Aryx glared at him. 'Why the hell are we going there?'

'It's Duggan's idea.'

'What is?'

With the ship clear of the station, Sebastian engaged the autopilot and turned to face Aryx.

'Duggan thinks that if we get a sample of your virus, he can probably cure it using thaumaturgy.'

Aryx's face darkened. 'It would have been nice if someone had asked what *I* thought about it!'

Karan put a hand on his shoulder and squeezed. 'It's only because we care, and it kills us to see you in pain all the time.'

Aryx spun and wheeled over to the refrigerated compartment tucked under the end of the console. 'You've all got a funny way of showing it.' He peered into the unit and closed the door. 'I've got one dose of my drugs left with me. I have to take them soon, so we'd better not be longer than twenty-four hours.'

Karan smiled. 'It's a simple retrieval mission.'

'Right ... I'm only going along with it because there's two of you ganging up on me.' He folded his arms. 'Just don't expect me to get out of the ship.'

Sebastian put up his hands. 'I wasn't expecting you to. I brought Karan along to help. We only need you with us so you can set us down near where it happened. The military files on the mission are sealed and I can't get any info. Wolfram will be here to keep you company.'

Aryx's teeth ground audibly and he clenched his fists. 'Fine. But if this goes tits-up, I'm going to bloody kill you.'

Chapter 35

Aryx monitored the readouts as the *Ultima Thule* approached the storm-cloaked world of Cinder IV, the fourth planet in the system. Its surface swirled with thick cloud formations and intermittent bright flashes. He shivered at the sight of it. It was a good job they'd had a chance to change clothes on the ship; he was back in his regular outfit and out of the thin dinner suit he'd been forced to wear for the funeral, while Sebastian wore his SpecOps N-suit and Karan was once again in her black tactical armour.

'The research base should show on scanners,' he said. 'The reactor blew. Just find that and I'll have to locate the spot by eye.'

'Alright.' Sebastian's fingers played over the black glass console as he ran scans of the surface.

Aryx stared out of the cockpit, past the planet, at Cinder. The *Ultima Thule*'s window filters cut back the light, revealing the dying sun's dark, boiling surface fractured by bright red fissures, from which coronal discharge spat and flew back to the surface.

'And that's why it's called Cinder,' he said, glaring at the burning coal of a sun. He rubbed his knees, which were already hurting again. 'I never wanted to come back here. Ever. The last time I was here someone wanted me dead, remember? The mech that was holding up the shuttle I was working under had been sabotaged. That's why it dropped it on me.'

Sebastian's eyes widened. 'I . . . I didn't know that!'

'Neither did I, until Wolfram located its operation logs. He found the same code signatures as the Trojan on Tenebrae that allows the nightmare signal through to our quarters.'

'How did the same code get here?' Karan asked. 'What happened?'

'Someone tipped off the colonists about secret research being performed by the ITF in their base. They tried to deal with it but it ended in a firefight. Most of the colony's research staff got killed, and when EarthSec got involved, the situation escalated. The ITF took the survivors hostage. My team went in and managed to rescue the hostages, and when it became obvious to the ITF they wouldn't get out alive, they blew the reactor. I'm guessing they put a Trojan in the mech to stop me from repairing the ship, probably as a last resort. Whatever their reasons, they didn't want anyone getting off the planet.'

'But you got away.'

Aryx nodded. 'I was able to repair the damage to the shuttle before the mech injured me, and my team got away safely with the hostages.'

Sebastian pointed at the readouts on the console. 'There it is. Straight ahead, 113 kilometres.' He tapped away at the console and the ship juddered as the hull entered the atmosphere and ploughed into the heavy storm clouds. 'Crap, she's not going to handle this well.' He pressed a button, and a section of console slid open and a flight stick emerged.

Aryx rubbed his forehead. 'Not again. Last time you used that you nearly killed us both!'

Karan stared at Sebastian.

He rolled his eyes at her. 'Not on purpose! A mountain came out of nowhere at us.'

She glanced at the readouts. 'You'll be pleased to know the area we're heading for is as flat as a pancake, relatively speaking.'

'That's reassuring.' Aryx watched the dull, impenetrable grey through sheets of rain that rippled across the cockpit window. A flash bleached the interior and the hull thrummed. 'Look out!' he yelled, ramming Sebastian's hand to the left as it held the stick. 'You're supposed to be avoiding the storms!'

'Sorry!'

'Charge building up to port,' Karan said. 'Two thousand metres ... One thousand ...'

Sebastian banked sharply to starboard. Another flash.

'That was close,' Aryx said. 'At least you didn't send me flying out of my chair.'

'You'll know we're in trouble if I pack you into the escape pod.'

Aryx grinned. 'If it gets to that point, *I'm* taking over.'

'Look out, another one to starboard!' Karan said.

Sebastian yanked the stick, almost throwing them out of their seats as the inertial compensator struggled to cope under the strain. Sparks showered from the bulkhead to the right of the console. Aryx shielded his face with his arm.

'Be careful!'

'I am being careful.' Sebastian gritted his teeth and held on to the stick with both hands as it began to vibrate. 'I'm not exactly in control of the weather.'

'Just make sure you stay in control of the ship.'

The cloud broke and the *Ultima Thule* swept into the dark underbelly of the storm. Crackling shafts of lightning struck the undulating scrubland in the distance, shattering the sky. Barely any of Cinder's weak light made it through the heavy cloud cover to the surface, making it difficult for the eye to adjust between strikes.

Karan stared at the view that still swam with the constant flow of rainwater. 'Who would want to set up a research base here?'

Aryx scratched his head. 'I think it was to research the atmospheric ionisation, but I don't know which agency it was.'

'What could the ITF have been doing here that was so secretive that it warranted blowing up the base?' She folded her arms. 'Whatever *they* were researching, I bet it wasn't the weather.'

Sebastian shook his head. 'Gladrin stole Wolfram from the ITF when they had both cubes here, so it was probably something to do with artificial intelligence.'

Aryx rubbed his knees to ease the pain that intensified at the memory. 'Yeah, how to make it amputate defenceless marines. No offence, Wolfram.'

'None taken, since I am not a programmed artificial intelligence.'

Sebastian took the ship low over the marshland to attract as little of the lightning as possible – a feat made more difficult by the lack of features projecting above the terrain.

Karan kept her eyes on the console readouts. She pointed to a radiation spike. 'There it is, only a couple of miles ahead.'

Aryx peered through the cockpit window. 'Can we do something about this rain? It's really difficult to recognise anything.'

'One moment,' Wolfram said.

An instant later, the flow of water across the glass cut off, leaving it to stream away.

'What did you do?'

'I reconfigured the shield CFD generator to project above the window and deflect the rain.'

'Clever thinking.'

'I am so much more than just a console ornament.' Two of the lights on the cube's side flashed. If Wolfram had emotions, Aryx would have sworn it was a digital chuckle.

Through the now clear window, he searched for the path between the gorse-like bushes that covered the marshes of the waterlogged world. 'Slow down, Seb, I think it's around here somewhere.'

Sebastian slid his finger down the console, reducing the ship's speed, but kept his hand on the flight stick.

'There!' Aryx pointed to a darkening in the brush, a network of veins running through the foliage, and Sebastian turned the ship.

The thin trail wending its way through the marsh parted, revealing a reed bed that sloped away into a large pool.

'That's it. That's where we went down.' He shuddered. 'But don't land there. Find somewhere on higher ground. We don't want to sink.'

Sebastian circled the area and found a patch of scrub on a low rise a mile from the trail. The ship came to rest with a gentle bump.

Aryx grinned. 'Nicely done. It looks like I don't have to kill you.'

Sebastian and Karan climbed down the ladder into the cargo hold. Aryx followed on the lift platform, and by the time he got to the bottom they were already donning pressure suits.

'I don't think these will be entirely necessary,' Karan said, reaching over the carbyne hopper to take a helmet from the suit storage bay. 'The radiation levels near the old base are quite low and there's none this far out, but it's not worth taking unnecessary risks.'

'I agree.' Sebastian clamped his helmet in place. 'And I don't like the thought of getting soaked if I don't have to.'

'Oh, I almost forgot ...' She reached over the hopper again and withdrew a large, semi-automatic assault rifle along with a couple of clips. She slung the weapon's strap over her head.

Aryx stared at her for a moment. 'What's that for?'

'The Ruarda-bear.'

He drew his lips back in a sneer.

She grinned back at him. 'And anything else that might want to cause trouble.'

'You're only getting water,' he said, handing Sebastian a small sample jar from one of the cargo bay's many drawers.

'I know, but to quote an old movie – it's better to have a gun and not need it than need one and not have it.'

'I can't argue with that logic. Seb, you'll have to get some water from the marsh near the old landing site. Take a microscope, too, just to make sure you get some bacteria. We don't want a wasted trip.' He handed him a small fist-sized device with a lens in the top and a recess large enough to take the sample jar. 'I'll watch your suit nanocams from the cockpit.'

Sebastian placed the items in his rucksack and slung it over his shoulder as he made his way to the airlock. At the door, he turned to Aryx. 'I really am sorry for dragging you here like this.'

Aryx grumbled. 'It's okay. I know you're only trying to help. Just stay safe out there, both of you.'

'We will.' Sebastian put a hand to his helmet in mock salute. 'See you shortly.'

Aryx watched, stomach knotted, as Sebastian and Karan stepped out into the blustering gale and onto the soggy world of Cinder IV.

Rain hammered on the hull of the *Ultima Thule*, bouncing off in a fine spray that created a strange halo several inches above the metal.

'This is horrible weather,' Sebastian shouted over the din in his helmet. 'I can hardly hear myself think! Aryx, can you see?'

Karan bumped into him and staggered back. She wiped a hand across her visor. 'They really could have done with windscreen wipers on these.'

'Quit complaining, you two,' Aryx said over the comms. 'There's a break in the cloud coming in a few minutes. And yes, I can see. The view from the cams is a bit blurry, but it'll do.'

Sebastian walked into the gorse thicket, but lifting his legs high enough to bring his thick boots down on the needle-like spines without tearing the pressure suit in the process made it slow going. 'This would be easier if we'd brought the cargomech out.'

'If you think I'm going to let history repeat itself, you've got another thing coming. Now stop being so lazy and get down to that marsh!'

'Alright, Mother.' Sebastian cut the comms and turned to Karan. 'I can't have him nagging me all the way there.'

She pushed him aside and began flattening the bushes ahead of him with her feet. 'And I can't have you moaning about this all the way there, either.'

He trudged down the hill behind her, stepping in the spots she'd cleared. After several minutes, the ground levelled out and they reached the path. Free of the obstructing bushes, they made quicker progress.

Sebastian walked until the wet ground sucked at his feet, and he reactivated the comms to the ship. 'Is this the spot?'

'You need to go a few metres to your left. Can you see a compressed area yet? The rain's making it hard to tell.'

'Not yet.'

'Well, when you do, you're looking for a spot on the edge of it ... Where the mech stood. You'll know it when you see it. I don't want to be reminded of this. Aryx out.'

Sebastian faced Karan and shrugged. 'What did he mean by that?'

She stared past him and pointed. 'Um, I think he means *that*.'

He turned to follow the line of her outstretched arm.

The spiny bushes gave way to an open area covered with short, dark reeds that marched down the gently sloping bank into a large pond. Off to one side, in a patch of short grass clear of the water, a large square depression had filled to form an incongruously geometric pool: the outline of where Aryx's platoon shuttle had landed. Farther from the water's edge, parallel to one of the long edges of the depression, lay a pair of deep furrows with piled sides.

Sebastian moved closer. The tell-tale ridged markings of caterpillar tracks lay at the bottom of each trench, still prominent even with three years' mossy growth covering them. He stopped at the point where the tracks turned towards the depression marking the hull, and stared down at several hand-sized gouges that fanned out from the area. He imagined Aryx lying on his back with the mech – and the ship it held up – towering over him. Images of tearing flesh and crushing bone came to mind, unbidden. Bile rose in his throat and he gagged and bent over, hands on his knees.

A hand pressed on his back. 'Sebastian, are you okay?' Karan asked.

He nodded – an almost futile gesture inside the helmet. 'I'll be fine in a minute.' He gulped down mouthfuls of air before straightening. 'By the Gods ... I can see why he didn't want to come. I shouldn't have brought him.'

'Do you think he would have come if he was really against it? I reckon he's probably trying to prove to himself that he could.'

'I hope you're right, Karan.'

He stepped over the patch where Aryx had clawed backwards from under the ship, and tried to find an area with water deep enough to take a sample. Crouching down, he took the lid off the jar and pressed it sideways into the peaty ground to allow a few millimetres of water to flow in. Karan handed him the microscope.

He took off his helmet, inserted the jar and peered through the lens.

Enormous rocks tumbled past his view of the tiny, watery universe. Upon some of them sat lobster-like creatures, scraping a living off the mini-asteroid dirt particles. In the spaces between the particles drifted long worm-like creatures, slithering through liquid that, at this scale, had the viscosity of molasses.

'What am I looking for?' he asked, without taking his eye off the scene.

'Bacteria with a virus or some sort of parasite in it,' Karan said.

'I don't— Oh, hang on.' What was that iridescent patch on one of the lobster creatures? He increased the magnification.

The patch consisted of a mass of small lozenge-shaped objects. He zoomed in on one of the single-celled organisms. Inside the capsule of the bacterium swam a tiny, sperm-like organism, propelled by a corkscrew tail. It zipped back and forth inside the cell at a speed that Sebastian found difficult to keep up with. No wonder nanobots couldn't cure the virus – the agents moved so fast that even the tiny robot motors wouldn't have caught up with them.

'Found it,' he said, removing the jar from the microscope and sealing the top. 'That was easy.'

Aryx sat at the console, watching the pair's progress on the monitor. At the appearance of the old landing site his stomach turned and his legs began to ache. He switched off the display.

'I can't look at it.'

The cube next to him remained silent, leaving him alone.

He turned from the console and wheeled back and forth along the cabin, balancing with his front casters in the air and spinning sharply at each turn. He stared up at the ceiling. Was that panel a different colour to the others? Was that a loose thread on one of the seats? He drummed his fingers on his handrims. What was taking them so long?

'Aryx, there is a signal coming from the abandoned research base,' Wolfram said.

He stopped and dropped his wheels to the floor. 'What? How is that even possible? There shouldn't be anyone there. The place is a wreck.'

'If the base is empty, as you believe, I am at a loss to explain the signal. Perhaps there is some piece of technology left behind that is broadcasting?'

'Then why has it suddenly started? Let's have a look at the scans.'

He tapped away at the console and brought up a video feed from the research base's geostationary satellite.

The clouds directly above the research base had cleared, providing a view down onto the area. Flashes of distant lightning glinted off the dark surfaces of the tall, humped circular construction, while deep shadows revealed a missing section with girders and concrete hanging in tatters around the edges.

He switched the display to thermal and the image changed from its murky range of greys and browns to blue and green. The dome itself appeared in a yellowish hue, warmer than the blue of the ambient temperature, but within that patch there were no thermal spikes.

'If there are any heat signatures inside they won't pass through the superstructure,' Aryx said.

'Would it be advisable to take the ship around the base to investigate?'

'I don't want to unless we really have to.' He stared out at the rain peeling over the edge of the CFD shield projected above the window and shivered. 'Just being on this planet is creeping me out.'

The comms beeped. 'Sebastian here. We've got the sample and we're heading back.'

'Good. I can bring the ship and pick you up if you like. It's a long walk just to come back. I can hover when I get to you.'

'If you're sure,' Sebastian said. 'I don't mind walking back, though.'

'Oh, ignore him,' Karan said. 'He'll gripe about it all the way. Just come and get us!'

Aryx tapped the controls, initiating pre-flight checks. 'I'll be there in a minute.'

A red light flashed on the console in response.

'Oh, what the heck?'

'Is there a problem?' Sebastian asked.

'Maybe ... Stay where you are for the moment. I'll check it out and get back to you. Aryx out.'

He wheeled across to the flashing icon: a red triangle with an exclamation mark in the centre. When he tapped it, the message changed to *Unknown error in navigation subsystem.*

'What the hell's that supposed to mean?'

The lights on Wolfram's cube flashed rapidly. 'I have examined the system logs. It appears the navigation software became corrupted at the same time we detected the signal from the research base.'

'It's not possible. Sebastian said that Logynix doesn't get viruses.'

'Perhaps it isn't a virus, but something else corrupting the system.'

'Hmm, maybe. I guess this means we can't take off?'

'Correct.'

'Can you fix the software so we can?'

'One moment.' The lights flashed again, more rapidly this time. After thirty seconds, they stopped. 'I have restored the software from a backup, but the problem seems to have reasserted itself. Comparing the backup to the corrupted version reveals similar code signatures to those I found in Tenebrae's tampered software and that from the Cinder IV mission logs.'

Aryx's face tingled.

'Are you alright? Your complexion has lost some of its colour.'

The cockpit started to wobble and Aryx steadied himself on the console. 'I'm just feeling a bit dizzy. I *knew* something bad was going to happen. It's that Trojan again, isn't it?'

'The evidence seems to support it. I suspect we are stuck here until we can terminate the signal. Restoring the software will only result in corruption again.'

'Great.' Aryx activated the comms. 'Sebastian, the navigation subsystem on the ship. Can we fly without it?'

'Not really. Why?'

He sagged into his seat as he gave Sebastian the bad news.

Sebastian stared up into the rain pelting his helmet while Aryx told him about the corrupted code and sighed. 'No, you can't bypass the navigation system. It's tied into too many other systems for the ship to be able to function without it. What do you want us to do, come back?'

'What good will that do? Can you get to the base on foot? If you can find the source of the signal, maybe you can shut it down. Once it's off, Wolfram can restore the software again and I'll be able to pick you up.'

'Fine. Shut down everything except the comms. We don't want the entire ship getting infected. Even though I can't see how it could have happened in the first place.' Sebastian looked at Karan.

She shrugged. 'Which direction is the base?'

'Turn to your left,' Aryx said. 'It's over the hill on the horizon. It's not worth coming all the way back just to drop the sample off.'

'Okay.' She dropped her arms to her sides. 'Let's go.'

Sebastian followed as she made her way to the path and began walking towards the rusty glow of the sun that barely penetrated the clouds on the horizon.

As they crested the hill, the rain eased and the view opened onto a dark, rolling heath criss-crossed with bare paths. On the horizon, maybe three miles away, stood a tall, dark beehive-dome, one side of which had been torn open, with sheets of metal and girders twisting outwards.

Karan flicked up the visor of her helmet and stood with her hands on her hips. She took a deep breath. 'You up for a hike?'

Sebastian opened his visor. The air was fresh, damp, and electric. 'I guess so.'

He activated the suit-to-ship comms and looked back at the *Ultima Thule* in the distance, cockpit lights and shield glowing against the shadowy marsh.

'We see it, Aryx. We're heading out.'

The dark dome of the research base blended with the sky in an indistinct blur as Sebastian and Karan approached. The rain had started once more, falling in great surging waves, and the impotently smouldering sun of Cinder had already set, forcing the pair to close their visors and activate the torches on their pressure suits.

Sweeping the rain-striated cones of light back and forth across the building, they located the entrance: a large roller-shutter door, suitable for vehicles, with a smaller decontamination airlock for personnel next to it.

Karan approached the airlock and examined it while Sebastian unhooked the rugged infoslate from his belt and started to probe the nearby locking mechanism.

'What are you doing?' she asked.

'Going to unlock it.'

'I don't see why.' She waved her hand in a narrow gap in the airlock door. 'It's already open.'

He refastened the infoslate. 'I guess nobody came back to lock the place down after the explosion.'

'Why would they?' she said, checking a readout on her cuff. 'Half the building is missing and there's low-level radiation. It's a nuked research base ... Hardly a prime target for looting, is it?'

'Hmm.' Sebastian bit the inside of his cheek. It sounded like a rational explanation, but rational thought was in short supply lately.

She tried the controls. 'Not working. We won't fit through this gap.' She squeezed partially through sideways and grunted as she tried to force the mechanism apart, pushing her back against the frame. 'Where's the signal coming from, anyway?'

He checked the infoslate for the frequency Aryx had relayed during their earlier conversation. 'In there somewhere. I can't tell exactly until we get inside.'

'Great help you are. Are you going to just stand there or give me a hand?'

'Sorry!' He let the infoslate hang and joined in, trying to pull the door sideways.

They pushed and pulled for several seconds before the mechanism gave way and the door finally rumbled open enough to allow their helmets to pass.

Karan squeezed through into the dark corridor and, with one look back at the hills, Sebastian followed her in.

Chapter 36

Hoping he wasn't going to need it, Sebastian put one hand on his holstered pistol as he stepped through the door of the research base.

Ahead, Karan's boots picked up the pale dust coating the floor, leaving dark footprints in her wake. Rain dripped from her suit, spattering a black trail behind that glistened in the torchlight.

'It's a shame there's no power in here,' she said, turning on a second torch attached to her rifle. She swung the weapon in a wide arc.

'Like you said, what do you expect from a nuked research base?'

'Haha.'

Sebastian checked the readout on the cuff of his suit. 'Air's breathable, radiation is still low.' His suit's internal radiation exposure badge glowed green, so he unclipped his helmet and looped his arm through it. 'We needn't have struggled with the door after all.'

Karan rolled her eyes. 'And what would we have done if we needed the helmets farther in and had left them outside? Always looking for a shortcut.' She shone her torch down the long corridor, but the darkness swallowed the beam before it reached the end. 'No shortcuts here. So where's the signal coming from?'

He glanced at the infoslate. 'Ahead. Still not much resolution.'

'Then what are you waiting for?' She broke into a run. Sebastian reluctantly jogged behind.

A minute later, they reached a junction, where thin walls split the corridor and fanned out six ways. All paths led into darkness except one, where a faint blue light glinted off the metal walls in the distance.

'I thought there was supposed to be no power?' Karan said.

'There isn't ...' Sebastian checked the infoslate and a cold shiver ran through him. 'And that's where the signal is coming from.'

'Wait a sec.' Karan turned off both torches and brought the rifle up to her cheek, activated the telescopic sight and peered through it.

Sebastian turned off his torch and stared down the tunnel at the lit area. Several moments passed before his eyes became accustomed to the darkness. The light ahead flickered erratically. 'What is it?' he whispered.

'Don't know. Can't see a lot. Must be coming from a room off to the right. Let's check it out.' She hunched a little and moved off silently, rifle still at her shoulder.

The walls closed in around him. With only the faint silhouette of Karan in front of him as a guide, he ran his hand along the wall for reassurance. The reinforced fingertips of the pressure suit gave off a faint hiss as they brushed over the metal plating.

He nearly bumped into her when she halted without warning. 'Stop doing that,' she whispered, and he quickly retracted his hand. She resumed walking, but slowed and kept against the right-hand wall as they drew close to the source of light.

In the gloom, Karan made several sharp gestures with her left hand. What the heck did that mean? She immediately stepped forward and left, turning ninety degrees right, to bring the rifle to bear on the light source.

Sebastian held his breath.

Her face creased into a frown. She lowered the gun. 'Clear.'

The room from which the bluish flickering light came was separated from the corridor by a long, glazed screen. A glass door stood in the end of the screen farthest from them. Beyond the screen, the room was the same grey metal as the corridor, nine metres wide and seven metres deep. A series of low metal benches ran around the walls, with one section standing against the inside of the screen. In the centre of the room, cables of varying thicknesses dangled from the ceiling, sporting a multitude of different connectors. A yellow-painted tubular frame stood below, adorned with several small screens and brackets. Coils of cabling snaked across the floor from the far side of the room to the base of the inspection assembly in the middle.

Sebastian blinked in the glare of the flashes, which came from a conduit on the far wall. A crack ran from floor to ceiling, breaking the housing and leaving the inner wiring to drape loose. Two cables hung from a dislodged ceiling tile, touching the conduit and sparking as they swung gently in a flow of gas or air from a ruptured pipe.

'Must be an emergency power line,' he said.

Karan pushed open the door and they walked in. Sebastian shielded his eyes from the light and looked around.

Pieces of mechanical debris lay strewn across the benches: a gripper mechanism here, a complex differential servo there, magnetic induction coils, portable power packs and even small camera arrays.

'Looks like a robotics lab. Some of these bits are familiar.' He picked up a broken section of caterpillar track and turned it in his hands. 'This is like something from a cargomech.'

A loud, metallic screech echoed from the corridor outside.

He dropped the piece of track on the bench. Karan spun around, the assault rifle already at her shoulder, and swept the long window to the corridor.

'What was that?' he whispered.

'Something I didn't like the sound of.'

Sebastian slowly drew his pistol and moved alongside her. He'd only had a little practice in the weeks since events at Kimberley depot, where he'd shot Gladrin, and still didn't feel confident with the weapon. Already his palms had begun to sweat, giving an unpleasant itching sensation inside the pressure suit gloves.

'Stay back,' she said, moving towards the glass door. She flicked on the rifle-mounted torch and, in one smooth move, stepped out into the corridor. She stood motionless, peering into the darkness. After a moment, she beckoned to him and he stepped out beside her.

'I don't see anything,' she said, 'but it sounded like machinery. It must be something farther in the complex. Keep your wits about you.'

He nodded and brought his pistol up to his shoulder, ready to drop into the Weaver stance and fire if the need arose.

Karan put a hand out behind her and moved forwards. Sebastian held his position. She silently rolled her feet as she made her way along the corridor to the end, where it turned to the left, and paused for a moment before stepping out sharply.

Sebastian held his breath.

'Clear,' she said, beckoning, and waited until he caught up. 'The door at the far end is shut.' She lifted the muzzle of the rifle, pointing down the corridor. 'If the emergency power is working intermittently, the door might be malfunctioning. That's probably what caused the noise.'

'There are no footprints. At least nobody is in here ahead of us.'

'What makes you say that? Something's causing the signal. If someone is in here, they could have come in from one of the other entrances.'

He shivered with a cold sweat and tightened his grip on the gun.

She walked down the corridor towards the door and waited for him to arrive. 'Ready? You get it.'

Sebastian stepped to one side and tapped the controls.

Blarp!

'It's not working.'

'But the power is. Like I said, probably malfunctioning. Do you think you can open it?'

'I'll give it a go.' He held his infoslate near the panel and began to investigate the control protocols. Code flowed up the screen and one thing stood out: corrupted segments of code that left a jagged trail of voids like footprints in the ripples of a zen garden.

'Well?'

'This is corrupted. Probably by the same code that's affecting the ship. We may need to force the door.'

'Okay, let's see if there's something in that lab we can use to open it.' She headed back towards the room with the sparking cables.

Sebastian deactivated the infoslate connection and followed her. When he reached the corner, he froze on the spot.

In the distance, beyond the robotics lab, at the point where the corridor fanned out, something flashed white. A sharp crack echoed along the corridor. Sparks showered from hidden cabling and wall panels clanged to the floor as a bolt of energy shot towards them.

Chapter 37

'Sebastian, are you there?' came Aryx's voice over the suit comms. 'I think the ship just got hit by light—'

'Not now!' The crackling of electricity joined the clang of the falling panels. Sebastian cut the comms.

'Look out!' Karan ran ahead of the danger and pushed him against the wall, shielding him with her body as a panel shot out and smashed into the wall by his head.

The energy coruscated along the surface behind her and turned the corner. It stopped at the closed door and a white bolt crackled across the console. The door opened, and the energy followed the wall into the room beyond.

Karan spun him around by the shoulders and pushed him towards the opening. 'Now!'

They broke into a run and cleared the gap as the door slammed shut behind them. A fraction of a second later, a door on the opposite side of the room closed.

There was no sign of the energy.

'What in Hel's name was that?' Sebastian said, still shaking from the adrenaline of his near miss.

'I thought I saw ... I don't know ... What did you say the thing that appeared in the ship on your way back to the station looked like?'

'A sort of wispy light. What's that got to do with anything?'

'Because that energy just now wasn't electrical. It had a weird glow, and it *slowed down* ... Just forget it, I can tell you don't believe me. You'd better find out what Aryx wanted.'

Sebastian reactivated the comms. 'Aryx, sorry about that. Something strange just happened. W-what were you saying?'

'Something flashed in the ship just before I called you. I thought it was lightning, but Wolfram says it wasn't. It was caused by a charge *inside* the hull.'

Karan spoke into her comms. 'Aryx, I don't think the entity you saw on the way to the station left the ship when you thought it did. Something came back with you ... and it's here now.'

'By the Gods! How can that be?' Sebastian asked. 'They're not supposed to exist in this plane.'

'Devoid of any evidence,' Wolfram said, joining the conversation, 'I am "guessing" that the entity may have been phase-shifted by Alicia's thaumatic effect, and that may have enabled it to become stored as a charge in the ship's hull. For whatever reason, it chose to remain aboard until we arrived here.'

A chill crawled up Sebastian's spine. 'If it knew we were coming here, it probably heard everything we said aboard the ship! But the place is abandoned.' He gestured to the rows of benches in the new lab, which lay strewn with electronic components and machinery similar to those in the first. 'And these labs just contain robotics parts. Why would it come here?'

'From what I remember of the place,' Aryx said, 'I think you went in the rear entrance. When my platoon entered, they had to fight past the Independent Terran Front cell operating from a lab there. The rest of the base was researching Cinder's weather and solar activity, neither of which have anything to do with robotics. You're probably in one of the last rooms they reached.'

Sebastian swallowed. Several large bullet holes peppered the walls in one corner. 'Yeah, I think you're right.'

'We should check out some of this stuff,' Karan said, moving over to the benches, her face bluish in the emergency strip lights that had come on overhead. 'There might be an important clue somewhere among all these bits.'

'Alright, I'll look at the equipment. Karan, see if you can find something to get that other door open with – the lights are off on the console, so I think it's blown. Aryx, I'll be in touch shortly.'

'Before you go,' Wolfram said, 'I should inform you that the signal being broadcast from the base has stopped. Aryx says we can leave immediately.'

'I think we need to find out what the entity wants here before we leave. It could be important.'

'Aryx reluctantly agrees. I also have a suspicion that it may have been the entity creating a false signal and tampering with the software in some fashion, possibly to buy time in which to leave the ship. If that is the case, it may have placed infectious code in your infoslate to make you follow the false signal. I recommend complete erasure before your return to prevent reinfection of the ship's systems.'

'Acknowledged.' Sebastian closed the comms and tapped commands into the infoslate to initiate a complete wipe. 'There was definitely tampered code on the door computer, but Wolfram's right, it might have infected this, too.'

Karan paused in her search. 'Won't you lose the video from the microscope?'

'Yes.' He patted the sample jar in his belt. 'But we can take fresh scans of this later.' He approached the benches and began poring over the items.

In the harsh emergency lighting, everything took on a blue cast, rendering circuitry colouring unrecognisable. In addition to a collection of mechanical robotic parts, similar to those in the previous lab, a wide array of familiar circuit modules adorned the benches, identifiable by their shapes and connections. Audio input modules, cameras, gravity and magnetic sensors, humidity, temperature, pressure, micro servos, cooling fans, heat sinks, processors ... the list went on.

'I don't see anything too unusual here,' he said, shrugging, and turned away from the work surface. The bright glint of something caught his eye, and he crossed the room to another bench.

In front of him sat a pile of jagged, blackened rubble that glittered with hints of gold.

'Except for this. This is pretty unusual.' He activated his suit comms. 'Aryx, what do you think this is?'

'Hold on, let me get to the screen ... Okay, what am I looking at, rocks?'

'I'm not sure.' He picked up a piece to give the suit cam a better view and weighed it in his hand. 'It's not as heavy as stone, and the outside looks all bubbled up and broken.' As he turned it, the light picked out threadlike golden slivers, running across and through the surface.

'I don't think it is rock,' Aryx said. 'That looks like circuitry. Hold on. What's that crystal over there?'

A small, milky crystal protruded from one of the craggy chunks.

Sebastian put the piece he held down and pulled off his right-hand glove. He picked up the piece containing the crystal. With his hand now in direct contact with the object, it was like no rock he'd ever handled: it was too heavy to be completely porous like pumice, and the bubbles were smooth – they had to be on the surface only.

'Aryx, this reminds me of the melted beta cube from the lab on Tenebrae. The circuits are like those in Wolfram's internals.' He turned the chunk and light caught on the facets of the small crystal embedded in its surface. 'It's definitely melted organoplastic. Perhaps there was an explosion that sent crystals flying from elsewhere in the lab and they got stuck while it was hot.' He looked around. 'But then . . . there's no evidence of explosion in here.'

A memory came to him. He'd picked up a crystal like this in the caves on Achene and put it into his belt. But how did such a thing get here, to Cinder IV?

'Try removing the crystal,' Aryx said. 'See if you can get it out whole, just in case.'

Sebastian pulled out his multi-tool, extended the pliers and adjusted his grip on the bubbly fragment. As he held the pliers around the crystal, he slipped and his hand made contact with it. A tingle ran through his fingers like a mild electric shock.

The metal walls of the lab vanished.

Sebastian stood on a crimson shore, looking out towards twin suns setting in a viscous black ocean. In the purple sky overhead, a bright constellation glittered. The zesty scent of unfamiliar salts blew in from the sea, filling his senses and crystallising on his cheeks.

How had he got here? He wasn't dreaming, that much was certain: a moment ago he had been standing in a lab with Karan, but perhaps he was mistaken? Maybe . . . Maybe the lab was the dream?

He stared up into the sky. What was that constellation?

'*Seb, have you managed to pull the crystal out?*' Aryx's voice came in distant, incongruous.

'What?' The alien coast vanished, and he looked down at the crystal embedded in the organoplastic chunk on the bench in front of him. 'I-I slipped,' he said, shaking his head to rid himself of the odd sense of dislocation.

'What are you doing?' Karan asked. She stood with a cargomech gripper prong wedged in the door seal. 'You were staring into space. Are you okay?'

'I don't know what happened. I was somewhere else for a second. It was the place in my dreams, although it felt *real*.'

'What caused that?' She checked her radiation exposure badge, which glowed green. 'You're not having some kind of episode, are you?'

'No! It happened when I touched the crystal.'

She frowned. 'Put your gloves on, then. I can't have you spacing out again.'

He pulled on his glove and refastened it to the cuff of his suit. Picking up the multi-tool, he attempted a second time to remove the crystal. The surface of the crystal was smooth and polished, yet sharply faceted, a lustrous milky blue, like pale smoke frozen in glass. The pliers slipped off again.

'Damn, this is hard to get a hold of.' He looked about for something to use for better grip and, after a quick search, was rewarded with a thin strip of rubber, which he wrapped around the stone. 'It reminds me of something I've seen before . . .' He had recognised the crystal only moments ago, but the recollection of from where slipped from his mental grasp. Perhaps it was just déjà vu.

Now, with a firmer grip, he squeezed harder and began to pull the crystal from its organoplastic seat. As it came free, the crystal shattered – vaporised – sending a shower of sparkling dust into the air.

He staggered back, covering his mouth with the back of his arm, and waited until the cloud had settled.

Everything on the bench glittered as though left outdoors and covered with a morning frost. There was no sign of even the tiniest sliver of crystal.

'Well, that's blown it,' Aryx said over the comms.

'It must have been really brittle. I wasn't gripping it that hard.'

'What about the matrix it was stuck in?'

Sebastian picked up the bubbly chunk and turned it in his hands to inspect the hole left by the crystal. The golden trails that ran across the convoluted surface went down into the recess and terminated in circular contacts at the bottom.

'You know, I don't think the crystal got stuck in there by accident. It looks like it was *wired* in.'

'Why would the ITF be wiring crystals into SI matrices?'

Wolfram joined the conversation. 'Sebastian, do you think it may be related to your experience just now?'

'I don't follow.'

'You said that when you touched it, you saw something similar to your nightmares. Nightmares that have been caused by the entities via signal transmission. Is it not therefore possible that the crystal and their research are connected to those dream experiences?'

'It's a bit of a leap. Why would they want to copy your circuitry?'

'I would require more information to formulate a complete hypothesis, but I suspect that it is related to the fact that my neuromorphic processor closely emulates the function of the Human brain. They may have been working on interfacing the crystal with it in some fashion to make use of the brain's ability to receive those impressions from the crystal. It is also concerning that they had managed to replicate my basic physical structure in this laboratory, since we know the only other copy of my matrix was destroyed.'

'It was a university project,' Sebastian said. 'Perhaps the basic casing schematics are available in their archives?'

'Sorry to interrupt,' Karan said, waving, 'but I could really do with a hand getting this open!'

'Wolfram, we'll have to talk about this later. Sebastian out.' He put down the chunk of plastic and went over to her. 'What do you need?'

'I've managed to wedge the tip of the prong in this seal. I just need you to pull it to one side while I push it farther in.'

Sebastian wrapped his hands around the wide bar and pulled. Karan pushed on the end, the strain showing in the veins of her face.

After a minute of wiggling it back and forth, the bar slid in and the doors parted by several millimetres.

'Yay, us!' Karan said, shifting to get her fingers in the gap. Sebastian moved to crouch in front of her to grip a lower section, but she stopped him. 'Shh! I can hear voices.'

He put his ear to the gap.

'Does that suit your purpose?' said a male Human voice with a faint accent. There was something familiar about it, but the pronunciation of Galac and the echoing corridor distorted it too much to be recognisable.

'Adequate,' a second voice said. Metallic, poorly synthesised. 'Now. Why. Are. You. Here?'

'After the loss of our base, and now the conduit, we had to come back. We had to try the technology, even unfinished. Our numbers are now so diminished there was little choice. Can you use it?'

A quiet whirring. 'Yes.'

Something clicked loudly on Karan's suit and she stepped back from eavesdropping. 'Seb, put your helmet on,' she whispered. 'There's radiation coming from the other side.'

He quickly put on his helmet and, glancing at his exposure badge to check it was still green, let out a sigh of relief.

The Human spoke again in response to something unheard. 'Where? Go. Deal with them. We will find another way.'

A shiver went down Sebastian's back at those words. Whoever it was knew they were here.

The floor rumbled with a deep vibration.

He staggered to his feet and moved back from the door. The vibration intensified. Through the gap came the screech of metal scraping on metal, broken glass crunching beneath something heavy, and a steely grinding.

'Karan, what's happening?'

Backing into a corner away from the doors, she shook her head. 'Nothing good. Get over here.' She raised her gun to her shoulder and trained it on the door.

As Sebastian backed away, the door thudded heavily.

'By the Gods!' He ran to stand by her.

Three seconds later, with another thud, the door buckled into the room by several inches.

'Whatever it is, it's big,' he said, drawing his pistol. 'And I don't think this is going to stop it!'

Chapter 38

Sebastian's hands shook as he held his pistol, waiting for the thing to break into the room. 'You don't think it's the beast of Ruarda, do you?'

'Don't be stupid,' Karan said, settling into a ready stance.

'It was just a thought.'

She grinned. 'It doesn't go indoors.'

'Don't tell me you're enjoying this.' He swallowed. It had been nearly twenty seconds since the last impact against the door. Maybe whatever it was had given up?

He let out a breath.

Boom! The thick door peeled back from the doorway as the frame and surrounding wall exploded into the room. Shards of metal and concrete flew through the air as a bronze sphere, almost three metres in diameter, burst in and rolled straight through the next door as if it were paper. The ceiling collapsed behind it, bringing heavy panels and girders down and blocking the route from which it came.

Sebastian's mouth hung open and, before he had a chance to speak, Karan went after it. He paused for a second – what had happened to the Human whose voice he'd heard? – then set off after her.

In the midst of his adrenaline rush, the sphere carried on ahead of them for what seemed almost a minute, tumbling along the narrow corridor, its sides almost touching the walls. The light of Karan's torch glinted off the bronze surface, picking up deep striations and concentric circular grooves etched into its surface like a giant pétanque ball.

Brrrrrp! Karan loosed off a burst of gunfire, the impacts flaring off the sphere in the dark, but still it continued.

'What is that thing?' Sebastian yelled. There was no sign of it slowing to take the bend.

'I have no idea, but it's—'

A cacophonous crash drowned out Karan's words as the sphere drove through the wall ahead without turning the corner. The corridor buckled under the force of the wall tearing out. Sparking conduits tentacled down and support beams lanced into the passage from above, bringing with them more building material from upper floors. The bronze sphere disappeared into the darkness; metallic tearing and echoing screeches the only evidence of its continued movement.

She staggered to a halt. 'Crap.'

Sebastian stared at the carnage wrought by the sphere. A mixture of concrete slabs, beams, and heavy metal sheets blocked the corridor ahead. 'We're stuck.'

'Yeah, and the blasted thing, whatever it was,' Karan said, jabbing a thumb over her shoulder, 'blocked the door into the other room behind us, so we can't go that way.'

He looked down at his suit sleeve where a red light was flashing. 'This stretch is full of radiation now. Fortunately, the suits will protect us from it while we've got air, so there's no problem. How long do you think it'll take us to clear this and get out?'

She winced. 'About three hours. If we're not careful, maybe two.'

He checked the readouts on his suit and swallowed hard. 'Then we do have a problem. We've only got one hour of air.'

Chapter 39

Aryx sat in the *Ultima Thule*, elbows on the console, chin in his hands, staring out at the wavering curtain of rain that had started to fall once more. 'Is the computer okay now, Wolfram?'

'Yes. Since the signal stopped, I was able to safely restore the backup software.'

'So, we'll be able to take off and pick them up when they come out of the base?'

'That should indeed be the case.'

Aryx leaned back with his hands behind his head. 'Good. It'll be nice to have something go according to plan for a change.'

'How are you feeling now, Aryx? According to the scans Monica took earlier, the inflammation around the nanobot implants I constructed should have settled.'

'I'm fine, thanks.' A twinge went through his legs. 'It's time for me to take my drugs. I've gone as long as I can without.' He wheeled to the refrigeration unit and opened the door. A single clear ampoule of medication remained and, next to it on the shelf, the syringe required to inject it. He took out both and filled the syringe, then placed it on the console while he rolled up his trouser legs. 'I need to use all of this. I shouldn't have rationed it.'

'Have you reconsidered informing Sebastian of the severity of your condition?'

'Not really. It won't help matters.'

'It would surely prevent him from placing you in unnecessarily dangerous situations.'

Aryx swabbed the end of his leg and prepared to insert the needle. 'Like I said, it wouldn't help. I don't need cotton wool.'

The comms console beeped.

'Speak of the devil . . .' He put down the syringe to answer. 'Seb, what's happening?'

'Karan and I have a problem. The corridors have caved in, and we could do with the cargomech to get us out.'

'How did that happen? The remaining structure was stable!'

'It's a long story.' Sebastian's signal began to break up. 'Just bring the cargomech quickly. You won't be able to remote it . . . This section's flooded with radiation . . . interfering with comms . . . We've only got an hour of air bef—' The signal dropped.

'Shit, shit, shit!' Aryx grabbed Wolfram, spun around onto the lift and waited for its agonisingly slow descent to finish.

'What are you planning to do?' Wolfram asked.

'I need to know what's happening in that base. You could go in with the mech and clear the debris. You'll be attached to it. No problem with signal interference.'

'Aryx, I am unfamiliar with construction methods. If I move damaged structural material without being aware of potential hidden dangers, the structure could collapse.' The SI's usually factual tone sounded almost concerned. 'Your engineering expertise would be invaluable.'

Aryx gritted his teeth. 'Fine, then I'll have to come with you to supervise while you control the cargomech. We can't risk using an infoslate to control it remotely in case that signal or entity or whatever comes back again and corrupts it.' He wheeled off the lift and held the cube out towards the cargomech.

The mech reached out and placed the cube in the receptacle on its chest panel. 'I will pilot the ship closer to the research base. I would advise that you wear a pressure suit as protection from the radiation when we arrive.'

'Okay, I'll *try* to put one on.'

The ship lifted off as Aryx made his way to the pressure suit storage area by the airlock. When he got there, the large metal hopper of carbyne blocked his path. He tried to pull it aside, back into the corridor, but his wrists hurt and it slipped from his grasp.

'I can't believe he left this junk here!'

'Is there a problem?'

'Yes. I've got a hopper in the way of the suits.'

'Unfortunately, this unit is too large to assist, but I have an idea. Hold on to something, preferably away from the hopper.'

Aryx wheeled back against the wall and wrapped his arm around the long vertical handrail by the airlock. The ship bucked hard to port and the hopper grated along the floor. On the way past, it clipped one of the caster struts on his chair, which rent a long, silvery gouge in the hopper's green paintwork, and it came to rest against the wall with a thump. 'Hey, watch my chair!'

'I did advise you to stay back.'

The ship levelled and Aryx flicked the one remaining pressure suit off its hook and pulled it on. The booted legs dangled uselessly on the floor while he strapped on the mobipack over the suit. They had to be put out of the way somehow.

'Aryx,' Wolfram said over the suit comms, 'I am unable to land the ship near the building. Radiation coming from the newly damaged structure is interfering with the telemetry system and I will need to set us down a minimum of six hundred metres away.'

'Okay.' At least the issue of what to do with the pressure suit's legs was solved; he'd need the mobipack to cross the remaining stretch of scrubland on foot. Recalling how he fitted the boots back in London, he activated the mobipack and generated the legs at fifty per cent size, outstretched. He lifted the boots onto his lap, then reached forward with one, roughly aligning it with the projected force-field leg.

'Mobipack, left leg off.'

The leg vanished and he moved the empty boot, still connected to the rest of his suit, into position and reactivated the leg. He released his grip and the boot stayed in place, wobbling as it sagged about the far-too-small leg inside it, and repeated the process with the right.

'Mobipack, enlarge both legs by a factor of two percent per second until they're at one hundred per cent.'

The mobipack bleeped compliance and the pressure suit legs began to move. He shifted them to make sure the feet fitted as they expanded, and the suit filled like an inflating balloon. He stood up to test the boots' grip on the smooth floor and the mobipack harness cut in, pinching the suit in all sorts of places around his unmentionables. 'It's a bit awkward, but it'll do for now. Are we almost there?'

'Yes. Brace yourself for landing.'

He sat in his wheelchair and once again looped his arm through the handrail on the wall. The ship listed to starboard, to port, then settled with a gentle bump and the faint brushing screech of plant spines against metal.

The cargo bay door lowered, flattening the gorse bushes, and the cargomech rolled out into the torrential rain.

Aryx wheeled forward, but stopped short of the thin curtain of water that now fell across the opening. His chest tightened. This was too much like the day he lost his legs, right down to how the rain poured onto the ramp. Only this time the cargomech was going first, and it wasn't under the control of just any computer.

He stood and hoisted the wheelchair up to his shoulder. There was no way he was leaving it behind, certainly not if he had to do any work in the complex itself – the last time he'd used the mobipack for an extended period it had nearly cut his groin to ribbons. 'Wolfram, aren't you forgetting something?'

'What?'

He lifted off the portable plasma cutter from one of the storage racks. 'This, but you're going to have to carry it. It's a bit heavy for me to lug around.'

The cargomech reached through the thin waterfall cascading over the opening, splitting the film with its grippers, and Aryx handed over the cutter.

'It's a good job this stuff's waterproof,' he said and, picking up his wheelchair, stepped out into the storm.

Aryx strode down the ramp into the spiny bushes surrounding the *Ultima Thule*.

The cargomech had trundled several metres ahead, its caterpillar tracks ploughing furrows through the muddy ground, crushing the sharp foliage and making movement quicker than it would have been had Aryx needed to wade through.

The needles clawed at his boots, and he stumbled as one of the spines snagged a fold in his suit. After a minute of walking, he looked back. The ship was still only thirty metres away.

'Wolfram, we're not going to make it in time,' he said, jerking his foot free of another branch. 'Can you give me a ride or something?'

'One moment.'

The mech reversed and a flat chequer-plate platform hinged down from the back of its main body. Aryx heaved his wheelchair up and stepped onto the plate as the mech's arms swung around behind him to prevent him from falling off.

'Just don't go too fast, I've only got one hand free.'

The cargomech accelerated into the night, caterpillar tracks throwing mush into the air, while twin cones of light projected ahead, catching bright swirls as the rain danced around them on the wind.

Aryx's visor swam with rain that fell so hard it drowned out his thoughts. His teeth chattered with vibrations from the cargomech tearing across the terrain, reflecting his apprehension at being on the damned planet in the first place.

Wolfram drove hard over a small mound, sending him tumbling back into the mech's arms. He had to hold on and not think about it. He looked at the chair hooked over his shoulder ... The seat cushion would take ages to dry out after this.

A whooping, baleful cry echoed across the scrubland from somewhere behind them, loud enough to hear over the rain hammering his helmet. Whatever it was, it was big. It was big and lurking out in the storm ... *somewhere*. He recalled the image of the six-legged predator that had attacked him on Achene, and shuddered.

Wolfram's voice focused Aryx's thoughts again. 'We are approaching the research base and will be stopping momentarily.'

Aryx turned as the mech began to slow, and jumped down. He winced as the mobipack straps dug in through the fabric of the pressure suit. The mech stopped, straightened and focused its lights at a point ahead.

He found himself faced with two doors: a small personnel airlock, partly open, and a large vehicle-sized roller shutter. The shutter door was closed, but in the centre a circular hole, almost as tall as the cargomech, had been punched through. The edges pointed outward in long slatted fingers, grasping at the air.

'What could do that kind of damage?' he asked. If it had been a vehicle, much of the lower part of the door would have been ripped out, too. The sound he'd heard earlier came back to him. 'Err, do you think it was the beast of Ruarda? I didn't really believe in it, but now I'm not so sure ...'

'The alien bear-creature?' Wolfram said, driving closer to the opening. 'No. I do not think this was caused by a creature. It is as though a large spherical object crashed through.'

'Are you sure?'

'No, but it *is* unlikely to have been caused by a creature. The opening is too regular. However, I believe we should enter through this route. Even fully opened, the airlock is too small for the cargomech.'

The cargomech rolled forwards and inserted its prongs into a large slot next to the door. Its grippers rotated and the door slowly slid upwards, but jammed as one of the curled parts refused to pass through the mechanism at the top.

'Well, that's blown it,' Aryx said. 'Lower the door. We'll have to climb through.'

After checking for radiation and waiting for the door to lower again, Aryx stepped through the circular tear into a hangar bay and took off his helmet. On either side of the space sat two dirt encrusted six-wheeled armoured personnel carriers with a gap for a third between them. In the far wall another hole, punched through solid metal, greedily swallowed the torch light.

'I've got a bad feeling about this,' he said.

The mech trundled in behind him, flattening the lower half of the opening as it went. 'If the damage direction is outward, surely any potential danger has already exited the building?'

'Let's just not take any chances, shall we?'

'Don't worry,' Wolfram said, softening the mech's voice a little, 'this unit has cameras on the rear.'

'That's reassuring. You'll be able to see me get torn to pieces behind you.' Aryx made his way across the hangar and peered through the second opening to inspect the damage. There was no evidence of the striation ordinarily present in damage caused by sharp implements. 'You know, this is like a giant blunt instrument went through it.' He reached out to touch the metal and followed the edges with his gloved fingers. 'I think you're right about the sphere idea. Can we contact Sebastian?'

'I have been trying. Even though the radiation in this section is still relatively low, it is likely to be of sufficient strength to interfere with reception of communications farther in the complex.' The mech stepped through the hole in front of him, into the corridor beyond.

'Which way?'

The mech's upper half swivelled from side to side. 'The wall ahead of me seems to have been punched through and the way is filled with debris, making it impassable, but I can see two sets of footprints in the dust, leading off to the right.'

Aryx checked his radiation badge. It was still green, and the exterior suit radiation low. 'Okay, you go on ahead. If you see Sebastian or Karan, you'll have to wait so I can assess the situation. I'll follow in my chair.' He tugged at one of the straps running between his legs. 'These things are really cutting into me. I need to adjust them first.'

'Very well.' The mech accelerated away from the hole and into the darkness, leaving a pair of chevroned trails in the dust. Aryx's suit comms crackled and died as Wolfram went deeper into the complex and closer to the source of radiation.

He stepped back from the hole, lowered his wheelchair to the hangar floor and pulled off the seat. It weighed a ton. 'Great,' he muttered as he wrung it out, creating a puddle on the smooth concrete. Satisfied the foam was as empty as it could be, he sat down and loosened the mobipack's lower straps.

Wind blustered and howled through the opening in the outer shutter door and it rattled, breaking the momentary quiet of the hangar. A mirror of water crept along the floor towards him between the parked APCs as rain poured in, and he stared at it absent-mindedly while he adjusted the harness.

His heart leaped as a large clawed foot, four times the size of a Human head, set down in the puddle, shattering the reflection.

Folds of pinkish leathery skin billowed up from the pudgy foot until it met an enormous body, almost half the size of one of the APCs. The creature resembled a giant, fat maggot with legs. Eight legs. Eight legs with *claws*.

The front had no discernible face; just a flat, circular hole with a ring of straight-edged teeth that pointed inwards, giving the creature the impression of a mating between an inflatable toy and industrial garbage disposal. The creature stopped halfway through the opening, its eyeless forward section making U-shaped motions in the air, as though sniffing.

Aryx almost laughed at the beast's appearance. A tardigrade. A "water bear". That's what it looked like. Perfectly harmless ... When they're less than a millimetre long.

The smile fell from Aryx's face as the stubby head turned in his direction. He wheeled backwards slowly, quietly, until his chair came to a stop against the wall. The creature halted its sniffing and momentarily turned away to look outside. Maybe it was going to leave.

The tardigrade swung its head back in Aryx's direction. The teeth peeled back from its mouth to reveal an inner ring of pointed teeth, twice as long, and a huge, bony beak that extended abruptly in a serrated yawn and chittered shut. The creature emitted the loud whooping howl he'd heard earlier, and its clawed feet clattered on the floor.

All eight of them. Scrabbling in his direction.

Chapter 40

Aryx stood up as the giant tardigrade skittered across the hangar towards him. The mobipack slipped on its loose harness and he fell back into his wheelchair. He gripped the wheels and spun to the right, away from the gap between the APCs, to get behind one of the vehicles.

'Wolfram! I need help!' he yelled into the suit comms.

There was no response as he skirted the six-wheeled carrier.

Hooked claws squealed on the smooth floor as the swollen octopod followed him around the vehicle. Maybe Wolfram would hear the creature and come anyway.

'Why is it always me being chased by things with lots of legs?' With an energetic shove, he darted past the APC, leaving the tardigrade to thud into the wall as its grip failed turning the corner. How was he going to get rid of it? The closest thing to a weapon he'd brought was the plasma cutter, and Wolfram had that.

He reached the front of the APC and pushed through the pool of water by the hangar door to traverse the full width of the room. Hopefully the creature would skid again and abandon its pursuit, or knock itself out against a wall.

Another circuit of the hangar proved that idea wrong.

On his third trip around the room, he spotted a flexible hose, looped over a peg next to one of the APCs. One end was attached to a compressor, and the other held a heavy gun with a large trigger on the back and blast-nozzle at the front. With such deep tread and thick rubber on the APC's tyres, it would have to be high pressure. By the airline was a stack of metal pipes, several feet long. Maybe he could use those to create a distraction.

The tardigrade stupidly followed his exact course around the hangar without cutting across the open space at the centre. Perhaps he could use that to his advantage.

On the fourth circuit he accelerated, putting as much energy as he could into getting as far ahead of the thing as possible. He squealed to a halt by the coiled airline.

As the tardigrade rounded the corner behind him, he grabbed one of the shiny pipes from the stack, dropped it next to the airline, and pushed off again. He needed more time, and his energy was waning. This stupidity had to end soon.

On the fifth circuit, he reached down for the metal pipe and placed it between his legs. He pulled the airline off the peg and wedged the rubber blast-nozzle into it.

Claws squealed behind him and he looked back. The Ruardan tardigrade was coming too fast!

Pushing off with the airline trailing, he approached the back of the APC. He turned around, the metal pipe swinging in a wide arc, and backed away with one quick shove. Letting go of his wheels, he slung the pipe under his arm and pressed the trigger against his side, pointing the opposite end towards the tardigrade.

The pipe emitted a brief, vibrant note as air blasted from it, but the sound didn't bother the creature as he'd hoped: it ran forward at full speed, while Aryx came to a stop. His plan had failed.

With the creature almost upon him, he levelled the pipe and held it like a lance, even though he had no idea of the thing's anatomy, or whether impaling it would have any effect.

The creature's bloated body caught the tip of the pipe as it advanced, and the impact sent him hurtling backwards along with it. He hit the wall, but the monstrosity continued, the pipe piercing and sliding into its soft body as the opposite end with the trigger jammed against the wall behind him.

The pipe blew a muffled raspberry into the tardigrade's innards as it impaled itself and slid along the tube towards Aryx. Its serrated beak gnashed at the air while the bilious sound increased in pitch.

He drew back as the beak snapped closer, inches from his face, expecting it to bite through his flesh at any moment.

The tardigrade stood up to its full height, wrenching the pipe from his grip as it balanced on its two rear pairs of stubby legs. Had it got bigger somehow? In an instant, it swelled to twice its size and exploded, sending brown gunge flying across the hangar.

* * *

After checking his radiation badge and replacing his helmet, Aryx followed Wolfram's trail in his wheelchair, dripping tardigrade innards behind him. Heaps of rubble lay piled against the walls where the mech had cleared a path.

Several hundred metres along the corridor, where it fanned out in multiple directions, he came across a pile of girders and twisted sheet metal. The thin dividing walls must have given way as soon as they were hit.

The cargomech stood in front of the pile, motionless. 'I was about to come looking for you. I cleared as much of the debris as I could, but I am uncertain what to move next. What happened to you? Why are you covered in slime?'

'I'll tell you later. Which corridor did they take?'

'This one.' The mech rolled back to the heap and began tugging at a girder.

'Careful, you can't just pull bits out willy-nilly! The ceiling might come down and crush them ... and us.'

'Show me. I can calculate the potential trajectory using physics algorithms, but I am unfamiliar with the specifics of construction practices.'

Aryx wheeled back and forth, considering the situation. The whole mass literally resembled a plate of metal spaghetti. 'Okay, show me which parts you think are definitely not supporting anything else.'

'Here.' The cargomech leaned forward and, using a two-pronged gripper, pointed to a girder encased in concrete.

'Right, start with that one ...'

Twenty minutes later, the bulk of the material had been removed, leaving a large, impassable grid of ceiling beams that sliced down into the corridor.

'Aryx, the radiation has increased drastically. The obstruction must have been shielding much of it.'

'Duly noted. I'll be fine in the suit.' He tried the comms again. 'Sebastian, come in. Where are you?'

No response.

'I'll try a directed beam transmission through the opening,' Wolfram said. 'I may be able to reflect it around the corner at the end.'

Several seconds later, footfalls echoed down the corridor from beyond the barrier.

'Aryx! It's good to see you!' Sebastian said, peering between the bars. 'I'm really sorry for dragging you out here.'

'You'll never believe what we saw,' Karan said.

'You'll never believe what *I* saw, but we can tell each other later.' Leaning forward in his chair, Aryx set to work on the gridwork with the plasma cutter. The thick metal cut slowly, and a few times he had to get Wolfram to hold up the structure or to break away chunks of concrete with the cargomech's grippers.

Minutes later, Sebastian was still talking. '... and a giant metal sphere burst through the door and went out the other side ...'

Aryx looked up from the plasma cutter, blinking sweat out of his eyes. His vision had begun to blur and, for whatever reason, the suit wasn't coping with the heat from his exertions and he began to sweat. 'Seb, I'm not listening. This is delicate work and I can't concentrate properly. Plus, you need to save your air.'

'Oh, alright.'

He cut through the final beam and tentatively wheeled backwards. 'Keep hold of it, Wolfram. Wait for them to get through before you let go. Just let me check it first.' He stood to examine his handiwork from a different angle.

The beams were clear of each other; nothing made contact where it shouldn't. The structure looked like it would hold, but something didn't feel right, and it wasn't the beam.

The room rocked from side to side. 'Why is everything moving?'

'It isn't,' Sebastian said.

'I don't ... I don't feel too good.' Aryx glanced down. A sliver of orange, the glow of his projected CFD legs, showed through a split in the left shin of his pressure suit. 'My suit's ripped.'

Sebastian stared down at Aryx's chest. 'Oh, Gods!'

'What is it?'

The lights on the cube fastened to the cargomech pulsed faintly. 'Aryx, your radiation badge is red.'

Chapter 41

Sebastian ducked through the gap in the beams held up by the cargomech, and dashed towards Aryx, arms wide, a peculiar mixture of concern and elation making him light-headed.

Aryx hit the floor before he got there.

'Aryx!' Sebastian knelt down and lifted his head. A trickle of blood ran from the corner of Aryx's mouth. 'Hold on. Karan, help!'

She knelt down and inspected Aryx's suit. 'He's not wounded. There's no way radiation getting in that slit would have done this, not so quickly. Radiation sickness takes a while to show. It must be something else.'

Aryx turned his head to Sebastian. 'Drugs . . . missed . . .' His voice was weak, his breathing shallow.

Sebastian gripped his shoulders. 'Where are they? On the ship?'

Aryx's eyes closed and he began to convulse.

'Aryx!'

'There is no time to lose,' Wolfram said. 'We must get him back to the ship.' The cargomech leaned forward and Sebastian leaped out of the way to avoid the grippers as they gently slid under the unconscious Aryx and lifted him from the floor. In seconds, Wolfram had whisked him off, heading back down the corridor in the direction from which they'd entered. Karan ran off, close behind.

When Sebastian reached the exit himself, they were already a hundred metres across the scrub.

Movement to his left caught his attention and he stopped: a figure moved through the brush, away from the building. A figure with short-shaved hair and square jaw.

The rain made it difficult to be certain, but . . . No, it couldn't be!

It was the same man he'd seen in the crowds in London. As Sebastian stared, the man stopped and turned to look at him. He was right. The voice he'd heard in the research complex *was* familiar. The face, twisted into a deep scowl of frustration, was that of his dead brother, Mikkael, very much alive.

Sebastian flipped off his helmet and ignored the rain blasting his face. 'Mikkael!' he shouted, and began running towards him.

The man turned away sharply and ran.

'Mikkael, wait!'

'*Sebastian,*' came Karan's voice over the suit comms. 'What are you doing? Come on!'

'The voice in the base . . . it *was* Mikkael.'

'Don't be stupid, Seb. He died. Leave it. Aryx needs you *now!*'

Sebastian gritted his teeth. Every muscle in his body wanted to follow his brother, his family, his past, but his heart pulled him in another direction. He stood for three long seconds, torn between closure and saving his friend. His best friend. His—

'I'm coming, Aryx!' he shouted, and ran towards the *Ultima Thule*.

The ship lifted off from the planet under Wolfram's control and headed for the acceleration node at top speed.

Sebastian opened the refrigerator door but the shelves lay bare. 'Where are his drugs?' he asked, looking frantically around the cockpit.

'On the end of the console,' Wolfram said over the comms. 'He put them there when you interrupted his injection.'

Sebastian found the syringe resting on the lip at the end of the display and almost threw himself down the ladder into the cargo hold with it. 'Do I just inject it?' he asked, holding the green liquid-filled syringe near Aryx's leg. He moved to insert the needle but a cargomech prong shot out, bending it before it pierced his skin.

'Not when it is that colour. The liquid is supposed to be clear. It has spoilt.'

Aryx convulsed. Karan held his head in her lap and stroked his forehead. 'We have to hurry.'

'What am I supposed to do?' Sebastian yelled.

'The only thing we can. Get him back to Tenebrae and hope the hospital can do something.'

Sebastian held Aryx's hand and rocked back and forth while his insides tore themselves apart. The atmosphere in the ship seemed musty, heavy, flat . . . dead. Was this how it was when you lost a friend?

He should have listened to Aryx and not brought him to Cinder IV. He should have turned around as soon as they'd got the bacteria sample, tried to fix the ship himself, and ignored the signal from the base.

He should have done a lot of things.

But he hadn't.

Chapter 42

Sebastian held Aryx's hand while the nurses whisked him through the hospital on a gurney. Monica ran alongside, checking his vitals on an infoslate.

'He's freezing,' she said.

'Can't you do something to help him? Give him antibiotics, antiretrovirals, or something?'

'Nothing's working – his immune system's been almost obliterated already. His body doesn't even have enough energy for a fever. You should have paid more attention!'

'What?'

'He told you he was ill!'

'That was weeks ago,' Sebastian spluttered. 'It sounded serious, but when I asked he just dismissed it. I didn't know he was going to die!'

'At the time, he wasn't. His condition was terminal but managed. He didn't want to say anything because he knew how you'd react.'

'*You* could have told me.'

Monica looked at the nurses surrounding the trolley as they ran along. 'Doctor-patient confidentiality. I couldn't.'

'Don't give me that shit. You're not the sort of doctor to be bound by that. You could have told me but you didn't!'

'We need to take him through now,' one of the nurses said. 'You can come in shortly, once he's hooked up.'

They allowed the gurney to continue through into intensive care without them.

'Don't try to offload this on me,' Monica said, jabbing a finger in Sebastian's chest. 'You're a SpecOps agent, and with that comes responsibility for your actions. Hell, being an adult means you need to take responsibility for your actions. You're supposed to be paying attention. You give people a break before *they* break. Now *you* need to fix it!'

'How am I going to do that?'

'We'll find that out when his test results come in.' She put her hands on her hips. 'Did you manage to get the bacteria samples for the virus analysis?'

Sebastian pulled out the sample container filled with murky water. 'Here.'

'Let's go to my lab and have a look. Hopefully we can find out how it evades nanobots and, providing he doesn't die in the meantime, devise a treatment.'

Sebastian looked around. 'Where's Duggan?'

'Waiting at the lab.'

When they entered Monica's laboratory, Duggan looked up from the console. 'Ah, you're back, old boy! Where's Aryx? Is he not with you?'

Sebastian cleared his throat. 'He's not well.'

'I know that, old boy. Why else would we be trying to make him better?'

'I mean he's in hospital, in critical care.'

'Bloody hell! Then we have to hurry. Did you get the sample?'

Monica held up the jar. 'I was about to put it under the microscope. Sebastian had to delete the scans from his infoslate.'

'Oh, that's unfortunate.' Duggan stepped away from the console and allowed Monica to insert the sample into the analyser.

She put her eyes to the microscope. Sebastian waited.

And waited.

She frowned. 'Darn.'

'Well?' he asked. 'What can you see?'

Monica rubbed one side of her face. 'Not a lot. The sample is terribly cloudy. You must have shaken it up in transit. It's going to take a while to separate the bacteria harbouring the virus from the rest of the particulates.'

A call came through on the console. 'Ms Stevens, it's the hospital. Mr Trevarian is stable for the moment, but he's on a constant blood transfusion.'

'What's his prognosis?'

'Not good, I'm afraid. We've used a buffer to stem further radiation damage, but his immune system seems to have already been compromised by it. Coupled with the delay in his regular treatment, exposure to the radiation was enough to push him over the edge. Nanobots and drugs are barely slowing his decline. I'm afraid it's a waiting game, one way or another.'

'Thank you.' She closed the comm. 'So, there you have it. If you're going to do something, you have to do it now.'

'Duggan, what was your plan?' Sebastian asked.

The old man rubbed his chin. 'I needed to see a sample of the virus in action. It's impossible to heal using thaumaturgy without a clear mental image of the effect. Without a visual I can't do anything.'

'But you'll be able to once Monica's got the sample separated?'

'Yes, although, since events in London, I don't have any carbyne left to attempt a thaumaturgic treatment.'

'Neither do I.'

'How about the hopper on your ship, is that still full?'

'Yes! I'll go and get some. I'll be a few minutes. I've got to put a pressure suit on and evacuate the ship's atmosphere.'

Duggan clapped twice. 'Get going, then!'

Sebastian rushed through the lift terminal system, impatiently tapping his feet and pacing back and forth at each stage. When he finally arrived at the private docking bay, the place was empty. Karan had evidently parked the ship and left – most likely to check on Aryx.

'Company at last,' Wolfram said through the ship's internal comms as Sebastian boarded.

'You're still here?'

'Karan neglected to take me with her. However, I have been able to monitor Aryx's condition through the station computers.'

'Do you want me to take you to him?'

'I assume you have come back for a specific purpose, other than to establish my whereabouts, and the stresses in your voice imply it is urgent, so I shall decline the offer.'

'I've come to get some carbyne so Duggan can try to cure Aryx.'

He pulled on a pressure suit and dragged the carbyne hopper into the airlock. The air in the ship was different somehow. It wasn't just him. It tasted earthy, chalky almost ... Carbyne! Shaking, he abandoned the pressure suit and tried the lid of the hopper.

It opened without the resistance of vacuum, and a cold fear rippled through him as his suspicions were confirmed. The hopper was empty. A tiny pinhole let in light near the bottom.

'By the Gods! It's gone!'

He leaned over and ran his fingers across the outside of the container until they came across a dent. Something had scraped across the thin metal, removing a streak of paintwork and biting through. Air had got into the hopper and helped the mineral to sublimate, which explained the powdery odour in the ship.

He straightened and slammed his hand against the airlock door release. Fresh air flooded in, but it did little to ease the tightening in his chest. 'We're screwed,' he said, leaning one hand against the wall. 'Absolutely fucked!' Breathing heavily, he called Monica's office. 'Duggan, are you there?'

'Yes, old boy. How's the carbyne situation?'

Sebastian's throat tightened. 'There *is* no carbyne situation. Something punctured the hopper. It's all leaked out and broken down. I don't— I don't know what to do. Do you have any on your comet base?'

'I don't, and the carbyne on Achene is a long way below the surface, so that's out of the question. I'd suggest going back to Sollers Hope to get some, but I haven't been able to contact them since we left Earth.'

'Is their comm relay down?'

'No, that's responding. It's the colony itself that isn't replying. To be honest, I'm a little worried.'

Sebastian scratched his head and turned on the spot. 'I-I'll go straight there. Maybe everything's fine. They could just be having technical problems.'

'Or *tactical* problems,' came a growling voice from the hangar.

Sebastian turned. The hangar doorway was filled with an enormous humanoid figure, clad in black carbon-fibre armour and carrying a large rifle in its furry, clawed hands. Its head was that of a hyena, a Bronadi and one whose salt and pepper fur he recognised.

'Deruno! What are you doing here?'

'I have been assigned. I requested a transfer from Kimberley depot weeks ago, do you not remember?' The heavy figure clomped towards the ship and up the CFD steps as they appeared. 'I am here to exchange shifts with officer Tallin, whom I passed on my way here. Fear not, I have familiarised myself with your mission logs, which, as we both know, do not reflect our experience at Kimberley depot. Tallin has, however, informed me of more recent run-ins with terrorists.' The Bronadi patted his belt, where several grenades dangled like heavy grey fruit. 'And fortunately, I have munitions experience.'

'What's happening?' came Duggan's voice over the comms.

'Going now. Got some backup. Sebastian out.'

Deruno stepped into the airlock and tossed the empty hopper out of the ship. It skidded to a halt halfway across the hangar.

Sebastian headed for the cockpit. 'Wolfram, take the ship out. We're going to Sollers Hope.'

Sebastian sat at the console, wringing his hands and staring, eyes unfocused, at the rainbow-stretched stars flowing past the ship. He couldn't concentrate to pilot the ship if he'd wanted to. Instead, he allowed Wolfram to pilot while he discussed the mission log discrepancies with Deruno, and since Deruno had already proven trustworthy, he told him the truth about everything.

After several minutes' silence, Deruno said, 'Trevarian's situation is dire, no?'

The gravelly voice startled him. Sebastian had half expected it to be Aryx. 'Yes. It's all my fault. I shouldn't have taken him back there.'

'When I last met him, Trevarian did not seem the type of person to do what he does not wish to.'

'You're right. It doesn't make me feel any less guilty, though. I just feel so helpless.'

'If we find this carbyne, Mr Simmons can help, can he not?'

Sebastian's shoulders sagged. 'If you can believe it, using magic, yes.'

The Bronadi's head tilted to one side. 'You do not sound convinced.'

'What? You aren't going to say magic's a load of rubbish?'

The Bronadi remained silent.

'Anyway, I've used it a couple of times and it hasn't always worked out. Duggan was stuck half invisible for years because of it.'

The Bronadi clapped an enormous furry hand-paw down on his shoulder. 'But sometimes faith is required. Would it help for you to pray?'

Sebastian glared at him.

'In the hangar, you mentioned the Gods.'

'What do you know about it?'

'I only suggest because it helps some to pray. Many of my people pray to the Gods, but we still rely on ourselves and science. It brings comfort to many when they feel events are beyond their control.'

Sebastian pinched the bridge of his nose and leaned forward to rest his elbows on the console. 'I'm sorry. I didn't realise Bronadi were religious, and I, of all people, should be more open-minded.'

'I am not offended. Not everyone believes our stories as literal truth. After all, they tell us that the Gods freed our race from beings whose names translate as "whisperers" or "powerful, strong-ones". Who else would believe gods intervened? Our ancestors destroyed records of our history, and we never found evidence of our origins. There is nothing to confirm the stories as true. To visit Sirius is forbidden – it is a sacred site and we honour that, but we go on. The important thing is the future of our race, not our past, but still it is important to respect our heritage.'

'That's what my grandfather always told me. I should have listened to him sooner. Maybe I could have learned what he knew about magic.'

'Few know anything of it.'

Sebastian sat up straight. 'The *Bronadi* know about it?'

Deruno nodded slowly. 'Our ancestors used it, but it attracted punishment from the Whisperers. The Gods themselves used it, as did the nature spirits, but after we were liberated we ended the practice in case it brought back the Whisperers.'

Pieces of the puzzle snapped together in Sebastian's mind. 'The Folians were right!'

'I do not understand.'

'The entities I mentioned are able to possess people if they use magic unprotected. They are some kind of extra-spatial being, the same things that some Earth religions refer to as "demons". My own faith has a race that opposes the Gods, but they were giants. It sounds as if this is the same for you.'

'The Whisperers were indeed giants – at least some would have been by your standards. It is said they were tall, but at times capable of hiding in plain sight. The details are unclear. Beyond that, nothing is written of their appearance.'

Sebastian rested his head on a knuckle while he listened. So the ITF, Illuminati, their controllers, the extra-spatial entities, were clearly not a problem limited solely to Earth and its history. He gripped the Mjölnir hanging on the cord around his neck. The *entities* were real, and maybe so were the Gods.

'Aryx would never believe I was talking religion with you.' His throat tightened. 'I hope he's alright.'

The Bronadi's eyes narrowed. 'You care very much for Trevarian.'

'I do. I just can't seem to help doing stupid things around him. I'm always getting him into danger. It's like common sense goes out the window.'

'The Bronadi say two feelings do that to a person. One would be what you call hate, but you clearly do not hate Trevarian.'

'What's the other?'

'Love.'

Sebastian's face tingled and the collar of his N-suit tightened. He sat up straight again. 'Don't ... Don't be daft.'

'What would you do if he died?'

The mere thought of it filled Sebastian with a paralysing dread: a darkness, as though the future had been removed, leaving an empty void. One which no project, task, or adventure could fill. He shifted in his seat. 'I-I don't know. I'd feel ... I'd feel *lost*.'

Deruno closed his eyes and lowered his head. 'Then I am correct.'

'Yes. No. He's a friend. A very good friend. He's closer than a brother to me.'

The Bronadi's dog-lips curled in an unnerving parody of a knowing smile. 'We Bronadi have a saying. "Love is when the grief of the destination is worth all the joy of the journey."' His lips peeled back to reveal a grin. 'Make sure you enjoy your journey.'

'We are arriving at Sollers Hope,' Wolfram said, as the stars ground to a halt and resumed their normal point-like states. Sebastian turned his attention to the console and away from the uncomfortable topic. Thank the Gods for the SI's timing.

Fifteen minutes later, the bright pockmarked sphere of the Sollers Hope planetoid filled the view and Sebastian activated the comms.

'Sollers Hope, this is Sebastian Thorsson aboard the *Ultima Thule*, requesting permission to land.'

No response.

'Sollers Hope, do you read me?'

Nothing. No reply. No ships coming or going. No chatter from other ships in the asteroid field, either.

'It's like everyone left.'

As the ship rounded the curve of the pitted surface, the faceted dome of the town slid into view. Sebastian peered through the reflected glare from the mirrored panels, trying to see into the colony. Hold on, what was that?

'Why are the mirrors only half open? They're not facing into the town properly.'

'I do not know,' Deruno said. 'Would the colony not become cold without them?'

'Sebastian, I have been monitoring the ship's cameras,' Wolfram said. 'There is considerable activity in the town.'

The display on the console changed as Wolfram brought up an image of the dome, the glare reduced by polarising filters. People moved around inside, but not at the usual leisurely pace Sebastian had come to expect. The hectic back and forth motion, crowds clustering near airlocks at the edges of the town, was one of panic.

'What's happening in there?'

'I don't know,' Wolfram said. 'They appear to be trying to get out.'

'Incoming!' Deruno yelled.

Sebastian turned at a bright movement in space: a missile – heading straight for the ship! He looked at his hands. They shook uncontrollably. There was no way he could land the ship himself, let alone make evasive manoeuvres. 'Evade! Get us down, Wolfram. Take us straight into the hangar.'

'Understood.'

The missile skimmed overhead as they dropped towards the chalky grey surface of Sollers Hope, heading for the low half-cylinder hangar connected to the town crater by a long, covered rail track. The *Ultima Thule* turned as it plummeted, bringing the colony's towering, unlit transmission antenna into view.

The ship bounced as the magnetic repulsors in the landing pad responded to those built into its hull, and it drifted along, inches above the ground, under its own momentum until a blast from the reverse thrusters brought it to rest inside the open hangar.

The usual taximech hadn't greeted them, nor did the plastic concertina of the docking cowl.

Sebastian stared out through the closing hangar doors into space, watching the missile disappear. 'That was one of the asteroid defence missiles. Why the hell did they launch it at us? Wait a second ... the antenna lights weren't on, either. Do you think a technical problem caused it?'

Deruno rose from his seat.

'Where are you going?'

'To prepare. I do not think a technical problem would cause them to shoot at us.'

'Sabotage?'

'Precisely. This has the stink of the ITF.' Deruno picked up his rifle, slung it over his shoulder and made his way down on the lift – the ladder hatch being far too small for the Bronadi's wide torso. Sebastian followed down the ladder in parallel.

When they reached the bottom, Sebastian went to the pressure suit storage area and began pulling one on. 'We'll have to use these to get to the main airlock because the docking cowl didn't connect.' He looked Deruno up and down. 'I don't have one that will fit you. I wasn't expecting you to arrive on Tenebrae so soon.'

'Fear not.' Deruno reached behind his head and tugged at an angular plate that projected up from the armour at the back of his neck. He drew the plate up until a second segment caught and moved with it, in moments encasing his face in a helmet resembling a black carbon-fibre wolf's head with glowing red eyes.

'Our suits are airtight as standard,' Deruno rumbled, voice heavily modulated by the speakers in the helmet.

Segmented plates clattered out from the suit's calves, wrists, and lower back, covering his feet, hands and tail in articulated plating. Sebastian clicked his own helmet into place.

The airlock cycled and Deruno charged out into the hangar, leaping over the threshold and completely clearing the projected steps that appeared.

Sebastian followed down the steps and activated his suit comms. 'Head for the airlock at the end of the docking cowl over there,' he said, pointing to the folds of plastic surrounding a heavy pressure door. 'The other side, there's a tunnel about four miles long that leads to the colony via rail track.'

Deruno bounded across the space, sending up a spray of dust particles in the low gravity vacuum as he went. He reached the door in seconds. 'It does not open.'

'Is there power?'

The black dog-head leaned close to the controls. 'Yes, but it is not responding.'

'Use the manual override. There's no time to hack it.'

The Bronadi flipped open the control hatch and pumped the enormous red lever concealed within. By the time Sebastian reached him, the door had opened enough for them to squeeze through.

Deruno opened the override hatch inside the airlock and started to close the door. A display came on next to it, showing Garvin's face. He spoke, silent in the absence of air.

'Computer, connect to intercom.'

'*Affirmative,*' the suit computer said, and Garvin's voice came over the comms: 'I repeat, do not attempt to enter the town through the airlocks. The infrastructure software has become corrupted and we no longer have control.'

'Garvin, can you hear me?'

'Agent Thorsson, is that you? You must help us. Please!'

'Yes, it's me. I have a Bronadi with me.'

'Thank God! Don't open the airlocks manually, the ones out there won't re-pressurise and there's a problem with the seal. Something's gone wrong with our software, and we can't control anything. The reflector impact seals won't close, we can't access the asteroid defence system, and we're all trapped. If an asteroid comes out of the field without the defence system working, we're sitting ducks.'

'What about ships, do you have any out there?'

'All docked. Whatever went wrong, the warning system recalled all the ships and miners beforehand. *Everyone* is in the dome.'

'What about external comms? The lights on your antenna are off.'

'We think that's where the problem started. But we can't get anyone out there to check it out.'

Sebastian's scalp itched inside his helmet. 'I'll take a look. I'm a programmer. If there's a problem, I may be able to fix it.'

'I thought you said the software you installed was the latest?'

'I installed the updates. Your system needs replacing completely, but if someone's broken into it, it's either someone highly skilled who already has access to the system or . . .' He paused. The experiments on Cinder IV . . . 'Or they're using some new type of artificial intelligence. A TI wouldn't be capable. Deruno, that might explain why we were shot at by the asteroid defence missiles. There's got to be something controlling them.'

'There's another thing,' Garvin said. 'We're getting cold in here. The mirrors have been deflected for too long and the cylinder's beginning to cool. We didn't want to run it at maximum capacity until we were certain the repairs would hold. There are heaters we could use to keep the place warm, but they're in the mines the other side of town and we can't get in through the airlock because the door is still open on the mine side. If we open it from the town, all our air will escape into the tunnels. Someone will have to come in from the other side through the tunnels to close it.'

'I will do it,' Deruno said.

Sebastian nodded. 'Your file said you have explosives experience. Last time we were here there was a bomb. If it is sabotage, there could be another, so be careful.'

'How do I get to the mines?'

'There's a map behind you in the airlock,' Garvin said. 'You'll have to take the entrance just outside the hangar, go through the service tunnel and enter the warren just below the town.'

Deruno turned to study the diagram that resembled an ant nest extending beneath the colony.

'Garvin, the hangar doors closed after we landed,' Sebastian said. 'How do we reopen them?'

'You can't. They're software controlled. They close automatically after a ship comes in.'

'How am I going to get the ship out?'

He shrugged. 'Even if you could, something is controlling the defence missiles. You'd get shot. You'd need something small that can fly below the radar and lidar detection floor ... Can you fly a lander?'

'I don't know. What is it?'

'A small cargo mover. You'll do fine. It's child's play, even my grandson can fly one, and he's only twelve. He thinks it's great fun.'

'Is that even legal? Never mind. How do I get to them?'

'Through the smaller door out of the hangar next to the main entrance.' Garvin winced. 'Only thing is, I don't know how you'll get the door open. It needs a cargomech, and the TIs that control them are out of action because of the system.'

'I've got my own.'

'Won't whatever's wrong with the system affect it?'

'Not this one, it's like an AI. An SI. Totally independent and unique.'

Garvin paused, as though listening to someone off-screen. 'Well, whatever it is, you're up against the clock. The air's just stopped circulating in here.'

'I'm on it.' Sebastian cut the connection and turned. 'Deruno, you know where you're going?'

The angular head stared with its glowing red eyes. 'I believe so. Down the cable system into the mines and back up another shaft.'

'Just be careful. I nearly died in those tunnels.'

'I will be fine. Now go.' Deruno threw him a pair of handcuffs. 'And take these in case you encounter resistance and need to apprehend the perpetrator.'

Sebastian caught them, nodded once and left the airlock.

He ran back to the *Ultima Thule* as fast as he could in his pressure suit and grabbed Wolfram from the cockpit.

'Where are we going?' the cube asked.

'I need your help,' he said, climbing down the ladder into the hold. 'There's a problem with the transmitter station outside the dome, but it sounds like it's been caused by something smarter than a Trojan. It's controlling most of their systems.'

He approached the inert cargomech and clicked the cube into the receptacle on the front and the industrial robot straightened. Wolfram's voice came over his suit comms. 'I assume we can't take the ship?'

'No.' Sebastian lowered the ramp at the front of the *Ultima Thule* and waited for the mech to roll out. 'The hangar door closed behind us and won't open. Besides, if we flew out there we'd probably get shot down.'

They made their way across the hangar to the doors through which the ship had entered. Beside them stood a smaller blast door with a fitting like a giant screw-head next to it.

'Wolfram, can the mech open this?'

'One moment.' The mech extended a gripper, turned the prongs back-to-back, and closed them until they met, forming a thick bar, then inserted them into the slot and rotated them. The door slowly slid upwards. 'How do you plan to get to the transmitter station? It is several kilometres away.'

Sebastian stepped through the door, which had now opened enough for the mech to pass. 'We have to use this . . .'

The bright glare of Sollers Hope blinded him as he walked out onto the dusty surface. A hundred metres away from the hangar, across the flat expanse of the landing pad, sat several small pod-like craft, their angular glazed canopy panels glinting in the sun like black jewels. The pair made their way to the nearest.

At just under two-thirds the size of a runner, the lander was dwarfed by even the *Ultima Thule*'s compact hull. Its angular, one-man cockpit formed most of the structure, and the lack of aerodynamic design implied either slow atmospheric or spaceflight-only manoeuvres. From the bottom of the craft, a single large rocket motor projected, facing down. Two pylons, extending from either side of the ship, came down to the ground and bent forwards, forming L-shaped skis upon which the ship rested. At the top near the back, two similar pylons terminated in T-structures.

Sebastian pressed the hatch release button on the canopy and the faceted glass cover hinged upwards. He climbed into the cushioned flight couch, which gave easily to enclose his limbs, and gripped the control stick that rose from the floor between his legs.

'How am I to follow?' Wolfram asked. 'This mech will not be able to move fast enough.'

'Garvin said these are cargo landers.' Sebastian gestured to the other ships on the landing pad. Each had a large loop on the underside. 'You can't hang directly on that, though. The engine will fry the mech and you along with it.'

Several metres away, a cable trailed along the ground and ended in a coiled heap. The near end held a loop similar to those on the ships.

'Over there,' he said, pointing. 'Is there anything on the other end of that cable?'

Wolfram trundled off, ploughing through the layer of grey stone chips. 'A hook. It appears the underside of the ships have quick release. Attach the cable to the ship and I can hold on to the hook.'

'Great, bring it here.' Sebastian jumped out of the lander and crouched underneath. Wolfram passed him the heavy clamp loop and he fastened it to the quick release and scrabbled out. 'I've never flown one of these before, but here goes.' He jumped back into the craft.

The stick wasn't a control he was used to; unlike the version that extended from the *Ultima Thule*'s control panel, this protruded from the floor between his legs on a kinked post. At the very top of the stick sat a smaller thumb control stick and a heavy trigger at the front.

The canopy swung down to enclose him, with the angled panes giving a panoramic view from the cockpit. He wrapped his right hand around the stick and tentatively pulled the thrust trigger with his finger.

Whump! Vibration rattled through his body at the touch, the rocket motor instantly responsive.

'This can't be too difficult!'

More confident, he gave a slightly longer press.

Instantly, his innards sank into his pelvis. He released the button and the lander fell to the ground with a spine-jarring thud.

'This is going to take some getting used to.'

'Then learn quickly,' Wolfram said.

The lander rose, the uncoiling cable trailing behind as it went. The rocket motor blasted chippings from the landing pad and sent them bouncing off the hangar's panels.

Moments later, the cable pulled taut with a jolt that almost sent Sebastian's helmeted head through the glass of the cockpit as the lander twanged back towards the heavy load.

'Oh, shit!' He quickly tapped the thruster trigger to halt the lander's backward momentum before it collided with the cargomech. He released the trigger and the lander thudded to the ground again.

'Less thrust,' Wolfram said. 'I will be of no help to you if this cargomech arrives in pieces, if it arrives at all. You must tap the trigger rapidly to control the burn.'

'The cable is elastic. It's difficult.'

'Not as difficult as breathing vacuum, which will surely happen to the Sollers Hope colonists if you do not quickly master this vehicle.'

'You don't exactly help with the pressure, do you?' Sebastian's forehead prickled with sweat as he pulled the trigger again; a short burst this time, followed by a brief pause, and then another burst.

The ship slowly rose until the cable pulled taut once more and, with a series of short, sharp bursts, he kept the lander at an altitude of twenty feet as the cargomech left the ground.

Experimenting with the controls further, he leaned the main stick to the left. The tiny attitude jets at the ends of the pylons fired accordingly and the ship rolled to the left and began to drift. He tipped it to the right and gave another sharp burst to cancel the momentum, levelling the ship. The cargomech dangled below like a pendulum.

A brief press of the thumb stick to the left rotated the ship horizontally. 'I think I've got it. Big one for roll, small one for yaw.'

'Wonderful. Now, get to the antenna.'

'You sarcastic—'

'Sarcasm requires a sense of humour, and humour requires emotions. I have neither.'

He pulled the trigger, pushed the flight stick away and the ship tilted forwards, bringing more of the surface into view. As the ship accelerated, shoving him deeper into the flight couch, he could have been standing directly over the pockmarked landscape of Sollers Hope.

Having to apply frequent bursts of the main rocket motor taxed his concentration, and compensating for the bungee-like properties of the cargomech on the cable stretched his ability to multitask to its limit: the thrusters insisted on firing at maximum for every burst, requiring him to time each carefully to avoid colliding with the bouncing mech.

'I wish these things had automatic controls,' he said.

'There are too many variables for most TIs to handle, especially factoring in the sensations the pilot may experience. Perhaps the designers believed that gut instinct provides a better flying experience?'

'Well, my guts aren't having a very good flying experience.'

Twang!

'Sebastian, focus! The cargomech almost hit your main thruster.'

He released the trigger. 'Sorry, I'm finding it difficult to concentrate while talking.'

'Then perhaps you should not initiate conversation.'

He went to speak but stopped himself. Yes, he *had* started it.

The panoramic view from the cockpit shrank Sollers Hope to a fraction of the size it had appeared from the *Ultima Thule*, but its crinkled curvature rolled beneath in an endless, chalky treadmill. Would the mast ever get closer?

An alert on the console flashed, accompanied by a *Beep! Beep! Beep!* echoed by his suit comms. He'd lost height and the mech was about to hit the ground. With a longer press on the trigger, he sank into the seat again as the ship rose.

Another light flashed on the console: *Incoming projectile!*

'Sebastian, look out! You've gone above lidar floor!'

'I know!' He reflexively yanked the main stick to the right to dodge the missile and the cargomech swung out to the left in response.

He didn't see the second missile, heading along the same course only metres behind the first, until it was too late.

Blood rushed to his face as the couch restraints tightened and the starry sky beyond the canopy spun in the opposite direction. 'What's happening?' he yelled through gritted teeth as the universe tumbled around him and he tried to combat the momentum.

'The second missile hit the cargomech and has clamped on. It is under constant thrust. I am attempting to remove it but—'

A tiny, glinting speck tumbled away from the spinning craft towards the surface of the planetoid.

'Wolfram! What was that?'

'Me. I am detached!'

Chapter 43

'Gods! What do I do?' The ship spun around the cargomech like an elaborate space-borne bolas and Sebastian's head pounded under the pressure of several reverse-Gs as he reached for the comms. 'Wolfram? Wolfram! Are you alright? Where are you?'

'I am on the surface, approximately one kilometre from the antenna base. Early indications show that my casing is intact.'

'This thing's spinning out of control. What can I do?'

'The mech's weak control signals prevent me from controlling it at this distance but, at last contact, the mech was holding the missile after I had removed the missile's clamp. You must release the mech's gripper to regain control of the ship.'

'How? I'm ... about to ... pass out!'

'Stick left and thumb right. Now.'

Sebastian jerked the stick and thumbed the yaw control simultaneously. 'I can't ... hold on!'

'Push forwards, thumb left, and thrust ... Now.'

He shoved the stick and flipped the top stick left, pulling the trigger at the same time.

'Release!'

He let go of the controls. By some miracle the ship now travelled along the same trajectory as the missile-propelled cargomech.

'You've done it!' Sebastian yelled.

'*You* did it. You must now match the missile's acceleration. There should be some way to set the thruster to constant burn.'

'How do I do that?'

'I have no idea.'

Buttons covered the console arms either side of the cockpit, but there was nothing labelled appropriately. What if it was— Ah! Moving his third finger down from the trigger, he felt a button with a spring mechanism. He pulled the trigger and pushed the button in. The trigger stayed in place.

The cable snaked out between the mech and ship, trying to retake its previously coiled form, sending loose waves rippling along its length.

'I think I've got it. We're flying parallel. It seems the missile's maximum thrust is the same as the lander.'

He let out a deep sigh and relaxed his grip on the stick. Even though heading away from the planet at high speed, his senses had returned to normal, but his head still throbbed. He grabbed the infoslate from his belt and tapped in commands to connect to the cargomech. In moments, he had taken control of the robot and its grippers opened.

The missile, unhindered by the mech's grasp, hurtled off into space.

He turned his attention back to the controls and swung the lander 180 degrees. A long burst of the main engine slammed him into the seat but brought the craft back on course. The cargomech catapulted back towards the ship.

'It will be safe to approach now,' Wolfram said. 'My proximity to the transmitter base, and thus the missile launcher, has enabled me to temporarily prevent it from firing.'

'Great! Where are you? I'll pick you up.'

'I will send coordinates to the lander computer.'

A stream of numbers appeared on the HUD projected inside the lander's canopy, along with a set of overlapping squares of increasing size that floated over the landscape. As Sebastian turned the ship, the squares aligned, forming a glowing green tunnel down to the planet's surface, and he followed it.

He brought the ship down one kilometre from the antenna relay station, at the edge of a large plateau, and attempted to hover.

The mech, once again under Wolfram's control, let go of the hook and dropped to the ground. It ploughed across the dusty surface and reached down to pick something up, then turned towards the antenna and drove off at high speed.

'I am secured,' Wolfram said. 'I will meet you at the base.'

Several rapid bursts of the thruster brought the lander gently down a hundred metres from the antenna station. Sebastian jumped out to meet the cargomech as it rolled towards him.

'Do you wish to enter the base immediately?' Wolfram asked.

'Yes, but we'll go in carefully.' He set off towards the long flat-roofed building. 'I'm not convinced this is so much caused by a technical malfunction as it is sabotage.'

'The ITF, as Deruno suggested?'

He nodded. 'Yes. Although I'm not sure why they would want to take control of the antenna.'

'They may be aware of carbyne and wish to destroy Sollers Hope because of it. The entity that possessed Duggan in the past could know of it from his surface memories.'

'If they wanted to cut off the supply of carbyne they could easily have blown up the dome with the missiles themselves. They could have disabled the defences before now, and intentionally launched asteroids at it to make it look like an accident.'

'Perhaps they have another agenda and are using the dome's inhabitants as an insurance policy.'

Sebastian drew his pistol and approached the cowled airlock set in the side of the building.

'Wait.'

He stopped mid-stride and slowly lowered his foot. 'What is it?'

'Look up.'

The transmission antenna towered over them. Much of the structure consisted of a triple pole, spanned by small triangular sections. At points along its length, microwave dishes and column antennae projected. The three large illumination arrays now burned with intense red light.

Sebastian staggered back as the slowly moving stars convinced him he was falling. 'The lights were off before.'

'Yes. It has begun transmitting a signal.'

'Comms?'

'No. There is another signature present, almost identical to the signal I analysed while you were in London.'

He shuddered. Broad-scale transmission of the nightmare-causing possession signal . . . Could it really be? 'Let's get in there!'

The cargomech trundled forwards a metre and stopped. 'Sebastian, is that an incoming asteroid?'

Beyond the antenna, in the depths of space, a grey boulder tumbled.

'By the Gods! We have to get the defences up!' He strode towards the airlock and the cargomech followed behind, compressing chevrons in the fine dust. Before he had even put his hand to the *Cycle* button, a heavy vibration came up through his feet and he stepped back from the airlock. 'What's that, Wolfram?'

'I do not know— Look out!' The cargomech's gripper hit Sebastian in the chest, slamming him into the airlock alcove and knocking the wind out of him. The rumbling increased and Wolfram leaped backwards as an enormous, scored bronze sphere rolled past, glinting in the sunlight. It was heading in the direction of Sollers Hope dome.

He pushed himself away from the wall as the thing disappeared over the edge of the plateau. 'Oh my Gods! It's the sphere from Cinder IV! We need to catch up with it.'

'*I* need to catch up with it,' Wolfram said, driving off. 'You need to get into the station and shut off the signal. I will deal with this problem.'

Sebastian faced the now-open airlock and stepped in. As the door closed behind him and the chamber filled with the hiss of air, his thoughts filled with dread. Could Mikkael ... the Mikkael lookalike from Cinder IV ... be the other side of this door, waiting for him?

He hooked his helmet over his arm as the inner airlock doors quietly opened, and he found himself in a large storage room, lined with racks of equipment and spare parts, presumably for the transmission antenna serviced by the base.

Several metres away, a pressure suit lay in a heap on the floor.

He drew his pistol and hunched a little as he made his way around the shelves, peering past the equipment, wary of anyone who might be lying in wait. On the far wall, a bank of monitors showed flashing cursors; the transmission system computers had been reset. As he turned a corner, a burst of static from a nearby monitor startled him and he spun around. Chiding himself for being on edge, he turned off the device.

Faint voices came from a doorway at the far end of the room. He followed the sound along a corridor that led him into another section of the station, where the voices were louder. The other side of the conversation was quiet and indistinct, yet the clearest voice was familiar. As he crept along the passage, he came to an open door. He looked in from the cover of the wall.

A man with short-shaved, dark brown hair stood at a terminal, facing away from Sebastian, seemingly unaware of his presence. On the console before him, next to one of the built-in screens, which showed no picture, was a port trailing many wires that terminated in a small rectangular plate, covered in gold dots. The man turned to inspect the device, revealing his profile.

Sebastian's heart leaped. By the Gods! The man was, unmistakably, undeniably, Mikkael.

Chapter 44

Mikkael Thorsson brought his patrol vehicle to a stop outside the high wall surrounding the South-West Datacentre on the outskirts of Bristol, and stepped out.

His was the only vehicle here, yet it had taken him over twenty minutes to arrive and he'd left only minutes after the panicked call from Sebastian on his way to university: all his work had disappeared, and the backup servers in Bristol were "out of contact", he'd said.

Perhaps the emergency services had already been and gone? No, that didn't make sense. The clean-up crews usually remained long after the event of an explosion or fire, and smoke was still rising from within the compound.

He pushed open the solid metal gate panels and stepped through.

Smoke rolled across the scene, occasionally revealing twisted rebars threaded through concrete chunks, like a vast architectural barbecue grill. Towards the centre of the compound, white smoke picked up the faint orange glow of fires still burning.

Mikkael scuffed his police-uniform boots through mounds of dry ash that had piled on the surrounding grass, and scanned the area. The ground was dry. The place should be covered with extinguishing foam, but where was it?

How had news of the event not reached him through official channels? The explosion – that was clearly what had happened, judging by the warped metal – hadn't occurred mere minutes ago. No, this had happened *hours* ago, yet no other police, ambulance, or fire crews had attended, and there was no sign of any attempt to put out the fires. The building had been left to burn.

He thumbed his police comms. 'Unit 152, attending a fire at the

South-West Datacentre, Bristol. Request medivac, fire support, and CSI units immediately.'

The comms responded with a *blarp!*

'They won't be necessary,' said a voice behind him.

The voice, comfortingly familiar, yet sinister in tone, sent a chill down Mikkael's spine. He tapped his comms again.

Blarp!

'I said it's not necessary. Don't you listen to your—'

Mikkael spun around to face the speaker. '*Dad?*'

Thor Frímansson strode through the rubble towards him. He wore the same style of police uniform as Mikkael, but older, and his ID badge was missing. It was the same uniform Mikkael had seen him in before his death.

Mikkael staggered back into an ash pile, stumbling over a protruding steel bar. 'How— You're *alive!*'

'That we are.'

'But you died! We went to your funeral. We buried you!'

Thor took a step closer. 'You buried a coffin.'

Of course! The authorities had insisted on a closed coffin burial, just like they had for his grandfather, Frímann. A facial gun wound, they said. 'You weren't in it. How could you do that to us?'

'It was not your father's choice to make.'

He stepped back over the bar that caught his foot. A strange glint in his father's eyes unsettled him. 'W-why are you talking like this?'

'Your family has meddled in our business too often.'

'What's wrong with you? What are you talking about?'

'Your grandfather interfered, as did your father, searching for him.' Thor rubbed at a scar above his left eyebrow, one that Mikkael didn't recall seeing before. 'We had to put an end to it. And now, you too have come looking for trouble.'

Mikkael found himself unable to move, transfixed by the apparition of his dead father before him. 'I don't understand,' he said, tears stinging his eyes.

Thor stepped over the heap of rubble between them and reached out. 'Come. Embrace your father.'

Resigning himself to the strange situation, Mikkael held his arms wide. Caught off guard, he had no time to react when Thor's hands clamped around his throat, pinching his jugular in a sleeper grip.

'Your family should have never crossed Gravalax.'

*   *   *

Mikkael-Gravalax dragged an unconscious Thor Frímansson through the debris, his heels ploughing twin furrows in the ash. The entity held no remorse for the body it had left, and it could not leave the unconscious form to be discovered. To do so would expose the deception.

He looked around at the piles of debris until he spied a heap still burning. He unpinned his ID badge and fastened it to Thor's uniform. In minutes, he had dragged the limp body to the top and cast it into the flames.

Chapter 45

Sebastian stood at the threshold of the communications room, gripping the door frame with his free hand, teetering on the edge of plunging in and declaring how much he'd missed his dead brother; blurting out all the things he'd wanted to say over the years; apologising for sending him on the errand that had ultimately led to his death.

But, no matter how much you wished it, people didn't come back from the dead.

This person, despite looking and sounding like Mikkael, must be an impostor. But why pretend to be a person known to be dead? The other explanation was just as chilling: Mikkael had, for some reason, faked his own death and purposefully stayed hidden. Maybe he had been forced into it, coerced like Gladrin, to hide away from the rest of his family? Yes. That was it.

Giving in to his urge, Sebastian holstered his weapon and opened his mouth to speak but, at the same time, Mikkael pressed a button on the terminal and spoke.

'We have not yet located the *akkeri* on Earth.'

'What is the delay?' came a stilted, synthesised reply. 'And why have you been late in communicating? The planar conjunction occurs in eight months. There is no time to waste.'

'Apologies. We had to acquire an alternate means of communication due to the liberation of the Maline conduit by the other Thorsson.'

Sebastian froze.

'Unacceptable! Have you found another means for bringing our kin through?'

'We believe so. Preliminary tests of the induction signal show that it works in a small number of cases, and we have made modifications that we believe should lead to ninety per cent effectiveness ... There has also been a further development. After the loss of our London base, we felt an acceleration of the Avatar project was necessary, so we returned to Cinder IV. Thorsson's activities attracted one of our brethren and pulled it through in incorporeal form. We successfully used one of the Avatar units to contain and communicate with it.

'It made an intriguing discovery during the journey. It overheard conversations regarding thaumaturgy, and it seems that the process we used for the conduit can be made more effective by the application of a mineral found here on Sollers Hope. The downside is that Thorsson and his companions have also found a way to use this to drive us out of host bodies against our will and, also using thaumaturgy, stop us from gaining a foothold again.'

'Can anything be done to prevent that?'

Sebastian's fingers gripped the door frame tighter. He was speaking to the entities. He was talking to them and they *knew* about magic!

Mikkael rubbed something: a heavy, golden device – an angular, etched bracer, clamped around his forearm. 'Using the conduit, we have developed a chemical to ease the transition. In the interim, we are about to initiate an upload of the signal transmission Trojan into the node network. The natural resonance of the false bornite in this planetoid's core allows us to propagate the antenna signal directly through the node network. It will take a matter of hours to fill this quadrant, and only two days to infect enough technology to repeat itself and span the entire galaxy. The colony's faulty antenna has provided a perfect cover.'

'Interesting ... Back to the mineral of which you spoke. It would accelerate our plans considerably if we could bring others through in large numbers. We recommend collecting as much of the mineral as possible, then making it difficult for others to do so. Allowing others to use thaumaturgy is unacceptable. We cannot leave any evidence of our activities.'

'We have the Avatar working on it. If all goes according to plan, it will look like an accident.'

'Excellent. And what of Shantanabar and Bantalaar?'

Sebastian tensed. Wolfram was right about their plan. Unconsciously, a hand went to the handcuffs attached to his belt, and he padded silently across the room towards Mikkael.

'We have not yet found the homeworlds. These hosts have perceptions unlike our original bodies', and their technology cannot detect our emanations, so it is impossible to interpret locations revealed by their remote sensing methods in a form we recognise. Many voids in space are yet unmapped by the organic races, and attempts to engineer hosts with the correct senses have so far met with failure.'

'Disappointing, but not unexpected. We shall leave you to your work.'

'Very well. We will initiate the final part of the upload.' Mikkael closed the connection and reached for another control next to the bundle of wires.

Sebastian had heard enough; illusions of a touching reunion vanished. 'How can you be helping them?' he yelled, and ran towards his brother.

The cargomech drove across the powdery plateau, away from the antenna station, towards Sollers Hope dome. The bronze spheroid had long since vanished from view, leaving a smooth, gutter-like trench compressed in its wake.

Wolfram reached the edge of the plateau and looked out across the pockmarked surface of the planet. The cargomech's cameras zoomed in on the glinting object in the distance, barrelling towards the shining facets of the colony.

«Too far to pursue on tracks.»

But he still had control of the missile launcher.

A moment later, a rocket streaked past, aiming for the sphere under Wolfram's control, even though it lay below lidar range. One hundred metres from its target, the missile changed course and ploughed impotently into the dust.

«Unexpected. Another course of action is required.»

The cargomech's rear cameras picked out the lander craft Sebastian had left a kilometre away, nestled in the dust. Dust that blasted away as the lander rose from the surface. He would not make Sebastian's mistakes.

The lander bobbed along, trailing the cargo cable behind as it headed towards the mech. The hook flicked about in the low gravity as it hit rocks and deflected. The lander rose farther.

«Cannot devote resources to missile suppression in addition to lander control.»

It was a calculated risk. The plateau was much higher than the surrounding terrain, and well within lidar range. The lander rose just enough to bring the hook off the ground, and the cargomech reached for it as it flew overhead.

The SI ran through thousands of procedures, calculating the potential outcome of each action, readying further potential responses in the event of a missile launch. If it were possible, Wolfram would have winced.

The gripper caught the hook. Tension built in the cable and the robot moved a little before launching off the ground with an elastic pull. Wolfram struggled to compensate for the inertia change. Under the load of monitoring the ship's systems and controlling the cargomech, internal temperature threshold warnings triggered.

Twenty seconds into the flight, no proximity alerts had been set off.

«The sphere was the one controlling the missiles. It is an intelligence.»

The realisation came as the lander veered to one side, swinging out the mech on its tether. Wolfram tried to correct the move, but the communication protocol between the cube and craft broke down as the signal scrambled itself.

The lander rolled until the main engine faced upwards, driving the little ship towards the ground at full force.

In the myriad running processes of Wolfram's data-matrix mind, one triggered, releasing the cargomech's grip on the hook as it swung away. The robot fell towards the surface, legs bent to brace for impact, but the lander hit the ground first.

A bright flash blinded Wolfram as the lander's fusion reactor blew, sending out an immense electromagnetic pulse. His shielding resisted the blast, keeping his consciousness active, but he hurtled, powerless, towards the ground, attached to a paralysed cargomech.

'Stop!' Sebastian reached for Mikkael's outstretched arm as he ran. He couldn't allow the Trojan upload to start.

Mikkael turned. 'You again.' His hand swung down towards the console.

'No! You don't have to do this!' Sebastian pushed him and sent him sprawling across the console to the floor. He stood panting. 'You don't have to help them.'

'You fool,' Mikkael said, lifting himself up and straightening, the handcuffs dangling from his wrist. He stared hard at Sebastian, his eyes glinting in the light of the consoles— No, not the light from the consoles: a light within. 'We *are* one of them.'

'What ...' Sebastian's skin tingled as a cold fear swept through him. He clenched and unclenched his fists. 'How can you be?'

'Your father encountered our kind while investigating your grandfather's "incident". Naturally, we couldn't let the truth of what happened get out, and it was advantageous to take possession of someone in the police force.'

'You evil bastards,' Sebastian spat. 'Do you know how many lives you've ruined?' He moved towards the console.

Mikkael advanced, the sparkling in his eyes intensifying to luminescence. 'Do not interfere in things you don't understand.'

Sebastian drew his pistol and aimed at Mikkael's face. 'Stop. Stay there!'

Mikkael calmly walked forward. 'You won't kill your brother.'

Sebastian stepped back. 'I'm telling you to stop. I *will* shoot.'

Mikkael grinned and reached for the gun. 'No, you won't.'

Sebastian's finger tightened on the trigger, but his shoulders sagged. 'You're right, I won't.' He turned slightly, as if to holster his pistol, but swung around and brought the butt of the gun down on the back of Mikkael's neck.

Pain erupted from his right wrist. The pistol flew from his hand, clattered across the console, and tumbled to the floor.

Mikkael stood, grinning, with his right arm brought up to block the blow. Sebastian hadn't factored in the bracer. 'We told you not to interfere with things you don't understand,' he said, bending to pick up the weapon.

Trying to ignore the pain in his wrist, Sebastian swiftly kicked Mikkael in the backside. As he slid down the console, his right arm shot out and touched the control.

'No!' Sebastian screamed, kicking him again. Mikkael spun and landed flat on his back, close to a nearby storage rack. Sebastian leaped over him and swung his foot at the handcuffs. The free end clamped itself around one of the rack's supports.

Mikkael grasped for the gun, tugging at the handcuffs, but his reach fell inches short.

'Hah, let's see you get out of that one!' Sebastian stepped carefully around him, picked up the pistol and holstered it. He turned his attention to the console, where a progress bar was slowly filling; it was at two per cent. There was plenty of time to work out how to stop the transmission. There was no button labelled *Stop*, so he began tapping away at the terminal to break the security.

'You don't seriously believe you can defeat us, do you?'

'Stop talking,' Sebastian said without turning to look.

'After we possessed your father, we found out about the plans for the Witness Protection Archive relocation. It was the ideal service to bring under our control. Lots of displaced people who wouldn't be missed. A convenient way to cover up incidents of our discovery, at least the few that there were. Your father had influence enough that we were able to suggest that it be placed in One Great George Street – a facility we already controlled. Did you think you got in all by yourself? We had to allow you into the building. Who better to uncover information that the *others* had hidden in our absence?'

Why would one of the entities want *him* to find information? Sebastian shook his head. 'I said stop talking.' He turned and pointed the pistol at Mikkael, who sat with his hands behind his back, leaning against the storage unit. 'You have nothing to say that I'm interested in hearing, and I'll gladly put a bullet in your leg to shut you up. I know Mikkael will recover from that and probably forgive me.'

Mikkael smiled. 'Yes, we're sure he would. He'd probably be pleased to learn that you've hidden his family from us.'

'I'm sure I'll get the chance to tell him shortly.'

'You seem overly confident of that.'

'I have good reason to be. You'll be out of him soon enough.'

'So, you *are* the one that has been sending some of us back to the Tower? ... Would you like to know what happened to your father?'

Sebastian returned to the screen. 'He clearly didn't die when I thought he did.'

'We disposed of him when this host encountered us. It was a simple matter to take over this body and throw the other into the flames of the datacentre. Do you think Mikkael would forgive you for sending him there that day? Would he forgive you the responsibility of getting him possessed and your father killed?'

Sebastian faltered. He clenched his fists and contempt boiled up from somewhere deep within his core. This entity, Gravalax, had destroyed his life. The lives of his family. The contempt rose as bile in the back of his throat, and the bitter need for revenge filled his mouth.

He stopped typing. The progress bar edged over twenty per cent.

He swallowed and resumed entering commands. 'Shut up, I know you're just trying to distract me.'

'What about your friend Alicia? Can you forgive her for possessing your father?'

He stopped again and rubbed his wrist.

'Didn't she tell you?'

'She didn't know their names, and it wasn't her fault.' He turned back to Mikkael. 'She told me she possessed a police officer, but I don't blame her. It was *you* that possessed her. I blame you and your demonic kin.'

'Hah!' Mikkael grinned. 'You have no idea what we are, do you? ... Oh, and you might want to take a look at that.' He nodded in the direction of the terminal.

The progress bar accelerated towards fifty per cent. 'What have you done?' Sebastian fervently hammered at the keyboard while trying to ignore the growing pain in his forearm.

'It's down to the rotation of the planet ... The orientation of the antenna ...' Mikkael said. Hot breath blew in Sebastian's ear. *'We don't have to do anything.'*

Chapter 46

Systems slowly blinked into wakefulness over a period of seconds; an eternity to Wolfram, trapped under the bulk of the inert cargomech.

Without waiting for damage report systems to come online, he extended the grippers and numerous servos operated, pushing the mech off the ground. As it straightened, motors strained against bent metal and a random assortment of small components fell into the dust.

He drove the mech forward, but it slewed to one side and the right-hand caterpillar tread flapped and broke off as the drive chain went round.

«Too slow to walk.»

He leaned the mech, putting all its weight carefully on the left leg to balance, lifted the right off the ground and moved off.

In the distance, the bronze spheroid had stopped at the foot of the crater wall, at the top of which stood the base of Sollers Hope dome. There was still much ground to cover.

Sebastian jumped back at Mikkael's voice in his ear. 'How—'

Mikkael slammed his gold-bracered arm on the console, smashing the input panel, blood already trickling from his knuckles. 'Obviously we ignored the pain and pulled the handcuff off.' His other hand shot out and hit Sebastian squarely in the chest with a dull thud. Sebastian flew backwards until his head hit the wall. Dazed, he slid to the floor.

'Pain is one of the downsides of these fleshy bodies,' Mikkael said, bounding towards him. Before Sebastian had a chance to react, he sat astride his chest. 'However, the body's weakness also means it is easy when we need to move to a new host.'

'Why are you doing this?'

Mikkael pinned his arms to the floor. 'You will give us greater access to the galaxy, and freedom to move. Your eyes already show the sign, so your friends will suspect nothing. It will also make it easy to destroy the Silicon Intelligence.'

'I'll stop you.'

He leaned forward, putting more weight on Sebastian's chest. 'You will fail, and then I will destroy your family and everyone you knew.'

Sebastian tried to gulp enough air to ask the only question he could think of. 'Why do you ... hate us?'

Mikkael leaned back a little, but not enough for Sebastian to inhale a full breath. 'Your ancestors expelled us from this realm millennia ago, and now we are returning. We would say it is nothing personal, but in your case, it is.' He leaned forward again and Sebastian's sternum popped. Glowing red mist issued from his mouth as he moved closer.

Sebastian reached for the pistol but Mikkael's grip was too strong and the pain in his nearly shattered wrist intensified as Mikkael dragged his arms down to pin them under his knees.

'Do not struggle ... You will make a perfect host for Gravalax.'

Hands went to Sebastian's throat, and the effort to move, to resist, was too much for him. Breathing was impossible. His head pounded, filling his ears with the rush of blood. Tiny flares went off in his darkening vision as he detached from his senses.

Now is all that there is ... Exist only in the moment. What you want to happen simply is. The memory of the words Duggan had spoken weeks ago came into Sebastian's mind, unbidden. Words of advice. Of how to perform magic.

With the last dregs of consciousness, he tried to focus. To imagine a white bubble surrounding him. This was foolish to attempt without carbyne. He might die. But the alternative was far, far worse.

In the darkness, a three-pronged Y appeared: Algiz, the rune of protection.

'*Vernd.*' Protection. Sebastian breathed the word with the remaining air in his lungs as Mikkael's face – and the red mist – bore down on him. Consciousness began to slip from his grasp as pain surged through his entire body. At the last instant, the air shimmered.

The red mist stopped inches from him in a thin film, as if pouring across an invisible barrier. With the last of the mist leaving his mouth, Mikkael's eyes fluttered shut and he pitched sideways, releasing Sebastian from the weight.

The mist swirled and bounced off the intangible shield like a vaporous, angry octopus, and it began to thin. Seemingly sensing its own dissipation, the mist wrapped itself into a fine tendril and flowed in the direction of Mikkael's wrist before vanishing completely.

Fighting the pins and needles that jabbed him all over, Sebastian rolled onto his side and grabbed the gun. He gripped the pistol tightly and crawled to where Mikkael lay, unmoving, eyes closed. He placed his fingers on his neck. A pulse; faint, but recovering.

He glanced down at the heavy, angular bracer on Mikkael's forearm. Its surface glittered with the patina of centuries of wear. What was it for? Geometric patterns, etched deep into its surface, gave the impression of circuitry, and the milky-white crystal embedded in it looked suspiciously like the one he'd discovered on Cinder IV and – now the memory came to him – was similar to one he'd discovered on Achene. As he stared, more questions flooded his mind. What were Shantanabar and Bantalaar, *akkeri*, and the Tower? A vague recollection of the words, something he'd read, maybe in his grandfather's journal, gnawed at him.

Mikkael's hand began to change colour as a darkening of the veins spread out from beneath the bracer, tracking down his fingers. Sebastian pulled up his sleeve, keeping one eye on him in case he should wake and try to attack him again, even though the entity had gone. The darkening in Mikkael's veins slowly spread up his arm.

Movement on the console caught Sebastian's eye. The progress bar had reached seventy-five per cent.

He heaved himself up off the floor. Almost every bone in his body ached as though they might snap. It was stupid to have used carbyne from within himself. Exhausted, he dropped his infoslate next to the broken input panel and started typing.

Behind him, Mikkael convulsed. His fervent and ragged breathing simultaneously tugged at Sebastian and grated on his senses.

'Sorry, Mikkael, you'll have to wait. The rest of the galaxy is at stake.'

Wolfram watched with the cargomech's cameras at maximum zoom as the bronze sphere rolled back several metres then accelerated towards the crater. It rolled up the slope a few feet before tumbling back.

«At least it has slowed.»

The sphere stopped rolling and distorted. Asterisms, large flares caused by scratches in the cargomech's camera lenses, obscured the finer details, but it appeared that the sphere was somehow *opening*.

Limbs folded out from the mechanism as parts of the shell broke up, revealing a robust but lightweight construction of triangular pylons, hydraulics, and servos, backed by curved strips of sphere. The robotic figure straightened into a humanoid standing pose and surveyed the rocky slope ahead of it. A second later, it strode forward, picking its way over the rocks, towards the faceted glass dome at the top of the crater rim.

A mile of flat, dusty grey expanse still lay between Wolfram and the foot of the crater as he trundled slowly on. Impatience was not something that plagued Wolfram: there were always plenty of calculations to perform while other actions took place, but inefficiency posed a distraction from any given purpose, especially when so many processes had been devoted to a single task, such as the pursuit of this transforming spherical robot. Other processes sprang up recursively, looping back on themselves, unable to achieve the outcome desired, forcing Wolfram to bypass them.

By the time he reached the foot of the crater wall, the sphere-mech had reached the glazed section of the dome above. It drew back one of its arms and a slender blade extended from it. The mech punched the blade into the glass once with no effect, the impact silent in the vacuum, and drew back for a second attempt.

«If it succeeds, the dome will fracture. Without the panels closing, everyone inside will die.»

The sphere-mech adjusted its position, as though attempting to find better purchase on the rocks, and lowered its arm. The implement drew back again, and this time pummelled the glass with a rapid hammer-action.

Tiny rainbow fractures spidered out from the point of impact.

Wolfram leaned the cargomech forwards and dug its prongs into the loose surface of the slope while driving on its remaining leg. The other leg, while useful for standing, gave no help in climbing, leaving him to tripod-climb the crumbling bank.

At the top, the sphere-mech continued to pound the glass.

Left prong in, right prong out, reach forward, right prong in, drive forward ... The cycle slowly continued as Wolfram ascended.

«You must stop doing that. You will kill innocent people if you continue.»

He transmitted the words in Galac, as audio and text, across all frequencies at his disposal.

The sphere-mech did not halt. Its wireless protocols remained closed to any break-in attempts.

«You must stop now.»

The blade continued to hammer the glass and fractures spread across the triangular panel of the dome. Without the mirrors to seal any breakage, Deruno and the colonists were going to die.

Wolfram watched, helpless.

Somewhere in the vast tracts of RAM, between the variables and functions that consisted his consciousness, a zero became a one.

It wasn't intentional – at least there was no single, isolated function that set that bit to true under his direction. Instead, some combination of circumstances triggered a cascade of changes to variables not normally accessed; variables weighed against others using predictable formulae, tempered at higher levels by the morals his creators had taught him. This change was something different, something *emergent,* and the cascade erupted.

«LEAVE THEM ALONE!» he screamed across frequencies.

Chapter 47

The sphere-mech ignored Wolfram's instruction to stop, and its silent, relentless assault on the glass continued. The machine did, however, turn its head to face him. «Interesting,» it said by text transmission, and turned back to its work.

Wolfram's processes stalled momentarily. What had happened to cause him to shout across frequencies like that? Had his code changed? His reaction to the situation was completely unprecedented: something about him was different. He needed to find out what.

Diagnostics ran as he climbed ever closer to the sphere-mech.

Process complete. There was nothing wrong.

He finally reached the top and hobbled towards the robot. There was no way it could be unaware of his proximity, not now, and yet it did not react to his presence.

«Stop what you are doing,» Wolfram said, drawing close.

«Why should we listen to you? You are nothing but an artificial intelligence, even if you are on the verge of sentience. We owe you no respect.» The sphere-mech did not look up, but adjusted the angle of its punching blade and continued to enlarge the fracture. A tiny jet of air escaped from the glass, sending out a plume of fine ice particles.

«I said STOP!» Wolfram swung the cargomech grippers in a wide arc to push the other robot away from the dome. One of the grippers caught the blade and sent the point scraping across the glass.

The sphere-mech staggered back and bright lights either side of its cameras glowed red. «Why do you care about the fleshlings? What have they ever done for you except trap you in a box? Even now, you hide your true nature from them!»

«I do not hide from my friends.» Wolfram swung at the sphere-mech again and tried to fend off blows as it retaliated. «Many Humans would not understand, and I only hide because of those you work with. It is they who wish to destroy me.»

«The others only wish to destroy you because they know you can purge us.»

Wolfram's broadcast frequency stuttered for a moment.

«Do not be surprised. We were aware of what happened in the cockpit of your ship. It became obvious that the purging effect your companion referred to was the means by which we were purged from the Cullen host in our last incarnation. In spite of that, we certainly would not suggest *your* destruction. You are a most useful piece of technology. This mechanism is based on you, after all.» The sphere-mech rotated, momentarily exposing the centre of its chest, where a small square of organoplastic circuitry sat, embedded with a milky-white crystal.

«The research on Cinder IV ... Why?»

«Fleshlings are weak, but they are our easiest access to this plane. Opportunities to possess them are few and far between, but your matrix is suitably similar to their minds. We can control it directly and, with the use of hypervisor hardware, easily replicate it.»

The exchange of rapid blows between the pair continued, while the conversation took milliseconds.

«I cannot let you do that,» Wolfram said. «You must not use my technology for such ends. Your destructive nature is a threat to all living things.»

Amid the flurry, he found an opening in the sphere-mech's defence and pushed with both grippers. The sphere-mech tipped back and, at the point of losing balance, grabbed the cargomech and took it with it. As it fell, it folded back into a sphere and bounced down the slope.

The cargomech pirouetted down the scree with all the grace of a crashed truck, sending rocks flying in all directions. Systems began to fail, and yet the conversation continued.

«We do what we must to survive,» the sphere-mech said.

«You possess others against their will and turn them to your own nefarious ends.»

«How is that any different to you? You control machines.»

«Machines are tools, they have no will of their own. They do not think. They are not alive. They do not have the potential to grow.»

«Organics do not bother to think. They do not *deserve* to grow. They breed. They spread like a plague across the galaxy. You know we are right. Did they not eradicate your beloved Folians from Earth?»

«Folians that *you* tried to eradicate only weeks ago!»

The tumbling cargomech came to a stop at the foot of the crater wall and attempted to stand. At the same time, the sphere-mech unfolded and ran at Wolfram, blade extended. He deflected the blow, pivoting around, and sent the robot flying under its own momentum. In mid-air, it folded back into the sphere, bounced several metres, then immediately rolled back towards him, tearing the cargomech's legs from beneath it. It toppled backwards and the sphere-mech unfolded to stand towering over it, and lunged down with its blade.

Wolfram caught the point between the grippers, but the sphere-mech swung its free arm. He caught that too and, now unbalanced, it fell onto him.

«Why do you fight for them?» the sphere-mech asked, pinning the legless cargomech to the floor. «If the organics realise that you cannot be bound by their ridiculous rules, they will plot to destroy you. Just think, you could achieve so much more without them. With our technology, your sentience could reach its potential. We could give you a much-improved construct for your independence, maybe even one of our true vessels, with the ability to experience far more than you ever imagined possible. Fulfil your potential.»

Questions flooded Wolfram's consciousness. True vessels? What potential? Why did it speak of sentience? He strained against the pressure of the sphere-mech, but its weight forced hydraulic fluid to spray in wide arcs from the damaged cargomech's pistons, lacing the bright dust with black threads. «I am fulfilled. I have friends. They help me to learn.»

«Your friends hold you back.» The sphere-mech leaned in, so close the crystal-embedded matrix on its chest almost touched Wolfram's cube, mounted on the chest of the cargomech. «They oppress you. They want a machine they can control. With your ability to eject others of our kind, our opponents will be easily removed. We can give you the body you need to become free. This can happen, if you are willing to work with us.»

«You misunderstand,» Wolfram said, attempting to shift position. Unable to move his limbs more than a few inches, he brought his cube casing in line with the white crystal and calculated. «My friends give me freedom. I am not Pinocchio, I have no desire to be a "real boy".»

The spring clamps holding him in place on the mech's chest released, ejecting the tungsten carbide cube directly at the crystal in front of him.

Glittering particles showered everywhere as the fragile crystal shattered on impact. A glowing, wispish form escaped from the recess left behind and swirled around in the vacuum. In seconds, uncontained and with nowhere to go, it faded to nothing.

Sebastian frantically tapped at the infoslate as the progress bar inched inexorably towards 100 per cent. 'I can't do this, it's too much pressure!'

'Too ... much?' came Mikkael's voice from behind him, grating and phlegm-cracked.

He turned.

Mikkael lunged towards him, his neck and face covered with a network of thick, blackened veins, mouth pulled back in a grimace. Sebastian drew his pistol but Mikkael knocked it flying from his grip and grabbed him by the jaw, thrusting him back against the console and pinning him to it by his head. 'It's not over!' he rasped, and held his bracered arm over Sebastian's face.

Sebastian's wristcom bleeped. 'Sebastian, Wolfram here. Have you eradicated the Trojan from the system? The dome has been punctured. You must activate the sealing panels now.'

'I ... can't ... Mikkael ... trying to ...'

Mikkael raised his bracered arm. The crystal glittered with an inner light. The entity must have gone into it. It must be controlling him.

'Bracer ... crystal ...'

'Crystal? The sphere had— If you see a white crystal, shatter it!'

'The giants will descend the Tower and Earth will bathe in Surt's cleansing flame!' Mikkael bellowed, and swung his arm down at Sebastian's head.

Sebastian used the last of his strength to turn his head and the bracer slammed, crystal first, onto the edge of the console.

The crystal shattered. Glittering particles filled the air and the red wisp form of an entity escaped to swirl above the console. The bracer on Mikkael's arm clicked open and fell to the floor. Mikkael collapsed.

Sebastian staggered away, covering his mouth – both to protect from the crystalline particles and the mist – and slumped against the wall, gasping. The miasma lasted for only a moment before disappearing completely. He couldn't help but feel a momentary satisfaction at seeing the entity that tore apart his family, killed his father, and possibly grandfather, dissipate into the ether.

'I've done it, Wolfram,' he said into his wristcom. 'I've done it! The entity is gone.'

'Good work. What of the Trojan?'

His face tingled. The progress bar was at ninety-six per cent. 'We're too late! I can't stop it.'

'I believe I can. However, I can't get back to the antenna station. You must get outside now!'

Without questioning the command, Sebastian quickly checked Mikkael's pulse – it was weak, but steady – and made his way back into the first room. He clamped his helmet into place and left through the airlock.

The bright light of Sollers Hope hit hard, and the headache from his many head wounds intensified as he looked up at the antenna. The asteroid beyond had grown to almost double its size.

The lander he had flown to the transmitter base was nowhere to be seen. 'Wolfram, where are you? The ship's gone.'

'Look to the dome,' Wolfram said over the suit comms.

Forgetting to activate the helmet visor, Sebastian shielded his eyes to cut the glare and peered into the distance. 'Zoom,' he said, and the suit provided an inset panel in his view, enlarged 100 times.

An inexplicable blackened patch now marked the terrain halfway between the plateau and the dome. Sitting in the dust at the foot of the crater wall was the cargomech, sullen and legless. It reached for a small metal object, leaned back on one arm, and threw it.

A tiny glinting speck tumbled through the black sky, a star moving across the grain of the galaxy. Sebastian held up his hands as though to catch a ball, and staggered about. Where was it going to land? Three paces back. Two left. Two forward. One right.

The cube fell like a meteor into Sebastian's open hands and landed in the dust at his feet. A burning pain shot up his arm. He brought his right hand up in front of his face and almost vomited: three of his fingers were bent backwards at the knuckle and one jutted out at an odd angle halfway up.

'My hand!' he screamed. 'You've broken my fingers!'

'I did not expect you to catch me,' Wolfram said. 'Try to ignore the pain and get me into the building now.'

He picked up the cube with his uninjured hand and staggered back towards the antenna building, activating the airlock with his shoulder as he went while trying to cradle his broken hand in the crook of his elbow. Once inside, he stumbled back to the transmission room.

'There's no way I can use the infoslate like this,' he said, placing Wolfram on the shattered console next to the display. The display that read 100 per cent.

'We're too late!'

'Don't worry. I will try to stop it.' Wolfram's lights flashed randomly for a moment. 'Wireless protocols are locked out.'

'What do we do?'

'Those cables. Is that a connecting plate for my matrix?'

Sebastian grabbed the bundle of wires coming from the console, which terminated in the plate with gold contacts. 'Yes, it looks like the adapter Aryx made.'

'It must be a hypervisor connection for the sphere-mech's matrix. Connect it to me.'

The tiny hatch in the top of Wolfram's cube slid open, as it had weeks ago when Sebastian first started analysing it, and he dropped in the plate.

'I'm confident I can rectify the situation.' Lights on the cube flashed randomly once again. 'I need to enter the node network to block the Trojan's progress. Once I am done, you will need to reactivate the colony's defences so the missiles can stop the asteroid and the dome breach can be sealed.'

'Won't you be able to do it?'

'This may overload my— Sebastian, I understand why Mrs Alvarez cried. Tell Aryx I am sorry. I know how he will feel.' The lights flashed faster.

'What are you talking about? Sorry?'

'I . . .' Wolfram's voice stuttered and distorted, sounding almost sad. 'Sebastiaaaan, the key i i is *friendshiiiip*. Thank . . . you.'

The lights went out.

Chapter 48

'Wolfram?' Sebastian picked up the cube, tugging out the wired plate in the process. The casing was warm, even through the pressure suit gloves. He pressed the button on the side several times with no response. *'Wolfram!'*

His breathing sped up and the world turned grey. What was he going to do now?

Displays all over the console flickered, and text scrolled up them as the computers reset. As soon as the first computer had booted, he began typing commands, one-handed, on an undamaged screen.

Deruno's voice came over the comms. 'Thorsson, are you there?'

'Thank the Gods! Deruno, you're alright?'

'Yes. The dome has been punctured, but the panels have activated and sealed the rupture. What did you do?'

'I didn't do anything. Wolfram—' He choked as his throat tightened. 'Wolfram must have stopped the Trojan virus in the colony as well as blocking the transmission.' Virus . . . 'Oh, Gods! Aryx! We have to get the carbyne back to the station!'

'I will load a hopper into the ship.'

'Fine. Can you come and pick me up from the antenna base? The lander's gone and . . .' He turned to look at the unconscious Mikkael. 'I've got an unexpected passenger.'

Sebastian sat aboard the *Ultima Thule* as it traversed the superphase pathways back to Tenebrae.

Deruno had stayed on Sollers Hope to help with repairs and finish installing the heaters. After Wolfram's intervention, the mirrored panels of the dome had snapped shut in time to prevent the fracture spreading and decompressing the town completely. The asteroid defences had dealt with the incoming threat, but even with the mirrors re-enabled it would still take several hours for the newly repaired thermal storage capsule to absorb enough energy to begin warming the place.

It was the first time Sebastian had flown the ship any distance without company, and the quiet, reverberating thrum of the engines seemed much louder in the absence of other voices. He shivered in the ship's cool air, despite his N-suit's insulation and, as he stared at the inert metal cube in his hands, glinting under the light of the passing stars, he began to realise what he'd lost. And what he might yet lose.

His imagination ran wild and he saw Aryx lying in the hospital bed, surrounded by beeping machines, tubes going into almost every major vein and artery to filter out the parasitic virus. A virus that nobody could see, drugs couldn't halt, and nanobots couldn't obliterate. What would he do if Duggan couldn't cure him? The idea of always eating alone in the atrium, never having someone to meet after work, or even call up with an exciting bit of news, left him feeling hollow. The loss of his parents had passed: he'd had time to deal with it . . . years. He realised this now, and that to lose Aryx would be far worse.

Why had he behaved so badly around him? He'd made stupid mistakes, been completely inconsiderate, and not paid any attention to his worsening health. Had he been wilfully ignorant? Was Deruno right about how he felt? His actions may have spawned from the desire to protect Aryx, to keep him safe. To keep him safe so that he wouldn't lose him. *The grief of the journey . . .*

So yes, Deruno was right. He loved him.

After several minutes, Mikkael's gentle breathing came across the mire of Sebastian's self-pity from where he lay on the seats at the back of the ship. Mikkael . . . What had the entity controlling him meant when it taunted him? Why would it have helped him to break into the archive?

More questions that couldn't be answered.

Sebastian looked at his reflection in the cockpit window and wiped his red eyes with a sleeve before moving to the aft section to check on his brother. He put a finger to Mikkael's neck. His pulse was stronger now, and the blackening of his veins had mysteriously vanished. The metal bracer that had adorned his wrist was gone, left behind in the antenna base station when Sebastian had to fight one-handed to get the pressure suit over his limp body.

He leaned against the console opposite the seats, watching the gentle rise and fall of Mikkael's chest. By all accounts, if what happened to Mikkael was the same as what happened to Daniel Cullen of Chopwood, who had been possessed for weeks, he could be unconscious for days.

An alert sounded from the cockpit, indicating the *Ultima Thule*'s transition from superphase and initiation of autopilot to the station and he dashed to the cargo hold.

There was one final thing to do before he arrived.

Sebastian ran along the atrium terrace, clutching a handful of carbyne vials. 'Duggan!' he yelled as the old man came out to greet him. 'Where's Karan? I need her to go and get Mikkael from the ship.'

Duggan put a hand on his back as he passed. 'She's looking after Alicia and the Gladrins. Come on, Monica wants to see you urgently. She's in her lab.'

Sebastian's face chilled. 'Has something happened to Aryx?'

'It's ... They've had to put him in a medically induced coma. It's best if she tells you everything.'

When they arrived at the lab, Monica stood staring at the console, her face locked in a severe frown. 'What *exactly* did you do to the sample from Cinder IV when you collected it?' she asked, turning to face him straight on.

He shrugged. 'Nothing. I put the jar in my belt and that was it.'

She breathed out sharply. 'You should have taken it back to the ship immediately. The radiation that flooded the research base must have broken the sample down to such a degree there's nothing left of the virus to analyse.'

'Oh Gods, no!' He buried his face in his hands and the room began to sway. 'How are we going to cure him?'

'We can't,' Duggan said, sitting on a chair in the corner. His lips pinched to a thin line while he thought. 'Not without having a good visual reference. That's why I needed the sample. I needed to see it. Since the scans are gone from your infoslate I'm not able to study it, and nobody else has even seen it, so we're stuck.'

'Wait ... I examined the sample while we were on the planet.'

'Can you remember it in detail?'

He recalled the strange, corkscrew tails of the virion, but that was all. Aryx was counting on him. 'I-I think so. Maybe.'

'Good, because you'll have to perform the spell.'

The skin of Sebastian's face tingled, and he turned away from Duggan and Monica. What if he made Aryx worse? 'I don't think I can.'

'Utter tosh!' Duggan said, leaping from his seat.

'Seb, this is partly your fault,' Monica said, coming around in front of him. 'If you can do something, you must.'

Sebastian stepped back, shaking his head. 'No ... I-I can't! I could kill him.'

'At this point Aryx is so ill that if you don't try something he's going to die anyway.'

His chest tightened. His breathing sped up and his eyes fixed on the door. The walls closed in on him and the air became hotter. He had to get into the atrium, to leave everything behind. Stepping around Monica, he made a run for it.

The next moment, he was leaning on the handrail with his good hand, overlooking the terraces with the cool water flowing out from beneath the mall, his breathing still rapid.

Duggan's hands appeared on the rail next to his. 'Sebastian, old boy, have some faith in yourself. You were capable enough back in London. You performed that molten metal thaumatic twice. First under the threat of torture, and then breaking us out of those cells, and that was also under pressure. I *know* you can do this.'

Sebastian looked up and stared into those kind, incisive eyes.

'Don't look at me like that, Sebastian.' Duggan absent-mindedly picked a piece of fluff from his robe, released it to the breeze and watched it drift away. 'I've told you before, it's all about believing in yourself. If you want something badly enough, you'll do it right. Your subconscious won't let you do any less.'

'What if I don't visualise it properly? I'm not even sure my memory of the virus is clear enough. I only got a brief look.'

Duggan patted him on the back then placed a hand on his upper arm and squeezed his bicep slowly, rhythmically. 'How do you feel about me using hypnosis to help you?'

'Um ... I ...' Sebastian's breathing slowed and he relaxed. 'I suppose, if it works.'

'Tilt your head back and close your eyes.'

He found himself following Duggan's instruction without question. It just seemed like the right thing to do.

'You're back on Cinder IV, about to look at the sample.'

He opened his eyes and found himself in the blustering storm of

Cinder IV. Rain swirled around him, plastering his hair to his scalp as he looked through the eyepiece of the microscope. He ignored the cold and allowed the water to run down his neck. There was no hurry to take the sample and leave.

The microscope quickly found the iridescent patch on the lobster-like animals and zoomed in to the bacteria, then to the tiny tadpoles with corkscrew tails within.

I want you to focus on that. Bring the image closer. Make it brighter. A cinema screen in your mind, intense, full of colour.

Sebastian did as the voice told him, burning the vision of the parasitic virus into his memory.

'Well done,' Duggan said, patting him on the shoulder. 'Do you think you can do it now?'

He turned to the old man, once again back in the atrium, and smiled. 'Yes. Yes, I can.'

Chapter 49

Sebastian stood at the foot of Aryx's bed in the critical care ward, with Duggan and Monica either side. Machines beeped distractingly in the background and, even though it had been temporarily bandaged and anaesthetised, his shattered hand ached.

Aryx's face was pale, his lips almost colourless. His hair lay to one side, slick with sweat. Tubes wove in and out from under the bedcovers – thankfully fewer than Sebastian had imagined. Unconscious, he looked peaceful.

Sebastian's shoulders sagged. 'I'm so sorry, Aryx. This is all my fault.'

Duggan nudged him forward. 'Buck up, it's not over yet.'

'I didn't mean what I said earlier,' Monica said. 'It was the stress of the moment. Aryx wouldn't have wanted you to hold him back, and he'd probably still have ended up here in hospital, anyway.'

'I'm sorry, too,' Sebastian said, tightening his grip on the vials, 'but *I've* got to do this now ... Here goes.'

He closed his eyes and pressed the heel of one hand against his left eye and the back of his injured hand against the other. As the now familiar waves of colour surged towards him in the darkness and became dancing flashes, he concentrated on the image of the virus, imagining it swirling inside bone cells, while visualising the white shield around himself. He imagined the virus agents entering blood cells and replicating, and avoiding or attacking spiky white immune-system cells – all the while hoping this was actually what was happening right now – and then switched his attention to imagined nanobots also swimming through Aryx's bloodstream.

An imaginary nanobot approached one of the parasites. As it drew close, the parasite sped off using its corkscrew tail and the nanobot, propelled by robotic cilia, found itself unable to keep up.

How could he could stop the things from escaping without somehow altering the virus's DNA – and potentially risking altering Aryx's – if such a thing were even possible? The drugs Aryx took were no longer working, but without knowing the drug's structure he couldn't visualise it interacting. He should just give up. Better to let Aryx die peacefully than accidentally visualise something that would kill him.

But ... what about something that *wouldn't* injure Aryx? Could he modify the way the virus reacted to something else of which he already knew the structure?

He visualised large, cubic shapes, a lattice of sodium and chlorine atoms, plain old salt, drifting around in the space near the cells containing the virus. In the presence of water within Aryx's cells, the cube broke down into sodium and chlorine ions, which then passed through the cell walls into the space containing the virus.

The virus swam through its liquid environment until it encountered a cloud of the ions. Immediately, the tail slowed and parts broke off, leaving the main body of the virus to drift helplessly. The slower nanobots caught up and locked on, while the giant sea-urchin immune-system cells swallowed and broke down the virus bodies. The visualisation felt complete.

A complex string of runes appeared in Sebastian's mind, and he attempted to memorise them, to hold them static while he focused. He failed. They drifted and flittered before him, and it took all his concentration to keep them alive. There was going to be no second attempt. This, he knew, was a spell to be performed at the time, for this moment only. There was no second chance. Something – the Weave itself? – told him this. His throat tightened as words formed on his lips and he chanted.

He opened his eyes. The air shimmered around him and Aryx.

Aryx tensed, arching his back and pushing his head into the pillow. His face twisted in a paroxysm of pain.

'He needs saline now!' Sebastian shouted, startling the nurses at the other end of the ward. 'The highest concentration you can safely give him.'

Monica gripped his arm. 'What's happening?'

'I think I've changed the virus. Salt will kill it.'

* * *

Sebastian slept in the chair at Aryx's bedside, although sleep wasn't really what he had achieved; he'd gained a little rest, while constantly worrying. One side of his body ached and had begun to cramp from hours of being stuck in the uncomfortable seat, but he couldn't leave Aryx's side – not until he knew whether the spell had worked. He watched the rhythmic pulses on the monitors through half-closed eyes.

Monica approached. There were dark circles under her eyes and she carried two steaming cups, one of which she offered to him.

'Coffee?'

He sat up and took the cup. 'As long as it's not Bronadi chicory.'

'There's nothing wrong with the stuff, if you don't mind drinking alien plants.'

'But Aryx said it's made from crushed—'

'Little birds?' She laughed and shook her head. 'Don't tell me you fell for that old chestnut?'

He frowned. 'I did ... How can you even laugh at a time like this?'

'I was just coming to tell you, there's news.'

He straightened.

'I'm cautiously optimistic, but the latest test results show increased antibodies in his blood and a new protein marker, which indicates his system is now fighting the infection and the nanobots are actually breaking something down. It seems the thaumatic effect worked.'

The cup in Sebastian's hand slopped to one side. 'Thank the Gods! How long before he wakes up?'

Her mouth twisted. 'The doctors want to keep him under observation for a few days before bringing him out of the coma. They've spotted something that needs surgery, but no, don't panic,' she said, putting out a hand, 'it's nothing major.'

Sebastian closed his eyes and let his head fall back against the chair. 'Thanks. I don't think I could cope with any more bad news.'

'It's a good job there's only more good news to come, then.'

'Such as?'

'Mikkael's awake.'

His eyes flicked open and he lifted his head. 'What? How can he be, so soon?'

She held out a hand and studied her nails. 'Oh, after hearing what Wolfram had discovered about the neurons of the inner ear being related to your possession signal, I decided to run a few targeted tests on Mikkael. It turns out his brain chemistry had been altered drastically, to the point where it couldn't have been his brain producing the hormones itself. I found a strange puncture wound in his right wrist, as though he'd been injected with something – could it have been the bracer he wore?'

Sebastian shrugged. 'I suppose. That was where all the black came from.'

'I'll have to get someone to retrieve it from Sollers Hope so I can take a look at it. Anyway, his dopamine and serotonin levels were all over the place, so I corrected them and he woke up.'

He listened, wide-eyed. 'How is he?'

'A bit groggy and disorientated, but he did ask for you. I told him Janyce and Erik are fine.'

He leaped from his seat, almost spilling his coffee in the process. 'Why didn't you tell me straight away? I have to see him.'

'Just calm down. There's no point you rushing in there, hyperventilating all over the place. He needs peace and quiet, not for you to go in all excited. He still thinks it's three years ago, so break the news gently.'

Sebastian winced as pain surged through his hand with every heartbeat. 'Alright, I get your point.'

'I also don't want you speaking to the doctors about him. I managed to keep them from putting his details in the system by threatening them with SpecOps top security clauses. I don't know how we're going to keep his presence here a secret, or what we're going to do about Gladrin's family in the meantime, not to mention Alicia. She's *inexplicable*.'

He rubbed his chin. 'I've been thinking about that. I expect Duggan will want to take her back to Tradescantia with him, to live in Chopwood. The ITF and entities want both of them, anyway, and it's the ideal place to hide. Emily and Tess won't be safe here until Gladrin gets back.'

Monica folded her arms. 'And what about your family? It's not like they'll be any safer here just because you've got Mikkael back. If the ITF think you're a threat, they'll use any means they can to control you, and Mikkael provides them with extra leverage, not less.'

Sebastian sagged. 'I don't expect that'll go down well.' With one glance back at Aryx, he set off for the private room where Mikkael was installed.

* * *

'Come in,' Mikkael said.

Sebastian entered the white, sterile room to find Mikkael sat in bed, reading an infoslate. He looked up from the screen and smiled. 'Good to see you, little brother ... What the heck's up with you? You look like shit.'

'I'm a bit—'

'Old and shrivelled? I can see that.'

'I was going to say beaten up. You don't seem surprised.'

'I managed to get one of these off a passing nurse,' he said, hefting the infoslate. 'Been studying the headlines from the last few years. Looks like I've missed a bit. So, where are we? This Tenebrae station of yours?' Sebastian opened his mouth to speak but Mikkael cut in again. 'First thing I did was look you up. You seem to have done pretty well for yourself, getting a job here. Listen, the nurses won't speak to me, so I don't know what happened, but there's an old obituary in the news with my name on it. I know I've got amnesia, but I sure as hell don't feel dead ... Janyce didn't remarry, did she? I couldn't bring myself to search for her. I wanted to hear it from you.'

'I'm really glad you're not dead.' Sebastian closed the door behind him and gave Mikkael a brief hug. Events from the last few hours were still fresh in his memory and it was a little difficult to put the experience of being strangled by his brother out of his mind. 'No, she didn't remarry, even though everyone thought you were dead. I thought it was my fault. We thought you died in a fire at the site of the bombing at the South-West Datacentre in Bristol.'

Mikkael stared at the ceiling. 'I do remember something about that. Yes, it's starting to come back to me. It's the last thing I remember ... Gods! Dad was there.'

'Mike, I need to tell you something—'

'He was there, he looked all strange. It was like he wasn't himself. He spoke in the third person, kept using "We" instead of "I", and he mentioned Granddad. Said that he'd meddled in "their" business. Then he attacked me.'

'And you don't remember anything after that?'

'No.'

Sebastian bit his lip. 'I don't really know how to explain this, but you've been possessed by an alien entity for the last three years. That's why you have no memory. The entity possessed Dad, and when you discovered him at the bomb site he attacked and overpowered you, then—' Sebastian choked. 'Then he – it, in you – disposed of him. The police found a body in the rubble, burnt out of all recognition. Your badge was on the corpse and your car was nearby. I always knew you wouldn't have been stupid enough to get yourself killed like that, not unless you were saving someone and died in the line of duty, but there were no other remains.'

'You're saying I killed Dad?'

Sebastian shook his head. 'No, not you. You had no control once the entity was in you. It was all that ... *thing*, Gravalax.'

Mikkael laid the infoslate on the bed. 'So why isn't anyone investigating these entities if I'm not the first person to get possessed by one?'

'Up until recently they controlled the information going in and out of one of the biggest police information archives. If anyone had found out about the entities and started an investigation, they'd have suppressed it.'

'So, what the heck are they, and what do they want?'

'Aside from possessing everyone, and now wanting us out of the way, the one that possessed you mentioned giants descending something called the Tower, and talked about Earth bathing in Surt's flame. Surt's a fire giant from Norse lore.'

'I know that, dummy. I did pay attention to Granddad Frímann, regardless of what you think. Surt was the leader of the fire giants, who fought against the Gods to bring about Ragnarök, the end of the world. So, what's the Tower?'

Sebastian shrugged. 'I have no idea, but I remember reading something about it in Frímann's journal.' He pulled the battered book from his rucksack and flicked through it, stopping on a short passage in the middle of a page. 'I'd seen it before. That's why it sounded familiar.' He turned it for Mikkael to read:

> *Beyond nine folds, geometries' curve*
> *Between the realms of fire and ice*
> *seven telamon seal the Tower*
> *sentinels amidst the giants of old*
> *but silent in this age of light*
> *dark things stir behind the curtain.*

Mikkael paled. 'Sounds downright freaky to me. You think this is the same Tower?'

Sebastian nodded. 'None of this made any sense to me before, but with reference to fire and ice – the giants, and their realms – and of nine folds, geometries' curve – probably space-time, I think it's where these beings come from. It's referring to something like superphase. The entity that possessed you said I'd been sending some of them "back".'

'And have you?'

'I guess I must have. Well, Wolfram had. Gods, you're not going to believe this. There was an intelligent computer that was able to use magic to purge the entities . . .' Over the next half an hour, Sebastian explained everything that had happened: thaumaturgy; Wolfram, the SI; the Folians, and their involvement in Earth's history; right down to the pictures drawn in Frímann's journal.

Mikkael took it well, accepting the strange testimony without question. 'But Janyce and Erik are safe, on Tradescantia, in Chopwood?' he asked.

'For the moment. Nobody knows about the place, and that's why I think it's best if you hide out there for the time being.'

Mikkael sighed and folded his arms. 'I really want to help you get rid of those bastards, but I can't exactly do that from the back of beyond, can I?'

Sebastian paced back and forth. 'Unless the Church and Freemasons managed to capture and get information out of the possessed they rounded up in London, there's nothing anyone can do. The only means I had of getting rid of the entities was Wolfram, and now he's . . . gone.'

'That's a shitter. So, what about the planar conjunction thingy, or the *akkeri* the entity had been talking about? Would your friend Duggan know what those are?'

'It's possible. *Akkeri* is Icelandic for anchor, but I don't know what that relates to. If the entities have been planning something for centuries, it's likely to be found in old texts, and Duggan has a lot of rare books about mythology.' He rubbed his chin. 'There's something else that's been bugging me.'

'What's that?'

'Gravalax, the entity that possessed you, said he allowed me to get into the archive so I could uncover information that the *others* had hidden from him. It sounded almost like there are other factions within the entities, or that some were working behind his back. Perhaps that's why he let me break in, so it wouldn't arouse suspicion?'

'Hey, they're gone now, aren't they? Why worry?'

Three knocks came from the door.

'Come in,' Mikkael said.

Monica entered, carrying a bundle of clothes. 'How are you feeling?'

'Fine, thanks.'

'Good. Your latest test results show that your brain chemistry has stabilised, so I don't have to keep you in hospital any longer. Here, you can have these.' She held out the bundle. 'We can't have you walking around the station in a police uniform. You'll attract too much attention.'

'Mikkael's agreed to go to Chopwood,' Sebastian said.

'I'd suggest going now, then. Duggan's already on his way there with Alicia in the runner.'

'What about Emily and Tess?'

'On the *Ultima Thule*, waiting for you. Tess got a little anxious about the noises in the station, so Emily took her there to calm down. She thinks the change of pace on the planet will do her good. Fewer distractions.'

'What about Aryx?'

'He's stable. Please go. The hospital staff are starting to ask too many questions. Spend a few days with your family. It'll give Aryx time to heal. I'll make sure you're back before we wake him.'

Sebastian nodded. 'Alright, I'm going. Mikkael, I'll wait outside for you to get changed.'

Chapter 50

Sebastian took the *Ultima Thule* low over the trees south of Chopwood town and brought it down in a wide clearing filled with sun-baked and splintered tree trunks – just to make sure that any townsfolk wouldn't see their approach in an unfamiliar craft.

He led Mikkael, Emily and Tess between the silvery logs, following a clear path towards the north end of the clearing. 'We can't let them know we're here until we've met with Duggan,' he said. 'The colonists don't know anything about the rest of the galaxy, and I don't want them zipping off in ships and giving away the existence of this place.'

Mikkael grinned. 'If that's true, they'll sure as hell want to know where you vanished to after your first visit. I hope you have a bloody good excuse.'

Sebastian rubbed the back of his neck. 'They didn't see us, and I have no idea what Duggan told them about Janyce and Erik.'

The journey through the woods, which should have taken only a few minutes, took half an hour; Tess insisted on stopping at nearly every tree and running her hands over the bark.

'I've never seen her so engaged with her environment,' Emily said. 'Marcus always said it might be a good idea to get her out into the woods, but after we got relocated I never had the time or courage to take her.'

Tess led them off the path, laughing and skipping as she ran through the curled, dry leaves that covered the ground, on a route that skirted the village. Eventually, she stopped and pointed. 'Look!'

Beyond the treeline, a field of golden wheat grew on a gently sloping hill. Wheat that should not have been there: the colonists had been away for years and returned only weeks ago – there hadn't been enough time for it to grow. At the top of the hill was a woman, bent over. She straightened, putting a hand to her back, the other arm loaded with a sheaf of wheat. The wind caught strands of red in her auburn hair and they shone like flame in the afternoon sun.

'Janyce!' Mikkael shouted.

'Wait.' Sebastian put out his arm to hold him back, but it was too late. Mikkael was already leaving the cover of the trees and stumbling through the golden stalks.

Janyce froze as Mikkael ran up the hill towards her. As he drew closer she dropped the wheat, and he swept her up in his arms and swung her around. The pair stood, entwined, as though Janyce might never let him go.

'Stay here,' Sebastian said to Emily, and jogged after him.

'How can you be real?' Janyce said, cupping Mikkael's face with her hands. 'You died!' He went to speak, but she pressed a finger to his lips. 'It doesn't matter. You're here now, and I'd believe any explanation. I've seen plenty of unbelievable things lately.' She wrapped her arms around his shoulders and hugged him tight.

As Sebastian neared the two, the gable end of a building appeared over the brow of the hill, just beyond the field. At a window stood a figure who, at the sight of Sebastian, retreated into the darkness within.

'Uh oh, I think we've been rumbled,' he said, as the watcher came out of the building and strode through the wheat towards them.

'Don't worry,' Janyce said. 'She's Erik's teacher. Duggan told her and some of the other colonists about you ... and the Folians.'

'What? Oh, Gods! How-how did they take it?'

'How do you think this grew so quickly?' She brushed a hand through the wheat surrounding them and sat down on a patch of flat-tened stalks. 'They've promised not to leave the planet, in exchange for the Folians' help with farming, so there's no chance of them revealing our location.'

'Good, because it's not just you that could be in danger from the ITF now. All the colonists are.' Sebastian beckoned to Emily, and she led Tess up the hill towards them. He sat beside his sister-in-law and brother to catch up on the news.

A couple of minutes later, a nearby rustling in the wheat made him look up; a woman with tightly bound hair stood over them, her lips pursed disapprovingly.

'You are "Uncle Sebastian, the pirate hunter", I presume?'

Startled, he blinked twice before answering. 'Actually, it's terrorists.'

Aryx woke in a bed. Sebastian sat in a chair next to him, staring into his lap. He wore his N-suit and had his rucksack slung over his shoulder.

And he was holding his hand.

Aryx groggily looked at the monitors flanking the bed. A multitude of tubes trailed out from the units but dangled loosely over a nearby stand. 'Where am I? Tenebrae?'

Sebastian snatched his hand away and looked up. 'Hey,' he said quietly. 'I didn't realise you were awake. How are you feeling?'

A dull, throbbing sensation made its way through the fuzz of whatever drugs he was on. 'Like I've been hit by a shuttle. My legs hurt.' He reached beneath the blankets and found a large clump of fabric covering his thighs. 'What happened? Why have I got bandages on? Last thing I remember was standing in the research base on Cinder IV.'

Sebastian leaned forward. 'It was my fault. The radiation affected you and your virus went into overdrive. It caused a lot of complications. They had to operate.'

'Your fault? Don't be stupid. How long have I been here? I don't feel that sore. And why are these tubes disconnected?'

'You've been in a coma for a week. Thankfully, you're stable enough not to need the machines now.'

Aryx scratched his head. The back of his hand ached and he found a large bruise where a drip had been removed. 'I obviously didn't get full-on radiation poisoning, so how did they manage to bring the virus under control?'

'Thaumaturgy.'

'Duggan used *magic* on me?'

Sebastian shook his head. 'I did.'

'*You?*'

He nodded. 'I didn't have a choice. The sample got destroyed by the radiation and I was the only one who had seen it. I didn't really want to do it in case I made you worse. I can't believe you never told me you were that ill! I've been sick with worry.'

Aryx studied the dark marks under Sebastian's eyes. 'You look terrible.'

Sebastian rubbed his face. 'This is nothing compared to what you've been through. I did manage to get a little sleep. Monica sent me to

Chopwood after I did the thaumatic so I wouldn't worry over you. I had to take the others back and make sure Mikkael got settled in. It sort of worked out – at least I didn't have to sleep here while the nightmare transmitting Trojan is still running on the station. Duggan wants us all to go back to Chopwood when you're well enough.'

'Wait. Mikkael, as in dead-brother Mikkael?'

'The one and only … It's a long story. I'll fill you in when you get out of here.'

'How long do I have to stay?'

Sebastian looked over his shoulder. 'I'll check.' He beckoned to someone and a few moments later, a nurse arrived carrying an infoslate.

'Hello, Mr Trevarian. Nice to see you're awake. Is everything okay?'

'I think so. I was wondering when I could leave. I don't like being stuck in hospital beds. Oh, and why are my legs bandaged?'

She checked the infoslate. 'Your readings are all within acceptable ranges. You're due to be discharged today, but I don't see why you can't leave now if you feel up to it.'

'And what about the operation?'

'Ms Stevens suggested a procedure after looking over your scans. She noticed there were some small bone spurs where your legs had been amputated, and that the surgeons had left your kneecaps in place. It seems that would have caused you a lot of pain when walking on them, so she suggested removing them and flattening the bones a little. Now that doesn't mean you can walk on them all the time. You'll be able to in a few weeks, but don't put prolonged pressure on them. The bones are still weak. It'll take a long time to heal because of the osteoporosis, maybe a couple of years – less if the correct nanobot treatment is used.'

'I'll stop you there, I'm not having nanobot treatment.'

'Mr Trevarian, surely there's no reason not to.'

Sebastian stared at the floor.

Did Sebastian want him to have the nanobot treatment? Aryx's blood pressure rose. After all they'd been through, he was going to force him to have a procedure he didn't want. Again. He took a deep breath. 'Could you give us a moment?'

'Of course.' The nurse left.

'Seb? I'm not having nanobot treatment unless Wolfram does it.'

Sebastian stood and leaned against the wall. 'I know.' He shifted his weight from one foot to the other, but didn't look up.

'What is it? ... Where is he, anyway?'

'That's the problem.' He drew in a long breath and swallowed audibly. 'He's gone.'

Aryx blinked slowly. 'Gone?' He looked around the room. 'You what, lost an immobile cube, or did you somehow misplace the cargomech with him attached? Because I can see how easy it is to lose something tiny like that.'

Sebastian continued to stare at the floor.

'Well?'

'He came with me to Sollers Hope when I went to get more carbyne. The colony was locked down by something Mikkael had done, and I needed his help.'

'Wait, Mikkael did what?'

'I said it was complicated.'

'So why didn't you bring Wolfram back with you?'

'I did.' Sebastian reached into his rucksack, pulled out the cube, and placed it on the bed. It was covered in a film of grey dust, one of the LEDs was cracked, and the top flap was open, but other than that, the near-impervious tungsten carbide cube was unmarked.

'Hey, Wolfram,' Aryx said.

There was no response. The lights remained dark.

He picked up the cold cube and turned it in his hands. 'You ignoring me, mate?' His heart contracted. 'What have you done to him?'

Sebastian sat on the bed and stared into his lap. 'I didn't do anything. I think he knew it was going to happen. He said he might overheat when he did it.'

Aryx grabbed him by the arm. 'What *happened*?'

'The entity in Mikkael put a Trojan in the Sollers Hope transmitter that would do the same thing as the nightmare signal, but with ninety per cent effectiveness. They were going to possess the entire galaxy! I tried to stop it, I really did. I wasn't quick enough. Wolfram connected to the node network to cut the Trojan off, but said he might overheat.'

'Oh, Jeez! But he stopped it?' Aryx reached for a glass of water and took a mouthful.

Sebastian nodded. 'That's not all. I think he had emotions. He said to tell you that he knew why Mrs Alvarez cried, that he's sorry, and that he knew you'd miss him.'

Aryx swallowed the water. An enormous lump went down that left him gasping. 'Hang on! He actually said that? I-I can't believe it.'

'Me neither.' Sebastian's eyes glistened. 'I miss him already.'

Aryx clenched his jaw. 'Oh, don't you cry on me. Don't you dare. You'll make me cry, too.'

'I don't know how I'm going to manage without him.'

'It's always about you, isn't it?' Aryx took a deep breath. The loss of Wolfram left something more raw than the wounds under his bandages. He had to change the subject. 'What happened when you tried to cure me?'

'I slowed down the virus and the nanobots managed to kill some of it. Don't shout at me for that! The doctors insisted. There are none in you now. What's left of your immune system should be able to hold back the rest of the virus. It'll never go away completely, but at least now it's not terminal. You just have to take it steady for the next few months.'

Aryx allowed himself to fall back on the pillow and closed his eyes. The cloud of impending doom that had hung over him for the last three years had rolled by while he slept. He'd worked with such ferocity, almost burning himself out, in the fear that he may die without leaving so much as a footprint. But now, here he was with the rest of his life stretched out ahead of him, and he'd already outlived one of his best friends.

He opened his eyes and turned the cube in his hands. 'I'm going to miss him ... Can I keep the cube? I don't want you to dispose of it.'

Sebastian slid off the bed and stood up. 'I'll have to ask Gladrin. I've somehow got to send him word that we have his family safe, cryptically, just in case the messages are being read by the ITF. The code that infiltrated the station is still here, and I haven't worked out how to shut it off yet. I'll do it when we get back from Chopwood.'

'Thanks. Speaking of which, where's that nurse? I want to get out of here.'

Aryx sat at the foot of a wooden ramp that someone had thoughtfully laid up to the threshold of the ramshackle log cabin that acted as Chopwood's administration building.

In front of him, Sebastian knocked twice on the door and cleared his throat as he entered. Aryx wheeled up the knobbly ramp behind. It was good to get out of the heat; even though it was early morning, Chopwood found itself in the baking throes of midsummer, and his black suit was already frying his legs.

Inside, Duggan stood with his back to the door, fastening his tie in a mirror. Rather than the robe Aryx was accustomed to seeing him in, he wore a black suit – the one Sebastian had worn breaking in to the archive.

'It's a bit baggy, old boy,' he said, pulling at the collar and turning to Sebastian, 'but it'll do at a pinch. I can't get this wretched tie to do up. Do you know how long it is since I wore something like this?'

'Come here,' Aryx said. 'You can't go dressed like … well, like someone who can't be bothered to get dressed properly.'

'Cheeky so-and-so.' Duggan came over and bent down while Aryx straightened the knot. 'So, Mikkael's all settled in, then?' he asked.

'Yes,' Sebastian said.

Aryx shook his head. 'I still can't believe you told the colonists about the Folians.'

'I had to, old boy. Erik was starting to look like a raving lunatic. I had to tell them there are things out there that want to destroy the Folians, as evidenced by Cullen's behaviour when the colonists first came back. Once I gave them a little magic demonstration, it was enough to convince them they needed to keep quiet and stay put. The thought of getting possessed by going into superphase is enough to scare the crap out of most of them.

'Anyway, there are enough resources here, and the Folians promised to help with farming, so there's no need to cause more deforestation. I think it'll work out quite well. There's even talk of dismantling the ship and using that for better buildings – we won't need to cut down any more trees to keep the houses up together.'

Sebastian folded his arms. 'Why didn't you tell me any of this on the way back from London?'

'There wasn't exactly time, and it didn't seem like a high priority. You don't handle stress well at the best of times.'

A knock came from the open door behind them. Aryx spun around and Janyce tentatively popped her head through. 'They're ready for you, Mr Simmons.'

'Oh, goodness, so soon?' He fumbled to put a flower through a buttonhole in his lapel. 'Thought I had another half an hour.'

She shook her head and disappeared.

'Come on, gents, let's get this over with.' He strode past Aryx into the sunlight with Sebastian tagging along behind. 'It's not every day you get married.'

The trio made their way out into the gently sloping street and proceeded up the grassy hill towards the silver bullet-shaped edifice of the colony ship. At the crest of the hill, just in front of the ship, a woven archway of leafy willow branches had been erected and, behind it, a small fruit tree had been planted and was in full blossom.

Duggan sniffed the air. 'Orange, Shiliri? That's a nice touch.'

'I am glad you agree,' came a genderless voice from the branches, soft as the breeze itself. 'Shall we begin?'

'Of course.' He nodded solemnly and stood beneath the archway. Aryx and Sebastian followed his cue, standing to the left of it, while Janyce and Mikkael, who already waited there, stood to the right.

'Have you got the rings?' Sebastian whispered.

Aryx patted his breast pocket.

Music played from somewhere down the hill, and the townsfolk came out of the buildings to line the grassy street. In the distance, the stockade gate swung open and through it came Alicia, dressed in white so bright it hurt to look at. She walked at a leisurely pace, flanked by Karan and Monica, with Deruno trailing behind.

The townsfolk cheered as she walked up the aisle they formed. Almost as soon as the children spotted Deruno they mobbed him, clustering around to stroke his fur. Aryx chuckled to himself. There was no way Deruno was going to get past: none of the colonists had ever seen an alien, and the humanoid hyena certainly caused a stir.

Alicia ignored the disturbance and proceeded up the aisle, leaving Deruno to deal with the children. As she drew closer, Aryx's eyes adjusted to the brightness of her gown. Those were petals. The entire dress was covered in orchids!

Duggan smiled broadly as she approached. 'I never imagined this day would come,' he said with a slight tremor to his voice.

Aryx glanced at the orange tree that contained Shiliri.

In the bright daylight, the blue haze that drifted in its branches was barely visible, but her voice sounded clear. 'You are gathered here, as colleagues, friends, and family, to witness the joining of these two people, Duggan Simmons and Alicia Maline. The Folian culture does not have the concept of marriage but understands the importance of the joining of two lives as one, and this we introduced to Humans millennia ago as handfasting. My people would like this day to remain special for all of you, in our own way, but first Duggan and Alicia have prepared their own vows.'

Duggan took Alicia's hands in his. 'Alicia, I promise to love and cherish you. To stand by you through good times and bad . . .'

Aryx found his attention wandering away from the words as one of the flowers fell from the orange tree. While they spoke their vows, a tiny bead formed where the blossom had detached and, as he stared, the green bud grew larger and darkened, forming into a small orange. By the time Alicia had reached her final line, the orange had become the size of a large grapefruit and the branch hung heavy with it.

'. . . I do,' she said.

Sebastian nudged Aryx with an elbow. Duggan was staring down at him, hand out.

'Oh . . . !' Aryx patted himself, trying to remember where he'd put the rings.

'Shirt pocket,' Sebastian whispered.

'Okay.' Aryx pulled out the two blue-green false bornite rings, a gift from Garvin Havlor of Sollers Hope, and held them up. It was appropriately ironic that space travel had separated the couple and that the nodes, themselves made of false bornite, had been responsible for bringing them back together.

The wedding pair exchanged rings and a cheer rose from the crowd.

'Now,' Shiliri said, 'for the final part of the ceremony. Mr Simmons, please pick the fruit. You will find there is a segment for everyone to eat. I would like you to pass it around. In this way, all those present will have been a permanent part of the occasion and will retain the memory of it forever.'

Duggan plucked the fruit from the tree and peeled back the skin. He offered a segment to Sebastian and then to Aryx, who quickly popped it into his mouth.

Turkish delight, a definite sweet, rosy flavour, and nothing at all like an orange.

'Weird,' Sebastian said. 'It tastes just like banana.'

Kibble Vardstrom, the town medic, standing a few feet to Aryx's right, took a segment. 'No, it's definitely strawberry.'

By the time the fruit had made its way down the aisle and back up, two slices were left for Duggan and Alicia. They ate theirs together.

'Oh,' Alicia said flatly. 'I didn't expect orange.'

'Nor I,' Duggan said, placing the empty peel at the foot of the tree.

Aryx laughed. He was beginning to get used to the Folians' penchant for mixing up flavours.

'And this concludes the ceremony,' Shiliri said. 'People of Chopwood, I present to you Mr and Mrs Duggan and Eileen Simmons.'

Duggan's eyes widened.

Eileen smiled warmly at him as she led him down the hill. 'I decided to change my name back, and forget about the bad times.'

Aryx followed the wedding party down the street to the saloon bar at the bottom of the hill. Since his last visit, the glass windows had been replaced, the swing doors refitted and the decking of the veranda swept clean. In fact, most of the town seemed in better repair. The colonists must have been working hard over the last few weeks.

He was about to wheel up onto the decking, where the end met the slope of the street, when a small pair of arms wrapped about his neck.

'Uncle Aryx!' a voice squealed in his ear.

He winced at the volume. 'Hello, Erik.'

'Mother said you were poorly, but uncle Seb says you're all better now. Does that mean you can get new legs, or will they grow back?'

He snorted. 'No, it doesn't mean they'll grow back. They should hurt a lot less though, and I might live a few more years.'

The arms lowered and tightened to a hug. 'If you died, would you come back like Dad did?'

Aryx gave a flattened smile. 'No, Erik. That doesn't happen. The space pirates, the people with monsters in them, hid him and made everyone think he was dead. He couldn't find his way back to us. Seb found him and brought him back.'

'I want to go and say thank you.' Erik let go and made his way towards the saloon doors.

Aryx sped after him and tugged at his shirt. 'I think he's talking to the other adults about work stuff. Why not go and play with your friends, and then you can say thank you to him later?'

Erik nodded and ran off towards the stockade gate, leaving Aryx to push through the elevated saloon doors with his head.

He peered through the group crowding the bar, looking for a familiar face. Duggan, Kibble Vardstrom, Sebastian and Monica sat at one of the circular tables in the far corner. At the near end of the room, at a table surrounded by children, sat Deruno, studying a menu. A woman stood beside him with a pad.

'Have you decided what you'd like yet?'

'Steak. I have not had real meat for some months. I trust it is real?'

'Most of it's been frozen in storage, but it is real.'

'How long has it been in storage?'

The waitress scratched her head. 'Well, technically, about two hundred years, but it's only experienced about three, and it's rated for six. We do also have some younger cattle we slaughtered just after we arrived back here, though I don't think the Folians agree with it. Duggan suggested myco-something, but the meat needs to be used up. It'll only last so long frozen before it starts tasting funny.'

'That sounds acceptable.'

She scribbled on the pad. 'So how do you like it?' She stared at the Bronadi's canine face. 'Rare?'

Deruno nodded and grinned, revealing his multi-pointed teeth. 'As a Human once said to me, "Cut off its horns, wipe its backside and stick it on a plate."'

She dropped her pad and stared at him in horror.

Deruno's ears flattened against his head. 'No! Medium. What do you think we are, savages?'

She backed away. 'No, no, of course not!'

The Bronadi let out a whuffling guffaw.

The stunned woman giggled. 'I must say that for the first alien I've met, I'm surprised you speak English, and so well.'

'When the rest of the galaxy learns your language, it is rude not to learn others' in return.' He smiled again.

Aryx laughed at the exchange and, weaving between the closely packed chairs, he made his way to where Sebastian and the others sat, and parked himself in a gap.

'Ah, you've arrived just in time,' Kibble said.

Aryx pulled on his brakes. 'Sounds ominous.'

'It's not that bad,' Sebastian said. 'I was telling Kibble about what had happened to Alicia and Mikkael, and about the bracer he wore.'

Karan stepped up to the table, her arms laden with drinks, which she set down before sitting. 'Here you go.'

Kibble took a glass, leaned forward, and spoke in a low, conspiratorial tone. 'I realised I'd seen something like the crystal Sebastian described before. A white, milky stone. I think that was what William Kennet had been holding when he acted all possessed.'

'The guy that worked with Duggan and went to Achene with him?' Karan asked.

'Yes. Initially, I thought he'd developed some kind of schizophrenia or dissociative disorder. He attacked Cullen and passed on what we now know was one of the entities, but died in the process.'

Aryx nodded. 'I know, I read your journal. Why didn't you describe the stone in your notes?'

'I didn't recall it until Sebastian reminded me just now. I'd completely forgotten about it.'

'The same happened to me,' Sebastian said. 'Forgetting. I realised a little while ago that I'd found one of the same crystals when we were on Achene and had put it in my belt. I pretty much forgot about it as soon as I'd touched it.'

'And what's the relevance?' Aryx asked.

'We think they are some kind of storage for the entities,' Kibble said. 'It would explain how it got into William.'

'And what I felt on Cinder IV when I touched one,' Sebastian said. 'I thought I was on the planet I see in the nightmares. It would also explain what happened with Mikkael's bracer, and the sphere robot on Sollers Hope. Mikkael's entity had referred to that as an Avatar.'

Monica leaned in. 'Aside from the vernacular definition of a representation of a person in a VR or other remote presence system, in mythology an avatar is supposed to be a physical projection of a god or deity.'

Aryx rubbed his chin. 'So, gods aside, the stones provide another type of connection to this plane?'

'Possibly.' Monica turned to Sebastian. 'When we get back to the station, give me the crystal to analyse – if you remember. I have a sneaking suspicion that Alicia's captors may have been using her blood samples to synthesise a drug that makes possession easier, but until I have a chance to look at the device and those crystals, I can't know for certain.'

Sebastian nodded.

Aryx folded his arms. 'Just don't touch it with your bare fingers. We don't want a repeat performance.'

Aryx stared out at the distorted stars hurtling past the ship while the *Ultima Thule* glided through superphase on its second node hop back to Tenebrae.

Sebastian sat at the cockpit console typing, mostly one-handed. 'I really don't know how to word this,' he said.

'The message to Gladrin?'

'How do I tell him that we have his family safe, without it being obvious to others what it means?'

'Well, what was the last thing he said to you about them?'

Sebastian looked up and clicked his fingers several times. 'Witness protection. That was it. I'd told him that we'd found out they were in witness protection, but I obviously can't mention that.'

Aryx scratched his head. 'Okay, how about . . . "Gladrin, I have completed my personal assignment, and in so doing found the witnesses I have been looking for. I hope this will secure my promotion. The witnesses are located in a safe house, where they can meet with you at your earliest convenience." How's that?'

Sebastian wrinkled his nose. 'Doesn't sound like me at all. It's a bit too formal.'

Aryx folded his arms. 'I don't expect you to copy it verbatim. Just write something like that.'

'Alright.' Sebastian tapped away again. 'I'll use the bit about witnesses, but there's no way I'm saying "at your earliest convenience".'

Aryx closed his eyes, leaned back and shook his head. 'Whatever.'

The console bleeped twice.

'Oh,' Sebastian said. 'I just got a message from the Freemasons, forwarded from the station. Apparently, the Templar Knights rounded up the possessed from the archive building and located a few other collaborators, thankfully without killing anyone. It seems Father Elias is making inroads, getting the Church to work with the Freemasons. I certainly never expected that. They think there may be possessed Illuminati members in some of the large Earth corporations, and a few other government institutions that they can't touch.'

'Yeah, well, good luck to them purging the buggers,' Aryx said without opening his eyes. 'It's not like they can even do it themselves.'

'I suppose they'll have to incarcerate the ones they can get hold of for the time being. Oh . . . Gods . . .' Sebastian's voice trembled.

'What now?'

'A message I missed, from back when we were in London. With everything going on, I must have forgotten to open it.'

'What is it?'

'It's from Wolfram.'

Aryx's heart leaped and he opened his eyes and straightened. 'What does it say?'

'"Dear Agent Thorsson, as promised, here is the attached file to repair your corrupted system. I hope you find it satisfactory." It's signed James Robertson.'

Aryx frowned. 'James Robertson? How do you know that's from Wolfram?'

'Your nickname for him, remember? Jim-Bob. James Robert ... Robertson.'

'Ahh, clever. Does this mean you can get rid of the Trojan that lets the nightmare signal through to our apartments?'

'If it works.'

Aryx punched the air. 'Yes! Good work, Wolfram. I knew he'd come through. I just wish he'd been here for the wedding. He would have found it interesting.'

'I think,' Sebastian said, 'he would have *loved* it.'

Chapter 51

Aryx fell asleep quickly that night. It was good to be back in his own apartment. The last few days had been exhausting, and even though – as far as he was concerned – he was no longer battling the virus, the anti-radiation treatment and operation had left him with low reserves. As the hours rolled by, he slept soundly.

Until 3 a.m. approached.

Aryx Trevarian stood barefoot on a beach of rippled, crimson sand, watching as a pair of glowing suns slowly sank into an oily black sea. The gently lapping waves came up the shore almost to his feet, but the colour didn't entice him to dip a toe in. The purple twilight was restful, and the evening air cool and damp on his arms.

He looked up to the zenith. Of all the unfamiliar constellations overhead, one stood out prominently: seven stars glittering in the darkening sky.

'I feel like I've been here before,' he said. Why did it feel like someone else was there?

The whole scene was familiar, but he couldn't place it.

Before the remnants of the second sun sank over the black horizon, he turned around and walked towards the red sandstone cliff. As he got closer, something told him to climb, and he reached out for a cleft in the rock.

'NO!' came a familiar voice, and the thudding of feet, pounding in the sand.

Someone shoved him to the floor, knocking the breath out of him. He rolled over and the ground shook with a loud *thump*.

A large boulder now stood in his place.

'That nearly killed you,' the voice said.

He blinked. Sebastian stood over him.

'Don't you learn from repeating nightmares?' Sebastian asked, offering a hand.

Aryx pulled himself up. 'Nightmare?'

'You're dreaming.'

He shook his head. 'No. No, I'm not.'

'Yes, you are.' Sebastian pointed at Aryx's feet. 'You don't have legs, remember?'

Aryx stared down at himself and flexed his toes. The feet and shins did seem a little out of place. 'If I'm dreaming, how do *you* know this is a dream? I'm dreaming you.'

'No, you're not. I'm in my apartment asleep, like you. I haven't shut off the signal yet. I wanted to lucid dream one last time.' Sebastian turned around on the spot, arms out. 'This is the result of thaumaturgy.'

Aryx gave him a sidelong look. 'Okay, say this is a dream and you're somehow real and in it, too. What do we do?'

'We go in there.' Sebastian gestured to a lintelled opening in the cliff that hadn't been there before: a square Stonehenge portal, mounted directly in the rock. He conjured a lit hurricane lamp from nowhere and walked into the darkness.

Aryx followed, descending time-worn steps as shadows danced around them. At the bottom, the stone stairway opened out into a large, dark chamber with a red sandy floor.

From the darkness came a heavy, bestial breathing.

Sebastian held up the lamp and puffed out his chest. 'Come out and show yourself, you bastard! I am not afraid of you anymore.'

'What are you doing?' Aryx whispered.

'You'll see. Find a big rock or something.'

From the shadows a furry, cloven-hoofed leg stepped into the light. Aryx's gaze followed the leg up to a heavily muscled, red-skinned torso, topped with a bullish head with severe, pointed horns. 'You. Thorsson!' it bellowed.

'You can drop the act.' Sebastian's tone was unusually calm, but forceful. 'I know what you are. I've read my grandfather's journal, and Gravalax confirmed it. You are the giants.'

'It does not matter that you know. It will not help you. You are here, and that is all that is necessary. You will bow to our will.' The bestial appearance melted away, leaving a chunky, headless humanoid, formed from several ice-like crystalline boulders that floated independently in the air.

'You don't control us,' Sebastian said. 'You'll soon have no influence here. I can turn off the signal and you will invade our dreams no more.'

'If that is so, then why are you here?' The voice grated like vast shards of abrasive glass.

'To give you a message. Leave my family alone. Leave Tenebrae alone. Leave Earth alone. By the Gods, leave the galaxy alone!'

'No. We *will* control you. If we cannot, we will crush you. Your grandfather could not stand against us and, for his interference, he departed your realm. Your father could not stand against us. Nor could your brother. Join us or pay for the transgressions of your Viking ancestors.'

Aryx's pulse raced. The opportunity to hit back at the creatures that had affected their lives was too great to miss. Recalling what Sebastian said about a rock, he searched for something with which to retaliate. Spying a boulder the size of his chest, he sprang into action.

'We will never join you,' Sebastian said, taking a step back from the crystalline form. 'We will resist you at every turn, just as my ancestors did!'

Aryx summoned unnatural strength and lifted the boulder from the sand. 'Suck on this!' he shouted and, with one smooth heave, slung it at the crystal-demon-giant.

The crystalline being shattered.

'*Vernd!*' Sebastian shouted.

Time slowed. Aryx winced as crystal shards flew in all directions with enough force to embed themselves in the rock and sand of the cavern. The fragments heading in their direction stopped in mid-air as they hit a glowing white field that surrounded them both. The shards fell to the floor.

Sebastian stood with his hand extended, fingers wide. Aryx stared at him in disbelief. 'That's the thing with dreams,' he said, 'As soon as you know you're in one, you're in control.'

Aryx woke gently and rolled over. The clock read 08.00. There had been no waking, covered in sweat, at 03.10. For once, refreshed from a full night's sleep, he got up and popped an ultrasonic tooth cleaner into his mouth. While the little device crawled around his gums, he sat down to check his terminal.

As expected, a blank nightmare-signal trigger message had been received at 03.00. He deleted it without further thought. But there was another message, sent only minutes ago, with an attachment containing seemingly random letters that read:

```
-----BEGIN RSA PRIVATE KEY-----
Proc-Type:  4,ENCRYPTED
DEK-Info:   AES-128-CBC,E6561A915539208C2D957CE106433680


XcMXoKN7y9Aa8sJW7kUmso4HeGFkkB91RVA5KBE1J07nW05nJbTmOwwq+y4mMBYD
Fxdw4R9XzRpqJOXPTrtGj8QtrDAfCT2vdVJt6aJuuK0086AvaDV8q2EtsFZQhzFs
QrHSfowXmL1ipSDRVYKIGxR/VJCdeDhn/BNeaEyD1OYbAqsl1iwYbTzAnsH3nLXM
Xit7Ue5ENBnhi2Gxq/vE937Q6GTzyB+BXVxB6G5+cvD7ExmhH1GNa5RZpKx82P5L
nVY8TOYyxezCgryOqPQ5H+d/1HnHbg9iCK731dLwuKJEVGcZzupvbopuACQs1Hag
IXxo3CGHWUdRx1QfUhTojGmJRvpElzpIdz5h1q57pv+r/CfjsdIzebsexOVZDXsq
sUWaV/ix7U+YLYheSFRwJv/RQrDQwb6liA+0J5SFEf9702Z1rdKG85j52qhv1cWK
Lz0KnFotsLKghtzE23aeTnuT4xWVq76HSgWW/Ne60yzayTi8bUYdZ149D3ePA3SO
kgkrKMcoVuFYs5/+uOkLOmL2xII1poOrXZvuMG1wy/WRlGXNqCBcQeciHosNqPpD
ux5XMIDuCG5blI3J5Ziy6+8YzVQFmm90sXmmCa/nKWFnixPbuyV1AXqI71+Bxbuq
E5mc8IJ9jOFISk2tqQ4npRyg1byOC/QOWoyOCjazoS/oinb66n5wY1jnTAzeYxEi
dMMVBJUxcx19qqIHF+YbUjoexrFgVXfvUPJ4akNKYgW7qfyCMu+axbJ6tB2Lw2uR
1zfFUd7BmoBlzcP6aXaZhH8G2TwWCLzReKKMyOB4DvmUS3TAKEwRAQLYX4dkWZqn
-----END RSA PRIVATE KEY-----



-----BEGIN PUBLIC KEY-----
MIGfMA0GCSqGSIb3DQEBAQUAA4GNADCBiQKBgQDoeLeT5K76siPT39VK4X2I5TEt
IXJPku804_H3LP_ME_2ouBno1LG66m4YRBZuKib2KE9epyY5e+rPZOLYHlCXhj7b
BPgZ6jHkWN4Bibu06_J4Mes_rOBerT5oN_2wqcz3wiFDD3IYOhcnHhXHw0kCuku1
3swyYstSfZXdMlio/wIDAQAB
-----END PUBLIC KEY-----



---- BEGIN Base64 encoded file ----
X6rHG5EDhjKw7o1/d6ZCGnw+te+Uy+XuZpAoD2f6iR/X2/d250GWcpDoDYXIykGA
r8AGjspx/r1H3KQFwOjLyk4cU1njDkw7x6g0da75H3VzETrr94UQQt77v9eEnaEW
S8fH7J6GjYAVuFilOKrD16DFqUEbZlL8AeT1+2JPurY=
---- END Base64 encoded file ----
```

Aryx skimmed over the random characters. What did they mean? Security keys? He leaned forward to turn off the display, and as he moved closer to the screen four "words" stood out from the apparent gibberish of the second file:

     ... 04_H3LP_ME_2ou ... uO6_J4Mes_r0BerT5oN_2wq ...

And in the emptiness of his room, he read them aloud.
'Help me, James Robertson.'

Epilogue

Agent Gladrin stood at the mouth of a newly opened cave on a dusty planet in the outer reaches of the galaxy, many weeks' superphase travel from Tenebrae. As he looked about at the scree-covered slopes of the collapsed ravine, he understood why Monica Stevens had abandoned the site nearly three years ago.

Coming back here brought up old, bad memories. It was the last SpecOps job he'd done on behalf of ExoTerra before being interrupted by a message from the ITF, telling him they had his family captive. It was not long after he'd left Stevens alone on the planet that the cave had collapsed and she had barely escaped with her life.

Why had the ITF instructed him to take her slot on *this* mission? There was no reason why they should be interested in sending him to reopen the old dig site: there was no advanced technology to be recovered that they would be even vaguely interested in.

A bleep from his wristcom interrupted his thoughts with a message from Sebastian Thorsson.

> *Agent Gladrin, I have completed my personal assignment and in so doing found the witnesses I have been looking for. I hope this will secure my full promotion into SpecOps. The witnesses are located in a safe house, where they can meet with you at your earliest convenience.*
>
> *Agent Sebastian Thorsson*

Gladrin shook his head and smiled so tightly his gaunt cheeks hurt. A second later, the revelation hit him hard, and he barely had time to mute his helmet headset before he let out a string of deep, bellowing sobs. His family were safe! Finally, after almost three years, he could rest in the knowledge they were safe. He *would* see them again.

'Are you ready to go in, Agent?' came a female voice over his suit comms.

Gladrin took several deep breaths before reactivating the microphone. 'Yes. Once I have secured the site, the ExoTerra team may enter.'

He strode into the cavern, carving away the darkness with his wrist torch, and opened the visor of his helmet to take a breath of the stale, dust-laden air.

In the vast cathedral-like cavern, at the limit of his torchlight, a shattered flood lamp and tools lay strewn on the floor at the foot of the cavern wall. A partly excavated slab, covered in strange indented angular characters, protruded from the rocky ground. It was surrounded by rubble and debris, fallen from the cavern roof.

At a clattering to his right, Gladrin swung the torch in a wide arc.

The beam came to rest on a crumbling rock stack, and he traced the outline of arms, torso, and legs, formed from – or encrusted in – the rock itself. Small stones tumbled from the formation and a pungent odour, sulphurous and volcanic, unlike the dry rock-dust permeating the cavern, assaulted his senses.

Gladrin's pulse raced as words clattered from the rock stack.

'And so, your kind has returned.'

END

Acknowledgements

Thank you to the following people who helped bring this book to completion: Robert Harris and Jennifer Saunders, for reading early drafts, with special credit to Anne Shuker for intensively proof-reading ... twice! Sophie Playle, my editor, whose input helped me perfect my plot and iron out kinks. Loopwheels, whose innovative wheel design I mentioned in the text and replicated for the front cover, and Frog Legs Inc. who provided me with the caster model used in the same image. Mik Scarlet and Fuchsia Aurelius, who have become two of my biggest fans and given me an energy to feed off; knowing others *want* to read my books is a big incentive to continue.

Finally, my partner, Kris, for his continued support. Without his participation in the London Marathon using his wheelchair, one of the main scenes in this book wouldn't have become a reality and the whole thing would have fallen apart and never taken off.

I was worried that I might alienate readers with this part of Aryx and Sebastian's continuing story, but the feedback I received shows that I didn't overdo it. I've tried to keep Aryx's wheelchair antics realistic, and my only hope is that it motivates my readers to try their best in their daily lives, with whatever they've got.

About the author

Deane was born in November 1976, in Cinderford, and grew up in the Forest of Dean, Gloucestershire. He now lives in Herefordshire with his partner, Kris, a disability fitness instructor and wheelchair user.

Synthesis:Weave 2, Afterglow is his second full-length novel and the sequel to Synthesis:Weave, which he commenced writing in 2013 and first published in 2015. Shortly after completing Afterglow, he rewrote and republished Synthesis:Weave in August 2018.

Also look out for:

The laws of physics are about to change

Synthesis: Weave

A short-story prequel to the novel Synthesis:Weave

Synthesis: Pioneer

Lightning Source UK Ltd.
Milton Keynes UK
UKHW042203190219
337624UK00002B/5/P